They play                here was some rhythm               next-to-last ball was             on the wall before Kartor could get to it. Lesset intercepted, and flung it purposefully but far too hard toward Roni. Roni bobbled the ball; the spinning goal rejected her throw and her rebound. By then a green ball was in the tubes. Roni called for the blue ball again, but Anj had it and made the goal with a casual one-handed toss.

Theo started moving, trying to position herself, but as the ten-tick gong sounded the ball found a slot and launched itself toward Kartor. He managed to push it to Theo, while the sound of approaching footsteps grew louder.

"It's mine, give it to me!" Roni's voice was loudest; but the others were calling out "Time!" and "Shoot!" and over it all Viverain bellowed, "Now, Theo!"

Theo ignored the sounds of steps and the shouting; brought the ball up and threw it at the spinning top goal—

Kathunk! Something hard slammed into Theo; she flung her hand out, grabbing for balance—there was a squeal of shoes, and a splat! Roni's voice went from screech to howl.

"You killed me! Blood! Blood! I'm bleeding!"

Knocked breathless by the fall, Theo stared up at her, seeing blood all over the other girl's face. She tried to get up, then rolled away, arms folded over her head to protect it from Roni's kicks.

"Killer! Sociopath! Killer!"

**BAEN BOOKS by**
**SHARON LEE & STEVE MILLER**

**THE LIADEN UNIVERSE®**
*Fledgling*
*Saltation* (forthcoming)
*The Dragon Variation* (forthcoming)
*Mouse and Dragon* (forthcoming)

*Duainfey*
*Longeye*

# FLEDGLING

## A New Liaden Universe® Novel

# SHARON LEE & STEVE MILLER

## WITHDRAWN

BAEN

A Baen Books Original

Baen Publishing Enterprises
P.O. Box 1403
Riverdale, NY 10471
www.baen.com

ISBN: 978-1-4391-3343-9

Cover art by Alan Pollack

First Baen paperback printing, March 2010

Library of Congress Control Number: 2009018224

Distributed by Simon & Schuster
1230 Avenue of the Americas
New York, NY 10020

Pages by Joy Freeman (www.pagesbyjoy.com)
Printed in the United States of America

The authors would like to extend special thanks to the
following people, all of whom made Fledgling richer,
and without whom you might be
reading some other book.

Mike Barker, for his unflappable good
nature, and deft touch with a wiki

Sam Chupp, the voice and the will
behind the Fledgling podcast

Shaennon K. Garrity, who was kind enough
to lend us the Antonio Smith Method

Donna Gaudet, for naming Melchiza

Robert Parks, for taking it to the street

Shawna Camara and Angela Gradillas,
for their promotion work in Second Life

Toni Weisskopf of Baen Books, our patient editor

Jennifer Jackson of the Maass Agency,
our marvelous agent

The many, many supporters of the Fledgling
on-line project, and especially the denizens
of the Theo_Waitley Live Journal Community,
who made it all happen, and happen well

# ONE

· · · · · · ·

*Number Twelve Leafydale Place*
*Greensward-by-Efraim*
*Delgado*

"WHY DO I HAVE TO GO WITH HER?" THEO DEMANDED, and winced at the quaver in her voice. She'd meant to sound cool and remote and adult. Instead, she just sounded like a kid on the edge of a tantrum.

Housefather Kiladi looked up from his work screen and regarded her just a shade too seriously. Theo bit her lip.

"Because," he said in his deep, calm voice, "in the culture predominant upon Delgado, children—by which I mean those persons who have not attained what that same culture deems as their majority—are understood to be submissive to, and the responsibility of, their biological mother." He raised a strong eyebrow. "Surely you are aware of these things, Theo."

Well, she was. But that didn't mean she had to like them. Or live with them.

"You're the one who taught me that accepting

cultural mores is *a choice*," she said, pleased that her voice was steady now, if still more heated than she would have liked. "I don't choose to accept these particular conditions."

"Ah." He leaned back in his chair, hands folded on the edge of his desk, considering her out of thoughtful black eyes. "But a decision to rebel against predominant standards is only half a decision. What will you do instead?"

"I'll stay here. With you." There. She'd said it.

Both eyebrows rose, and he tipped his head to one side, consideringly. Theo felt a brush against her knee, and a moment later black-and-white Mandrin leapt to the top of the desk and sat down primly next to the keyboard.

"A bold and straightforward plan," Father said eventually. "My congratulations." He reached out to scratch Mandrin's ears. "I must ask, however, if you have considered all the ramifications of this choice."

Theo eyed him. "What do you mean?"

"Decisions have consequences," he murmured, his attention seemingly centered on the cat, though she knew better. Jen Sar Kiladi had been her mother's *onagrata* for as long as Theo could remember. She knew him every bit as well as she knew her mother— *and I like him better, too,* she thought rebelliously.

"For instance," he told Mandrin. "Your mother will certainly be both shocked and saddened by this decision. She may exert her influence. Ethics and law are, as you know, on her side. How will you respond? To what extent are you willing to fund this choice? How much sorrow are you willing to cause? How much disdain are you willing to bear? Surely, your friends must recoil as you step beyond that which they feel and know to be proper. Your mentor may consider it incumbent upon her to alert the Safety Office, and the Safeties deem it their duty to intervene."

Mandrin shook her head vigorously, as if these possibilities were too awful to contemplate. Professor Kiladi smiled slightly and refolded his hands, gaze settling on the untidy stack of hard copy on the desk-side table.

"In fact," he told the papers gravely, "such deviance from the norm might come to the attention of the Chapelia, who would perhaps feel Moved to send a Simple to you, to ascertain if your rebellion might Teach."

He glanced up and pinned her in a sharp glance.

"If you were to ask me—which I note that you have not—I would say the price seems excessive for what may be. at most a few months' inconvenience." He inclined his head. "You must, of course, please yourself."

Theo swallowed. "You don't *know* that it's only for a few months," she said, her voice unsteady again.

"Do I not?" he murmured in that over-polite voice he used when he thought you were being especially stupid. "How inept of me."

Theo looked down at the floor and the blaze of galaxies dancing there. Father's study floor usually projected the star fields; he said they helped to put his work into perspective. Theo's mother said they made her dizzy.

"Do you," she said, raising her head and meeting his eyes. "Do you know *for certain* that it's only going to be a couple months?"

"Child..." He came out of his chair in one of his

boneless, catlike moves, flowing toward her across the pirouetting stars, silent in his soft, embroidered slippers. "Nothing in life is certain. Your mother tells me that she requires a few months to concentrate on her own affairs. She is, I believe, at a delicate point with regard to her career, and wishes to do all that she may to advance herself."

He paused, head cocked to one side. "Who am I to argue with such excellent reasons? Kamele is scrupulous in these matters, and I, at least, admire her determination. For I don't hide from you, Theo, that I am a lazy fellow. Indeed, if I did not already enjoy tenure *and* a position I would surely be too indolent to seek them."

"You're not lazy," she said sullenly, and took a deep breath. "And the fact is, you don't know when— or if!—she'll decide to come back here. She might decide to, to . . ."

. . . to choose another *onagrata*, which was— unthinkable. Theo took a hard breath. *I won't cry,* she thought. *I won't!*

"She may decide to remain separate from me," Father said, completing her thought smoothly, like it didn't matter. "She may decide to seek another arrangement for herself and for you. These things fall within her rights as an adult in this society. However, if you will give the matter only a little consideration, I believe you will discover that you have some rights, as well. For how long have we enjoyed our private dinner on Oktavi evening?"

She blinked at him. "Ever since Kamele started teaching the late seminar," she said. "Years and years."

"So, it is a long-standing arrangement to which your

mother has given her consent. There is therefore no reason to discontinue our pleasant habit, unless you wish to do so."

"I don't!"

"Then there is no more to be said." He tipped his head, consideringly. "This is not, I think, something for Delm Korval."

He wanted her to laugh, Theo thought. Treating her like a kid. Well . . . she *wouldn't* laugh, that was all.

But she did feel, just a little, relief, knowing that the just-them Oktavi dinner would stand, no matter where Kamele—

The ancient mechanical clock wall mounted over Father's desk struck its two notes just then—one for the hour, and one for the eighth, which was seven— and a muted *thweep* from her pocket registered her mumu's agreement.

Professor Kiladi moved his shoulders in his familiar, supple shrug, and reached out to tousle her hair, like she was six instead of fourteen.

"The hour advances, child. Go finish packing. Your mother will wish to leave for the Wall before night opens its eyes."

"I—" She cleared her throat. "I'll come by your office on Oktavi, at the usual time."

"Indeed," he said solemnly. "I anticipate the occasion with pleasure." He smiled, then, gently. "Take good care, Theo. We need not be strangers, you know."

"I know," she said. Mustering her dignity, she turned to go, only to find her body overruling her mind, as it so often did. She spun, flinging herself against him in a hug, squeezing tight, feeling strong arms hugging her in return.

"You take care," she muttered fiercely into his shoulder. "*Promise me*, Father."

"I promise, child," he murmured, his deep voice a comfort. He released her, stepping back out of the embrace.

"Go, now. Be on time for your mother."

Theo dropped the case containing her music slips into the packing cube, narrowly missing Coyster's inquisitive pink nose.

"Keep out of there!" she told him, turning back toward the desk. "You don't want to get packed, do you?"

Coyster didn't answer. Theo swept up her biblioslips, the extra thread and her back-up hooks, and went back to the cube, walking so hard that the simulated koi swimming in the floor mosaic dashed away to hide under the simulated lily pads.

Bending, she put her things *carefully* into the cube and sighed, staring down into the half-empty interior. Beside her, Coyster sighed in sympathy and settled onto the rippling blue waters, white paws tucked neatly under orange chest, amber eyes serious.

"Hey." Theo knelt and tickled him under the chin. "I'm going to miss you, cat," she whispered, blinking hard. "Don't play with Father's lures, 'k? You'll get in trouble if I'm not around to untangle them for you."

Coyster squeezed his eyes shut in a cat-smile, and Theo blinked again before giving him one last chuck under the chin and rising to her feet.

Her bed was stripped and folded away; the desk was clear. The desk itself, and the bed, were staying right here; all the faculty apartments in the Wall were furnished, Kamele had told her, adding that one desk was as good as another.

Theo doubted that, but Kamele had made it clear that the discussion period was closed, so she'd kept the thought to herself.

She took a deep breath. Really, she was almost done. All that was left was to take the pictures down, fold up the closet, and decide about her old books—and the mobile.

The mobile—that was hard. She'd made it herself for an art project, back when she'd been a kid. It was the Delgado System, with its space station and twin ringed ice giants, built to micro-scale. With Father's help, she'd hung it up where the air from the vent would move it. Coyster had discovered it as a kitten, and had hatched all kinds of plans to reach it—from leaping straight up from the floor, to taking a running leap off the top shelf over the desk—but the mobile remained uncaptured.

Lately, he'd gotten above trying to capture it, but Coyster still harbored a fascination for the flying, spinning thing. Theo would entertain him—and herself—by changing the speed or direction of the air flow from the vent, to make the mobile twirl wildly, or spin *verrrrry* slowly. She turned her head. Yes, he was watching it now from his tuck-up next to the cube, ears set at a calculating angle.

Theo grinned, then nodded. That settled it. The mobile stayed; it would give Coyster something to do besides stalking Mandrin and playing with Father's fishing gear.

The books... She wandered over to the shelf, koi beneath her shoes, and fingered the worn spines. *Mr.*

*Winter and the Mother of Snows*; *The Shy Kitten*; *I Can Find It!*—stories for littlies, that Kamele and Father had read to her until she could read them herself, and did until she'd memorized them. Her fingers moved on, tarrying on *Sam Tim's Ugly Day*, and a smile tugged at the corner of her unwilling mouth. "Is it worth taking to Delm Korval?" she whispered, and shook her head, eyes blurring again.

"Well." She turned away from the shelf and looked down at the koi making lazy circles inside the floor. "No sense cluttering up my new room with books I never read anymore," she said, maybe to the simulated fish, or maybe to the cat drowsing by the cube. She sniffled a little, and turned on her heel.

Her clothes hung orderly in the closet: dark green school coveralls with Team Three's red stripes on shoulder and cuff; sweaters, jerseys, and slacks. She pulled her favorite sweater off its hanger, and slipped it on, her fingers stroking the border of bluebells 'round the cuff. It was too early for bluebells in the garden, of course, but—

She swallowed, blinking hard to clear her vision, and slapped the side of the closet harder than was really needed. It began to compress, hissing a little as the air squeezed out of her clothes.

Next stop was the control unit over the desk. She put her fingers against the keys, eyes closed so she didn't have to see the picture of Delgado from the space station's observation tower snap out of existence, or the picture of Zolanj, who had been Father's cat before Mandrin, and who had sometimes agreed to sit on Theo's lap, but never on Kamele's. Or the picture of the river camp where Father went to fish, or . . .

Her fingers moved across the keypad with cold deliberation, like they belonged to someone else, while Theo bit her lip and reminded herself that they were stored in the house bank, and that she could easily retrieve them when she came...back.

Her fingers touched one last button; she took a deep breath and opened her eyes, to look 'round at her denuded room.

It looked...peculiar...with blank walls and floor, without all of her things spread around—like a stay-over room on the station. She blinked again, reminding herself for the hundredth time that she *was not* going to cry.

"Is this move really necessary?" she asked Coyster, but he was absorbed in watching the mobile and didn't answer.

Theo shook her head. Something was wrong—*really* wrong—and whatever it was, the adults weren't talking to *her* about it.

"Pack up, Theo, we're moving to the Wall," she said, in a wicked—and deadly accurate—imitation of Kamele in her *I-am-the-mother* voice.

And Father—Theo sniffed. She'd been *sure* he would understand her position. But he was just as bad as Kamele—*Don't be late for your mother*! Treating her like she was a kid—

And that was wrong on a whole 'nother level, Theo thought, as she leaned over the ambiset again, turning off the aromatics, white noise and breeze. Father *never* treated her like a kid—even when she acted like one. *Especially* when she acted like one.

She chewed her lip, staring down into the blank floor. Kamele wasn't *stupid*—and neither was Housefather

Kiladi, despite his frequent claims to the contrary. If whatever was going on was so twisty that *they* couldn't untwist it . . .

"Maybe we ought to take it to Delm Korval, after all," she said over her shoulder in Coyster's general direction. He sneezed, and she grinned, reluctantly.

Behind her came the snap of the closet's magnetic locks meeting and sealing. At that instant, her mumu *thweeped* its reminder—her mother would be waiting downstairs, with new keys in hand, and a determination to leave the house on Leafydale Place, where Theo had lived her whole life. 'Til now.

"Chaos!" Theo muttered. She grabbed the closet's handle and dashed back to the cube, sealing it with one hand while she dragged her bag over a shoulder with the other.

One last look then around the blank, bleak room. Then she took a firm grip on closet and cube and hurried out. Behind her, in the empty room, the left-behind storybooks trembled on their shelf, and one tumbled to the featureless floor.

# TWO

........

*University of Delgado*
*Faculty Residence Wall*
*Quadrant Eight, Building Two*

"YOUR ROOM'S JUST DOWN THE HALL." KAMELE WAVED vaguely to the right. "Why don't you take your things in and get settled? I've sent out for dinner—our first meal in our new apartment! An inauguration!"

Theo, closet and cube in tow, looked around the tiny, severely squared receiving parlor. The walls and floor were white ceramic—fireproof, explosion resistant, and certified safe, just like the whole rest of the Wall. Three plastic chairs sat in a semi-circle around a battered table that looked like it might actually be wood. The smooth floor was partially covered with a rug Theo had last seen rolled up in the storage bin at...home. Kamele had probably intended it to soften the space, but the faded yellow and red flowers only looked sad and beaten down by the shiny whiteness.

"Theo?" Her mother's voice had that bright, brittle quality that meant she was 'way too tired and stressed out. *Not* a good time to ask if the joke was over and could they could go home now.

"Sorry." Theo took a deep breath and got a firmer grip on the leads of her luggage. "I'll just go set up the closet."

Kamele gave her a too-fast smile and nodded. "I'll call you when dinner gets here."

"Great," Theo said, trying not to sound as worried as she felt. She steered her stuff carefully across the old rug and down the narrow hallway. When Kamele got into overdrive at home, Father would sit her down in the common room, bring her a glass of wine, and talk to her—about nothing, really. The weather. The cats. The fishing rod he'd seen in Nonactown. Theo wasn't sure if it was the wine, or Father's voice, or the warm, flowery breeze only he could coax from the ambiset, but whatever it was, all the bright, strained energy melted away and Kamele would fall asleep, and wake up her normal brisk and efficient self.

Theo wondered if there was any wine in the apartment—and then forgot about it as the door slid back to reveal her so-called "room."

The desk was directly across from the door, molded out of the wall, three short shelves above it, and two drawers below. Next to it was the bed, decently folded up at the moment, which was a good thing, Theo thought darkly, or else *she* wouldn't have fit inside, never mind her stuff.

She left the closet in the open doorway and gingerly maneuvered the cube into the corner to the right of the door, where it would be out of the way, more or less, dumped her pack on the floor beside it, took

off her shoes, and threw her sweater over the back
of the chair. Then she turned to survey the situation.

On inspection, there was only one possible place
for the closet—the end wall to the left of the desk.
Biting her lip, she shifted the folded-up closet back
and forth between the narrow hall and the narrow
doorway, trying to line up the the angle of entry.

Finally, she got the thing into the room and posi-
tioned it against the wall with a sigh of relief. She
blew her bangs out of her eyes with a *fuff*, reached
to the controls—and hesitated, reassessing the available space by eye.

Yes, she decided, again. The closet *would* fit.
Just.

While the closet expanded, she inventoried the desk,
approving the neatly labeled connectors. She could
hook up her school book, no problem; there was a
socket for her mumu, and an extra, labeled "research."

Theo frowned. At home, she'd done all her research
through the school book connection. She wondered
if there were different protocols inside the Wall residences. A quick search of the desk drawers failed to
turn up either hard-copy instructions or an official gold
infoslip. Fine, then. She'd just ask the Concierge, the
next time she jacked in her school book.

She turned to look at her pack, sitting slumped on
the slick white floor next to the still-sealed cube, and
frowned. Her solos were done; she'd made sure to
finish them early, so she'd have time to pack, or—if
Father had taken her side, which, in retrospect, she
should've known he wouldn't—time to cook dinner
and do a little recreational reading afterward.

"I'll get it tomorrow," she said to the room at

large. "If it was *that* important, they would've left the instructions out where people could find them."

From the left came a bump, a wheeze, and a *ping!*, which was the closet's way of announcing that it was accessible, now. Theo went over to inspect, shaking her head. It fit, all right. Both ends were as tight against the corners as they could be.

"If I get another sweater, I'll have to keep it in the desk," she said, and bit her lip. She was used to talking to whichever cat happened to be in her room—lately, that had been Coyster, though Mandrin, Father's white-and-black, sometimes came by for a visit. Here in this new place, though, she was all by herself. She had to remember that. Chaos! Her mentor *already* thought it was weird that she talked to cats.

"Grow up, Theo," she muttered—and brought her fingers up against her lips.

Fingers still pressed to her mouth, she turned, skidding slightly on the slick floor, and wished *she'd* had the foresight to bring a rug. Maybe she could buy one at the co-op tomorrow. She had plenty of credit on her card; and if she could find one cheap enough, she wouldn't even have to have her mother's countersig. Now that she was fourteen, she could spend up to fifty credits a day on her own sig, *much* better than when she'd been a kid and had to have Kamele's sign every time she wanted to buy a fruit bar, or—

A gong went off, loudly. Theo jumped and spun, sock-feet slipping on the slick floor. She twisted, managing to stay upright more by luck than intent, and by the time she was oriented again, Kamele was calling her.

"Theo! Dinner's here!"

✳    ✳    ✳

They ate at the meal bar in the alcove between the common room and the shuttered kitchen, teetering on tall stools in the dim, directionless light. Kamele had ordered ginger soy noodles and plum soup, with juice for Theo and coffee for herself. Ginger soy noodles being one of Theo's favorite meals, her portion was quickly gone, and the plum soup, too, both reduced to smears of sauce at the bottom of the disposable bowls. She sat then, her hands tucked around her cup, recruiting, as Father put it, her courage.

Across from her, Kamele had eaten a few ginger noodles, and given the soup a long, thoughtful look. Mostly, she was drinking coffee, her movements sharp and not quite steady. Theo thought again about wine, but didn't quite know how to ask if there was any in-house, let alone suggesting if it might be a good idea for Kamele to have some.

The other question hovering on the tip of her tongue... She *did know* that this wasn't the optimum time for asking questions, with Kamele trembling at the edge of a crash. But she had to know—she had to know *why*.

Her mother ate another few noodles, washed down with a large swallow of coffee. Theo took a hard breath.

"Kamele?"

Over-bright blue eyes focused on her face. "Yes, Theo?"

"I'd like to learn the reason why we've moved here." *There*, she thought, *that sounds calm, and grown-up, and non-judgmental.*

The bright gaze dropped. Kamele used her hashi to poke at the noodles in her bowl.

"We've moved here so I can do my work more efficiently," she said quietly.

Theo blinked, thinking of the high-end access available at Father's house.

"You can work from home," she blurted, "and a lot more comfortably, too! Kamele, your office at home is bigger than this whole apart—"

"Precisely." Her mother was looking at her again, cheeks flushed and mouth tight. "A true scholar must value her work above all else. Living in Professor Kiladi's house, I—we have grown . . . accustomed to certain luxuries that are not necessary for—and indeed may be inimical to—the process of orderly and analytical thought."

That, Theo thought, sounded like a rote response, and if it had been Kamele asking and Theo answering, the rote response would have only earned her a closer interrogation.

Theo took a breath.

"Kamele—"

"I am not done answering your question yet, Theo," her mother said coolly. "Or have you decided that you don't wish to learn, after all?"

*Oops.* Theo bent her head. "I framed the question," she said quietly, like the well-brought-up child of an academic from a long tradition of Waitley academics, "because I wished to learn."

There was silence while Kamele drank more coffee, then pushed the considerable remains of her meal to one side.

"Research, study, and teaching are only three-quarters of what a scholar must do in order to . . . become prominent in her field," she said slowly. "A scholar must have contacts, allies; colleagues who support her work and whose work she supports in return. These associations cannot be built, or strengthened, by living retired in the suburbs. I need to be *here*, at the intellectual heart of the planet, in order to make the contacts I need to... The contacts I will need to further my career."

Theo opened her mouth, and hastily raised her cup for a swallow of juice.

"I've gotten out of touch," Kamele said, slowly. "And it has cost me. Cost us all. We can recover, of course. With work. Hard work. Work that must be done from the Wall." She looked up, bright eyes fierce. "I am a scholar of Delgado. I must be resolute."

She might have seen Theo staring, because she smiled suddenly—a real smile, tired as it was. "So, we will take up the professorial lifestyle, as our mothers and grandmothers have done before us. It will be an adventure, won't it, Theo?"

Applying Father's definition of an adventure being a series of unlooked-for and uncomfortable events, Theo guessed that it would be.

She cleared her throat, suddenly wanting to be by herself to think, even in that nasty little den of a room. Pushing back from the table, she barely remembered to say, "Thank you for sharing your thoughts, Kamele."

"Of course," her mother said. "You're not a child anymore, Theo. It's time you began to ask these questions and to plan how you'll manage your own career." She waved an unsteady hand.

"I'll deal with the clean-up. Go and get your rest. Tomorrow's a school day."

Like she didn't know that, Theo thought, but she slid off the stool without any other comment than, "Good-night, Kamele."

"Good-night, Daughter," her mother murmured, but she was looking down at the tabletop, her brows drawn together in a frown.

· · · ·❊· · · ·

"Who knew that two people could make such a noise," Jen Sar Kiladi murmured, "that the house is so silent in their absence?"

He put his palm against the door to Theo's room, and paused on the threshold as the lights came up.

"Thorough," he noted. "We can hope that she spent most of her angst in turning off her room, and has none left over for her mother."

*She is*, the voice that only he could hear commented, *right to be upset. And she will ask questions.*

"Agreed," he murmured, crossing the room to pick up a fallen book. "Only they might, might they not, be *gentle* questions?"

He sighed down at the book: *Sam Tim's Ugly Day*. An unfortunate translation, but a useful conceit that had delighted a much-younger Theo. Though she appeared, he thought, stretching to put the book up with its fellows, to have outgrown the conceit, yet she might still recall the lesson.

"An awkward time for a separation," he said, perhaps to himself, "with the child dancing on the edge."

*Yet Kamele's reasons are sound*, countered the voice inside his head. *You, yourself, encouraged her to do what was needful.*

"Oh, indeed! Every bit of it—and more." He shook his head at the bare room, and turned to retrace his steps.

"Does it seem to you, Aelliana," he asked as

he stepped out into the hallway, "that I may have become—just a thought!—meddlesome?"

His answer was a peal of laughter.

· · · ·✳· · · ·

The 'fresher was at the end of the hall. Theo showered and returned to her room, closing the door and unfolding the bed. It didn't take up quite as much room as she had feared, which was a blessing in a space where centimeters mattered.

Having put the bed down, though, she didn't immediately retire. The glare off the floor and walls set her teeth on edge. She went over to the desk to check the ambiset. If she could get some pictures—or at least some color!—into the walls; put a mosaic into the floor, it would make the place seem more like home, cramped as it was.

Except—there was no ambiset to be found. Theo went out into the hall, but there was no ambiset there, either. She actually compressed the closet, thinking that she must have placed it in front of the control center—but the only thing behind was more featureless, white wall.

"I do *not* believe this," she said loudly, her voice sliding off the walls and tumbling into the glare. She ran her hands through her hair and stared around the tiny room, even casting a not-exactly-hopeful look at the ceiling.

No ambiset.

"And this is supposed to *focus* my mind?" Theo asked the air.

The air didn't bother to answer.

All right. She took a deep breath. At least she knew

what to do to about the jitters. She needed some handwork, that was all. Her needles and thread were in the cube. She'd lay down a couple lines of lace. In fact, there was that idea she'd had about making a lace flower like the new ones Father had planted in their garden.

She knelt by the cube, unsnapped it and lifted the lid, looking down into a dark maw lined with numerous needle-sharp teeth.

"Hey!" She dropped the top, caught it before it hit the floor and laid it gently down. Inside the cube, Coyster yawned again.

Theo sat back on her heels and shook her head, feeling the grin pulling her mouth wide.

"You're going to get me in *so much* trouble," she said.

Coyster shook out a dainty white paw and began to wash his face.

# THREE

· · · · · · · · · · ·

"IT'S TIME TO GET UP!" THE CLOCK ANNOUNCED IN A cheery sing-song.

Theo snuggled tighter into her pillow, getting a face full of fur in the process.

"It's time to get *up!*" the clock sang again, slightly louder this time.

Theo sneezed and opened her eyes, coming nose-to-nose with Coyster, who was propped up on the pillow like a miniature—and very furry—human.

"It's *time* to get *up!*" The clock was beginning to sound a little testy.

Theo sneezed again. Coyster put a paw on her nose and looked disapproving.

"Theo Waitley," the clock said sternly. "If you do not get up within the next *thirty seconds,* a note will be inserted into your file. Mark."

"Gah," Theo said comprehensively, and flipped the

blanket back. The floor felt cold and creepy against her bare feet as she crossed to the desk and pressed her thumb against the clock's face.

"There," she muttered. "I'm up. Happy?"

The clock, duty done, didn't answer. Theo sighed hugely and wandered out to the 'fresher to wash her face.

A few minutes later, slightly more awake, she pulled out a pair of school coveralls. She dressed, hasty in the cool air, and touched the closet's interior mirror.

The dark surface flickered to life, and she sighed at what she saw. There were dark circles under her dark eyes, like she hadn't slept at all, and her face was even paler than usual. Her light yellow hair was wisping every-which-way, which was unfortunately just the same as always. When she was a littlie, she'd been convinced that she'd wake up one morning to find that her fluff had been shed, like duckling down, and she'd grown sleek, dark brown hair straight down to her shoulders.

She combed her fingers through the fly-away half-curls, trying to make them lie flat, which never worked, and didn't this morning. Grumbling, she tapped the mirror off and turned away.

Coyster was still lounging against the pillow, half-covered by the blanket, eyes slitted in satisfaction.

"Get up," Theo said. "I've gotta put the bed away."

He yawned, pink tongue lolling.

Theo hooked him under the belly and dropped him to the floor.

"If *I* can't sleep all day," she said, pulling the blanket straight, "*you* can't sleep all day."

Coyster stalked away, tail high, and jumped onto

the desk. By the time the bed was put away, he was curled and sound asleep, like he'd been there for hours. Theo shook her head—then bit her lip.

Last night, she'd filled a disposable bowl with water and shredded some old hard copy from a school project she was done with into the cube's inverted top. Coyster had let her know that he would tolerate these primitive arrangements for a limited time only, so Theo had added proper cat bowls, a litter box, kibble, and a can of his favorite treats to her growing after-class shopping list. She felt bad about leaving him all day without anything to snack on, even though she knew he wouldn't take any harm from it. Father always left cat food and water out in bowls in the kitchen, for Coyster and Mandrin to graze at their leisure.

"If *I* have to get used to everything being new..." Theo let the sentence drift off, blinking a sudden blurriness away.

She was going to have to tell Kamele about Coyster, she thought, considering the slumbering furry form on her desk. She hoped her mother was in a less edgy mood this morning. A good night's sleep... Maybe Kamele had had a good night's sleep.

Yawning, she bent down to retrieve her school bag.

"I'm going to school," she told Coyster. An orange ear flickered and Theo grinned. Not so sound asleep, after all.

Bag over her shoulder, she slipped out of her room, closing the door firmly. She didn't want Kamele finding out about Coyster until she had a chance to explain the situation.

Chaos, she was tired! Which was, she acknowledged as she headed down the hallway toward the kitchen, entirely her own fault. She'd spent 'way too much time working out the pattern for the lace rose she wanted to make. By the time she'd given up and tucked her traveling kit away into her bag, it had been late. Not as late as general lights out—*that* was a note-in-your-file—but well beyond the Strongly Suggested bed time for juniors who hadn't yet had their *Gigneri*.

Yawning again, Theo dumped her bag on the meal bar and put her hand on the kitchen door. Tea, she thought, was definitely in order. Some of Father's strong black tea with the lemony after-note. She'd just put the kettle on and—

"What!" she stood, staring stupidly at the bland lines and blank screen of a standard kaf unit. There was nothing else in the alcove. No stove, no cabinets, no refrigerator, no tins of tea lined against the back of the counter...

"Good morning, Daughter." Kamele sounded as tired, or tireder, as Theo felt, so it probably wasn't the smartest thing she'd ever done to turn around and point at the poor kaf like it was disorderly or something, and demand, "Are we supposed to *eat* out of that?"

Kamele frowned.

"Don't roar at me, Theo."

She swallowed. "I'm sorry. I was just—expecting a kitchen."

Kamele's frown got deeper, and Theo felt her stomach clench.

"This is the kitchen that most people *eat out of,*" she said sternly. "It amused Professor Kiladi to bypass the kaf and cook meals from base ingredients, and I saw no harm in allowing him to teach you something of the art, since you were interested. If I had foreseen that you would scorn plain, honest food out of the kaf—"

"I'm not," Theo interrupted. "Kamele, I'm sorry. I'm not—scorning—the kaf. It was just...a shock. I was looking forward to making a cup of tea, and—"

"The kaf will give you a cup of tea," her mother said, interrupting in her turn. "All you need to do is ask."

Tea from a kaf unit was not, in Theo's estimation, *tea*. It was a tepid, watery, tasteless beverage that happened, via some weird and as-yet-uncorrected universal typo, to be *called* tea. Real tea had body, and taste, and—

Her mumu *thweeped* the eighth of the hour.

"I suggest that you choose your breakfast quickly," Kamele said, and stalked past her to confront the kaf.

Two sharp jabs at the keypad, a flicker of lights across the face screen, a hiss when the dispenser door slid up. Kamele slid the tray out and carried it to the bar. Acrid steam rose from the extra large disposable cup.

Theo wondered if kaf coffee tasted any better than kaf tea, but it didn't seem like the time to ask. Instead, she stepped up to the machine, punched one button for juice and another for hot cereal, and very soon thereafter was sitting across from her mother at the bar.

Kamele was drinking the coffee, though not like she was enjoying it, and staring down into her bowl so intently that Theo knew she couldn't actually be seeing it or her cereal. She sighed and dug into her own breakfast. Father and Kamele were both prone to sudden fits of intense abstraction, when they would simply...step away from whatever it was they were doing to pursue a certain fascinating thought. Theo guessed it came of being a scholar and having so many interesting things to think about, and she had early learned not to interrupt a fit of abstraction with small talk.

The cereal wasn't too bad, though it was sweeter than she liked; the juice was room temperature and astringent. Theo ate quickly, keeping an increasingly worried eye on her mother, who continued to drink coffee and stare a hole into her cereal.

Theo cleared her throat.

"Early class this morning, Kamele?" she asked, trying to sound bright and interested—and hoping to bring her mother to a realization that her cereal was getting cold.

Her mother glanced up, her eyes soft and not really focused.

"Yes," she murmured. "I do have the early class this morning, Theo. Thank you for reminding me. I'd best be on my way." She slid off the stool, carried her untouched bowl and the half-empty cup to the disposal.

*Well*, Theo thought, *that didn't work, did it?*

Kamele bent to pick up her bag.

"Don't dawdle," she said, slinging it over her shoulder. "I'll be a little late this evening—there's a meeting. If it looks like it'll go long, I'll text you." She bent and brushed her lips against Theo's cheek.

"Learn well," she murmured, and was gone, moving quickly toward the receiving parlor, her footsteps sounding sticky against the slick floor. Theo heard the outer door chime and cycle.

*This*, she thought, finishing her cereal hurriedly, *is not good*. She sat back, reaching for the leg pocket where her mumu rode. She'd just text a quick message to Father, and ask him to—

*Or,* she thought, hand poised above the pocket, *maybe not.* For all she knew, Kamele wasn't speaking to Father, and would refuse anything he sent to her. She was certainly behaving like— Theo took a breath. Until somebody *told her* something, she couldn't dismiss the possibility that Kamele had—had released Father. There were signs, she thought carefully. Before last night, Kamele had always referred to Father as "Jen Sar." "Professor Kiladi," in all its stiff formalness—that was how a junior academic referred to a senior, not how a woman spoke of her *onagrata*.

Theo sighed. She *hated* not knowing what was going on. Maybe the best thing to do was wait for Oktavi's dinner with Father, and ask him again.

Maybe he'd even give her a better answer than "local custom."

Grumbling to herself, she stuffed the disposables into the receptacle, shut the door to the kitchen, and glanced at the readout set into the top of the table. Still plenty of time to meet Lesset before class, if the bus didn't run late.

"Bus!" she said out loud, and smacked fingertips against her forehead. She didn't have to catch the bus today. She lived inside the Wall now; school was just a belt ride away.

"Great," she muttered, and slung her pack over her shoulder. "So I'll be early."

She was at the Team's usual table in the Ready Room, working on the lace flower again, her tongue between her teeth as she tried to figure out how to make it 3D *and* all one piece, when Lesset wandered in—and stopped just inside the door, blinking.

"Theo! What're you doing here this early? Is something wrong?"

Theo frowned up at her. "If something was wrong, I'd be late, wouldn't I?"

"It would depend," her friend said reasonably, "on what was wrong."

"I guess." She sighed and reached for her pack. "Actually, something *is* wrong. Kamele moved out of Father's house. We're Mice now."

"You're living in the Wall? *Really?*" Lesset blinked, then grinned. "That's tenured!"

Theo eyed her sourly. "No, it's not." She bent to put her hook and thread away into her bag.

"*Seriously* tenured," Lesset insisted. "Where's your nest?"

"Quadeight Twobuild, right on the belt."

Lesset's grin went from wide to round. "Fact?"

"No, theory!" Theo snapped. "What'm I gonna do, make up the direction?"

"But that must be—it's *gotta* be. . . . Chaos!" Lesset sat suddenly, her pack bumping the table, and there she continued to sit, staring right through Kartor and Roni when they came in. Kartor flopped into the chair on Theo's right, his eyes pinned to the screen of his mumu. Roni dropped her bag on the table and went over to Team Two's table, just like she always did.

"Any time you're ready," Theo muttered, and Lesset turned to her, putting a quick hand on her arm.

"I'm sorry," she said, though she didn't sound particularly contrite. "It just came to me that you're living—you must be living in, you know—*her* apartment."

Theo sighed, and wished she hadn't put her hand-work away. "*Her* who?"

Lesset frowned. "Don't you *ever* read *The Faq?*"

The *Faculty-Administration Quarterly* carried the daily university news—lists, mostly. Lists of people who were applying for grants. Lists of people who had gotten their grants. Lists of people going on sab-batical. Lists of people coming back from sabbatical. Changes of address.

Kamele said that once, in the long ago past, *The Faq* really had only been published once a quarter, but the level of news generated by such a large faculty and administration forced a more frequent publication schedule. She read it, and Father, too, though Theo thought they had different reading experiences. For instance, Kamele called it *The Faq* or, sometimes, *The News.*

Father called it *The Scandal Sheet.*

"I skim it sometimes," Theo said, and made a face. "Bor-ing."

Lesset sighed and shook her head. "Information is never boring," she said in a prim voice that made her sound exactly like her mother.

"Long lists of names are boring," Theo answered, then prodded. "You were going to tell me who *her* is."

"Well . . ." Lesset chewed her lip. "Professor Flandin—the sub-chair of the History of Ed—"

"Lesset, I *know* who Professor Flandin is! Kamele's in EdHist!"

"All right, don't roar at me! How'm I supposed to know what you know?"

"I'm sorry," Theo said, noticing that her shoulders had climbed up nearly to her ears. She relaxed them, deliberately, and looked at her friend. "So you think we're in Professor Flandin's apartment? Why? She go Topthree?"

"Topthree!" Lesset laughed and patted Theo's arm. "You really *don't* read *The Faq*, do you? Professor Flandin didn't get promoted. She got *disbarred*."

Having delivered this last in a penetrating whisper, Lesset folded her hands on her knee, and gave a single, solemn nod.

"Disbarred?" Theo frowned. Now she came to think about it, she'd heard *some*thing . . .

"Falsifying data," she said, suddenly remembering. She looked at Lesset. "She falsified cites in her last two pubs."

Lesset smiled. "You *do* pay attention sometimes! So, anyway, if Professor Waitley's been assigned— Quadeight's only two ramps down from Topthree!— been assigned to Professor Flandin's apartment, that must mean the dean approved her temp-posting to sub-head. *That* wasn't in *The Faq* yet!"

"Maybe they're waiting to make the announcement at the Faculty Meeting," Theo said, but she was thinking about Kamele—Temp Sub-Head!—and she hadn't said anything—not a word. That felt pretty bad, like Kamele didn't trust her. But, Theo thought, her spirits rising considerably, if the temp appointment was the reason Kamele had moved to the Wall, then that meant they could go home after the search was finished and the department had appointed someone permanent!

The knot in her stomach eased, and she looked up with a smile as the first whistle sounded.

"Time to go," Lesset said, as she and Theo rose and shouldered their packs.

Roni rushed over from Team Two's table, grabbed her pack, and marched off, calling, "Don't be late!" over her shoulder.

Kartor rose automatically, his attention still on his mumu.

Lesset sighed, her steps not as brisk as they might've been. "Professor Appletorn first thing is cruel and unusual."

"He's not so bad."

"He's not so bad to *you*," Lesset retorted. "He doesn't loathe *you*."

"He doesn't loathe you, either," Theo said reasonably. "He's a teacher. His job is to make sure you learn."

"I'm so tense in his class I don't think I'm learning *any*thing," her friend said, as they moved out of the Ready Room. She shuddered.

That was serious, if true. Theo had noticed that Lesset wasn't at her best in Professor Appletorn's class, but if she was letting her tension get in the way of performance, that was bad. Theo sighed, worried.

Professor Appletorn taught Advertency, which was core. If Lesset didn't pass, she'd not only pull the Team average down, she'd have to repeat Fourth Form, *and* clear a higher achievement bar, to cancel out the note in her file.

She looked around, suddenly worried on another head—and spied Estan and Anj, the last two members of the Team, rushing toward them from the pass corridor from the belt station. There must've been another Crowded Condition on the Quad Six beltway. That had been happening a lot, lately.

"Maybe you should talk to your mentor," Theo said to Lesset, as they turned left down the hall. They were walking so slow now that lazy-moving Kartor was ahead of them, and she could hear Estan panting from behind.

"I did talk to my mentor." Lesset sighed gustily. "She said I was learning how to deal with adverse conditions."

"Oh." said Theo. She frowned. "Are you?"

"I don't think so," her friend said mournfully.

# FOUR

· · · · · · · · · ·

*Scholarship Skills Seminar: Advertency*
*Professor Stephen M. Richardson Secondary School*
*University of Delgado*

FOUR TEAM THREE CAME AROUND THE CORNER INTO
the seminar hall more like a loose gaggle than a team,
Estan and Anj still sweaty and breathing hard.

Theo cringed. Professor Appletorn paid attention to
such things, and graded for form. But Lesset's steps
had gotten slower and slower the closer they'd gotten
to the classroom, and Theo had lagged behind, too,
to show support for her friend. It was important to
support your friends, according their Social Engineering instructor. Even if you privately thought they were
being just a little too sensitive.

Four Team Six was ahead of them, which wasn't
unusual; their Ready Room was closer to Advertency
by a good three halls. They shouldn't be showing
bonus just for being ahead—fairness said that such
advantage would be factored in to the Team averages.

What *was* unusual was the fact that they were

standing in front of the seminar room like a bunch of random nonacs instead of a functioning Learning Team, blinking at the door.

Which was shuttered.

Theo frowned.

"What's wrong?" Lesset asked. "Why are they standing in the hall?"

"The door's closed," Theo said.

"Closed?" Lesset repeated. "But why would it be closed? We have a class. Professor Appletorn insists that the door be open until he starts teaching!"

"Did we all miss a schedule jump somehow? Is it locked?" Kartor asked, as their group joined Six in front of the shuttered door.

Several people snatched out their mumus, fingers flying.

"Sched clean," came a mumble, followed by a group sigh of relief.

"Is it locked?" Kartor asked again, since the crowd of Team Six blocked his view of the status lights.

"No-oo," Vela answered slowly, looking at him over the heads of her teammates.

"Then," Roni said impatiently, "open it!"

"Do you think we should?" That was Simon, Team Six's proceduralist.

Before Estan, Team Three's proceduralist, could answer, Roni sighed loudly and lunged forward over Vela's shoulder, smacking her palm against the plate. Somebody on Team Six—probably Simon, Theo thought uncharitably—squeaked nervously, like he expected alarm bells or a team of Safeties. All that happened, though, was that the shutter folded out of the way, showing the bright, empty room beyond.

"Was that so hard?" Roni asked, still impatient.

Team Six traded glances.

"No," Vela said quietly. "It wasn't hard. But we didn't have consensus, Roni."

"To open a door?" Roni shook her head in visible disgust, which, Theo thought, Vela didn't deserve. They *should* have reached consensus—or at least let the proceduralists talk. Roni was weak on consensus-building—and consensus-reading, too. Consensus was one of the things the Team was supposed to help her with.

"As long as the door's open," Kartor said, "maybe we should go in."

Team Six exchanged another round of glances, and Theo didn't blame them. The teacher always awaited the class. The seminar room was the instructor's space, and students only entered with permission.

On the other hand . . . Theo heard the muted twitter from her mumu, the tone she used to warn herself that she was about to be in trouble . . .

"If we don't get to our stations soon," she said from the back of the group, "the room will mark us all late—as Teams *and* as students!"

Simon bit his lip, but he turned to address his teammates. "She's right," he said. "It's the student's responsibility to be on time, no matter the conditions!"

Vela nodded, gathered her team with a nod and a hand-wave of consensus, and entered the room. Roni, Kartor, Estan, and Anj followed, with Theo and Lesset bringing up the rear.

There was the usual clatter as they got to stations, adjusted table heights, set up their 'books, and logged into the Learning Group Space. Then, it got . . . quiet.

Theo shifted and looked around, first at the empty teacher's station where Professor Appletorn ought to be standing, and then at her classmates—which was pretty much what everybody else was doing.

"Should we *tell* somebody?" Naberd asked. "Call the Safeties, maybe?"

Simon shrugged, and Estan looked up from his 'book with a frown.

"I can't find a procedure for what we should do if the instructor is..." his voice dropped, "...missing."

Silence. Then Vela spoke up. "I'm going to ask for consensus to call the Safeties."

"That won't be necessary, Ms. Poindexter."

There were quick loud steps and a clang and clatter as an Educator's Rod was tossed haphazardly into the corner, making everyone jump in startlement.

Professor Appletorn swept into the room, slapped the autoboard up and spun on the balls of his feet, a frown on his face.

"The correct and studied term would be *late*, rather than *missing*, Mr. Vanderpool, and within the bounds of my contract I am neither."

The professor stood there for some moments, hands behind his back, keeping the silent class rapt while he leisurely looked from face to face as if counting them, or verifying that both teams were in full attendance.

"Perhaps," he said suddenly, "Mr. Vanderpool will be so kind as to remind this august gathering of scholars of the basic tenets of Advertence."

Theo held her breath. Estan Vanderpool was a stolid, solid, meticulous boy who wasn't easily rattled. Normally.

"Well, Mr. Vanderpool?" Professor Appletorn's voice

was sharp enough to slice cheese, as Father said, and he hadn't waited the full thirty seconds, either. It was like he was *pushing* Estan, only of course he wouldn't do that. Not really. Pushing was Physical Intimidation and that was *'way* more trouble than just a note in your folder.

Estan took a breath so deep his shoulders lifted.

"Advertence is the quality of being heedful or attentive. It carries the connotation of consideration and deep thought. A scholar who practices advertency is a careful researcher who weighs what she has learned before forming a hypothesis to lay before her colleagues."

*Text perfect*, Theo thought with relief, *right out of the first lesson*.

Professor Appletorn rocked back on his heels, thumbs hooked into the pockets of his coveralls.

"Indeed," he said softly. "And what avenues are open to the study of an advertent scholar . . ." He paused, then stabbed out with a fleshy forefinger. ". . . Miss Tibbets?"

Theo frowned. Another of her teammates, not as stolid or as solid as Estan. Sometimes Anj was there, and sometimes—she wasn't.

This morning, though, she was home and answering her mail.

"The avenues of study open to the advertent scholar," she said crisply, "are: text, eyewitness, and primary source."

"Images?" Professor Appletorn asked, almost mildly.

"Images require an exacting level of observation and consideration, because they're so easy to manipulate. Primary source images, or those documented in the texts and which have provenance, are preferred, but even then the careful scholar will seek corroboration in another study-set."

Their instructor nodded in silent agreement, lips pursed, then jerked his head toward row three, toward...

"And what, *Miss Waitley*," he snapped, "do we say of the scholar who depends solely on primary sources, and shuns the validation of the texts?"

Theo blinked, and stupidly, the first thing she thought was that Professor Appletorn *was* targeting their Team, singling them out one by one.

"*Well*, Miss Waitley? Have you none of your price-less pearls to cast before us this morning?"

He wasn't just in a bad mood, Theo thought, he was *angry*. She took a breath, her fingers touching the keys of her school book, sending the link into the Learning Group even as she looked up into his big square face.

"Sir, I propose a textual validation as a starting point for forming an understanding of such a scholar." Her voice was cool and crisp, more like her mother's than her own. "I cite the paper published by Professor Monit Appletorn, an Acknowledged Authority in the field of research dynamics. Professor Appletorn tells us that those who seek out the treasure of the primary source are the most dedicated of scholars, instant Authorities, whose work validates the work of all those who come after."

Silence. Theo, watching the color drain out of his face, wondered if he was going to faint.

"Am I to understand, Miss Waitley," Professor Appletorn said, and his voice wasn't sharp, now; it was soft, almost a whisper. "Am I to understand that you have read and given consideration to this paper?"

"Yes, sir," Theo said, which was nothing less than the truth. Kamele would ground her for a month if she heard Theo claiming credit for research she hadn't done.

"Have you?" Professor Appletorn whispered. "Why?" *Why?* Theo blinked at him in amazement.

"I am waiting, Miss Waitley." His voice was stronger again, and Theo took a breath to steady herself before answering.

"I was doing my preliminary research for the course," she said slowly, trying to figure out how she'd managed to make him even madder; "and your paper was cited in several of the texts. I—it was only what an advertent scholar would do, to pull up and read the paper."

"I see." The silence stretched thin and cool while he stared at her. "You are either very stupid or very clever, *Miss Waitley*." He said her name as if it tasted bad! He turned his head suddenly. "Which is she, Miss Grinmordi?"

Lesset actually twitched, her mouth forming a perfect O. Her voice was surprisingly strong at first, then faded suddenly away—"I, she, well . . . evidently . . ." There was a pause, as if words—never her firmest friends—failed her. She threw Theo a helpless look and then looked back to their professor.

"It, um, depends . . ." she stammered finally.

The whole class held its breath.

Professor Appletorn seemed to . . . deflate. Not that he became less angry, Theo thought, but that his anger had used up more energy than he had available.

He sighed.

"That is correct, Miss Grinmordi," he said temperately. "Evidently, it depends. We do not yet have sufficient data to make a determination."

He turned and walked to the front of the room, putting his hand on the control for the autoboard, just as someone's unmuted mumu chimed the first eighth of the hour.

Uncharacteristically, Professor Appletorn ignored the sound, apparently giving the autoboard his whole attention.

"Simon Joniger," he said, finally naming somebody who wasn't one of Theo's teammates. "Please share your links for our last study assignment."

The rest of the seminar had been interminable, the students' mood not improved by the amount of solo work "for next time" in addition to that outlined in the syllabus. At the end of the session, the two Teams escaped as a group, silently, with only an exchange of glances in which relief and puzzlement were equally mixed.

Theo had to hurry to catch up with one of the victims, who was walking head down, eyes down, and at a dangerous clip.

"Phew. Lessie . . ." Theo ventured, finally gaining her friend's scowling attention.

"You see?" Lesset moaned as they got on the belt to the maths hall together. "I can't *think* when he snarls at me like that. My mind goes blank and I just want to be someplace else—"

"But you did fine!" Theo protested. Lesset blinked.

"I did? But he was so *angry* . . ."

"He was angry at all of us," Theo said, then shook her head. "No, he was mad when he came to class. Something must've happened before—the reason he was late, maybe. And he was trying to rattle us—*specifically* us, our Team." Which was, she thought, weird. What could Four Team Three have done to make Professor Appletorn so mad?

"But you said I did fine?" Lesset persisted. "How?" Theo sighed.

"*It depends* was the right answer," she said. "It was correct, exactly the thing an advertent scholar would have said." She gave Lesset a smile. "I wonder how much data you have to have to decide that somebody's a nidj?"

But Lesset was off in another direction, looking vacantly at the walls and people sliding by for a moment before gathering together another question.

"Did you *really* read that paper? The one you cited?" Theo turned to stare at her. "I said so, didn't I?"

Her friend lifted a placating hand. "You did, and I know you wouldn't ever lie about your research. It's just—*why*?"

"Because Professor Appletorn's an Acknowledged Authority," Theo said patiently, "and I kept coming across cites to his paper when I was scanning the prelim lit. Reading one more paper wasn't *that* hard."

"Fact?" Lesset obviously had her doubts.

"Fact," Theo said firmly, and, noticing that her friend still looked tense, tried a joke. "See what you could be reading instead of *The Faq*?"

"Oh!" Lesset's face went white, then red. "Oh!" she cried again. "That's just—antisocial!"

"Wait!" Theo held up her hand. "It was supposed to be funny—"

"To you, maybe! But I don't think it's funny to be laughed at." She took a deep, furious breath, and turned to walk away—or tried to, her upset making her oblivious to the direction of the belt's travel.

The ultra-safe, grippy surface of the belt would have assisted her flight, if she'd been properly balanced. Unfortunately, Lesset had thrown her weight at an angle to the direction they were traveling in, heedless of inertia. The resulting resistance knocked her off-balance; she staggered, her bag swinging forward over her shoulder, unbalancing her even more.

Theo snatched at her friend's arm just as Lesset threw herself backward in an awkward attempt to recover her footing, and the two of them went down in a heap, Lesset yelling.

The belt immediately slowed to a stop, and the other kids surged forward—then dropped back at the shrill sound of a whistle and shout of, "Safeties!"

"Stay where you are!" The taller of the two officials snapped when Theo tried to get up. "We have to run a scan."

This they speedily did, while Theo wished Lesset would get her bag off of her knee, and tried to figure out how late they were going to be for math.

"All right, you can stand."

Lesset stood first, head hanging. Theo flexed her bruised knee and followed.

"Names?" The shorter Safety asked, mumu pointed at them, the red "record" light showing.

"Theo Waitley," she said resignedly, and heard Lesset whisper her name.

"What happened?" The taller one asked.

Theo took a breath. "Lesset stumbled on the belt. I thought she was going to fall and tried to catch her."

"And instead of catching her, you *both* fell down, the belt stopped, and you, your Team, and all the rest of the students here are going to be late for class."

The taller one shook her head and tapped her mumu. "I see you're flagged as physically challenged, Miss Waitley. Next time, I suggest you pay attention to your own balance and let your friend help herself." She gave Theo a stern look. "Unless you were *trying* to be disorderly?"

Theo gaped at her. "No!"

"Thumb-prints here," the shorter Safety said, presenting his mumu, screen up. "Three downs for Four Team Three, and notes in your files, Ms. Grinmordi and Ms. Waitley."

The Safeties stepped off the belt. "Everybody face front. Motion beginning on the count of three—One! Two! Three!"

The belt started up, slowly, steadily gaining momentum. Theo faced front, bottom lip firmly caught in her teeth, and pretended that she didn't notice Lesset's downcast look, or Roni's loud whisper to her belt-mate.

"Oh, yeah—Theo Waitley. She's the clumsiest kid in Fourth Form!"

# FIVE

· · · · · · ·

*City of Efraim*
*Delgado*

"THEY DIDN'T HAVE ANY YUMMIFISH AT THE CO-OP," she told Coyster apologetically. He flicked his ears and looked at her reproachfully from his perch on the edge of the desk.

"I know, I know. I'm a bad provider. But, look. I brought you a ball." She put it on the desk by his toes, and gave it a push. It jingled across the surface, beady red eye-lights flickering enticingly.

Coyster yawned.

Theo shook her head in mingled amusement and irritation. "You're welcome," she said, moving across the room. She shifted the cube to the front wall, one end against a corner of the closet, picked up the lid and went up the hall to the 'fresher.

The shredded paper—unused, as far as she could tell—went into the disposal. The lid went into the sanitizer, just in case. She washed her face while it was being zapped and dragged a comb through her hair, wincing when she pulled knots, and wishing, not for the first time, that she had sleek, well-behaved hair like Lesset's.

The sanitizer pinged and she retrieved the top, wrinkling her nose in protest of the sweet, lingering antiseptic odor.

A rapid series of jingles greeted her as she opened the door to her room, but by the time she stepped inside, Coyster was sitting in the middle of the floor washing his face, his back to the ball.

Theo grinned, but pretended not to notice as she fit the lid onto the cube and crossed the room to her bag.

The Best in Five Worlds Kitty Pan had cost more than she'd expected—"Twenty creds!" she told Coyster as he inserted a supervisory nose into the assembly process. "I hope you're happy."

She pushed him gently out of the way while she finished programming the cycles, but he was inside almost before she'd gotten it into the corner.

While Coyster was inspecting his new facilities, Theo took the self-cleaning bowls out of their sanitary wrappings. She filled one with kibble from the sack she'd picked up—not, as it happened, the same kind that they fed the cats at home, but the only kind the co-op carried.

She stowed the resealed sack in the bottom drawer of the desk and went up the hall again to put water in the second bowl, coming back just as Coyster pushed his head through the crack between the door and the jamb. Theo frowned.

"Thought I'd closed that," she muttered, toeing him out of the way. She made sure the door was latched behind her before putting the water next to the food bowl, and sitting down on the cold, smooth floor.

The bowls were blue. In the co-op, they'd looked bright and cheerful; here, they looked—faded, and more than a little forlorn.

"It wouldn't be so bad," Theo told Coyster, who'd wandered over to sniff at the kibble. "If we could dial up a mosaic. All this white is . . . boring."

Coyster looked at her over his shoulder—accusingly, she thought.

"I *know* it's not the best kind, but it's all they had."

He blinked, executed one of his in-place precision turns and put his front feet on her knee, looking questioningly up into her face.

Theo smiled and rubbed his ear, smile wobbling wider as he pushed his head into it.

"If you *really* want to know," she said, "I had a lousy day. Professor Appletorn had a scope primed for our Team; I made Lesset fall on the belt, the Safeties gave the whole Team three downs *and* we were late for math, which was two downs more. Not only that," she continued gloomily, bending over so Coyster could butt her head with his. "Marjene wants to *have a chat* tomorrow after teamplay, and all the rugs in the co-op are made out of *plaslin!*"

Coyster burbled and tugged on a lock of her unruly hair.

"Thanks," Theo said, using both hands to stroke him down his whole length. Soft fur over wire-strong muscles. Not what you'd expect from a creature whose most strenuous activity was chasing a ball around the room for a couple minutes.

She stroked him again. He purred briefly, then backed gently from between her hands, executed another precision turn and faced the food bowl. He picked a single crunchy up in his mouth and munched it consideringly. Theo waited, wondering if she was going to get the emphatic left-hind-foot-shake that meant, so Father said, "This is *not* acceptable."

After a pause, Coyster bent his head again and began to eat.

Relieved, Theo rolled to her feet, socks slipping on the floor, requiring a quick twist of her shoulders to stay upright.

"Nidjit anti-social floor!" she muttered. "Whoever thought making everything out of ceramic was a good idea ought to be evaluated!"

She grabbed her bag and hauled it over to the desk, making sure to place her feet firmly. Most of her solo work was done, thanks to a double research period after math. She thought she'd go over the analysis trees for Advertency one more time, though—after today, she didn't want to do *any*thing to call Professor Appletorn's attention to her ever again.

"Though it would be useful," she told Coyster, as she unslung her school book, "to know what made him so mad." Or maybe not, she thought, jacking the 'book into the cable labeled "research." It wasn't as if the class could do anything to *prevent* whatever it was from happening a—

Coyster, momentarily sated, was sitting with his back half-turned to her, looking high into a corner of the room. Just trying to fool her into thinking there was something there, the way cats did—but no! If he'd been at home, and finished with his after-school snack, *that* would be when she'd change the airflow to the mobile that by all rights should be hanging in that corner. Too late to bring it, and besides, it didn't look like the mobile's kid-safe auto-attach would work on the slick ceiling anyway. Theo ground her teeth. Why couldn't things have just stayed the way they were? Everything had been *fine*—

Warmth spread from the utility pocket where she kept her mumu. She pulled it out, flicking the screen on with a practiced one-handed motion.

It was a text from Kamele, short and, Theo thought, terse.

*Agenda lengthy. Home before ninebell. Do your solos. Don't forget to eat.*

Eat. Theo sighed wistfully as she slid the mumu away. She didn't suppose the kaf would be able to deliver one of Father's melted cheese sandwiches and a mug of evening tea. Her eyes filled, blurring the desk. She bit her lip, turned, her foot slid and she went down, hard, on her rump on the cold floor.

"Chaos!" she yelled—and began, to her utter embarrassment, to cry.

She'd been lucky in her timing. Not only did she catch the direct bus to Efraim, which was Nonactown's official name, but she got a seat by the screen, where she could pretend to be absorbed in the map and condition reports and ignore the superior looks of the half-dozen Chapelia acolytes in their baggy gray uni-suits and half-face gauze.

She did bite her lip when the 'change for Greensward highlighted, but she didn't tap for a stop; she stayed in her seat, hands folded decorously on her lap, and only had to blink once or twice to clear her eyes as the bus continued on its way.

Strictly speaking, she should have had her mother's

permission, if not an actual bluekey, for a solitary expedition outside the Wall. She *had tried* to text Kamele. All she'd gotten was the "away" message, though, which meant the meeting with the lengthy agenda was level two confidential or higher, a fact that might have been more interesting if Theo hadn't been focused on other things.

In the end, and after a consultation with Coyster, she'd left a short message in Kamele's in-queue, grabbed a sweater, and ran for the bus. There should be no problem accomplishing her errand and getting back to the Wall before Kamele's meeting broke up.

She did think that her mother might not be delighted to hear that Theo had been out alone to Nonactown. But it wasn't, Theo thought, like she was *wandering*. She had a goal and a destination—Gently Used, on Merchant Street. Father had taken her there—if not *often*, then at least several times. He'd introduced her to the proprietor, too. While that didn't exactly put her or the shop on the Safe List, Theo felt sure that Father wouldn't have taken her anyplace *dangerous*.

Despite the bus being a Direct, transit time to Merchant Street this evening was slightly longer than she had estimated. The Chapelia de-bussed ahead of her, en masse and in step, going right while she would be going left, and she breathed a sigh of relief to see them go.

Her feet had barely touched the street when her mumu sang sevenbells. Still, she thought as she walked down the pathway—no belts in Nonactown—or in the suburbs where her—where Father's—house was, either—it shouldn't take *that* long to buy a rug.

The evening breeze made her glad she had her

sweater and reminded her that walking within the Wall, or in its shadow, made both time-keeping and weather-minding by sight difficult. Father did that—used the position of the sun in the sky to tell the time, and the type of clouds and wind-direction to predict coming weather—he said it "kept him close to the world"—and he'd taught Theo the way of it, to Kamele's amusement.

"We have devices called clocks, Jen Sar," she'd said, from her seat on the garden bench. "Which tell us the time when we're inside, too."

"Indeed," Father had answered gravely. "And yet sometimes—we are outside. And in some circumstances—rare, I allow!—devices fail."

Kamele had shaken her head with a small smile and returned to her book; and Father had continued Theo's lesson.

Speaking of time, Theo thought, shaking herself out of her memory, it was passing, and the clouds were moving from the west, on the back of the brisk evening breeze.

The street was busy this evening, light spilling out into the dusk from unshuttered shop windows and doors. Theo walked carefully, her stomach grumbling as the breeze brought the scent of frying spice bread to her. Almost, she crossed the street to buy a slice, but the recollection that there were only twenty-four creds left on her card moved her on past.

First, she told herself, she'd buy the rug. Then, she'd have a piece of fried bread.

The door to Gently Used stood open; on the walk outside, Gorna Dail was talking vivaciously to an old man with an electronic zither strapped to his back.

Theo slipped past the animated conversationalists and into the store. She passed the low counter with its light-guarded displays of rings, fobs, bracelets, and dangles with only a cursory glance. Father wore jewelry—a twisted silver ring on the smallest finger of his right hand—but Kamele said that honors were decoration enough.

The rugs were in the back of the store, piled together by size. Theo located the pile she wanted and knelt beside it, her fingers busy over the fabric.

"Is there something in particular you're looking for, young student?"

Theo gasped, and blinked up into the worn face and smiling eyes of Gorna Dail.

"Such concentration," the shopkeeper said, and the smile moved from her eyes to her lips. "Theo Waitley, that's your name, isn't it? Has the housefather commissioned you for solo flight?"

Theo looked down, and rubbed her hand over the nap of the rug she'd dragged across her knees. It felt good, springy and soft at the same time. Like Coyster.

"My mother and I have . . . relocated to the Wall," she said to the rug.

There was a small silence, then a neutral, "I see." Gorna Dail hunkered down next to Theo and ran her hand over the rug, like she was considering its merits, too.

"It's good to have something to break up all the white," she said, "inside the Wall."

Theo looked at her in surprise. "You've been inside?"

Gorna Dail laughed. "Long ago—and only for a semester. I was a Visiting Expert, so they gave me an apartment on—Three?—no, I'm wrong. *Topthree.*

It was well enough. By the standards of fourth-class ship quarters, it was spacious. But I remember those walls, and the floors—all white and slick. Easy to clean and to sanitize, I suppose, but not very restful." She glanced at Theo. "In my opinion, of course."

"Not only that," Theo said feelingly, "you can hardly stand up without your feet sliding out from under you!"

"Yes," said Gorna Dail placidly. "I remember that, too." She stroked the rug on Theo's lap again, frowning slightly, and reached out, running an expert thumb down the side of the stack.

"You were a Visiting Expert?" Theo asked, diverted.

"Oh, yes. Years and years ago. Before you were born, I daresay. It's what I did, in those days, to make a name for myself. You won't believe me, maybe, but I have *two* master certifications, from University itself."

Theo looked at her, but the older woman's attention was on the rugs. "But," she blurted, "what are you doing in Nonac—in Efraim?"

That got her a sideways smile.

"Hah. I *had* forgotten that... Non-academic! Everyone who is not studying or teaching is non-academic! Do you think I should be living inside the Wall?" She shook her head. "I'm retired, now."

"Then," Theo said. "Why are you on Delgado?"

Gorna Dail laughed. "Because, after all my traveling, I wanted to settle on a nice, quiet, boring little world, where nothing of note ever happens. And Delgado—aside the college and its great work, of course!—is certainly that. Ah." She slid her hand into the pile of rugs, and pushed them up. "Pull that one out, if you will, and tell me what you think of it."

Theo grabbed the rug indicated, and pulled. It was

heavier than she had expected, with a sheen to the mixed blues and greens that reminded her of water.

"Betinwool and silk," Gorna Dail murmured. "It's used, but whoever owned it before me took care of it. It could pass for new."

"New—" Theo snorted as she flipped the edge of the rug up and looked at the knots on the underside. "The new rugs at the co-op are all made out of plaslin."

"And you won't have that, eh?" Gorna Dail smiled again. "I don't blame you in the least, Theo Waitley. Now, tell me honestly—what do you think of this rug?"

Theo ran her hand over it, pleased with the way the nap silked along her skin, and smiled at the cool, swirling colors. It would almost, she thought, be like having her water mosaic again.

"I like it," she said to Gorna Dail.

"Good. Now, let's talk price."

"All right," Theo said steadily. "How much is it?"

Gorna Dail laughed, and sat back on her heels. "No dickering here, I see!"

Theo looked down, cheeks hot. "I don't know what you mean," she said, her voice sounding sullen in her own ears.

"A joke, Theo Waitley," the shopkeeper said placatingly. "Only a joke. On many worlds, in many cities, a price is . . . mutable. It changes with the weather, the time of the day, the demeanor of the buyer, the mood of the shopkeeper. It is not an entertainment of which Delgado partakes, more's the pity. So, for you, the price on the rug is forty cred."

Theo licked her lips, and ran her hand over the rug again, which was a mistake, because it only made her want it more.

"I can't spend that much today," she said, and looked up into the woman's face. "Could you—I can pay twenty-four cred today, if you can put it aside for me? And tomorrow—well, no, not tomorrow," she corrected herself. "I've got teamplay after class. But, I'll bring the rest the day after tomorrow for sure."

Gorna Dail tipped her head. "And carry the rug home on the bus?"

Theo paused, then found her solution "I'll take a cab."

"Excellent," the old woman said, with a slight smile; "but I think I may have a better answer, if you'll allow me."

"I'd be glad to learn," Theo said politely, and wondered why Gorna Dail chuckled.

"I propose this: I will charge your card for the full amount—" Theo opened her mouth—and subsided when the shopkeeper held up a hand. "Wait until you've heard it all. What I propose is charging your card for the full amount, *tomorrow*."

Theo blinked. "Can you do that?"

"Easily," the woman assured her. "Also, because you're such an accommodating customer, I'll throw in a pack of grippers, so your rug won't slide all over that slick floor, and—" She paused and smiled at Theo. "*And* I'll have them and this rug delivered to you tomorrow evening, after teamplay."

"Really?"

"Really. All you need do is swipe your card and give me your direction. Will that suit you, Theo Waitley?"

"It will!" Theo smiled, relieved. "Thank you!"

"My pleasure, child," Gorna Dail huffed as she pushed to her feet. "My pleasure."

# SIX

· · · · · ·

*History of Education Department*
*Oriel College of Humanities*
*University of Delgado*

"SO, THEN," KAMELE WAITLEY SAID, WITH A CALM AUTHority she was far from feeling; "we're agreed."

She looked carefully around the table at her colleagues, who had not seen the need, who had not wanted to commit the funds—and whom she had one by tedious one brought to her side. She wished that it had been finesse or gamesmanship, pure reason, or anything other than brute will that had carried the day. If she had come back to the Wall sooner or, failing that, taken the necessary time to strengthen her ties inside the department—but she had come late, and reluctant, driven by what Jen Sar dignified as "necessity." If it were discovered—and it would be!—that the Educational History Department at Delgado University had failed to pursue an investigation after one of their own professors was dismissed for falsifying data—they would lose students, funding; perhaps their accreditation! And it would not happen, Kamele had sworn—not on her watch.

*Your honor is in peril as much as the department's,* Jen Sar had said, after listening to her lay out her observations and her fears. *Of course you must do what is necessary to bring all into Balance.*

Balance, as Kamele had learned over the years of their life together, was the Liaden ideal. And it was deucedly difficult to maintain.

Which did not mean that it should not be pursued.

"It appears that we have indeed agreed to an *in situ* forensic literature search," Mase Toilyn said quietly from half-way 'round the table. "In order to be certain that the two instances of dishonest scholarship of which we have become aware are, as we believe, the only such instances."

"It's expensive," Jon Fu said, which had been his constant objection throughout the meeting. This time, however, the note of complaint had given way to resignation.

"Expensive, yes, but prudent," Ella ben Suzan, Kamele's oldest friend and her only ally at the table, concluded firmly.

"...prudent," EdHist Chair Orkan Hafley repeated, sighing as her hands fluttered over her note-taker. Flandin had been her protégé; that Admin had allowed her to remain as chair was, in Kamele's opinion, worrisome. It hinted at alliances extending into the Tower itself, but even so, Kamele assured herself for the twentieth time, it did not mean that Hafley's position was robust, or that true scholarship could not prevail.

"Yes," Hafley said, finally, frowning down the table at Kamele. "Yes, *Sub-Chair*, we're agreed that it's our duty to husband the reputation of the college and its scholars. What we *haven't* agreed upon is which of the numerous protocols should be implemented, or, indeed, who should do the work. Perhaps," she concluded, with heavy irony, "*you* have a suggestion."

Kamele forced herself to meet that frown and counter it with a smile.

"But remember that the Emeritus Oversight Committee was formed for this very purpose!" she said with false cheerfulness. "We'll apply to them for dispassionate searchers."

"Well," the chair sniffed. "And the protocol?"

Kamele reached to the notepad, fingers dancing over the lightkeys. Three blue links hovered inside the Group Space at the center of the table.

"Please," she said, looking 'round at her four colleagues once more, "everyone contribute three links concerning your favored protocol."

Fingers moved; a set of yellow links joined the blue, and a moment after, green, red, violet . . .

Kamele nodded. "Now, if we do a branch-search," she tapped the command into the notepad, and watched with satisfaction as the trees formed and connected, closer and closer, until, at base . . .

"As you can see," she said, keeping her voice pleasant and calm. "Each of our favored implementations has at root the Antonio Smith Method. That being so, I would suggest that the basic Smith Method, which has not only been proved in rigorous field conditions, but has also birthed so many daughters, is best suited to our purpose."

There was some discussion of the suggestion, of course, though briefer than it might otherwise have been.

She injected the possibility—nay, the probability!—that the search and approach they had agreed upon might eventually be adopted as an official protocol for the university entire, and with the calculating looks brought into some eyes and faces came a certain willingness to move at long last from talk, to action. When the chair finally adjourned the meeting, the responsibility for contacting the Oversight Committee rested satisfactorily in the hands of Ella ben Suzan.

"I think you handled that very well," Ella said as the door to Kamele's office closed behind them. She stretched with vigor before collapsing dramatically into the visitor's chair, her head against the back and her eyes half-closed. "And you were afraid you'd lost your touch."

"I *have* lost my touch," Kamele said, casting a half-amused glance at her friend. "Honestly, Ella, you should have become a professional actor."

"And been disowned? No thank you. I like my comfort—now as much as then. Besides, hadn't my best friend already set aside childish pursuits to aim for a more realistic goal?"

Kamele sat down behind her desk and tapped her mumu on without looking at it. "With my mother's . . . strong encouragement."

"Mothers exist to guide their daughters," Ella murmured. "I'm quite content with the amateur troupe." She opened her eyes and squirmed into a more upright position.

"But enough of youthful reminisces! This evening you not only manipulated our honored colleagues of the EdHist Department into consensus, but you got Hafley into a corner, so that she *had* to back you or risk an open divide within the department, which she can ill afford. All of that, and you still insist that you've lost your touch?"

Kamele sighed and leaned back in her chair. "I was clumsy," she said. "If I didn't push them, I certainly drove them, and you're not the only one who saw the manipulation. *Depend* on it—Hafley saw what I was doing, and she'll find a way to make me rue it. Having me shoved in as sub-chair over her candidate—"

"And wouldn't Jon Fu have made a wonderful sub-chair?" Ella interrupted. "*Yes,* Chair. Of *course,* Chair!" Her voice had gone all wobbly and unctuous. "The wisdom of a thousand grandmothers could not teach us better than you do, Chair."

"Stop!" Kamele laughed. She raised a hand. "Stop— it's too perfect! His own mother would be deceived."

"Or she would pretend to be, so she could be rid of a bad job," Ella said darkly, then waved. "Hafley's light was fading even before Flandin's perfidy was discovered. The Directors won't be long in replacing her," she said, and grinned one of her wide, lunatic grins. "*Kamele Waitley, EdHist Chair.*"

Kamele snorted. "Not likely."

"Nothing *more* likely, now that you're finally demonstrating the proper reverence for your career!" her friend retorted. "You'll see—and I expect my sabbatical to be quickly approved when you're made chair."

Kamele considered her. "Sabbatical? Isn't that out of sequence? In any case, it's *my* plan to name you sub-chair if your prescience is proven."

Ella shook her head in mock sorrow. "How many times do I have to tell you, love: *First* the sugar, *then* the rod."

"Yet you find hard work sweet."

"You know me too well," Ella said with a fond smile that slowly faded. "Speaking of hard work—how's Theo taking the . . . move?"

"She'll adjust," Kamele answered, surprised at the grimness of her own voice.

Ella laughed slightly. "Spoken like a loving and vigilant mother! And you?"

"I?"

"Don't be dense, darling."

Kamele glanced down and fiddled with her mumu for a moment. "I don't anticipate any problem readjusting to the Wall. I grew up a Mouse, after all."

"As we both did." Ella stood. "Well, you know where I am—not as high on the Quad as you, of course, Sub-Chair!"

She walked around the desk and bent down to give Kamele a quick kiss on the cheek. "I have rehearsal," she murmured. "You're not working tonight, I hope?"

Kamele shook her head. "Theo's home alone."

"Oh." Ella looked serious. "Well . . ."

"Ella . . ." Kamele said warningly.

Her friend raised her hands placatingly. "I know, I know! She's just a bit clumsy. It's a stage. She'll grow out of it." She sighed and lowered her hands. "If she doesn't do herself or someone else a serious injury beforehand."

"She'll be fine," Kamele said firmly.

Ella took refuge in a laugh, spun lightly on her toes and headed for the door.

"I'll see you tomorrow, Kamele."

The office door closed behind her and Kamele sank further into her chair, reaching up to rub her eyes.

Chaos and disorder, but she was tired! She'd crammed a week's worth of meeting prep into a working lunch and tea, and another week's worth of people-prep into odd moments before the meeting itself. She'd gotten what she wanted—what the department needed!—and the work ahead looked mountainous, indeed.

Among all the work that needed to be done, she had explicitly *not* needed Monit Appletorn importuning her in the break room this morning. Even if she had been disposed to consider him in the light of an *onagrata*, the timing and . . . boldness of his presentation would have given her pause.

Not that she considered Monit anything but a humorless, ambitious annoyance, or ever had. Kamele ran her hands into her hair, making the disorderly chaotic. Make that an egotistical, humorless, ambitious annoyance.

And then there was Theo. The child was nervy at the best of times, and she'd made it plain that the relocation had neither her approval or her support. Kamele sighed. Depend on it, had it been Jen Sar who had proposed they move to the Wall, Theo would have been brought over in a heartbeat, glowing with excitement and eager to help in any way she could.

Setting aside the fact that Jen Sar could charm wisdom from a Simple when he chose to, Theo adored him—a state of affairs that had previously seemed . . . benign. Surely, it was a good thing for a child to have a solid male role-model? Their remove to the Wall, however, suddenly threw Theo's attachment to her mother's *onagrata* into an awkward light. She had, Kamele admitted to herself, shirked her maternal duty. It was going to be bad enough after Theo's *Gigneri*—

"Which is borrowing trouble," Kamele said aloud. The earliest possible date for Theo's *Gigneri* was more than six months away. So much could happen in six months, when you were fourteen.

And when you were forty-four.

Her mumu chimed eight bells four. She'd told Theo she'd be home before ninebells. If she didn't leave soon, she'd break her word.

She reached for the mumu—and only then saw the Safety Office icon blinking ominously from the in box.

Her heart lurched. Gasping, she tapped the message open.

It was not, as she had foolishly feared, a note calling her to the infirmary or the hospital on her daughter's behalf—that was obvious from her first hasty scan.

Her second, calmer, reading revealed that the letter was a Parental Advisory. Theo had taken another fall on the belt between classes—and this time, she'd pulled someone down with her.

Kamele closed her eyes, recited the Delgado Senior Scholar's Pledge, and read the advisory a third time.

It would seem that Theo's victim was Lesset Grinmordi. Kamele grimaced; as thin as Theo's friend-loop was she could hardly afford to lose one, even a flutterhead like Lesset. Kamele sighed and looked back to her mumu. The report stressed that there had been no aggression involved, but was rather an accident, born of a lapse of judgment.

That much, Kamele thought, was a continuing positive point in her daughter's behavioral record.

Whatever Theo *was*—odd, clumsy, brilliant, sullen—she wasn't aggressive.

The Safety Office recommended that Kamele review Theo's physical limitations with her again. It further recommended that the two of them contact the infirmary for an overview of the various medications—all perfectly safe!—that might be expected to alleviate those same physical limitations.

"Physical limitations," Kamele muttered. Jen Sar would have one of his mannerly fits if—

But Jen Sar, she recalled, around a gone feeling in her stomach, was out of the loop; the courtesies paid to the Housefather were no longer his due.

Which didn't make the prospect of reviewing Theo's physical limitations with her any more appealing. And she would see the university in ashes before she drugged her daughter to make her orderly—perfectly safe, or not.

For a moment she closed her eyes, seeking a restful pattern and only seeing the slow twirl of a receding star field. Her sigh was loud enough to startle her eyes open. It would be easier if she knew she still had the luxury of the occasional casual glass of wine and exchange of small gossip with Jen Sar. But there—necessity. She had known what this quest would cost her; and believed it to be worth the price.

Kamele touched the mumu's screen, filing the advisory. The next letter in-queue was from Marjene Kant, Theo's mentor. Kamele sighed and tapped it open.

Marjene reported that she had arranged to chat with Theo tomorrow after her teamplay. She appended the Safety Office report of Theo and Lesset's fall on the belt, and added her own commentary:

*While it is not my intention to second-guess a mother's arrangements for her minor daughter, I cannot help but feel that this unfortunate incident would not have occurred if you had allowed me to prepare Theo for the upcoming alteration in her living arrangements. It's clear to me that her physical challenges are exacerbated by stress...*

Kamele touched the screen slightly harder than was strictly necessary, filing Marjene's letter away.

The last note was from Theo. It stated, very briefly, that she had gone out to buy a rug for her room, and expected to be back at the apartment well before ninebells.

Kamele closed her eyes. A rug.

On one hand, a mother in receipt of a message not respectfully seeking permission to buy a rug, but informing her of the act, might—ought!—to be...annoyed.

Yet, on the other hand, she could scarcely blame the child. Theo had grown up in a sensation-rich environment; Wall quarters must appear...stark and inhospitable to her. In fact, she admitted, their new apartment seemed a bit comfortless to her, who had been a Mouse for her first twenty-eight years.

"Life would have been much simpler," she told the empty office, "if I hadn't gone to the chancellor's reception."

But that was nonsense. She *had* gone to the reception, all those years ago; she *had* met Jen Sar Kiladi, then newly come to Delgado to take the Gallowglass Chair, been fascinated by him, and eventually offered him the opportunity to become her *onagrata*.

And the fact was—the *truth* was—that her life would

have been simpler, yes, and also much poorer. Leaving aside the mental, and physical, stimulation that came with his companionship, Jen Sar was a good friend—to her, and to Theo. The years she had spent in his company had been neither wasted nor extravagant.

Her mumu chimed again, warning her of the approach of ninebells. She stood, slid the device away into its pocket.

Time to go home.

# SEVEN

· · · · · · · · · ·

*Retrospection on an Introduction*
*Chancellor's Welcome Reception*
*for the Gallowglass Chair*
*Lenzen Ballroom, Administration Tower Three*
*University of Delgado*

"*WHERE,*" ELLA GROWLED, SHOVING A GLASS INTO Kamele's hand and grabbing her elbow, "have you *been*?"

"Rehearsal," Kamele hissed back, allowing herself to be steered into one of the ballroom's dimmer corners.

"Rehearsal?" Ella repeated blankly, and then, more sharply, "You're late for the Chancellor's Reception because of a *choir rehearsal*? Have you lost your mind?"

It was, Kamele acknowledged, taking a sip from her glass, a fair question.

"I didn't think it was going to last so long," she said mildly, and made a show of scanning the room. Scholars as far as the eye could see, the ranks of dusky formal robes broken here and there by the brilliant yellow of a Director's coat.

"So," she asked, "where is he?"

"Your collar's crooked," her friend answered. "And your robe isn't sealed."

Kamele raised her glass, taking care to *sip*. She wasn't nearly as cool as she wanted Ella to see— junior faculty simply were *not* late to a Chancellor's Reception. And junior faculty most definitely did not over-drink at so august a gathering. That was for after.

"Kamele . . ."

She sighed and put the glass into Ella's hands, turned so that she faced the corner, yanked the rumpled collar straight and slid her finger down the robe's front seam. Then she twirled once, slowly, as her friend's face threatened to add a wrinkle on the spot.

"All tidy, now, Mother?" she asked, taking the glass back and having another sip. She was, she told herself, calm. She had not missed the reception, and that was the important thing.

Well, one of the important things.

"Where is he?" she asked again.

"Who?" Ella blinked at her, and Kamele sighed.

"The new senior faculty member. Double—or is it triple?—Professor Kiladi. The Gallowglass Chair, remember? The reason this reception went to the top of your social calendar for the year?"

"Oh," Ella said, "him." She tipped her glass in an easterly direction. "Over at the receiving area, last I saw. Looks stiff and chilly and stern. He'll fit right in with the rest of the tenured."

Kamele grinned.

"I do feel for him," her friend continued; "just a bit. His back has got to hurt like destruction. Mine would, after all those bows."

"Bows?"

"One for each of the seniors, as they passed by on review," Ella said. "Very elegant, each one. The Chancellor and Director Varlin were positively *aghast*, you could tell by the way they just stood there next to him, like they'd been dipped in plastic and left to dry. I suppose they didn't go over protocol with him, or expect that he'd bring his own."

Kamele choked a little on her sherry.

"Did you introduce yourself?" she asked.

"I was waiting for *you*," Ella answered repressively.

"That was noble." Kamele had a last sip of sherry and regretfully placed the nearly full glass on a nearby tray. "Since I'm here, I guess we'd better do our duty and introduce ourselves, so we can be promptly forgotten."

"What else are junior faculty for?" Ella asked rhetorically, placing her glass on the tray as well.

"Waste of perfectly good sherry," she muttered, as she slipped her arm through Kamele's and the two of them stepped out into the light.

Gallowglass Chair Professor Jen Sar Kiladi was not a tall man; indeed, Kamele thought, he was slightly shorter than her own somewhat-less-than-average height. He was, however, *upright*, and wore his formal robes with an air; right hand resting lightly on the head of the black ironwood cane that was the badge of his station. His face was sharp-featured, and displayed a certain patient politeness. One received the impression that he could stand there, coolly elegant and not at all discommoded, the whole night through and into tomorrow morning.

Arm-in-arm, she and Ella tarried at a polite distance while a junior in the dusky purple robe of the Hard

Sciences offered a trembling introduction in a voice too soft for them to hear.

"Not a beauty," Ella whispered, leaning her head companionably against Kamele's. "More's the pity."

Kamele bit her lip. Ella had an eye for a pretty man, though surely Professor Kiladi was so far above either of them that it hardly mattered if he was easy on the eyes or a three-headed ogre.

The Gallowglass Chair had done with the trembling junior, who was walking rapidly in the direction of the nearest source of sherry.

"Our turn," Ella whispered. She slipped her arm free and stepped forward.

At the edge of the receiving area, she paused and brought her hands together in the Scholar's Text.

"Ella ben Suzan," she said, her voice perhaps, Kamele thought, a shade too crisp. "History of Education."

Professor Kiladi bowed, graceful as a dancer.

"Scholar ben Suzan," he murmured, his voice deep and grainy.

Ella gave him a firm nod and moved aside. Kamele stepped up to take her place.

Looking at a point just over his right shoulder, she brought her hands together to form the open book. "Kamele Waitley. History of Education."

Professor Kiladi tipped his head. "You are a singer, Scholar Waitley?" he asked, and for a moment she thought he had caught her out; knew of her lateness and the reason and was about to call her to the attention of the Chancellor.

Gasping, she met his bold black gaze—and managed a quick smile and a head shake.

"I'm a member of a chorale," she said, speaking carefully. "Recreational only, of course. My studies arc my life's work."

"Certainly," he replied, "study illuminates the lives of all scholars. Yet there must be room for recreation as well, and joy in those things which are not study. I myself find a certain pleasure in... outdoor pursuits."

"Outdoor?" She looked at him doubtfully. "Outside the Wall?"

He raised an eyebrow. "There is a whole planet outside the Wall," he murmured. "Surely you were aware?"

Was there, Kamele wondered, a thread of dry humor in that craggy voice?

"I've heard it said," she answered, matching his tone as nearly as she might. "But tell me—what manner of pleasure may be had outside of the Wall?"

"Why, all manner!" he declared, bold eyes flashing. "Gardening, fishing, walking among the trees and growing things, watching the sun set, or the stars rise..."

"Watching the sun set?" Was he having fun at her expense? "That seems a very... fleeting pleasure."

"I have heard it argued that the highest pleasures are ephemeral, and best enjoyed in retrospect." He paused, then added, softly, "Though there are those of us who disagree."

Kamele caught a motion of robes from the edge of her eye and turned to look. Ella was moving away with the new adjunct from Mathematics—Norz? Vorz? She couldn't recall, though he was excessively pretty. And that was doubtless the last she'd see of Ella tonight.

Abruptly, she recalled herself, and looked back, surprising a look of... sympathy on Professor Kiladi's face.

"Forgive me," he began, but she stopped him with a wave of her hand.

"I think we must have been the last faculty to introduce ourselves," she said seriously. "Would you like a glass of sherry? I'd like to learn more about the pleasures of watching the sun set, if you'd be kind enough to teach me."

Some time later, with the hall all but empty, they were still talking. Professor Kiladi had not grown prettier; indeed, the best that could be said was that he had an *interesting* face. Kamele found it became more interesting—found *him* more interesting—as they continued to talk. The black eyes were quick, and the humor disguised by the deep, rough voice surprisingly—and enjoyably—wicked. It was probable, Kamele conceded, that Professor Kiladi was something...less than...compliant.

"I have undertaken the impossible!" he declared at last, with a rueful smile and a regretful shake of his head. "I cannot *teach you* a sunset, Scholar. You must experience it at first-hand."

Kamele put her—second? third?—empty glass down on the tray and considered him. "All right," she said equitably. "Show me."

Both well-marked brows rose, and he lifted his hand, the twisted silver ring on the smallest finger catching the light.

"Scholar, you must forgive an old man his—"

He paused, his expression arrested, seeming scarcely to breathe. Concerned, Kamele dared to touch his deeply braided sleeve.

"Professor Kiladi, are you all right?"

He blinked as if he were bringing her back into focus and gave her a smile that seemed...less genuine than his other smiles.

"A consultation with my muse; I did not mean to alarm you." He glanced down into his half-full glass, then up into her face.

"If you wish it, I will be pleased to show you a sunset, Scholar Waitley. We merely need to find a time when our schedules—and the planet's rotation—align."

"Thank you," Kamele breathed, her eyes still on the violet-drenched horizon. "That was..." Words failed her; she smiled and turned to face him. "Thank you," she said again.

He returned her smile.

"It was no effort of mine, I assure you," he said. "You might experience a sunset yourself every day, if you wished to do so."

"Not every day," she said wistfully. "You saw my schedule!"

"So I did," he acknowledged. "But the fact that you are here proves that there is at least one evening when you may partake of this pleasure."

She nodded, her eyes drawn again to the horizon, where the gaudy display was deepening to black.

"And this is only one of those pleasures you told me of," she said. "Is watching the stars as...glorious?"

"The stars impart a different, but I find, equally satisfying pleasure," he said softly.

"I imagine it would be difficult to time that particular pleasure," she murmured. "Night Eyes open at tenbell."

"Surely the monitors would not consider someone quietly sitting and looking at the sky a danger?"

"It would be . . . odd behavior, even if it wasn't specifically on the danger list," she pointed out. "For the purpose of public safety, odd is dangerous."

There was a small pause, and a light sight. "I do keep forgetting," Professor Kiladi said ruefully. "Delgado is a Safe World."

"You say that as if it were . . . unsavory," Kamele said, turning to look into his face.

He raised an eyebrow. "Unsavory . . . no. Far different from other worlds? That . . . yes." He looked out though the final light had faded into night, and was silent long enough that Kamele dared a question.

"What are you thinking?"

"Eh?" He blinked and raised his head, offering her an absentminded smile.

"I was thinking that perhaps I should acquire quarters outside of the Wall."

She turned to stare at him. "*Outside* of the Wall?" she repeated, shocked to the core of her Mouse's heart.

"Indeed," he said coolly, as if there were nothing remarkable in the plan at all. "A small house, perhaps, down there—" He pointed downhill from their shared seat on the bench in the faculty green.

"In Nonactown?"

"Not, I think, in Efraim itself," he murmured; "the lights would spoil the stars. No . . . perhaps over there, to the right of town. A small house, with a walled garden, so that I might sit out all night if the fancy takes me, without embarrassment to the Directors."

"Would you do that?" Kamele looked at him doubtfully. His sense of humor was so dry that it was sometimes difficult to know when Professor Kiladi was joking. On this instance, however, he did appear to be serious.

He smiled at her. "I have, alas, been known to take odd fancies. Shall I escort you inside now?"

"Not . . . just yet," she said, looking down at the lights of the town. She struggled to understand him. To want to live outside of the Wall; distant by choice from one's intellectual colleagues. How odd. And yet—a sunset every day? That might tempt, she thought.

"Will you grow . . . crops in your garden?" she asked, as if it were the most usual thing imaginable.

He laughed. "Flowers, I assure you! Perhaps some shrubs. A tree . . ." He took a breath, and shook his head slightly, as if amused by his own plans.

"Is that another—Outside pleasure?" she asked. "Growing flowers?"

"I fear that it may be," he confessed.

Lights were coming up in the town below. A garden, Kamele thought, with . . . flowers.

"I would like to see that," she said finally.

"I would be delighted to invite you, once all is accomplished," he answered gallantly.

"And I'd be delighted to accept the invitation." She smiled and rose. "I have to go in and grade papers," she said. She held out a hand and he placed his palm against hers. "Thank you again, Professor Kiladi."

"Please," he said, his rough voice serious, "let me be Jen Sar."

That was another shock, but a pleasant one. She smiled.

"And let me be Kamele," she said.

"Assuredly," he murmured. He stood and offered his arm. Together they strolled back toward the Wall.

# EIGHT

· · · · · · · · · ·

*University of Delgado*
*Faculty Residence Wall*
*Quadrant Eight, Building Two*

THEO'S MUMU SANG ITS *YOU'RE-THIS-CLOSE-TO-TROUBLE* tune as the bus pulled into the Wall terminal. She threw herself down the exit ramp and ran across the plaza for the entrance.

"Chaos and destruction!" Night Eyes opened at tenbell, but Mice who hadn't had their *Gigneri* were supposed to be inside by ninebells, or they'd better have a bluekey to show the Safeties at the entrance. Being Outside after curfew without a bluekey—*that* was a trip to the Safety Office, Kamele and Marjene called in for an instant meeting with a Safety Liaison, and herself presented with a Plan of Behavior. At least, Theo thought, running as fast as she could, *that* kind of trouble wouldn't pull down the Team average.

"You didn't get enough notes in your file for one day?" she muttered as she slapped her palm against the scan plate and waited in an agony of impatience for the main door to open.

Open it did, painfully slow. She slid through when the gap was wide enough to admit her skinny self, took a breath and walked—*calmly*—past the Safety station and the Eye, toward the belt platform.

Her mumu thweeped ninebells as she stepped onto the belt for Quadeight Twobuild. Theo sighed in relief—then shook her head. She'd managed to dodge trouble with the Safeties, but she still had her mother to face.

"The bus was late," she said experimentally. While this was actually true, it sounded like an excuse. Kamele—and Father too, if it mattered—would say that it was her responsibility to be sure of the time-table before she traveled, and to plan in advance. She had just *assumed* that the evening bus would run the same route, and take the same time, as the morning commuter bus—and she'd been wrong.

Unlike the daytime commuter, the late bus wandered the streets of Nonactown, picking up and setting down an astonishing variety of passengers, most of whom stared at her coveralls and sweater like they'd never seen a student before, and two who were definitely the kind of people that Father *Looked At*. People Father *Looked At* inevitably looked—and often moved—away. Without Father there, they stared, and then they'd moved, all right. They came over to sit in the seat behind her, whispering loud enough for her to hear.

"Fluffy-headed dacky girls shouldn't be on the bus all alone, should they, Vinter?" the first whispered.

"Dacky girls think the whole world's safe," the

second, presumably Vinter, whispered back. "Dacky girls think the Eyes never close."

"The Eyes don't watch everything—even we know that!"

"Got another maybe," Vinter said.

"What's that?"

Vinter's voice sank, though it was still perfectly intelligible to Theo, where she sat very still, with her head turned toward the side screen, pretending hard not to notice them.

"Maybe not a dacky girl at all," he whispered.

There was a moment's silence, then the first one whispered hoarsely. "You mean—a Specialty? Down here?" As near as Theo could tell, he sounded genuinely awed.

"Happens," his friend said sagely. "Knew a techie saved up a whole half-year's cred to have a Specialty come down from the station all dressed up like a Liaden."

"But who'd *pay* for a fluffy dacky?" the first wondered, and the two of them laughed noisily. Theo bit her lip.

The route map she was staring at flickered, the upcoming stop limned in green.

"That's us, then," said the whisperer named Vinter. There was the sound of shuffling behind her as the two of them got up—while the bus was still moving!—and stepped toward the exit. Theo watched them out of the side of her eyes.

The first nonac looked down at her, giggled, and moved on, shaking his head, as he casually put his hand against the low ceiling, saying, "Wow, this is a rough section of road, ain't it? Hold on tight!"

As if his warning had made it happen, the bus hit a bump, bouncing Theo a little in her seat. The standing nonac slipped, and snatched at the ceiling, his hand covering the Eye mounted there.

The second . . . paused next to Theo. "Hey, dacky girl."

Theo turned her head carefully, trying to arrange her face into Father's *Look*. Judging by the way the nonac's grin widened, she didn't do a very good job.

"Be careful," he said, and before she understood what he was going to do, he'd put his hand against her shoulder and *shoved* her against the screen.

"Stop that!" Theo yelled, but the giggling nonac was already on his way to the opening hatch.

"Go back inside the Wall!" he called over his shoulder—"where a rough bus ride won't bang you around like that!"

His buddy smirked, took his hand off the Eye, and the pair of them were gone, down the ramp and into the low-lit night. The hatch rose, and with a whine of electrics the bus got moving again along its extended route.

Theo looked around her, but she was the last one on the bus. She settled into the corner of her seat, rubbing her shoulder where he'd pushed her. . . .

The Quad Eight belt stop was coming up, she realized, her attention suddenly on the reality at hand. She grabbed the bar and swung onto the platform.

For a moment she stood still, eyes closed while she took a deep breath, like Father had taught her to do. She tried to clear her mind, too, but all her mind wanted to do was try to figure out how mad

Kamele was going to be, and what she could say to defend her actions that didn't sound either stupid or antisocial.

*Well,* she thought, taking another deep breath; *I'll just have to improvise.*

· · · ·�֍· · · ·

"Theo? I'm home!" Kamele's voice slid off the slick walls, coming back to her in a faint echo. There was no other answer to her call.

"Theo?" Half worried and half irritated, she walked into the dim, untenanted dining alcove. The door to the kitchen was shut tight. Frowning, Kamele opened the door, and touched the kaf's query button. As she had suspected, the last withdrawal on record was breakfast.

Kamele shook her head, irritation edging over worry. This antipathy to the kaf—obviously, she needed to have a chat with her daughter—*now.* Kamele spun on her heel and headed for Theo's room at a determined pace.

The status light showed that the room was occupied, and Kamele's irritation spiked into anger. Sulking in her room, pretending not to hear—she slapped the entry override.

The door opened, displaying the desk, school book jacked in, but the student nowhere to be seen. A small ball winked red lights at her from beneath the chair. The closet was against the left-hand wall, and a packing cube, too; on the right were two bowls, one filled with water, the other with kibble, and a litter pan. Regardless of the assurance of the status light, the room was empty.

Or not.

"*Prrhp*?" the orange-and-white cat commented, strutting out from behind the cube. He wove a long, welcoming hug around her ankles before strolling out into the hall.

"Coyster!" Kamele called, but the cat, predictably, kept to his route. She took a breath, adding *smuggled cat* to the list of her daughter's transgressions. How long had the girl thought she'd get away with *that*? she thought, snatching her mumu out of her pocket.

She tapped up the parental oversight section and keyed in the tracking request as she walked back down the hall.

Her mumu squeaked.

Startled, Kamele looked down at the screen.

*Out of range.* The letters were red. Kamele tapped the query button.

*The unit you attempting to contact is not responding.* The help text scrolled, as if she didn't know that. *This may mean that the device has been damaged, or that it is presently located at a point outside the university network. A systemic lapse may, rarely, return a false negative. It is suggested that you wait a few moments and try again. If a second negative is returned, please contact the Office of Academic Safety.*

Out of range? Kamele eased down into one of the rickety plastic chairs in the receiving parlor, and pulled Theo's message out of archive.

*Gone to buy a rug, back before ninebells.* Terse to the point of rudeness, with no please or thank you or request for a bluekey...

Kamele bit her lip, staring hard at the blameless floor. Request for a bluekey... If Theo's mumu was outside the college's network—but surely not! No question that she was headstrong and willful—but even Theo wasn't foolish enough to go Outside without a bluekey—

Unless, she interrupted herself, Theo *had* a bluekey. What if she had applied to Jen Sar?

Kamele shook her head. No. Theo might have asked, but she would not have talked Jen Sar Kiladi into violating the proprieties. Which left two possibilities: Either there had been a rare momentary stutter of the Wall intranet, or Theo had gone Outside without a bluekey, without asking permission, and without telling her mother where she was going.

*Well,* thought Kamele, *there's a way to test that proposition.*

But she didn't immediately tap her mumu. Instead, she sat with it in hand, her eyes on the rug she had brought from home. She and Jen Sar had bought it together, at an eccentric little shop in Nonactown. They'd laid it on the floor of the common room in his house, and there it had stayed, a delight to the eye and the foot until—Kamele shook her head. They'd put it away years ago—she no longer remembered precisely why—and forgotten about it until—

The apartment door twittered, clicked and opened. There was the sound of quick steps, and a quiet, "Oh no, the door!"

Theo stepped into the room.

· · · ❖ · · ·

Her mother sat poised on one of the stupid plastic chairs, mumu in hand and an expression of cool remoteness on her face that Theo knew all too well.

Kamele was in what Theo privately called her Mother Scholar Mode. What it meant was that Theo was about to be questioned, lectured, then questioned again to be sure that she had internalized her lesson.

She felt her shoulders crawling up toward her ears, fingers unoccupied with handwork curling in toward the palms. She tried to take a deep breath, but her chest was so tight, it—

"*Prrpt?*" The query was followed by a vigorous bump against her knee. Theo looked down as Coyster finished weaving himself around her ankles. He sat on her foot and wrapped his tail 'round his toes.

*You should've told her about Coyster at breakfast*, Theo scolded herself. *She wouldn't have heard you, anyway.*

"Good evening, Theo," Kamele said coolly. "Would you like to tell me where you've been?"

*Well, no*, Theo thought; *I wouldn't*. Unfortunately, she couldn't see any way out of it.

"I left a message in your queue," she said, sounding sullen in her own ears. "I went to buy a rug."

"I saw that message. You promised to be back before ninebells, but you failed to tell me *where exactly* you intended to purchase this . . . rug."

Theo bent down and picked Coyster up, which at least gave her something to do with her hands. He hooked his front paws over her shoulder and stuck his nose in her ear, purring.

Kamele raised her mumu and Theo saw the glint of red letters on the screen and the unmistakable shape of the Safety Office logo. She swallowed. Had the Eye reported her, after all? But she'd been inside before ninebells!

*Perhaps a case of luck over intention, Theo?* Father's voice asked from memory, and Theo bit her lip. Great. Like it wasn't bad enough that *Kamele* was going to lecture her...

"Could you," her mother said quietly, "be a little more specific?"

*Might as well,* Theo thought, reaching up to stroke Coyster, *get it over with.* She raised her head and met Kamele's eyes.

"I went to Nonactown," she said. "To a store called Gently Used." She hesitated, then decided that explaining a bit further wouldn't seem to be a excuse. "Father had taken me there, when... *before.*"

Kamele... blinked, her expression wavering. She looked down quickly, and cleared her throat.

"I see," she said after a long moment. "And you went *alone* on this... expedition?"

"Yes," Theo admitted, adding, "I knew exactly where I was going," which might have been—just a small—excuse.

"Sometimes," Kamele said, glancing down again, "the unexpected happens, even when we know exactly where we're going." She sat up straighter in her chair and put the mumu on the battered table top.

"Traveling to Nonactown by yourself demonstrates an extreme lack of judgment, Theo. I'd thought you were more mature, but obviously I was mistaken. For the remainder of this grade-term you will go to school and to teamplay, and then *you will come home*. We'll revisit this subject at the Interval, and evaluate. If, at that time, I see evidence of more mature behavior, we'll discuss an adjustment to these arrangements. Am I clear?"

Theo stared. No lecture? And hardly any questions? That was so unlike Kamele that for a moment Theo forgot to be upset about being grounded.

"Theo," Kamele repeated sternly. "Am I clear?"

"Yes," Theo assured her, hurriedly. "However, I have . . . conflicts."

Kamele looked stormy. "And they are?"

"Tomorrow after teamplay, I have an appointment with Marjene," Theo said hurriedly. "And on Oktavi, I'm . . . Father and I meet for dinner."

Her mother sighed. "You may keep your appointment tomorrow with Marjene, of course, and will come directly home afterward. As for the Oktavi arrangement with Professor Kiladi . . ." She glanced down—maybe at the floor, or maybe, Theo thought, holding her breath, at the rug.

"I will consider that, and let you know my decision tomorrow. Is there anything else?"

"No, Mother," Theo said meekly.

Kamele nodded. "Where's your rug?" she asked suddenly.

"My—rug?"

"You went to Nonactown to buy a rug, you said. Where is it? Or didn't Ms. Dail have anything to your liking?"

"I . . . she . . ." Theo closed her eyes and concentrated for a moment on the solid presence of Coyster beneath her hands—soft over hard, she thought, and stroked him again before opening her eyes and looking at her parent.

"It's going to be delivered," she said steadily. "Tomorrow. After teamplay."

"Delivered," Kamele echoed, and sighed. Theo

waited, shoulders tense despite Coyster's warmth—but Kamele only sighed again and shook her head.

"Very well. My last subject for the evening." She frowned. "Smuggling a cat into this apartment shows another disturbing lack of judgment. How long did—"

"I didn't smuggle him!" Theo interrupted, stung. "He brought himself!"

Kamele frowned. "I beg your pardon?"

"He brought himself," Theo repeated. "I was packing—he must've jumped into the cube when I wasn't looking, and then I was in a hurry, so I just sealed the lid without—and when I opened it here, there he was!"

"And you didn't bother to tell me?"

"It was late," Theo said, trying to be as diplomatic as possible about her mother's state last night, "and you were—you were tired. I was going to tell you tonight, but—"

"But other matters intervened," Kamele finished for her, lips pressed tight. She sighed. "Call Professor Kiladi, please, and ask him to arrange to retrieve his cat."

Theo stared at her, tears rising, hands pressing Coyster so tight against her shoulder that he grumbled a complaint and squirmed. She let him go, barely attending as he dropped to the floor and strolled over to sit next to Kamele's chair.

"Kamele . . ." Theo began, horrified to hear her voice quavering. Her mother raised a hand.

"*Now,* Theo."

Bottom lip caught between her teeth, she pulled her mumu out, tapped the quick-key, and raised it to her ear.

"Good evening, Theo." Father didn't sound surprised to hear from her. On the other hand, he didn't sound pleased either. Neutral, that was it. Inside her head, she could see the bland expression that went with that tone.

"Father," she said miserably. "Um . . ."

She took a breath, ducking her head to wipe her damp cheek on her shoulder. No word from Father. He would, Theo knew, wait until she told him what she was calling for. Silence didn't bother Father, like it did some people. . . .

She cleared her throat. "Coyster's here," she managed, voice shaking.

"Ah. I'm pleased to know where he is. I'd thought he was angry with me for having misplaced you, and was sulking."

"No," Theo said shakily. "He packed himself into my cube and I didn't know he had come along until I opened it last night."

"I see. Well, he appears to have decided upon his posting. I can hardly argue with his choice."

"Yes, well . . . Kamele, um . . ." She closed her eyes, picturing him in her head, black eyes sharp, face attentive, waiting politely for her to continue. "Kamele asked me to call you and—and ask you to, to arrange to . . . take him back."

The silence from his side continued longer than she had expected. Her stomach had almost tied itself into a knot when he sighed.

"Theo," he said gently—no—*carefully*. "Please ask your mother if she will speak with me."

"Yes, sir." She diffidently looked to her mother. "Father . . . wonders if you'll talk to him."

For a second, she thought Kamele was going to refuse. Then she sighed sharply and thrust out a hand. Theo crossed the room and gave her the mumu.

"Jen Sar?" she began, in her briskest, coolest voice. "I—" She stopped. Closed her eyes. Coyster stood up, stretched—and jumped into her lap.

"Yes," Kamele said. "I am aware of your thesis that cats are symbiotic rather than parasitic. However, the fact remains that—" She stopped again, mouth tight. Coyster bumped his head against her free hand; she raised it absently and rubbed his ears. Theo held her breath.

"That's nonsense!" Kamele exclaimed. "There's nothing *strange* to her here! She has her Team, and her school work, and her—" Another sharp silence, while her fingers continued to rub Coyster's ears.

"Very well," Kamele said finally. "But *only* until the end of the term, are we— You're quite welcome, Jen Sar ... Yes, of course—and you, as well." She turned the mumu off, placed it on the table next to hers, and sat staring at the pair of them for a long moment. Theo kept as still as she could, hardly daring to breathe. Father had talked Kamele into letting Coyster stay, but that didn't mean that Theo couldn't talk her right out of it again by being a nidj.

Finally, Kamele looked up, and gave Theo a small smile.

"Professor Kiladi makes a strong case for the benefits of Coyster's continued residence here—at least until the end of the term," she said moderately. She picked Coyster up and put him gently on the floor, then rose, brushing cat fur off her coveralls.

"It's long past time for dinner," she said, and held

out her hand. "Shall we see if the kaf will provide anything moderately edible?"

That was a peace offering. Theo smiled, reluctantly, and came forward to put her hand into Kamele's.

"All we can do," she said, "is try."

# NINE

• • • • • • • •

*Teamplay: Scavage*
*Professor Stephen M. Richardson Secondary School*
*University of Delgado*

"FOUR TEAM THREE IS THE NEXT TO LOWEST RANKED team in Fourth Form," Roni said, loudly, as they left their Ready Room for the first class of the day. "Why do you think that is, Theo?"

*You know better than to answer that,* Theo told herself, and bit her lip. Roni wasn't just bad at consensus, sometimes it seemed like she was actively against it.

"I guess *you* never earned the Team a down," Kartor said, hotly. Theo blinked. Kartor never got into arguments.

"'Course I have," Roni snapped. "But even *you* have to admit that five in one day is...exceptional."

Kartor's ears turned red. "What's that supposed to—"

"Casting blame is antisocial," Lesset spoke up. "We're a Team; we're supposed to help each other." She stared at Kartor, which was, Theo thought, trying to ignore the knot in her stomach, not fair. *Kartor* hadn't started the argument.

"Are we supposed to pretend that we don't know which member of our Team is pulling the rest of us down with her?" Roni rounded on Lesset, her chin and shoulders pushed forward. "We're supposed to practice intellectual honesty, aren't we?" She threw a nasty look over her shoulder at Theo. "And *advertency*."

Theo felt a rush of heat, and looked down to make sure of her footing as she mounted the belt.

"That's aggressive, Roni," Estan said sternly. Next to him Anj smiled absently and nodded.

"That's all right," said a cool, amused voice that Theo barely recognized as her own. "She's just peeved because, without me, *she'd* be the one who'd earned the most downs for the Team. Isn't that right, Roni?"

Kartor laughed, Lesset gasped, Estan looked stern, Anj kept on smiling.

Roni's face turned an interesting sort of purple-red color. Her lips parted. Theo watched her interestedly, wondering what she would say next.

But apparently Roni thought better of taking the argument further. She closed her mouth and faced front, shoulders stiff.

Theo took a shaky, secret breath, and looked around at the passing corridor, pretending she didn't see Estan frowning at her.

In spite of the acrimonious start, the rest of the day went smoothly for Four Team Three. 'Course, Theo admitted to herself, as they filed into study hall, that was mostly because their Team mates had been very careful to keep Theo and Roni as far away from each other as possible. Theo did her part by grabbing the study table at the very back of the room, and opened her school book with a feeling of relief tainted by the knowledge that the worst part of the day was still before her.

She'd just have to hang back at teamplay, she decided. Four Team Three couldn't afford any more downs—Roni was right about that. The best thing to do would be to let her teammates play while she concentrated on not bumping into anybody, or falling, or tripping over the cracks in the floor. . . .

Theo sighed. For the millionth-and-twelfth time, she wished she wasn't so clumsy. In her head, she wasn't clumsy at all. In her head, she could see a pattern of how she and all the people and things in her vicinity *ought* to move, but when she tried to move like the pattern, she'd inevitably trip over a teammate, or pull them down, like she had done to Lesset yesterday. Teamplay was worse, even, than walking down the hall; and scavage was worst of all.

She sighed again as she remembered that she was supposed to have a "chat" with Marjene after teamplay. As her mentor, Marjene was committed to helping Theo negotiate and internalize the intricacies of social and intellectual interaction—that's what the Concierge said. Theo knew Marjene wanted to help make things easier for her, and she felt guilty—a little—for not liking her better and for not taking her advice more often.

Still, she thought, in an attempt to cheer herself up, after she lived through teamplay and her chat with Marjene, she could look forward to the delivery of her rug.

. . . which was good, she acknowledged, frowning at her 'book, but didn't quite make up for the fact that Kamele hadn't yet given her a decision about Oktavi evening. She *had* to see Father. The 'book's screen blurred, and Theo bit her lip, blinking hard—and blinked again, staring at the unfamiliar icon sitting in the bottom left corner of the screen.

It was a small, even a demure, icon, in official-looking dark green: a coiled Serpent of Knowledge, *Research* floating above it in precise green letters. Theo frowned. She was certain the green icon hadn't been on her screen yesterday, so it must've been downloaded from one of today's classes, but . . . All their Sci work was done in Group Space, and Professor Wilit, their Social Engineering instructor, hadn't shared any links with the class today. Though Professor Wilit didn't always announce downloads or extra work assignments.

*Well,* Theo thought, *it couldn't have gotten there by accident.* She must've just not noticed the download.

"Advertency," she muttered, remembering Roni's jibe. "As if."

She touched the green icon.

It unfolded, like a flower blooming, until the entire screen was limned in green, with a query box centered.

**Name?** The floating green text asked.

A quiz, Theo thought, staring at the familiar layout. How in chaos had she missed *that*?

She keyed in her name. The center box faded as a new one glowed into being at center top.

**Protocol**, the floating text said. **List primary line of inquiry.**

Theo closed her eyes, thinking back to Social Engineering. She didn't remember Professor Wilit saying anything about a solo quiz, or an unscheduled paper. On the other hand, she discovered to her chagrin, she didn't remember much about any of the day's classes; it was like she'd been doing the work in her sleep.

She took a breath and brought her attention back to the screen.

Primary line of inquiry, for a Social Engineering solo? She chewed her lip. It *had* to be a Social Engineering solo, she decided. It was just like Professor Wilit. So. The little bit she remembered from today's class had to do with the mechanisms that societies put into place in order to enforce the goals of that society. She probably couldn't go wrong by initiating a line of inquiry into an enforcer protocol. The problem was narrowing the subject.

*The Eyes don't watch everything,* she heard the bus whisperer's voice again. *Even we know that.*

Which was, now that she thought about it, kind of an . . . interesting . . . thing to know. Especially since *she* knew that the Eyes *did* watch everything. It was knowing that, as much as the Eyes themselves, that kept society safe.

Except . . . getting pushed wasn't exactly safe, was it? she asked herself, and reached for the keys.

**Primary line of inquiry:** *The Eyes, their purpose and their programmed watch cycles,* she typed, and paused . . .

The box closed.

"I wasn't *finished,*" Theo muttered, tapping the screen where the box had been. It did not reappear, but a third one did, at the right margin.

**Result Sought:** *A graph or map,* Theo typed rapidly, *illustrating unwatched areas, with timetable.*

The box faded, and a fourth came into existence on the left.

**Deadline?** it inquired, which gave her pause until she remembered that Professor Wilit never gave them deadlines for their work. She'd told them during their first class that she'd be doing a term-long study, and would share the results with them before the Interval. She'd said it would amuse them. Theo wasn't so sure—and, anyway, she liked to get her work done promptly. It wasn't like there was a lot of it, though if you listened to Lesset...

*ASAP*, Theo typed. The final box faded.

**Accepted**, came the message, and Theo nodded, fingering open a notepad and beginning to tap in a preliminary source list. She wondered if anyone at the Safety Office would talk to her about the Eyes, and if she should ask Professor Wilit for a study-chit. Each student got three per grade-term, and she'd already used one of hers. If the Safeties wouldn't talk to her, even with the chit, then she'd have wasted it, and would have only one in reserve for the rest of the term.

Her mumu was suddenly warm, signaling receipt of a message. Theo pulled it out of the pocket in her coveralls and thumbed the window up; her stomach clenching when she saw the text was from Kamele. If she couldn't see Father on Oktavi...

*Theo, you may keep your dinner engagement with Professor Kiladi.*

That was all.

Theo smiled and just sat there, holding her mumu and rereading that single line until the warning whistle sounded and it was time to pack up and go to teamplay.

✳   ✳   ✳

They'd changed clothes and got to the practice floor ahead of time with Roni's, "Don't be slow, don't be late!" echoing through the corridor the whole way. Of course they weren't going to be late—everyone on the team was trying to be on their mettle with the last few sessions worth of setbacks and point-bleeds threatening to drop Four Team Three to the lowest in the school for the year, much less to the lowest ever in the team's history. Seventy-eight Four Team Threes had come before them, and only five had had lower scores at this point in the year.

Father had once threatened to write a column for *The Faq* in order to gain, so he said, a greater audience for what he called the *Fallacy of Infinite Comparability*. Kamele had given him one of those frowns that quivered at the edges, like she was covering up a laugh, and said that if he wanted to commit academic suicide over a triviality it was up to him.

Apparently he had decided that publishing the *Fallacy* wasn't quite worth academic suicide, because the column never appeared. Despite that, Theo knew he had a valid point—comparing their team to teams from so long ago was . . . meaningless, really, given tech advancements, alterations in teaching theory and four dozen other facts. She felt the weight of team history anyway, and it wasn't made any lighter by the fact that *she* was the one holding the rest of them down.

Theo escaped the girls' dressing room with more relief than usual.

Roni'd been walking around with her shirt half-on explaining in a loud voice to the female team members the importance of bringing the Team average up, starting right now; and some more time complaining that she'd have to buy another new set of blouses, and maybe new shoes, too, because she was growing so much.

"Every one of us has got to start acting mature!" she'd said sternly, veering between topics like a honeybumble between two nectar-filled blossoms. "We've got to take responsibility for our own actions and support the team properly!"

Theo had tried not to cringe under the barrage of "mature, growing-up, and act-adult," sentiments Roni'd thrown around—it sounded like she was just re-broadcasting the last things she'd heard from her mentor. Worse, Roni had *particularly* stared at Theo's chest when when she'd said, "growing up."

It wasn't until Theo arrived at the game court that she realized why Roni had been talking quite so loudly and importantly. Normally, Roni wasn't much for the active games like Scavage—she said they made her sweat too much—but this was her second turn as captain, and Roni liked to be in charge!

*That's antisocial!* Theo told herself, and bent into her warm ups with a will, trying to focus on the Team, rather than the individuals.

As she warmed up, she heard the sounds of the balls being readied above the court; the slow clunks and chirps as they rode the ball-lift up to the ceiling feed tubes. Involuntarily, she looked up—but the launch bin wasn't open yet so she wasn't really trying to get a jump on the game.

The nearby smack of shoes against floor brought her attention to court-level again, stomach clenching as she saw that Roni was deliberately coming toward her. She was almost as noisy as Lesset, Theo thought, like she thought making noise was proof of effort. Roni came closer, the captain's band already around her arm, and her Team smile locked in place. Her forehead showed a sheen already, as if even the warm-ups were work for her.

"Theo, I just wanted to say—*I* don't believe those rumors that you knocked Lesset down on purpose," Roni said surprisingly. "I was right there and I saw the whole thing. It really was an accident! I think you really do *try* to be a good Team member, but you can't help it if you're clumsy!"

Theo stared, feeling her fingers curl in toward the palms. She *needed* her needle and her thread *right now*, she thought, or she was going to—going to—

Orange flashed at the edge of her vision. Gasping, she spun, and called out to the Team.

"Professor Viverain is on the court!"

Viverain was the acting head of the L & R department, but unlike Professor Appletorn, who held a full-time collegiate position, she was a traveling academic who sought work where she could now that her old college had been decertified. Viverain rarely instructed the Four Team students, but when she did she wanted them to play just as sharp as graduating Fifth Forms.

"Four Team Three, I expect everyone to be in position by the time the ball-bin is full!" Viverain called out. "We're going right to a game!"

*Groronk!*

The first round buzzer went off and the bin overhead emitted a rumplety-bumplety sound as the balls loaded. The Team members stared up into the bin, trying to get a look at the balls they'd drawn—and each called a number. The Team Captain would then make the consensus call. Together, they had all of ten clicks to bid.

"Fourteen," said Lesset, which was predictable, because fourteen was about the least you could score on a round.

The greens... Theo thought she saw a lot of greens! Green was a high score ball if you could get a good shot...

"Sixteen," said Kartor. Theo thought that was a mite low... but the balls still weren't finished loading.

"Nineteen!" Estan and Anj called at practically the same second. That was starting to be high, in Theo's opinion... but no, maybe they'd seen how many greens there were.

Surer now, Theo called out her bid—"Eighteen!"— just as the bidding clock hit eight.

Roni stared, soundless, at the overhead... the clock hit nine, then...

"Twenty-one!" she called; the official Team bid. Everyone else gasped. That hadn't been a consensus call!

The buzzer double-clucked and the first ball began to roll down the spiraling wire chute, dropping toward the launch spout. Roni hurried down court while her team members darted glances and shrugged shoulders at each other. Twenty-one would take *a lot* of luck.

Overhead, the chute vibrated and sang as the ball picked up momentum.

"Let's go!" Theo called. She pointed at Kartor, whose face was just shy of grim.

"Third Ring!" she said. "Estan, you back Lesset in

Second. Anj—" but Anj had already drifted dream-
ily off down-court. Theo sighed. The Team Captain
should've set the positions, but Roni didn't care where
the rest of them were, as long as she was in First
Ring, where scoring was easiest.

Roni liked to score.

They did work up a sweat on the first round, with
Theo's off-the-cuff positioning proving to be reasonable. She and Kartor were in the outer, largest, Ring.
They could, if required, dive or drive into Ring Two.
Ordinarily, you tried to get fast people into the middle
ring... but having Lesset on one side of Ring Two
wasn't too bad, because not only could Estan help
her when she flubbed, but Team members in Rings
One or Three could back her up, too. Depending on
how, and how bad, she flubbed, if the ball got back
into Two or Three on the other side of the court, it
might still be playable. Roni was hogging Ring One,
even though she shared it with Anj.

On good days Anj was their best player; and she
could rove into Ring Two at need. Playing at the edge
of Two, where Lesset should be, she could keep the
errors to a minimum. Estan played opposite Anj except
when back-up was required, and Lesset wandered
between her supposed posts, sometimes blocking good
passes and other times causing bad bounces.

On the whole, they did better then they had a right
to on the first set. A typical ball started out on the
spiral, gaining speed, rapidly, until one of the rotating
tubular launch points matched the slot the ball was
passing over. The circular court was entirely contained
within a tall thinly-padded wall and it was Kartor and

Theo's job to gather the ball off the wall, if that had been its trajectory, and sling it underhanded toward the center; or if it were falling elsewhere in the outer ring to make sure that it didn't continue to the outside or bounce away from the other team members.

Once in Ring One—or if lucky tossed or kicked from Ring Two—the ball had to be scored by getting it—for a single point—into one of the waist-high stationary chutes on a flaring parabolic column rising seamlessly from the floor and extending—with a similar flare at the top—to the ceiling. The three rotating chutes higher up the column scored more, with the highest, fastest and smallest chute scoring top points.

The column at school was well padded at the base and, like the spirals, formed of a lightweight open mesh fabric mounted on highly visible mechanicals. In the higher levels and in the pro game the column was a near invisible crystal structure which was often a nexus of collision, but which could be used to aim and deflect the ball to someone in better position for a shot. In *this* scholastic version, the column was less dependable as a tactic; its safety factor a minus rather than a plus.

Time was of the essence in *every* version of the game, because as soon as a ball crossed into Ring One, or numbered beats after it crossed into Ring Two, the next ball started down the spiral. It was bad form—and cost points—to scavage, or score, the second ball first.

They only did that three times, the scavage, and came out of the game with twenty-three points, which was good for a first go, and was aided by a lucky score on the part of Estan, who tossed the ball into the rotating upper goal just as the timer buzzed, and Roni calling for it from the other side.

The second round was a disaster.

Lesset managed to toss two balls in entirely the wrong direction, causing two double scavages early in the set after Roni had bid a slightly more conservative twenty in the face of her teammates' grumbling of how lucky they'd been in the first game. Everyone rushed to try to make up the difference, the sounds of their running sounding extra clumsy to Theo, and it didn't help that Viverain added to the noise and confusion, by leaning over the wall of the Instructor's Tower, shouting suggestions for all of them.

Twice, Viverain called encouragement, as Kartor and Theo got the ball toward the center, but once into the Lesset Zone things tended to go astray. Lesset's shoes constantly scraped and squealed against the floor as she tried to get back to where she wasn't, and Roni's footfalls sounded like nads slapping water in the pool. In the end, the team missed their bid by five, with the instructor counting out their errors, loudly, the while.

"Theo, you've got to get me the ball more!" Roni was panting, her face almost as red as her shorts. "I think if you hadn't kept passing to Kartor and Estan you really could have helped me score more. You know, maybe if you'd managed to get the ball to other *females* we'd've been in the game!"

Theo gritted her teeth. She'd *counted*. She'd passed the ball to Anj nine times, Kartor seven times, Roni five times, Estan four times, and Lesset three. Far more . . . oh, never mind. Roni's real complaint was that she hadn't scored when she had the ball, and that *wasn't* Theo's fault.

Viverain leaned over the wall. "Waitley, you've got a good touch on those passes. You might go to the inside a bit more, but otherwise . . . you're keeping Third Ring strong. And you, Grinmordi—you've got to keep an eye on where your tenders are. Instead of trying to intercept you ought to be letting some of those go through for the best shot."

Theo saw the look Roni gave her as Viverain clicked the remote for the round-buzzer. The balls tumbled into the rig and before anyone else could bid—without even looking up!—Roni called, "Twenty-five, Team, twenty-five!"

Theo caught the shock on Viverain's face, then she was running, because the first ball through was a blue one—the smallest and hence the fastest to the floor.

If the second set had been a disaster the third was always just one lucky move away from it. Lesset scored early on an improbable push shot using the column for a bounce-in, then Kartor went down against the wall hard digging another one out of the joint, his throw finding an off-balance Theo who managed anyway to fling it to First Ring, where Roni was in just the right spot to score.

They played hard, and finally it seemed there was some rhythm to what they were doing. Anj woke up, and they all started feeding the ball to her—everybody, that is, except Roni, who started calling for every shot to be sent to the captain. Three in a row went to her and were flubbed in a flap of mis-worn shoes, and suddenly there was a scavage, which was Estan's problem as he mishandled a cross circle pass from Theo, badly cutting their chance of making the bid.

The next-to-last ball was blue, bounding wildly off the wall before Kartor could get to it. Theo backed him up, snagged it and threw in the direction of Second Ring. It should've been Anj's play, but Lesset intercepted, and flung it purposefully but far too hard toward Roni. Roni bobbled the ball; the spinning goal rejected her throw *and* her rebound. By then a green ball was in the tubes. Roni called for the blue ball again, but Anj had it and made the goal with a casual one-handed toss.

Theo thought the green ball's momentum would likely bring it to her. She started moving, trying to position herself, but as the ten-tick gong sounded the ball found a slot and launched itself toward Kartor. He bobbled it, managed to push it to Theo, who was rushing toward Second Ring while the sound of approaching footsteps grew louder.

"It's mine, give to to me!" Roni's voice was loudest; but the others were calling out "Time!" and "Shoot!" and over it all Viverain bellowed, *"Now,* Theo!"

Theo's back was toward the goal; she held the ball lightly on her fingertips, and spun, ignoring the sounds of steps and the shouting; brought the ball up and threw it at the spinning top goal as hard as she—

*Kathunk!* Something hard slammed into Theo; she flung her hand out, grabbing for balance—there was a squeal of shoes, and a *splat!* The game buzzer went off at the same time as a high keening sound began and Roni's voice went from screech to howl.

"You killed me! Blood! Blood! I'm bleeding!"

Knocked breathless by the fall, Theo stared up at

her, seeing blood all over the other girl's face. She tried to get up, then rolled away, arms folded over her head to protect it from Roni's kicks.

"Killer! Sociopath! Killer!"

"That's enough!" Viverain shouted. The yelling and the kicking stopped, but Theo still huddled on the floor, wondering dully how many downs she'd earned the Team *this* time.

# TEN

· · · · · ·

A SAFETY ARRIVED WITH THE AID TEAM.

Viverain pointed one A-Teamer at Roni, hunched over on the bench with a wad of disposable towels held to her face, and the second at Theo, sitting on the floor with her back against the wall, and her forehead against her knees. Then she frowned at the Safety.

"What do *you* want?"

The red-headed woman raised her hands, showing Viverain empty hands. "You called for an Aid Team, which means injuries. Injuries usually mean an unsafe condition exists. And, since one of those involved is Theo Waitley..."

"Theo didn't do anything!" That was Kartor, sounding...angry.

*He better watch it,* Theo thought dismally; *or they'll put a note in his file.*

109

"I'm sorry, Kartor, but that's not correct," Viverain said sternly. "Theo *did* do something. She played the game, and she pushed herself to excel for the good of the Team. That's not 'nothing.'"

"She tried to kill me," Roni moaned.

Viverain *tsk'd*. "Nobody ever died of a bloody nose."

The A-Teamer knelt next to Theo, medscan in hand. "What hurts?" she asked, her eyes on the readout.

*Everything,* Theo thought. She lifted her head with an effort, and took a deep breath that ended with a wince and a catch.

"Ribs ache?" the A-Teamer asked.

"A little," Theo admitted, and held still while the other scanned.

"Nothing broken," the A-Teamer said slowly. "There's going to be some bruising, and some discomfort for the next few days. I'm going to give you an analgesic and a muscle relaxant right now to take the edge off the discomfort and keep you from stiffening up..." She unrolled her dart pack. Theo held out her hand, barely noticing the minor sting.

"How'd you happen to get those bruises?" the A-Teamer asked as she re-rolled the pack.

Theo shook her head. "I don't really—"

"Her teammate," Viverain said, suddenly appearing over them. "The *Team Captain*, in fact—kicked her while she was down on her back on the floor with the wind knocked out of her. She was on the floor because the *Team Captain* knocked her down, trying to grab the ball out of her hands. I was astounded; and I hope never," Viverain said, in her scavage-court voice, "I hope *never again* to see such a blatant and damaging display of ego over Team!"

The court was silent. Viverain hunkered down next to Theo.

"How're you doing, Waitley?"

Theo looked down, biting her lip. "I'm all right, ma'am."

Viverain sighed.

"Listen to me, Waitley," she said, as the A-Teamer rose and moved away. "This wasn't your fault. You were doing the job that needed to be done. Mason put herself in the way; she got hurt, and then she did her best to hurt you. It's not you who's anti-social—and it's not you who's getting a note in her file." She paused. "Theo, look at me."

Slowly, Theo raised her head and met Viverain's eyes. The L & R professor grinned.

"That's the spirit!" she said and rose, holding down a broad hand.

Theo took the hand and Viverain pulled her lightly to her feet.

"Take a couple deep breaths," she said. "See how those ribs're feeling."

Theo nodded, carefully filling her lungs. It hurt, but not so sharp. *Must be the analgesic,* she thought, and looked up as someone else approached.

It was the red-headed Safety, and she was frowning.

"You need to have a serious talk with your mentor, Ms. Waitley. You can't help having physical limitations. However, you do have an obligation to society to insure that your limitations don't harm other people."

Like she didn't know that. Theo took a careful breath.

"I have an appointment with my mentor right after

we're finished here," she said, her voice sounding thin and not too steady.

The Safety nodded. "I'll append my recommendations to Professor Viverain's report," she said. "Your mother and your mentor will receive both—and of course a copy will be placed in your file."

"Sure it will," Theo muttered, which was stupid, but if the Safety heard, she decided to pretend otherwise.

"All right," Viverain called as the A-Teamers and the Safety left the court. "Time to get going, people! There's another team coming in to play!"

Marjene's booth was in Grandmother's Library, all the way over in Quad Three. Theo arrived late, which Marjene was bound to mark her down for. At the least, it was disrespectful to be late to a meeting. At the worst, according to Dr. Wilit, being late to a meeting could be seen as an attempt to assert superiority over the other attendees.

She certainly didn't want to be disrespectful of Marjene. Marjene was there to help her. And as for asserting superiority—if her ribs didn't ache so much, Theo might've laughed. And she *really* didn't want another note in her file.

Still, she couldn't quite make herself hurry across the Service Zone's wide lobby. She set her feet carefully, and kept to the edge, where there was less traffic, rather than cutting straight across the middle to Grandmother's door.

Most of the traffic came from the Mother-Daughter Center, where women who were secure enough in their careers went to arrange for a child. They passed Theo briskly, some by themselves, some arm-in-arm with a friend, some with heads together, giggling; some serious. Theo bit her lip. Kamele would have taken Aunt Ella with her, when she decided it was time; they would have gone through the files, and checked them against Kamele's Daughter Book, where she'd written down all the hopes and dreams she had for her own child. They'd have made their choice; filed it, and paid the fee. After the mandatory three-day waiting period, Kamele would have returned for the implant, confident in her choice.

Theo sighed, wondering bleakly if Kamele would have continued, had she known that all of her careful planning would produce a physically challenged daughter who couldn't go three days in a row without getting another note in her file.

Probably not, she decided. And as for the unknown sperm donor . . .

The door to Grandmother's Library was just ahead. Theo took a deep breath, wincing when her ribs grabbed, and put her hand on the plate.

She hadn't gone two steps down the row, when her mentor swept out of the booth at the right rear, and folded her into a voluminous embrace, pack and all.

"Sweetie! You must be *exhausted*." She stepped back, to Theo's relief; Marjene's hug had hurt her bruised ribs.

"Come on back," her mentor was saying. "I've ordered us some juice and cookies."

Theo sighed. Marjene always ordered juice and cookies. Sharing food was a social method of reinforcing a personal bond, Dr. Wilit said. Following Marjene down the dim, carpeted hallway to her booth, Theo wondered what shape their relationship might have taken without the frequent application of sugared snacks.

*That's not fair,* she told herself sternly, as she slid her pack off, and swung up onto a stool. Marjene was here to help her.

"Here you are, sweetie." Marjene put a disposable cup in front of her, and Theo bit her lip. Two "sweeties" inside of as many minutes was not good news. Marjene must've already read the incident report.

Theo picked the cup up, more for something to do with her hands than because she wanted the juice. What she *wanted* to do was get out her handwork, and just . . . be alone . . . for a while. Unfortunately, it didn't look like she was going to be alone anytime soon, and as for the handwork . . . Marjene would be disappointed if Theo succumbed to her "nervous habit," and Marjene was already plenty disappointed.

Theo sipped the tepid, too sweet beverage, put the cup back on the table, and folded her hands tightly together on her lap.

"That's better," her mentor said, sitting back with a smile. "You've had quite an eventful few days, haven't you? Is there anything you'd like to share?"

*No,* Theo thought crankily; *there isn't.* She didn't feel like talking to *any*body. She wished she was sitting on the bench in the garden at home, the breeze in her hair, and the birds chattering in the jezouli bushes . . .

Marjene's face suddenly went all wavy and soft as Theo's eyes filled with tears. She tried to blink them away, but they spilled over. Horrified, she looked down, and the tears dripped onto the tense knot work of her fingers.

"I guess you've seen the reports already," she said, her voice wobbly. "How I made Lesset fall yesterday, and hit Roni with a ball just now at teamplay."

There was a small pause before Marjene said, "Well, yes, I have seen them. But they only tell me what happened. They don't tell me how you *feel*, Theo."

Theo sniffed and thought about Coyster, which was a mistake, because that made her think about her room at home, and her mobile, and her pictures, and the fish swimming in the floor . . .

"I feel bad," she said, and reached for one of the disposacloths Marjene always had on hand, dried her face and blew her nose. Her mentor waited until she had finished, and nodded encouragingly when Theo raised her head.

"Hurting other people does make us feel bad," Marjene said gently. She tapped the display set into the table before her. "Yesterday's incident report states that Lesset wasn't injured, which is very fortunate. Today, though—Roni was physically hurt, and badly frightened, too."

Theo nodded and swallowed. "She got in front of the ball."

Marjene looked at her with gentle disappointment.

"Roni may have gotten in front," she said, "but you threw the ball. I know you didn't hurt her deliberately, Theo, but you *did* hurt her. You must take responsibility for your own actions—and the consequences."

"I know," Theo sighed, and untangled her fingers so she could have another sip of too-sweet juice that did nothing to ease the dryness of her throat. "I *did* hit her with the ball. But she was in the wrong place—out of position. If she hadn't—"

"Theo," Marjene said sternly. "Are you about to *cast blame*?"

She bit her lip, put the cup down and stared at

it, hard, for several heartbeats, as she followed the thought to its conclusion.

"Stating a fact," she said slowly, looking up into Marjene's round brown eyes, "isn't casting blame. I threw the ball—that's a fact. The ball hit Roni in the nose—that's a fact. Roni was out of position—that's a fact, too. And it's *also* a fact that she wouldn't have *gotten* hit in the nose if she'd been in First Ring, where she belonged."

Marjene blinked, and looked down at her display, lips pursed.

"I . . . see," she said eventually. When she looked up again, her face was sad.

"Theo, I'm going to tell you something that maybe I shouldn't, but I can't just sit back and let you continue to hurt people—and yourself! I want what's best for you, and this—this isn't good for you." She leaned across the table and put her hand over Theo's.

"Sweetie, you know you're physically limited. Your mother and I have talked to you about it; you've seen the notes in your file. What you may not have known is—we can help you, Theo. You don't have to, to knock down your friends, or hurt your team-mates. There are medications—very simple, very safe medications—that can *cure you!*"

Theo wished Marjene didn't have her hand pinned to the table. She also wished that Marjene would stop looking at her like she was a wet kitten or something . . .

"The thing is, sweetie—your mother knows about these cures. The Office of Academic Safety has approached her *several* times, asking that she help you. And she's always refused." Marjene smiled, but even Theo could see that it was strained.

"I'm sure she has her reasons—very good reasons! But sometimes a mother's love . . . Well, we're not impartial about our children. That's why our children have mentors! And that's why I'm telling you this. You haven't had your *Gignert*, and your mother has the right to refuse in your name—without consulting you. But, now that you're informed, if you were to tell me, right now, that you wanted to accept a cure . . ."

Shock brought Theo up straight in her chair, her hand snatched from beneath Marjene's and fisted in her lap. Her mentor was trying to talk her into—what *was* her mentor trying to talk her into, anyway?

"Theo? I know it's brand-new information. Take a couple minutes to think about how nice it would be if you never tripped, or hurt anyone else, ever again."

Theo blinked. A cure, Marjene said. And Kamele had rejected it. Why would she do that? Kamele didn't like the notes and reports that came in every time Theo broke something, or tripped, or—any more than Theo liked being the cause of the reports. She'd leap at a cure, if there was one.

Wouldn't she?

"Sweetie?" Marjene murmured.

Theo shook her head. "I—I think I'd better talk to Kamele," she said slowly. "I need to understand why she decided not to accept the cure for me. And . . . I want to talk to Father, too." Yes, she thought, she *needed* to know what Father thought about this whole thing—the cure, Kamele's refusal, and especially Marjene's motivation for telling her something even she said she had no right to share!

"Theo!" her mentor snapped.

Sheer amazement brought Theo's eyes up. Marjene

never snapped! And—yes, her mouth was set in a thin, straight line, her big brown eyes glittering.

Marjene, Theo thought, beginning to feel a little irritated herself, was *angry*.

"Why shouldn't I talk to Kamele and to Father?" she snapped back. "I—"

"Stop that *right now*," Marjene interrupted, which was something else she never did. Theo bit her lip, took a breath so deep her bruised ribs protested, counted to twelve, and took another, slightly less deep, breath.

"Thank you," Marjene said more moderately, like she'd taken a couple of deep breaths herself. "Earlier in our conversation, you cited some facts for my benefit, did you not?"

Cautiously, Theo nodded.

"Yes, you did. Now, I'm going to cite some facts for your benefit. Listen closely." Marjene paused, as if to collect her thoughts, folded her hands firmly on the tabletop, and looked into Theo's eyes. Looking directly into a person's eyes was a domination trick, according to Professor Wilit, with the dominated being the one who looked away first.

Theo lifted her chin and looked right back.

Marjene's mouth tightened, but the only thing she said was, "It's a fact, isn't it, Theo, that your mother has taken a faculty apartment for herself and for you?"

"Yes," Theo answered, fighting the urge to look at her knees.

"Yes," Marjene repeated. "And is it a fact that Professor Kiladi did not accompany her to your new apartment?"

This not looking down was *hard*. Theo licked her lips. "Yes, that's a fact, too."

"It is therefore a fact that Professor Kiladi is no longer Housefather in your mother's establishment, is it not?"

"Yes," Theo whispered. Her stomach hurt.

Marjene nodded. "And it's a fact, isn't it, Theo," she said, gently now, "that you haven't yet had your *Gigneri*, or in any other way been entrusted with the record of your genes?"

Theo looked down at her hands, folded together so tight the knuckles showed white. "Yes," she said clearly, "that's a fact, too."

"And you do know that calling a man who is neither Housefather nor a Certified Biologic Donor by the honor-name of 'Father' is at the least disorderly, and possibly even anti-social?"

Theo closed her eyes.

"Really, Theo," Marjene said after a moment. "Do you need any more notes in your file?"

*I'm going to be sick,* Theo thought. She swallowed, feeling tears prickling the back of her eyelids.

"Theo? Sweetie, I know it takes time to get used to new arrangements. But you have to be flexible. You have to embrace change. You're entering a whole new chapter of your life, and that's exciting and a little scary. I know. But clinging to the past only makes the present scarier."

*No*, Theo thought. *I'm not going to be sick. I'm going to, to knock over the table, and throw things, and—*

Her mumu thweeped.

Before she realized what she was doing, Theo was off the stool and grabbing her pack. She made herself look up into her mentor's astonished face and say, as calmly as she could, "I have to go now, Marjene. I'm expecting a delivery."

She turned without waiting for an answer and all but ran out of Grandmother's, leaving her mentor gaping after her, and probably composing another note for her file.

# ELEVEN

· · · · · · · · · · ·

*University of Delgado*
*Faculty Residence Wall*
*Quadrant Eight, Building Two*

A SANDY HAIRED MAN WEARING A GREEN SWEATER AND gray work pants was turning away from their door. He had a large roll balanced on one shoulder, casually held in place with one big hand.

"Hey!" Theo jumped off the belt, not bothering with the safety grip, wincing when her sore ribs complained. "Sir!"

The man continued his turn, sandy eyebrows up and an amused look on his ruddy, unlined face. The sleeves of his sweater were pushed up, displaying muscled arms thick with blond hair.

"Student?" he said courteously.

"I'm Theo Waitley." She was panting a little, her face hot and her hair sticky, and she made herself walk slowly, to spare any more twinges from her bruises. "I think that must be my rug. I'm sorry I'm late."

"Theo Waitley's the name on the delivery slip, right

enough, and nobody said you were late." He gave her a cheerful grin. "Ms. Dail guessed fivebells would find you home after your game, and I'm a couple ticks early. Truth is, I was going to go looking for a cup of something cold and maybe a snack before I came back to see if you were home yet." The grin widened. "Ms. Dail pays half up front on delivery work, the rest when we bring her the signed chit. Untrusting woman. But smart as new paint."

"You're very nice to bring this to me," she told the man, whose name, she realized suddenly, she'd forgotten to ask. "Mr—?"

He laughed. "Just Harn," he said, and jerked his head at the door. "If you'll get the door, I'll walk this in and lay it out."

"Oh, you don't have to do that!" Theo protested.

"No problem at all," he assured her. "Besides, you might need some help getting it down right, 'specially since you're gonna be using stickystrips."

"Well, if you're sure you don't mind, I'd be glad to have your help." She stepped past Harn and opened the door. He walked in after her, deftly maneuvering the long roll in the small space.

"My room's this way," Theo said, leading him down the hallway. She triggered that door, scooped Coyster up as he made a dash across the threshold and swung out of the way.

Harn walked past her at the absolutely correct angle, dropped to one knee and let the rug roll easy off his shoulder onto the floor. He looked around.

"Gonna need them stickystrips on this surface."

Theo stepped inside and dropped her pack in what had become its usual place near the wall. Coyster squirmed against her shoulder. She put him down and he pranced away, tail high, gave Harn's knee an enthusiastic bump, and sniffed at the rug.

Harn grinned. "I got a cat," he said. "Not that friendly with strangers, though." He glanced at Theo. "Where d'you want it?"

Theo looked up at the folded bed. Harn followed her gaze, and nodded. "Like to have this under your toes when you get up in the morning. Good idea." He picked Coyster up and moved him out of the way before touching the bindings.

Released, the rug unrolled slightly, showing a flow of greens and blues around a plain white sealpack.

"All right, now, Theo Waitley," Harn said, reaching for the sealpacks. "I'm going to need your help keeping this friendly cat of yours out of my way while I'm working. We don't want him to get stuck in the strips, and I sure don't want to lay the rug over him." One of the packs unsealed with a loud *zzzzZZZIIITTTT* and Harn looked at her over his shoulder. "Can you do that for me?"

"I'll lock him in the 'fresher and come back to help," Theo said. Coyster wouldn't like that, but it would only be for a few minutes.

"Nothing to help with," Harn told her, rising and sending another calculating glance around the room.

Theo understood. Her room was so small, she'd only get in the big man's way if she stayed.

"Call if you need anything," she said.

He nodded, absently. She grabbed Coyster and carried him to the kitchen, despite his demand to be put down *this minute*!

"You heard what he said," she muttered, holding his

squirmy furry body against her shoulder one-handed while she punched the kaf's buttons with the other.

"Hey! Watch the claws!"

"*Gnrrrngh*," Coyster said, twisting so hard she almost dropped him. She counter-twisted, which hurt, but managed to hold on to him and to the cup of soy milk she'd taken out of the kaf.

"You *are not* going back there to supervise," Theo told him. "You'll get in trouble."

Coyster sighed, deeply. *Patiently*. Theo felt a grin wobble around her mouth.

"I know, you never get in trouble. Except sometimes." *Just like me*, she added silently. She grabbed a disposable plate from the kaf's supply shelf and knelt carefully on the floor.

By the time she'd poured a dab of milk into the plate, Coyster was squirming to get away again, the need to supervise Harn apparently forgotten. Theo let him go. He walked straight down her chest, until his face was in the milk, then stopped, back legs braced against her belly, barely shot claws anchoring him to her coveralls, visibly vibrating along his entire length. Milk was a rare treat; too much wasn't good for cats, Father sa—

Theo caught her breath against a pain that had nothing to do with her ribs. She counted to twelve, then drank some of the milk from the disposable cup.

*What does Marjene know, anyway?* she thought, and drank some more milk. Coyster, finished with his tithe, did an about-face, propped his paws against her knee and bumped her elbow with his head.

"No, you can't have any more," she told him. "And if you make me spill mine, I'll have to lock you in 'fresher while I clean up the mess." She looked at him dismally. "Maybe I'd better lock us *both* in the 'fresher."

Coyster's response to this was interrupted by a loud voice, echoing weirdly off the walls.

"Hey, Theo Waitley! Come see what you think of this!"

"That was fast." She gulped the last of her milk, and rose gingerly, careful of her ribs, dropping the cup in the disposal on the way by. Coyster galloped past her, tail up, and by the time she got to her room, he was on his back among the shimmering blues and greens, feet in the air, eyes slitted in a cat-smile.

"Looks like you made a good choice," Harn said from his lean against the desk.

"Ms. Dail made a good choice." Theo walked over to the rug, put her foot on it and deliberately shifted her weight. The foot braced against against the floor slid a little, but the rug stayed put.

Harn nodded. "Those stickystrips are top-grade. If you do ever want to move the rug, just roll it up, then peel the strips off the floor, reset 'em where you want 'em and put the rug over 'em." He pointed at the folded-up bed.

"What I did was make it so there'll be some rug on both sides of the bed when it's down."

"Thank you for your help," Theo said, "and for coming all the way from—from Efraim."

"What Ms. Dail pays me for," he said cheerfully, and pushed away from his lean. He pulled a datastrip and a light pen out of his pocket. "What I need you to do is sign that the delivery's complete, so I can get the rest of my pay."

"Sure." She signed the strip; he slipped it and the pen away, and gave her a nod.

"I'll be on my way, Theo Waitley. Nice meeting you."

"It was nice to meet you, too," she said politely, leading him down the hall. She stopped suddenly as they reached the parlor, suddenly remembering—

"I'm so sorry!" she exclaimed, feeling her face get hot. "I—did you want something to drink, or—"

Harn laughed, holding up a big hand. "I'll take care of that on the way home." He smacked his sizable chest. "Not gonna fade away for lack of food for a while yet, eh?"

In spite of herself, Theo smiled. "If you're sure," she said. "I really do thank you."

"No trouble at all," Harn assured her as she opened the door. "I like to deliver inside the Wall."

"You do?" Theo looked up at him. "Why?"

"Reminds me of why I live down in town," he said and stepped out into the hall. "Have a good evening, Theo Waitley. You and your cat together."

Coyster was right, Theo thought, the rug did feel nice. Just sitting on it made her feel better. 'Course, it also made her feel better that, except for Coyster, she was finally alone, with hook and thread in hand.

She closed her eyes, letting her fingers shape whatever they cared to, finding calm in the patterned movements. Her ribs hurt, and so did her head, and she should really get up in a minute . . . or two . . . jack in her 'book and finish her solos. Thread slipped between her fingers, the needle moved, and she sat cross-legged on the rug, Coyster's purrs helping the thread relax her; and relax her some more, until she was more asleep than awake, and—

Her mumu chimed.

Theo jumped, eyes snapping open; mumu at her ear before it sounded a second time.

"Theo?" Lesset whispered loudly. "How are you?"

"Terrible," Theo said. "Why are you whispering?"

There was a pause, as if Lesset had blinked. "I don't know," she said in a more normal tone. "But—terrible, you said. Is your side hurting you?"

"Some," Theo admitted, "but . . ." She bit her lip and looked down at the shape her fingers had been making. Not a flower, but something kind of uneven and blobby. An amoeba, maybe.

"I had to see Marjene after teamplay," she told Lesset.

"Oh, no! Did she already have the report?"

"Worse than that, she yelled at me—"

"Your mentor *yelled* at you?" Theo could picture Lesset's eyes getting round, rounder even than her mouth.

"Close enough. And she acted like it's some kind of Crime Against Society to call Father like I always have, and . . ." Theo paused to draw breath, and ran her hand over the rug, watching the nap flow from green to blue.

"Well, it is," Lesset said. "I mean, not that it's a Crime Against Society. But it is kind of . . . strange to hear you calling Professor Kiladi 'father' when your mother's set him aside and—"

"Kamele has not set Father aside!" Theo interrupted hotly.

There was a pause. "He's not living with you, is he?" Lesset asked pointedly.

Theo sighed. "He's not living with us right now, no," she admitted, feeling her stomach starting to cramp up again.

"Then she set him aside," Lesset said, like it didn't matter. "*My* mother says that's a good thing. Professor Kiladi has served his purpose, she says, and now Professor Waitley's sub-chair of her department, and—"

"That's only a temp assignment," Theo protested.

"*My* mother says Chair Hafley's out of favor with Admin. *Your* mother could be the next EdHist Chair. That would be tenured and published!"

Theo's stomach twisted.

"Will you invite me to your apartment on Topthree?"

"We're not going to Topthree," Theo said, breathless. *We're going home*, she told herself. *Kamele's going to finish her temp post and then we'll go home!*

"You don't think Professor Waitley's good enough to be chair?"

"She's at least good enough to be chair!" Theo snapped, then blinked, seeing the trap too late. "I just don't think Admin'll pick her, is all," she finished lamely.

"Well . . ." Lesset let the word drift off, unwilling to argue on Admin's side, and Theo grabbed at the chance to change the subject.

"What're you going to do for Professor Wilit's solo?"

"*Whose* solo?"

"Professor Wilit," Theo repeated patiently. Lesset tended to put off her work until the last second, which Theo had never understood. She probably hadn't even opened her 'book yet. "There's a—"

"Hang on," Lesset interrupted. A woman said something unintelligible in the background, to which Lesset answered, "Theo."

Something else from Lesset's mother, her voice fading as she moved out of mumu range.

"Yes, ma'am," Lesset said, and then, her voice louder, "Theo, I've got to go. I'll see you tomorrow, 'k?"

"Okay—" she said, but might've saved the breath. Lesset had already cut the connection.

Sighing, Theo put the mumu on the rug beside her. She picked up her handwork, but couldn't seem to focus on it. Finally, she put it next to the mumu and stretched out, carefully, on the rug.

*So soft* . . . she thought, and closed her eyes—then opened them as Coyster put his nose against hers.

"*Prrt?*" he asked, amber eyes staring down into hers.

Theo rubbed his cheek. "Quiet," she said. "I've gotta think."

"*Prrt!*" Coyster stated, and curled around on her shoulder, purring immediately.

The last thing Theo remembered was thinking how nice that was . . .

· · · ·✷· · · ·

Kamele dropped her research book on her desk, and rubbed her eyes. She was going to have to stop running at triple speed soon—but there was so much to do! If she could get a decent night's sleep . . . she shook her head, mouth wobbling. She'd thought the move back to the Wall would be . . . comforting. After all, she had come *home* . . .

. . . only to find that home had shrunk, or that she had grown in . . . unanticipated directions, so that the once-comfortable embrace of the Wall now chafed and irritated.

And it could hardly help matters that she had become unaccustomed to sleeping alone.

Her head hurt. She reached up and pulled the pins loose, letting her hair tumble down to her shoulders. It was so fine that she had to keep it pinned tight, else it wisped and wafted around her face and shoulders. Uncontrollable stuff. And Theo had inherited it, poor child.

Kamele massaged her temples, and finger-combed her wispy, unmanageable hair. She thought about going down to the faculty lounge to pull a coffee, and decided against it. She'd had enough caffeine for one day—no, she'd had *more than* enough—and caffeine was the only reason to drink coffee from the department's kaf.

She sat down at her desk, and pushed the 'book aside, glancing at the privacy panel as she did. Yes, the door status was set to "open." Office hours would be done by sevenbells and she could go home. Perhaps she'd stop at the co-op on her way and pick up a bottle of wine. She wrinkled her nose, remembering the last time she'd had wine out of the co-op.

Or perhaps not.

There being no students immediately in need of her attention and advice, Kamele pulled out her mumu and tapped the screen on.

There was a message from Ella in queue, assuring her that the Oversight Committee was already moving on their request for the forensic lit search. They, at least, said Ella, took the possibility of an accreditation loss very seriously indeed. Kamele nodded, pleased.

After Ella's note, there were a dozen or so routine messages from colleagues and Admin. Below them were two marked "urgent"—one from the L&R Department and the other from Marjene Kant.

Panic pinched Kamele's chest. She took a deliberately deep breath to counter it, and opened the message from L&R.

Professor Viverain wrote a clean, terse, hand, and Kamele was very shortly in possession of the facts of Four Team Three's scavage game. Viverain took the trouble to state not once, but twice, that Roni Mason had put herself into a position of peril, in defiance of the rules of both the game and of good sportsmanship, and, upon being injured, had immediately begun to kick Theo, who had already been knocked to the floor by the collision.

In summary, Viverain praised both Theo's teamwork and her growing skill in scavage and hoped that Professor Waitley would not hesitate to contact her with any questions she might have about the incident.

Kamele closed her eyes. Roni Mason was spoiled and unprincipled, following, Kamele thought uncharitably, properly in her mother's footsteps. Well. She opened her eyes. There was more, she was certain.

And indeed there was. The appended Safety Office report suggested that the incident might have been avoided, or at least stopped short of bloodshed, had Theo not been involved. The reporting Safety fielded the theory that Roni Mason had been trying to kick the dropped ball, not realizing, in her distraction and pain that (1) the game was over, and (2) that she was kicking *Theo*.

This was so transparently mendacious that it seemed

unlikely that anyone would believe it. On the other hand, Theo had a long string of notes in her file documenting instances of her horrifying clumsiness, all the way back to first form. Whatever her discipline problems—and Kamele had heard they were not inconsiderable—Roni Mason was not tagged as "physically limited."

Lips pressed tight, Kamele called up the A-Team report: Theo had suffered bruised ribs; the A-Teamer had administered analgesic and muscle relaxant, suggesting that the same be given before bedtime to prevent stiffness and to ensure a restful night.

Kamele took a deep breath and exhaled, forcefully. Unfortunately, the exercise did very little to prepare her for Marjene's message.

*I feel compelled to inform you,* it began without preamble, *that Theo ended our scheduled meeting this evening precipitously, standing up while we were in the middle of a discussion and announcing that she was expecting a delivery. I understand that her problem on the scavage court had distressed her, and that the topics we had before us were unsettling, but this sort of rudeness toward one who—*

Kamele closed Marjene's message and filed it. After consideration, she also filed Viverain's report, with attachments.

Half-a-dozen taps notified her students and the Department Chair that she had canceled what remained of her office hours. That done, she slipped the mumu away, changed the room status from "open" to "closed," gathered up her 'book and left the office, walking rapidly.

• • • ❖ • • •

Someone close by was singing something soft and abstract, like honeybumbles in the flowers. Beneath the song was the soft, familiar click of keys. Kamele sang like that sometimes, Theo thought, drifting comfortably awake, when she was concentrating. It was a different kind of singing than she did for the chorale—more like a cat purring contentment. Theo sighed, broke the surface of wakefulness and opened her eyes.

Barely two hand-spans away, Kamele sat cross-legged on the rug, her 'book on her knee, face downturned, fingers moving gently on the keys, her hair wisping around her shoulders in disorderly waves. Coyster was sprawled on the rug at her side, snoring.

Theo sighed again, and her mother looked up from her work, the song murmuring into silence.

"I'm sorry," Theo whispered.

Kamele's eyebrows rose. "Sorry for what?"

*Sorry for the song ending*, Theo thought, but what she said was, "There's another note in my file— probably two." She bit her lip. "I guess you got the report from Viverain . . ."

"Professor Viverain was extremely complimentary," Kamele said. "She praised your skill and your commitment to your Team."

Theo blinked. "She did?"

"She did," her mother answered, glancing down to fold up her 'book and set it aside. She looked back to Theo. "The Safety Officer was another matter."

"I know," Theo whispered, remembering the red-haired Safety. "She said I had a societal obligation not to hurt other people." She tried to sit up, gasping as her ribs grabbed, sending a bright spark of pain along her side.

"Easy." Cool hands caught hers, and Kamele helped her up. Theo closed her eyes, waiting until the sparks subsided into a sullen ache.

"The report said your ribs were bruised, and that the A-Teamer gave you an analgesic and a muscle relaxant. Have you taken anything since you've been home?"

Theo shook her head. "The rug got delivered, and then I talked to Lesset, and then Coyster and I . . . took a nap."

"An excellent idea," Kamele said, not even asking if her solos were done. "You haven't eaten anything?"

"I . . . had a cup of soy milk."

Kamele half-smiled. "That's something, I suppose. Well . . ." She pulled her mumu out, and sent Theo a questioning glance. "I'm calling for dinner. What would you like?"

"Um . . . veggie fried rice?"

Her mother nodded, tapped a quick message into her mumu and put it on top of her 'book. On the rug, Coyster extended his back legs, pink toes stretching wide, and relaxed all at once with a tiny, satisfied moan.

Theo smiled, and leaned over—carefully—to rub his belly.

"I went to see Marjene," she said slowly, watching Kamele out of the side of her eye. Her mother nodded, looking politely interested, which, Theo suspected darkly, she'd probably learned from Fa—

She took a breath and sat up, her hand braced on the rug next to Coyster's tail.

"Marjene says—she says there are drugs that can . . ."

She stumbled, not liking any of the words available. Marjene had said *cured*, but was being clumsy an illness?

"She said, if I may make a supposition," Kamele said coolly, "that there are drugs which can prevent you harming other people through your well-documented 'physical limitations.' Is that correct?"

Theo nodded, all the misery of the afternoon suddenly back, and her stomach starting to ache again. "She said that—you refused them—the drugs—for me?" She paused, took a breath and said, properly. "I'd like to understand why."

Kamele put her elbow on her knee and her chin in her hand. There was a tiny line between her eyebrows, and her eyes were serious.

"It's a complex issue," she said gravely, "but I'll do my best to answer, all right?"

Theo nodded.

Kamele sighed, then said slowly. "It is, of course, our obligation to do what we can to promote order and safety within our society of scholars. In a perfect intellectual society, such as the Founding Trustees envisioned, tending to our personal obligations and responsibilities would be enough to ensure that order is preserved." She smiled slightly. "Unfortunately, the Founding Trustees had been ... a little too optimistic about human nature. So, we created the Office of Academic Safety, to help us maintain the environment to which we aspire." She paused.

Theo nodded to show she was following this. She knew the story of the Founding, of course, but her teachers hadn't even hinted that the Founders were human, must less capable of what Kamele seemed to be saying was an . . . well, it was a protocol error, that's what—but Kamele was talking again.

"Sometimes, because it has so much to do, the Safety Office . . . becomes overzealous. When this happens, so some of us feel, it is our responsibility to oppose it, just as much as it is our responsibility to work for orderliness in our everyday lives."

There was a pause. Theo frowned.

"So you decided not to follow the Safeties' advice because of a . . . philosophical difference?" she asked slowly.

Kamele actually laughed. "Not quite. What I mean to say is that we're obligated to scrutinize the recommendations the Safeties make to us; to do our own research and to draw our own conclusions. We're scholars, and this is how scholars deal. So," she waved her free hand—maybe at her mumu, maybe at the desk.

"So," she said again. "When this issue of the drugs—of the so-called *cure*—first came up with the Safety Office, I did what any scholar would do; I did my research. And I found a number of . . . interesting . . . facts.

"The first is that there is a . . . small but significant . . . proportion of the population who share what the Safety Office terms your 'physical limitations' who . . . find that those difficulties resolve themselves at some point near their *Gigneri*."

Theo sat up straighter, ignoring the snap of pain from her ribs.

Kamele nodded. "Yes, that's an interesting fact, isn't it? But the second fact is even more so." She paused, as if to make sure she had Theo's full attention. "It seems that the recommended drugs are not . . . quite . . . as benign as the Safety Office assures us that they are.

Indeed, several of the offered 'cures' measurably limit learning, and make it difficult to concentrate. These findings also seemed significant, especially for a student who is in the process of acquiring her Core Learning."

On the rug, Coyster yawned, noisily, and rolled to his feet. He gave his shoulder a quick lick and headed for the back of the room, bumping Theo cheerfully as he passed by.

"Now," Kamele said. "Since Marjene has brought this issue to you and made it your responsibility, you may wish to exercise your right to research, and to form your own conclusions. I can, if you wish, send you citations from my own research, and that of Professor Kiladi. They may be helpful as a starting point, or you may wish to construct your own protocol, independent of our findings."

Theo licked her lips, thinking of Marjene, of how *certain* she'd sounded. Maybe, she thought, Marjene trusted the Safety Office too much? That was an interesting idea Kamele raised, the notion that the Safety Office could—in some cases should—be opposed...

"I'd like the citations," she said, "very much, please, Mother."

Kamele nodded. "I'll forward them to you tomorrow, along with the list provided by the Safety Office, of those drugs they deem safe and effective."

"Thank you," Theo said, around a slight shiver. *Hadn't,* she wondered, *the Safety Office done its research?*

She looked up. "I—Marjene's pretty...upset with me. If you haven't gotten a note, you will," she said slowly. "She—well, I left in the middle of our meeting. I didn't—"

"Marjene was *pushing* you," Kamele said tartly; "and interfering where she had no right. Perhaps a little distress will clear her mind." She straightened, stretching her arms wide.

A gong sounded. *Dinner,* thought Theo, suddenly ravenous, *is here.*

"Right on cue," Kamele said and rolled to her feet. She held her hands down, and Theo took the boost. "I'll meet you at the table," she said, heading for the door.

"Kamele!" Theo bit her lip, but it was too late. Her mother turned, one hand on her door.

"Yes, Daughter? Is there something else?"

"I—will you—" she took a breath, feeling perilously close to tears. "Are you going to, to take another *onagrata?*"

Kamele closed her eyes, and opened them, looking tired.

"Not right now, Theo," she said quietly.

The gong sounded again; she slapped the door open and was gone, her footsteps sharp against the ceramic floor.

# TWELVE

· · · · · · · · · · · · · ·

*Cultural Genetics Program*
*Bjornson-Bellevale College of Arts and Sciences*
*University of Delgado*

OKTAVI CAUGHT THEO CURIOUSLY OFF-BALANCE.
On the one hand, it had arrived with breathtaking speed, but on the other, so much had happened that it seemed years between the scavage game and the moment when she and the rest of the Team were finally able to close their 'books and put learning behind them for the day.

"See you tomorrow," Theo called generally, turning down the hall that led to the cross-campus belt, her pace increasing. She swung up onto the belt and winced as her bruised ribs protested.

"Ow," she muttered, and shifted the bag over her shoulder.

"If you keep jumping around like that," a husky voice said in her ear, "you're not going to give yourself time to heal."

"Kartor." Theo turned her head. "It's just bruises," she said.

He nodded, settling his own pack. "But there's bruises and bruises. If the bones are bruised, that's more serious than just surface bruises. Hurts more. Takes longer to heal."

"I don't *think* the bones are bruised," Theo said. "The doctor didn't say so."

"You're lucky she didn't break your ribs," Kartor said darkly.

"Oh, I don't think she could've done that…"

"You don't? Roni's 'way bigger than you are and she had leverage. Do the math, Theo. I betcha the Review Board will."

*He's really mad,* Theo thought, throwing a glance at him. His face was tense, with hard lines bracketing his mouth.

She bit her lip, not sure what to say to make him calmer. The scavage game had been *days* ago, after all. If he was still upset about it—and it seemed like he was—then he needed… Theo hesitated.

*Kartor needs to talk to his mentor,* she thought carefully, tasting the idea like it was brand-new, which was silly. Your mentor was there to help you work through bad feelings. Everybody knew that.

But what if Kartor's mentor was like Marjene?

Theo bit her lip. *The Eyes don't watch everything,* she heard the whisper from memory. *Even we know that.*

Kartor shook his head and gave her a sideways look, the corner of his mouth twisting up in a kind of lopsided grin.

"By the way, mind if I ride with you?"

"'Course not," Theo said, surprised. Kartor's mother worked in the Systems Group just off Central Station. He'd ridden the belt with her that far on more than one Oktavi evening.

"Notice how the Team's been working better the last couple days?" he asked, and Theo eyed him, wondering if he was going to try to pump her for details of the preliminary hearing, like Lesset had.

The hearing had been frightening and infuriating. Roni's mother had immediately requested that Theo be put into Remedial Tutoring "for the good of the majority" until the Review Board had time to rule. Breath caught, Theo'd waited, wondering around a feeling of sick dread what her mother would say.

But Kamele had only put her hand on Theo's shoulder, and hadn't said a thing.

The Review Chair, though, looked over the top of her glasses at Roni's mother, and said, her voice light and perfectly pleasant, "The Committee has not yet done its work, Professor Mason. However, if you feel that your daughter is at risk in the Team environment, we will entertain a plea for a Safety Order, and place her in Small Group Study until a ruling is made."

Roni's mother had gotten red in the face, just like Roni did when she was upset, but she hadn't had much choice, since she'd brought the issue up. She'd taken out the Safety Order, which stipulated that Theo and Roni would stay away from each other until the Committee ruled, and accepted a temporary place in Small Groups for Roni.

That had been more than all right with Theo. And, surprisingly, it had been all right with the rest of the Team, too.

"We don't seem to be—I don't know—*rushing* so much," Theo said slowly, as the belt whisked them past the Center Court Coop.

"We're not as *worried*," Kartor said firmly. "I've been thinking about it, and you know what? I think Roni's an—an unacceptable strain on the Team."

Theo blinked. "You think the match program made a mistake?"

"I know it's not supposed to," he said, shrugging. "My aunt's in Team Management, and she says the algorithm's pretty solid. If that's true—then they put Roni with us on purpose." He gave her an unhappy look. "Do you think they *wanted* us to fail?"

Theo thought about that as the belt slowed through Central Station, remembering the sets protocol from math. Where *did* you put the set of all things that didn't match anything else?

"Maybe they just lumped all the misfits together," she said, and bit her lip when Kartor laughed.

"I didn't mean—" she started, face hot, but he held up a hand, still laughing.

"No, you're right! Look at us! Anj has bad wiring in her on-off switch; Estan's lost without his rule book; Roni has to tell everybody else what to do; Lesset's butter-brained, and I'm a slacker. You're the only one who's normal!"

"Oh, I'm normal, all right," Theo muttered, but Kartor was laughing too hard to hear. Somewhat miffed, she looked out at the corridor. Two more stops until the Cultural Diversity Wing—she swung back to Kartor, pointing.

"Talk about being butter-brained—you missed your intersection!"

Kartor shook his head. "No, I've got an extra, down in the senior seminar space."

Theo eyed him. "I thought you said you were a slacker."

He grinned at her. "Yeah, but I'm not stupid."

They rode for a few minutes in silence, before Theo's curiosity got the better of her.

"So, what's your extra?"

Kartor looked down at the belt, like he was suddenly embarrassed, then looked back her. "*You* won't laugh at me," he said, with emphasis, and took a deep breath. "Etiquette."

"Etiquette?" Theo blinked. Etiquette was pre-Team. Kartor couldn't be doing a make-up on *that*, could he? And then she remembered the other thing he'd said—

"The senior seminar room," she said out loud, and looked at him. Kartor looked back—warily, she thought, like he wasn't sure after all that she wouldn't laugh. "You're taking *Traveler's Etiquette*? With Professor Sandaluin? Kartor, that's a *restricted* senior seminar!"

"Well, I'm only auditing," he said, sounding apologetic. "It *is* supposed to be restricted, but my mentor applied for me to sit in without grades, as long as I keep up. If I do all right, Professor Sandaluin'll give me a letter, and that's really all I need, 'cause I'm going to have to pass the corporation's training, anyhow, after I'm accepted."

"Accepted where?" Theo asked.

Kartor's grin was tight at the edges, his voice a little too bright. "I'm going to get a job on the station."

Theo thought about that. Kartor's family was only accidentally academic. His mother, his aunt, and his oldest sister were all in Information Systems. They had more of a knack for doing than for teaching—she'd overheard Professor Grinmordi say so, but not like she thought having a knack for *doing* was a particularly good thing.

"Doesn't your mother want you to go into Systems?"

He shrugged, looking uncomfortable. "My firstap's been accepted, and I'm scheduled to take the tests at the Interval." He shrugged again. "Ilsa's *Gigneri's* coming up, and my mother's pretty involved in that. I told her about the tests and she said it might be good if I was out from under foot for a couple days."

"The tests are given on-station?"

He nodded. "The corporation tests in groups over the Interval, so it's not like I'll be unsupervised. And if I can get a letter from Professor Sandaluin, that'll be a good note to have in my file!"

"It sure will," Theo agreed, remembering Father's comments about the professor in question. "She expects perfection, is what I heard."

Kartor shrugged again. "She's no worse than Appletorn," he said. "And I don't need a letter from him." He looked around, hitching his bag on his shoulder. "I get off here."

"Me, too."

They swung off the belt together and strolled down the long hallway, red, green, orange, and blue status lights twinkling at each door.

"Here's my stop," Theo said, turning right toward the door marked *Jen Sar Kiladi, Gallowglass Chair, and Professor of Cultural Genetics.* As she approached, the status light snapped out. The door opened and the man himself stepped into the hallway, his stick in one hand and his bag in the other.

"Theo," he said gravely, then looked to her companion. "Good evening, Mr. Singh."

"Professor Kiladi." To Theo's astonishment, Kartor bowed, wobbling a little because of the pack on his shoulder, and straightened.

One strong eyebrow rose. "Ah." He returned the bow, fluid and effortless despite his own burdens, and straightened while Kartor considered him ruefully.

"I see that I've got to work on my timing," Kartor said wryly.

"Indeed. But you must be of good heart. I swear to you that the thing can be learned."

Kartor grinned. "Thanks," he said, and raised a hand. "I'll see you tomorrow, Theo."

"See you tomorrow," she answered, and turned to watch him walk away, in his loose-jointed, careless way. She turned back to a pair of noncommittal black eyes in a perfectly composed face, and had time to wonder what she'd done that was *interesting* before he inclined his head.

"Where shall you like to eat this evening, Theo?"

She hesitated, biting her lip, not knowing whether she should even ask...

"Speak," he said lightly. "If the scheme is more than my aged self can support, be certain that I will tell you so immediately. My sense of self-preservation is strong."

"All right," Theo said carefully. "I'd like to—" She cleared her throat. "I wonder if we can't just go—go hom— to your house and have toasted cheese sandwiches and tea?"

He tipped his head, eyes slightly narrowed, then nodded.

"A rigorous course, but I believe I may withstand it," he said, motioning her to walk with him. "If we stop at the fresh air market on our way, we might also have a salad, if you'd like it."

Theo let go the breath she'd been holding. "I'd like that," she said. "Very much."

"Then that is what we will do." They turned right into the service hall that led to the tiny faculty parking bay.

"Does your friend aspire to anthropology?"

Theo blinked. "Kartor? No . . ." She sighed and shifted her bag, wincing. "He's auditing Traveler's Etiquette. He wants to get a job on the station."

The click of the stick against the surface of the hall echoed oddly, almost as if he'd used it to punctuate something he'd thought but forbore to say aloud. His words, when they did come, were fluid and thoughtful.

"Does he indeed? But surely his mother will want him with her in Systems."

"I think his mother is . . . more concerned with his sisters," Theo said slowly. "It sounds like, from things he's said, that she doesn't much care what he does, as long as he doesn't . . . get into trouble."

"Well, you mustn't blame her for that. I believe that many parents wish that their off-spring would refrain from getting into trouble."

Theo bit her lip, and the two of them strolled down toward Father's pride-and-joy—the car he delighted in describing to new acquaintances as a "burnished green neo-classic rally coupe."

Some of his new acquaintances returned from his show-off ride smiling, others . . . did not. But he was serious about his joy, and periodically engaged in events put on by Delgado's only road rally club.

"How have you occupied your time during the last few days, Theo?" he asked, opening the little car's boot.

Theo slid her pack off and put it into the boot next to his bag, then straightened and met his eyes.

"I haven't exactly been trouble-free," she confessed.

"Splendid!" He gave her one of his brilliant grins, slammed the boot, and waved her to the passenger's side. "You must tell me all about it."

Theo slid into the low seat, snapped the safety belt into place, then sat with her hands in her lap, chewing her lip. *This isn't,* she thought dismally, *going to be easy.* She'd *tried* to prepare; reasoning it out, reminding herself that she had been willfully ignoring social cues, like Coyster pretending that he couldn't see a bowl full of substandard cat kibble.

*You've got to do this,* she told herself; *you can't keep on not calling him anything, and besides, it's probably . . . upsetting to him to be called Father when he's not anymore, really, and he's just been too kind to say so.*

That this particular variety of kindness was hardly a hallmark of her companion's character did not occur to her until she had licked her lips and made herself say, "Professor Kiladi?"

He turned his head, one eyebrow well up.

"Dear me," he murmured. "I apprehend that I have fallen into your black book, Theo. You must tell me how."

Theo considered him warily. "Black book?" she repeated.

"Ah." He inclined his head. "The reference is to a notebook in which the names of all those who have done one a mischief are recorded. Allow it to be one of those quaint off-world customs of which Delgado does not partake."

"Delgado doesn't seem to partake of many off-world customs," Theo commented, thinking of Gorna Dail.

"Yes, but it has a plenitude of its own, similarly quaint, not to say infuriating." He settled back into his seat without pressing the starter switch.

"That was a very credible attempt to change the subject. My congratulations. Now, if you please: *Professor Kiladi?*"

She took a breath and met his eyes. "I—Marjene said that, since you're not Housefather now, I—that it's antisocial to . . . to call you 'Father.'"

"Ah! Marjene." He sighed the name, elongating it into something comically musical. "All is explained. And yourself?"

She blinked. "Pardon me?"

"Do you find Marjene's argument resonates with you?"

"Well . . . I—no!" she said suddenly. "I mean, she's *right*—I've been ignoring a social cue. And that's not . . . honest. But, if I'm being honest," she continued in a rush, "I'd rather *not* call you Professor Kiladi, unless—unless you'd rather I did."

"I am compelled to meet honesty with honesty: I'd rather you didn't." He touched the starter. The car shifted slightly as the engine engaged, like it was a live thing that gone from sleep to alert. Father went through a similar change—as if being in the driver's seat brought him to a higher level of awareness. Eyes front, he scanned the parking bay, and when he spoke, his voice was grave.

"Theo. Far from being offended, I would be honored if you choose to continue addressing me as 'Father.' If, after due reflection, you find that you cannot in propriety allow it, then I suggest 'Jen Sar' as comfortable for us both." He flicked a quick, dark glance at her. "Is that plain?"

Chest tight, she nodded.

"Good. Unfortunately, and as much as it costs me to say so, Marjene's appeal to local custom is legitimate. Our relative positions being what they are, I see no choice but that Professor Kiladi must be fielded when we meet in public. I would consider it a kindness if you do not invoke him often."

That made sense, thought Theo, and formed a workable compromise. She and Father could be comfortable—and so could Marjene and Lesset.

"All right," she said, and, with a vast feeling of relief, smiled. "Father."

"Hah." He put the car into motion with a touch. "Is that the awful whole, or is there more to your not-exactly-trouble-free existence?"

Theo sighed, her momentary glow of comfort fading. "There's more," she said dolefully. "A lot more. And worse."

"You must not keep me in suspense a moment longer, then! If you please, the round tale—and leave no detail unturned. I must have it all!"


There was a House Rule against talking about "critical matters" during the making and the eating of meals. "Too much angst curdles the milk," is what Father said.

When she'd lived in the house, Theo had thought that particular rule was . . . stupid, especially since Father's rulings on what constituted "critical matters" tended to be frivolous. In her opinion.

This evening, though, she was glad of the rule. Father had taken them the long way home, winding 'round the outskirts of Nonactown while she told the whole tale of the last few days—well, except for the bus ride; she had a feeling that he'd like that even less than Kamele had. He'd listened quietly, but with a worrisome sort of . . . immediacy, like he was *experiencing* everything she told him. She'd never felt anything like this from him—not anger, exactly, but—

She wasn't really sure.

Whatever it was, she was glad to be free of it for dinner prep. She set the table—the blue-and-white dishes and the faded blue cloth napkins, on the little table in the corner of the kitchen, next to the window that looked out over the garden.

While Father tended the sandwiches, Theo got out the wooden bowl, swooped Mandrin from the work counter onto a nearby stool, and mixed the greens together.

Across the kitchen, Father reached for the spatula. It slid out of his fingers, skittering away almost like it was alive. In her mind's eye, Theo saw it twirl and arc for the floor. She turned away from the salad, slid forward and captured the spatula in a left-handed snatch.

"My thanks," Father said solemnly, receiving it from her.

"Welcome," she answered, and got back to the work counter just in time to yank the bowl out from under Mandrin's nose.

"Cats are carnivores," she said, reaching for the oil. "That means you don't eat vegetables; you eat kibble."

"And the occasional toasted cheese sandwich," Father added. "You are a pampered house-bound creature, Professor Mandrin, who has never known the bounty of the land, nor the joy of dining on fresh-caught rodent."

"Father!"

He shot her a wicked look. "Does your appetite desert you? Will I be forced to eat two toasted cheese sandwiches myself?"

"You don't get mine that easy!" Theo told him, though, in fact, the idea of Mandrin eating a rodent did make her feel a little queasy. Well, the trick was not to think about it. She finished mixing the greens and carried bowl and tongs to the table. Picking up the sandwich plates, she took them to the grill, where Father bestowed a golden brown, and slightly sticky sandwich upon each.

At the table, Mandrin was inspecting the arrangements, her back feet on Theo's chair and her front feet set daintily between the silverware.

"You're more trouble than Coyster," Theo said, unceremoniously dropping her to the floor. Whether it was the insult of being compared to a cat so much her junior and orange, besides, or Theo's continuing interruptions of her business, Mandrin stalked off, the tip of her tail twitching.

Theo grinned, the teapot hooted and she turned back, only to find Father ahead of her, reaching up to the shelf where the cups were kept. He grabbed one, but jostled the cup next to it, which spun, wobbled and danced dangerously toward the edge. Father had

already turned away. Theo jumped forward, catching
the dancing cup just as it leapt for the floor, then
did some dancing herself, to keep from knocking into
counter or stool.

"That was close!" she said.

Father looked at her over his shoulder, and plucked
the cup out of her hand with a murmured thanks.
Theo frowned at his back.

"Are you all right?" she asked, which got her another
over-the-shoulder glance, as incurious as the first.

"Perfectly. Why do you ask?"

"Well," she said, following him to the table. "You
dropped the spatula and knocked the cup off the
shelf—and you *never* drop things!"

"Ah." He set their cups down and slid into his seat.
Theo sat across, watching his face as he surveyed
the table.

"This is very pleasant," he murmured. "It wants
only some flowers, but in this season—"

"*Father.*"

He looked at her, his face perfectly composed.
"I'm a little tired, child. Nothing to signify. Thank
you for suggesting the meal and the venue. Excellent
choices, both."

She smiled. "I think so, too."

"We have an accord. Delightful. Eat, do!"

Theo took a bite of her sandwich and sighed aloud
in sheer bliss, her eyes on the garden, where the
shadows were already growing out from the walls.
She had another bite of her sandwich, served herself
some salad and continued to eat while on his side he
talked about the weather and how it had been a bit
too dry for the sinneas to get a good start, though

there was a persuasive front on the way which he hoped might deliver rain overnight...

It wasn't until Theo had finished her dinner, feeling calm and almost sleepy, that she realized what he'd been doing.

"I'm not Kamele!" she snapped, sharply interrupting a discursive and lengthy wondering about the hedge on the southern side, and whether it ought to be removed or simply trimmed.

He blinked, searched her face earnestly, and inclined his head. "I concur. You are not Kamele."

"You're talking to me just like you do—did—when Kamele would get upset..."

"...and would require assistance in achieving calmness," he finished, and set his tea cup down decisively. "Consider it a service of the house. Are you done with your meal? Would you like more tea?"

"I'm done with my meal," Theo said, and pushed back her chair. "I'll get some more tea after I clean up—"

"Leave it," he said peremptorily. "I suggest that we adjourn to the common room, with the teapot. We will wish to be comfortable for this."


"Let us, by your kindness, deal with the simplest matter first," he said some minutes later from his accustomed chair next to the fireplace.

Theo nodded, and sipped her tea, wondering what was simple about any of her recent messes.

"It seems that Ms. Kant has been very busy on your behalf." He settled back in his chair, tea cup cradled in long fingers. "We shall leave for the moment the question of whether she has been *too* busy and if, indeed, it is your welfare which concerns her."

The blinked. "Marjene's supposed—" she began, and stopped when he raised his hand.

"I have read the same pamphlets that you have, Theo; though I have perhaps drawn different conclusions, old cynic that I am. To continue: Have you pursued the citations your mother has given to you?"

"Yes!" Theo assured him. In fact, she'd read the information with an increasing feeling of alarm. Even the mildest of the recommended drugs seemed to promise terrifying side-effects, up to and including slight, though apparently permanent, cognitive impairment.

"And has Marjene also shared her information with you?"

Theo snorted. "I read the files the Safety Office has on public key. Either they haven't done their research, or they chose to ignore contrary information..."

"...in the service of the greater good," Father finished, with the air of quoting someone who was not entirely in good taste. "You'll find, I think, that Delgado has a bias toward the greatest safety for the greatest number."

"Kamele says that the Founders...made a mistake," Theo said tentatively, belatedly thinking that the relationship of this comment to their topic might not be as plain to him as it was to her.

Father, however, had no trouble making the conversational leap. He cocked his head interestedly. "Does she, indeed? She had used to walk out only so far as undue optimism. In any wise—you *will* find that Delgado errs on the side of safety for the greater number. It is therefore up to you, and to such trusted advisers as you may gather, to protect yourself and your interests. Which may, indeed, not always be either safe or best for all."

Theo blinked. "I don't think I—"

Father raised a hand, the twisted silver ring glinting on the smallest finger of his right hand. "The rules of society exist to make it possible for individuals to work together in harmony. There is, however, a tension between the rules imposed by society and the necessities accepted by individuals. When that tension fails, society declines and the individuals become at risk."

She thought about that, while Father finished his tea and put the empty cup on the side table. Mandrin jumped into his lap and he stroked her, waking loud purrs.

"I consider you to be one of my . . . trusted advisers." she said slowly, silently adding, *no matter what Marjene says*.

He inclined his head. "You honor me," he said gravely.

She eyed him, suspecting sarcasm, or at least irony. "That doesn't mean you're not annoying."

He laughed. "Entirely the opposite, in my experience!" He shook his head at her. "Please, I am serious. You honor me with your trust and I will strive to be worthy of it."

"All right." She tasted her tea, which was cold, and put the cup on the table. "I intend to do my own searches, but—based on what I've read so far, I . . ." She took a breath and met his eyes, which was both easier and harder than keeping Marjene's gaze.

"My preliminary finding is that . . . accepting even the therapy the Safety Office lists as 'mildest' is . . . not a good idea." She paused.

Father tipped his head, waiting for her to go on.

"What I want to ask, is what you think I should *do*,"

Theo said, suddenly plaintive. "Roni's mother wants me in Remedial, the Safeties think I'm a menace, and so does Marjene. I've *got* to stop hurting people, or the Safety Office is going to call *Kamele* up for harboring an unsafe condition, and that's just not—I can't do that!"

"Ah. I see that you have indeed been doing your research. You are correct; additional pressure can be brought to bear upon you, through your mother. I believe you are wise to think proactively in this case." Father sighed and rubbed Mandrin's ears, staring off into some distance visible only to himself.

Recognizing the signs of deep thought, Theo folded her hands on her lap and tried to be patient.

"My suggestion," Father said, just as she had decided that it wouldn't be . . . too rude to go look in the any-thing drawer for the extra needle and spool she kept there, "is that you take up dance."

Theo blinked. *"Dance?"*

"It may, for the moment at least, answer the call for rehabilitation," he said slowly. "Certainly, it will dem-onstrate that you are taking the concerns of the Safety Office to heart." He looked up and met her eyes. "In a word, it will buy time, giving you and your mother the opportunity to plan a strategy. It would seem that simply holding line until you are considered old enough to speak on your own behalf may no longer be possible."

"Why?"

He looked up and gave her a brief smile. "Because you have achieved enemies—people who actively wish you harm, as distinct from those who would cause you harm out of a sincere, if misguided, concern for your safety."

"Roni?" Theo asked, thinking that *enemy* sounded so . . . grown up. "But Roni's only a kid."

"True. However, Roni's mother—is not."

Theo stared.

Father bent forward to place Mandrin on the floor. He stood, in one of his flowing, effortless moves, and smiled down at her.

"Be easy, child. You have your own corps of defenders. And yours, may I say, are somewhat more able than the honored Professor Mason."

The mechanical clock in his study called ninebells, its chimes echoing through the house like a familiar, comfortable voice. Theo's eyes filled.

"I wish I could stay," she said, knowing she couldn't.

"I wish you could stay, too," he answered softly.

He held a hand down to her. "I'm afraid I've kept you late," he said suddenly brisk. "Come along."

Theo let him pull her to her feet, like she had when she'd been a little kid. She went in search of Mandrin, finding her sprawled on the table among the dinner dishes.

"You are so bad," she said, and skritched the black-and-white chin. "I'll see you soon." Mandrin sighed and squeezed her eyes shut wearily. Theo grinned and followed Father out to the yard.

"I hope you don't mind a ride in the dark," he said, as he strapped in.

"Oh, no!" she assured him. "It'll be much more comfortable than the late bus!"

She felt his glance on the side of her face.

"Have you taken the late bus recently, Theo?" he asked politely.

*Nidj!* she scolded herself; but there was nothing for it but to tell him, now.

"I went to Nonactown to buy a rug," she said,

trying to sound like it was perfectly reasonable, "and took the bus back."

"How exciting your life has become, to be sure!" he said lightly, guiding the car out into the dark street. "I'd be interested in your impressions of the long route, if you would honor me."

*Kamele's already grounded you,* Theo thought; *he really can't do anything else.*

Except give her one of his quiet, incisive lectures that were always, somehow, much worse than Kamele's.

*And it's not,* she admitted, *like he didn't have cause.*

So, she took a deep breath as the car swept 'round the corner of Leafydale Place and told him about the bus ride.

# THIRTEEN

· · · · · · · · · · · · · · ·

*History of Education Department*
*Oriel College of Humanities*
*University of Delgado*

"THANK YOU, PROFESSOR WAITLEY," SINDY CLEMENS said, soft-voiced and grave, as always. "I appreciate your time."

"It's my pleasure," Kamele said sincerely. "That's an interesting line of inquiry you're pursuing. I'd very much like to see the completed project."

Sindy smiled and ducked her head; she was a gifted researcher with a knack for slicing through airy euphemism and into the bone of the matter. Unfortunately, her social skills were not as well-honed as her intellect. And she would soon, Kamele thought unhappily, watching the best student she'd been privileged to guide walk out of the classroom, have to acquire the means to defend herself, or academic politics would destroy her before she'd properly begun her work.

Of course, Kamele acknowledged, as she packed up her 'book, Sindy might choose to go elsewhere to pursue her researches. Many did. Delgado University sent dozens of brilliant students out into the wide galaxy every year.

On the other hand, the letters she had from her own mother, who had removed to Serpentine to take up the directorship of a moribund diaspora studies program shortly after Theo was born, didn't encourage her to believe that a talent for pure scholarship was *by itself* enough to prosper in a community of scholars.

She put her hand against the door to sign out and stepped into the hall, leaving the room to shut itself down. Kamele yawned as she walked toward the main hallway and the belt station. The senior seminar was in the last class block of the day, and her consultation with Sindy Clemens had kept her another four eights beyond that. At least Theo would have spent most of the evening with Jen Sar.

Kamele sighed, wishing she could have done the same. It would have helped, just to talk over the recent rash of . . . mess . . . as Theo styled it, with him. Not only did he know how to listen, but he brought what was very nearly a woman's understanding to certain matters. Talking with him, she had thought more than once, was like talking with a sister.

However, as Jen Sar was demonstrably and delightfully *not* her sister, spending time with him was a luxury that she certainly couldn't afford, not with Hafley just looking for a reason to bring all of the decisions made by her new and unwelcome sub-chair under review. Ella had reported that the Forensic Committee was moving with unprecedented haste. In fact, she was supposed to meet with Ella to—

"Destruction!"

Kamele yanked out her mumu, muted for the class period, grimaced at the reminder blinking on the screen, and touched Ella's quick-key.

"I regret to inform you that Professor ben Suzan has perished while awaiting a call from her adored sub-chair—"

"I'm sorry," Kamele interrupted. "Sindy Clemens wanted my input on her latest research and I couldn't—"

"Clemens scraped together enough courage to bring herself to your attention?" Ella interrupted in her turn. "Of course you needed to stay!"

"To bring *her work* to my attention," Kamele corrected. "The one hope I have for her eventual success is that she will dare much for her work."

"That may be enough."

"Geography," Kamele said darkly, "is everything."

"Speaking of geography, I'm in my office, if you'd like to reschedule our meeting for right now, give or take the time it takes you to get here. I'll get us some dark chocolate and coffee from the all-nighter."

Kamele laughed as she rounded the corner to the beltway.

"I have to teach tomorrow morning—and so do you!"

"Bah. I can give them a reading to parse. And so can you!"

The beltway was all but deserted. Kamele brought her mumu away from her ear, glanced at the time and shook her head.

"It's late," she said. "Let me apologize profusely and offer to meet with you over breakfast at Citations."

"I must find what the sub-chair's draw is," Ella said musingly.

"I'm sure Hafley will tell you if you ask, and then be very pleased to add that she thinks it improper for a temp sub to access those monies."

"Oh, for—" Ella sighed sharply. "Come to the office, Kamele."

There was an edge of . . . something in her friend's voice that caught Kamele's ear.

"It . . . can't . . . wait a few hours until breakfast?" she asked tentatively.

"I'd really rather it didn't."

Kamele frowned, identifying that *something* all at once. Ella was worried.

"I'll be there soon," she said. "Add some protein to the sugar and caffeine, will you? I'm starving."

"All right." Kamele sat in the visitor's chair in Ella's office, sipping all-nighter coffee, a tofu-and-mushroom sandwich still in its wrapping on her knee. "What is it that can't wait until breakfast?"

Ella shook her head and pointed. "Eat your protein; it'll wait that long."

Kamele sighed, leaned forward and pushed a pile of infoslips aside so she could set her cup on a corner of Ella's spectacularly messy desk. "I don't have a lot of time," she said, breaking the freshseal on the sandwich. "Theo . . ."

"Yes," Ella said darkly. "Exactly Theo."

Kamele looked up. "You don't know me nearly as well as we both know you do if you think I'm going to quietly sit here and eat this dreadful thing while you glower over my daughter's name."

"I'm not glowering," Ella objected. "As it happens, neither of my bits of news are particularly appetizing."

Kamele frowned at her, raised the sandwich, and still looking directly into Ella's eyes, took a large bite. It made the coffee seem like fresh roast. She waved her hand at her friend and reached for the cup.

Ella sighed. "Well, if you will have it—Lystra Mason has given Theo's name to the Chapelia."

Kamele inhaled—coffee, unfortunately. By the time she'd gotten her breath back, Ella had twisted her untasted sandwich into its wrappings and thrown the untidy ball at the disposal. She missed.

"Vile thing," she commented, though it wasn't clear if she meant the sandwich, the disposal, or Lystra Mason. She sipped her coffee and eyed Kamele. "All right, now?"

"No, I am not *all right*! Theo's name to the Chapelia?" She pressed her lips together until she'd swallowed what she'd been about to say, and satisfied herself with, "That woman is a fool."

"Yes, but a vicious fool. I happened to see her going into the Central Square Simple Circle and thought it odd enough to follow. She made the request to the person on duty at the desk, and was even so kind as to spell 'Waitley' for him."

"She's a *child*," Kamele said. "She hasn't had her *Gigneri*."

"A child," Ella intoned. "But steeped in the evils of complexity."

"You're not helping."

Her friend sighed. "In that case, I will helpfully note that you are of course correct. Theo is a child, and subject to the discipline and control of her mother.

Who, being the wise and sagacious woman I know her to be, will forthwithly make a donation appropriate to the sin and see the Call struck."

"Blasted nuisance," Kamele muttered.

"Exactly—done with malice aforethought, deliberately to shatter your attention and undermine your scholarship. Nothing that we haven't seen from Lystra before." Ella pointed at the sandwich wilting in Kamele's hand.

"Are you going to eat that?"

"No." She rewrapped it untidily and threw it at the disposal, where it hit the rim and tumbled in.

"Well, now that we've gotten the meal out of the way," Ella said brightly; "would you like to hear news of the forensic team?"

Kamele eyed her. "You know—something tells me that I don't." She leaned back in the chair and waved. "Go ahead. Spoil a perfectly lovely evening."

"If you insist." Ella reached to her 'book and tapped a quick series of keys. "Ah, here we are . . ." She cleared her throat and began, quietly, to read.

"Despite the fact that our team has not been long on its quest, we have identified certain matters which are of themselves unsettling, and, taken with the incidents of unethical scholarship perpetuated by former Professor Flandin, potentially dangerous to the entire academic structure of the University of Delgado. While fully cognizant of the many and heavy demands on the time of Sub-chair Waitley and Professor Liaison ben Suzan, the forensic search team does most earnestly seek a private meeting at the earliest possible moment. The committee holds itself ready to meet at any hour. We have nothing on our schedules that is more pressing than this unfortunate and complex issue."

Kamele closed her eyes. Ella, uncharacteristically, was silent.

"All right," Kamele said with a sigh. "My office, tomorrow—"

Ella cleared her throat. "I'm sorry to be wearisome, beloved, but, given the other hints and allegations contained within the committee's report—which I have forwarded to you—it might be best to meet somewhere . . . else."

Kamele opened her eyes. "Citations private parlor?"

Ella nodded. "I'll make the reservation for breakfast and let the search team know."

"Thank you." Kamele stood. "I've got to get home, Ella. Theo—"

"Kamele," Ella interrupted; "about Theo . . ."

"I'll handle the Simples tomorrow morning, after—"

"It's not just that," Ella interrupted again. "It's—you can't afford this. Not now."

Suddenly cold, Kamele looked down into her friend's face. "Ella—"

The other woman raised her hands. "Hear me out. You have a lot on you right now: Hafley's trying to discredit you; Mason's trying to discredit you—not to mention whatever has the forensic team in a panic. You must appear solid, strong. Purposeful. Releasing Jen Sar was brilliant—absolutely the correct move. And, while I don't expect that I *do* know how hard it was, I know that it was hard, yet you haven't wavered. You've shown the world that you can step away from personal considerations and take up the Scholar's mantle. You must take a similar step with Theo, or your work—all of your work, all of your care—all of your *sacrifice*!—is for nothing."

"What," Kamele said quietly—too quietly, to judge by the way Ella's eyes widened, "would you have me do?"

Her friend sighed and let her hands fall, fingers slapping the edge of the desk noisily.

"Play along with the Safety Office," she said, meeting Kamele's eyes defiantly. "Accept the therapy."

"You counsel me to drug my daughter."

Ella's gaze never wavered. "Six months. Schedule her *Gigneri* on the first possible date. Six months. It's not so much, Kamele, set against your career."

"It's *too* much," Kamele answered, the cold feeling in her chest infusing her voice. She picked up her 'book and turned toward the door.

Ella's mumu whistled cheerfully.

"Blast—it's Crowley—the forensic lead," Ella said, and thumbed the answer key. "This is serendipitous, Professor. I was just preparing to call you to schedule a breakfast meeting tomorrow—*Now*?" she asked, sharply, and then said nothing else.

Kamele turned away from the door. Ella's face tightened, lines etching between her eyebrows.

"Just a moment, Professor," she said eventually, and sounding much subdued. "She's right here." She tapped "mute" and looked up, making no attempt to hide her concern.

"Crowley says it's just gone from bad to worse," she said tiredly. "Apparently Flandin wasn't just falsifying her cites; she was tampering with the accredited texts."

"*What?*" Kamele walked to the chair and sat down again. Her stomach fluttered, but she didn't think it was lack of food. She had thought—but this was worse than she had thought. "Flandin didn't have an archivist's key."

Ella sighed. "Then it's all the more worrisome, isn't it? What should I tell Crowley?"

Kamele pulled out her mumu. "Tell him five minutes in the forensic committee's research room. Tell him I'll want to see everything. I'll be with you as soon as I text Theo."

· · · ·✳· · · ·

The little car zipped into the Wall's front drive, chasing the beams of its own headlamps up the twisty ramp. Father accelerated through the last triplet of ever-tighter curves, designed to force moderate speed. Theo laughed—and laughed again as the car sped toward the far wall and stopped gently just before its nose kissed ceramic.

"Well!" Father sounded like he was laughing himself. "We're a sad pair of scamps, I fear, and deserve whatever scolding your mother cares to deliver us."

He touched the controls and the doors opened.

"She won't know you've been racing unless we tell her," Theo commented, reaching into the boot to retrieve her pack.

"If only that were—" he began—and stopped.

Pack in hand, Theo looked up at him, but he only murmured, "Well," and closed the boot, shifting his stick to his right hand as he turned.

Turning, Theo scanned the area to see what might have given him pause, an exercise that was, for once, easy. A Simple in full regalia stood in a pool of red light next to the door, a 'book held open between mittened hands.

"Theo," Father said quietly. "Give me your mumu."

It was almost, she thought, as if he were still in the driver's seat. That level of awareness, but . . . sharper. Not a time to argue, she judged, or to ask him why. She pulled her mumu out and handed it to him.

"Thank you. Now, let us return you to your new home, where your mother will doubtless fall upon you with gladdened cries, while she heaps scorn upon the head of he who has led you along the paths of—"

"I am shown a name!" the Simple called out from the pool of red light. The amplified voice hurt Theo's ears. It was the same voice all the Simples had—sexless and without inflection. Initiates accepted a talky-box implant; that's what she'd read. It was supposed to facilitate their melding with the group. Walking at Father's side, Theo wondered if it worked, and how it felt to hear your voice coming out of the mouths of everybody around you.

"I am shown the name of one who has supped with complexity!" the Simple called again. "Theo Waitley!"

"What!" She stopped, felt a strong hand connect with her elbow and move her along.

"Don't stop," Father murmured. "Don't stare. Don't give them an advantage. You are an honorable person going about your honorable, unexceptionable—and private—business."

"Theo Waitley approaches!" the Simple shouted. "My work begins!"

If it had been up to her, Theo would have bolted for the door then, but Father's hand on her elbow held her to a deliberate, unhurried walk. The Simple stepped forward as they came into her pool of light, extended a mittened hand—and pointed directly at Father.

"Theo Waitley." The Simple's voice was quieter, now, which didn't, Theo was surprised to note, make it any more appealing.

"I am on a simple mission," Father said, never slowing down.

"What mission?" The Simple stepped into Father's path. He stopped, and Theo with him, her stomach tight.

"This minor child must be returned to her mother."

"One Chapelia will escort her."

"One will not," Father returned sharply. "That would invite complexity. My feet are upon the Path."

"What do you know of the Path, who goes uncovered and unique?"

"The Path is the journey and the journey is the Teaching," Father said, with the air of a student reciting a received formula. "Those whose feet are upon the Path must neither be brought aside nor delayed." He tipped his head.

"And," he continued, in a more conversational voice, "if your colleague at my rear and to the right does not cease her approach, regrettable things may happen. I protect this innocent child with every means at my hand." He hefted his cane, and . . . smiled . . . at the Simple.

"He has studied," came the voice—the same voice, but from behind them. "Perhaps he is on the Path."

"Consult the Name-Keeper while you await my return," Father suggested cordially. "Again, I escort this innocent to her mother." Theo jumped as his hand came under her elbow again, urging her to walk with him.

"Come, child."

"Yes, sir," she said meekly, and concentrated on matching his pace exactly. The back of her neck prickled and she wondered what the Simples were doing.

"Do not," Father murmured, "look back."

"What—" she began—

"And do not speak until we are inside."

The doors opened. They passed beneath the Eyes and walked past the Safety Station. Father nodded casually to the woman on duty as they mounted the belt for Quad Eight.

"What're you going to do if they *are* waiting for you when you leave?" Theo demanded.

He looked down at her, one eyebrow raised. "Don't be silly, Theo. I'll go out by another door."

"But your car!"

"The car is locked, and its owner well-known. It will be quite safe."

She took a breath. "How will you get home?"

"The bus." He inclined his head gravely. "I will, of course, be in no danger."

Theo knew better than to take *that* bait. "Could I have my mumu back now?"

"Ah, yes. How careless of me." He pulled it out of his pocket and gave it to her. "You are aware that your mumu—I should say, that everyone's mumu— emits an ID?"

"I'm not a *kid*," she said impatiently. "And the Simple was just reading the IDs out of her 'book. What I can't figure out is why she didn't realize you were carrying two mumus."

"But, you see," Father murmured, "the ID emitter on my mumu is...turned off."

Theo blinked.

"They turn *off*?"

He sighed. "Mind you, I don't say it's easy. Is this our stop?"

"Yes," Theo said, as the belt slowed. She swung off, Father at her side. "Would you have . . . hurt . . . that Simple, really? If she hadn't stopped."

He looked down at her. "Yes," he said seriously. "I would have hurt her, really. Liad, I fear, is a barbarous place, where people defend their honor and those who fall within it by any means, including physical force. Even having been so long embraced by the enlightened customs of Delgado, I find that I cannot wholly put these violent tendencies behind me." He lifted an eyebrow.

"You have now been fairly warned. Do you wish to run away?"

"From you?" Theo shook her head. "Don't be a nidj, Father."

He cleared his throat. "I will," he said, so solemnly she knew that he was trying not to laugh. "Do my best not to be a nidj, Theo."

He turned to survey the row of almost-identical beige doors set in at identical intervals into the white wall.

"Now, here's a pleasing aspect. Which door is yours?"

"Right the—" Her mumu warmed in her hands, and she glanced down, touching the screen. "I've got a text from Kamele," she said, and felt the full weight of his attention fall on her.

"Do you, indeed? Does she wonder when I'll bestir myself to return you?"

"No-oo . . ." Theo read the text again. Short as it was, it seemed . . . much less calm than Kamele's usual messages. She looked up into Father's black eyes. "She says she has a very important meeting that can't be put off. I'm to stay in, lock the door and not answer, if someone should ring."

"Perhaps she has received news of the Chapelia's interest," he murmured.

· "Looks like," Theo agreed, chewing her lip and glancing down to read the message a third time. *Would it be so bad,* she wondered irritably, *for Kamele to part with a little information now and then?*

"Why?" she asked suddenly, looking up. "Why did the Chapelia have my name in their book?"

Both eyebrows rose. "Theo, you astonish me."

"No, I don't," she said shortly. "You and Kamele are always telling me to question things."

"Indeed, but the quality of the question must also count for something—and of late yours have become... most interesting. So. Shall you let me in and show me this rug Gorna Dail has sold you?"

She considered him warily. "I'd like that. It's pretty late, though, and if you're going to have to go all the way around to the East Door..."

"It's scarcely late at all," he interrupted, and of a sudden gave her a smile. "I see I am found out. If you must have it, I crave a moment of Coyster's attention."

"Oh!" *Of course he wants to visit with Coyster,* she thought, turning toward the door; he was used to having the younger cat underfoot. And her, too. And Kamele.

"Is it... very lonely... with just you and Mandrin?" she asked, putting her hand against the plate.

"It is... quiet," he allowed, following her into the apartment. He glanced around the little hall while Theo locked the door. When she turned back, he was looking down at Kamele's rug.

"I think she meant it to . . . cheer the room up," Theo said awkwardly, unable to read the expression on his face.

"I'm certain that she did," he answered, his eyes still downcast. "Well." He swept a hand out, inviting her to lead on, and followed her down the hall.

"This is very pleasant," he said a few moments later as they sat together on the blue-and-green rug. Coyster was on his back between them, paws waving in ecstasy as Father tickled his belly. "Ms. Dail has done well by you."

"I hope so," Theo said, running her hand over the nap and watching the fascinating, waterlike flow from green to blue. "Do you know how to—to *dicker*?"

Grinning, he gave Coyster a final chuck under the chin. "In fact, I do. However, I believe that your mother would not thank me for introducing you to the art at this point in your education. First, master consensus and teamwork, then apply to me again."

She grinned. "Done!"

He laughed. "I see that you came away not entirely unmarked." He sobered. "It is, as you mentioned, quite late. Perhaps even late enough for a young student who has had a remarkably adventurous few days to seek some well-deserved rest."

"I'm . . ." Theo hesitated. She was sleepy. A little. But—

"I think you ought to stay here," she said, "until that Simple forgets about you. They probably put somebody on the East Door, too, you know . . ."

Father tipped his head, his face serious, though she could see the smile in his eyes.

"Well, lacking appropriate encouragement, she's

not likely to forget about me; nor are they likely to have forgotten the East Door. Which is to say that I agree with you. I should, indeed, stay here for a time. Thank you."

Theo considered him doubtfully. She could usually tell when Father was joking. "I—"

He raised a hand. "No, Theo. I am quite serious. Thank you for your care." He rolled to his feet and extended a hand to help her up.

"So," he said, smiling fully now. "Shall we say next Oktavi, same time?"

"Yes . . ." She blinked and cleared her throat. "Yes!"

"Good." He touched her cheek, his fingers warm, then ruffled her hair like she was a kid. "Sleep well, child."

# FOURTEEN

. . . . . . . . . . . . . . . . . . .

*History of Education Department*
*Oriel College of Humanities*
*University of Delgado*

THE COFFEE IN THE RESEARCH ROOM WAS FRESH-brewed. Kamele sipped hers and sighed aloud. *Some*one on the forensic team had her priorities straight.

Unfortunately, the pleasure of real coffee was negated by the methodical unveiling of data in the Group Space at the center of the table.

"As you can see," Professor Crowley murmured, tapping the light keys, "we have located no further discrepancies between Professor Flandin's publications and the material she cites. Everything, in fact, checks perfectly, and the committee had all but achieved a consensus accepting that those two . . . erroneous citations which resulted in the professor's loss of tenure were the only two incidents in existence."

Kamele sighed quietly, sipped coffee and recruited herself to patience. To judge from the patient expressions of his two team members, Professor Crowley was one who must tell the thing in whole and in order. And who for all of that, she thought, would not have insisted on a meeting *right now* only to say that the committee had found that there was nothing to find.

"In fact," Crowley continued, "the committee was well on its way to declaring that there was nothing else to find. It was only..."

"It was only," Professor Emeritus Beltaire spoke up from her seat at the far end of the table, "my own vanity, colleagues, that led us to explore what at first appeared to be the most minor portion of Professor Flandin's work: an encyclopedia entry on the subject of Vazinty pelinTrayle."

"The Saint of Panvine?" Ella sounded startled, as well, Kamele thought, she should. The Saint had been...opposed to the diversity of thought which the University of Delgado—for instance—held to be the treasure of higher learning.

To put it mildly.

"The so-called Saint," Professor Beltaire said dryly. "As it happens, my family holds the dubious honor of having once been enclosed by the pelinTrayle phu-lon. When the Beltaire patriarch embraced schism as preferable to genocide, he wisely brought away such papers, documents, and primary sources as he could lay hand to—for protection, you understand, should he need to place his jenos under a patron strong enough to withstand what blandishments Vazinty might make." She smiled.

"As it happens, Vazinty shortly had many more problems to deal with than the repatriation of an errant jenos. Beltaire settled upon Melchiza and eventually the original papers passed into the House of Planetary Treasures there." She paused to sip coffee. "Before surrendering them, the patriarch of course made copies, which the jenos retained, as part of our private archives. Eventually, the patriarch's great-granddaughter, who naturally had access to the history of the jenos, became, more by accident than design, an expert on Vazinty pelinTrayle."

She raised her cup again. Professor Crowley folded his hands, his eyes dreaming on the cluttered Group Space.

"So," Kamele said to Professor Beltaire, "you were uniquely placed to recognize an error in the relevant citation."

The elder scholar nodded. "Indeed I was, and I flagged the passage. Imagine my . . . surprise . . . when Professor Able—" she nodded at the last member of the committee, who appeared to be napping with her eyes open—"told me that the cite matched . . . precisely."

Kamele put her cup on the table.

"An error of memory, perhaps?" Ella murmured. "Even an expert is sometimes mistaken."

"My precise thought was something less gentle regarding the memories of old women, but—yes," Professor Beltaire said. "Cursing my failing faculties, I checked my hard copies . . ."

"She *can't* have altered the source documents!" Kamele protested. "That would have required an archivist's key." Or an archivist, brought in on the plan, and if that were the case—Kamele shivered.

"But she did just that," Professor Able said, apparently not napping, after all. "I have no idea *how* she did it, but I went through those documents line by line, comparing every word, and—the library sources have been altered. Only a bit, mind! Nothing more than a few words; sometimes only a point of punctuation."

"Nothing *important*," Professor Crowley said, leaning back in his chair, and looking 'round the table at them. "Taken in isolation."

"In sum, however," Professor Beltaire murmured, "these... corrections... draw a portrait of Delgado and Panvine standing... much closer together, philosophically, than we know to be the case, and, indeed, suggests that the current head of the Panvinian Administration is an adviser to the Delgado Board of Trustees."

"*What?*" Kamele looked at Ella, discovering an expression of bewildered outrage on her face that was probably, Kamele thought, a mirror of her own. She leaned forward, pressing her palms against the cool surface of the table as she ordered her thoughts.

"What I hear the committee say is that there is strong evidence that a... series? of source documents have been tampered with. Leaving aside for the moment the *how*, I would ask *why*."

Professor Able shook her head. "Flandin is the person to give the definitive answer to that. Unfortunately, we let her go."

"Though compelling, *why* does not fall within the scope of this committee's work," Professor Crowley added. "We were charged to survey the literature in order to ascertain if other... scholarly transgressions had been made which might damage the university. Evidence of such tampering has, alas, been discovered."

Professor Beltaire shook her head. "With all respect due to my honored colleague, I must disagree. What this committee has discovered is a discrepancy between the documents maintained by the research library and the documents held in private by an acknowledged expert. It is worth noting, colleagues, that *both* sets of documents are—copies."

"Certified copies!" Able corrected.

"As you say. But copies nonetheless. There is room for doubt. The copies are demonstrably not identical. What we cannot demonstrate from where we sit is—which set has been altered."

There was silence in the research room. Kamele closed her eyes, but she still felt the weight of her colleagues' regard. She was sub-chair; this investigation was her responsibility, begun for the best and most noble of reasons. The reasons for carrying through had just become...an imperative. If a whisper that Delgado's most closely held records had been altered escaped into the academic universe...

"I understand and value your argument," she said slowly, opening her eyes. She let her gaze go round the table, touching the face of each in turn: Beltaire grimly amused, Able only grim; Crowley resigned; Ella plainly horrified.

"I would be interested in hearing the committee's suggestions for a...quick and quiet resolution of this situation."

"Quiet will be difficult," Able said, "but I don't despair of finding the proper public relations angle."

"There must be an absolute determination made *first*," Crowley said sourly. "The copies *must* be compared to the originals."

"I agree," Beltaire said crisply. "If it is found that Delgado's copies have been compromised, *then* it is time for public relations to bake us an airy confection, and for the university to purchase a comprehensive doc-check of its archival material."

Kamele's stomach sank. The cost! And yet, the cost—if students stopped coming to the University of Delgado, if the results and facts reported by Delgadan scholars were automatically assumed by their colleagues elsewhere to be erroneous...

"Where are the original documents?" she asked Beltaire.

The old woman smiled. "Why, they are still safely locked up in the treasure house on my homeworld, Professor Waitley. Melchiza."

· · · · ✦ · · · ·

*She is not ready!*

Horror—hers, though it scarcely mattered—flooded him. He closed his eyes and spun a Rainbow; the very first thing taught to hopeful scoutlings, and perhaps the most useful. Together, he and Aelliana relaxed inside the benevolent colors.

"Tell me," he murmured, when his heartbeat had steadied; "upon what day and hour did I become a monster?"

*If her* Gigneri *is brought forward...*

"...which we will only suggest if it transpires that I have accurately recalled a particular bit of trivia I read years ago while in pursuit of something else entirely. It could be that I am mistaken; and in any case, the final word rests with Kamele—in whom I believe you repose complete confidence?"

*I repose complete confidence in no one,* Aelliana stated with an airy bravado that almost had him laughing aloud.

"That is, of course, very wise," he murmured, quellingly. "Now. If I might have a moment's peace in which to pursue my research?"

*Certainly,* his lifemate replied, and faded from his awareness.

· · · ✳ · · ·

She had the entirety of the committee's notes, recommendations and matches in her 'book. She had Ella's promise to get Hafley, the forensic team, and the Dean of Faculty into the same room tomorrow, utilizing whatever means seemed good to her. She had a hastily downloaded schedule of the current Quester's Fees, and the location of the nearest Simple Circle.

She also had a bottle of deplorable wine from the Quad Eight all-nighter, with which she hoped to counteract the jitters bestowed by adrenaline and too many late-night cups of coffee.

Her hair was wisping into her eyes. She shook her head, which of course only resulted in bringing the rest of it down. Well, the door to the apartment was scarcely six steps away. She'd be inside before she frightened the neighbors.

The at-home light was dark. Kamele blinked, her heart suddenly in her mouth.

Theo wasn't home yet? Surely Jen Sar wouldn't have kept her this late! What—

She slapped the lock without any memory of having crossed the intervening distance. The door opened, she swept inside—and stopped so suddenly her shoes squeaked against the floor.

Jen Sar looked up from his mumu. A smile glinted in the depths of his dark eyes, though his sharp-featured face was grave.

"Good evening, Kamele. Theo asked me to stay."

She let her breath out all at once, and raised her

free hand to shove her hair out of her eyes. "She's home, then. The door—"

"Forgive me. I felt it reasonable, in light of... certain events... that the door be persuaded to something less than complete candor," he said. Despite the rote "forgive me" he was as unapologetic as always for his tampering. "I'll put it right before I leave, if you wish."

"I don't know," she said shortly, and sighed, suddenly feeling all the hours of her day. "Jen Sar. We have to talk."

"Indeed we do." He rose, neat and supple, his grace making her feel even more disheveled and grimy.

"Come now," he said snatching the thought out of her head as he so often seemed to do, "I've had an hour to sit and recoup my strength after an evening with your daughter, while you are obviously newcome from some chancy venture." He tipped his head slightly. "Shall I pour wine while you refresh yourself? My topic will wait, if yours will."

*A shower, her robe, and, after, wine in the garden with the stars spread above like some fantastical tapestry*—Kamele spared a sigh for the impossible, and handed him the bottle.

"That is, hands down, the best thing anyone has said to me today."

His eyebrows rose as he took the bottle and walked with her toward the dining alcove.

"A chancy venture, indeed," he murmured, so seriously that she had to laugh, though it sounded a little high in her own ears.

"I'll be out soon," she said, dropping her 'book on the counter.

Jen Sar moved his shoulders. "You needn't rush on my account. I'll sit here quietly and plan my retreat."

That brought her around to frown at him.

"Jen Sar?"

He glanced up from his perusal of the wine label, face attentive. "Yes?"

"Why," Kamele asked, "did you gimmick the door?"

"Ah. Because the Chapelia have Theo's name and I couldn't be certain that they would not come here, since we had thwarted them at the gate. While your instruction that Theo not answer the door was sage, I felt it would be far less fatiguing for all if the door merely . . . discouraged visitors."

Kamele felt her shoulders sag. "I didn't expect them to be that—wait!" She reviewed their conversation thus far, and unhappily concluded that at no time had he *said* that her daughter was home. It was important, when speaking with Jen Sar, to keep track of those things that had *not* been said, as well as those which had. In fifteen years, she had acquired some facility, but tonight she was so tired . . .

"Where," she asked firmly, "is Theo?"

He sighed, deeply. "It is my fate to be found an abuser of youth."

Kamele took a breath. "Does that mean she's with some Simple, being—"

"It means that the child is asleep in her bed, with her cat on her pillow," he interrupted sharply. He threw his arms wide, theatrically. "I am altogether cast down and forlorn! Who could have supposed but that I would have been so incompetent as to allow a brace of unranked Simples to bear a child of my house away from beneath my very nose?"

Almost, she laughed, which was of course what he wanted her to do. She bit her lip and tried to look stern. "How much did you pay them?"

He gazed at her reproachfully. "Kamele, the exigencies of the day have disordered you. Surely you are aware that a mere male cannot buy a minor child from the Simples. That is for her mother to do."

"Yes . . ." she said, with strained patience. "So why didn't the Simple 'escort' her?"

"Because the Simples believe *me* to be Theo Waitley," he said, with the air of confessing all. He folded his hands before him and gazed up at her, his face bearing an expression of improbable innocence.

Kamele closed her eyes. Opened them.

"I am going to take a shower," she said, enunciating every word clearly.

"An excellent plan," he answered gravely, and gave her a small bow.

# FIFTEEN

· · · · · · · · · · · · ·

*University of Delgado*
*Faculty Residence Wall*
*Quadrant Eight, Building Two*

FEELING CONSIDERABLY LESS GRUBBY AND SOMEWHAT refreshed, her hair in a loose damp cloud around her robed shoulders, Kamele paused to survey the dining nook.

Two places had been set, a disposable cup, plate, and napkin at each. The wine bottle was unsealed and sat ready to hand, as was a kaf-dispensed "hostess tray" of assorted crackers and cheeses. Jen Sar sat in what had already become "Theo's place" in Kamele's mind, his back against the wall and his attention almost palpably on his mumu. She loved to watch him this way, wrapt so close in thought that he seemed to quiver, oblivious to all and everyone around him.

Of course, Jen Sar was never entirely oblivious to his surroundings.

He looked up, blinking as if just roused from a pleasant sleep, and gave her a dreamy smile.

"There now, that's more in the mode."

She laughed slightly and slipped onto her stool. "You have a very odd idea of mode, sir."

"No, there you are out!" he answered. "I have an expert's idea of mode."

He reached for the bottle, the twisted silver ring that he never took off gleaming on his smallest finger. "Wine?"

"Please," she said with feeling.

"This day of yours begins to take on the proportions of an epic," he murmured, pouring for them both. "Or was every sweet fruit served at the late meeting?"

Kamele took the cup from him and sipped, womanfully not wrinkling her nose at the taste. She had gotten much too accustomed to Jen Sar's wines, purchased from a merchant in Efraim, who imported cases from mountainous Alpensward. Jen Sar's draw, as the Gallowglass Professor of Cultural Genetics, was dizzying levels above hers as a newly minted full professor, even counting the absent sub-chair's percentage. The annual bonus he inevitably collected for his part in attracting quality students to the associated colleges comprising Delgado University didn't hurt either.

Carefully, she sipped her wine, hoping it would taste less dreadful this time. It had been a long time since she'd chivvied herself for resting comfortably on the laurels of her *onagrata*. She must be more tired than she'd thought.

"The day," she said, putting her cup down, "was long. The meeting," she looked into Jen Sar's attentive face, "was both unexpected and ... horrifying."

"Dear me." He pushed the cheese tray toward her. "Please, fortify yourself and tell all."

"I think you would have needed to be present for the full impact of the horror," she said, absently choosing a pepper cracker and a slice of soy cheese. "The telling of it is short enough: Flandin—the forensics team believes it was Flandin, and I hope their instinct is right. I'm really not equipped to handle a university-wide conspiracy! But, the sum is that Flandin appears to have gotten into the college's archives and altered the documents on file to match the citations published in her papers."

"I'll allow that to be terrifying." Jen Sar sipped his wine; Kamele thought he put the cup down with a bit more alacrity than usual. "How was the deed discovered, if the source matched the cite?"

"Professor Beltaire is an expert in the subject of one of the . . . falsified cites. She had her own copies of the material held in the archives."

Jen Sar tipped his head. "Copies."

"Yes, precisely. The originals are on Melchiza."

"Ah." He gathered up a cracker and a bit of cheese.

"Professor Beltaire describes herself as too elderly to undertake the journey," Kamele said, glancing at her cup and then away. "I think there may be some . . . political . . . anxieties there, too. Crowley will go, and Able."

Jen Sar sent her a sideways glance from beneath thick dark lashes. "And yourself?"

"Oh, yes," Kamele said, grimly. "I'm going. After all, I started this; it's up to me to see it done, and done correctly." She rubbed her eyes and against her better judgment reached again for the wine cup. "Which brings me to my topic. I'd like to leave Theo with you while I'm gone."

Both eyebrows rose—never a good sign—and a shadow of what might have been shock passed over his face.

"Leave Theo with me!" he exclaimed.

She raised a hand. "I'll take care of the paperwork, if you agree. Normally, of course, I would leave her with Ella, but after this evening—" Her voice caught and she looked away, raising the cup for a swallow of wine.

"Ella, this evening," she told the tabletop, unable to quite meet Jen Sar's eyes; "counseled me to accept the Safety Office's *therapy* for Theo. For the good of my career."

Jen Sar would hear the hurt in her voice, and she was sorry for it. He and Ella had never become comfortable with each other, though they tried, for her sake. But Ella—she and Ella had been friends since secondary school; they'd shared junior scholar quarters in the Lower Wall. In the normal way of things, Ella would have been Theo's secondmother, as involved in her education and well-being as Kamele herself...

"I can't leave Theo with Ella," she finished, finally raising her eyes to meet his.

"I understand," he murmured. "Certainly you would not wish to place your daughter into a position of potential peril." He frowned slightly. "What I fail to understand is why you must leave Theo on Delgado."

She stared at him. "But—take Theo to Melchiza?"

"Melchiza is hardly the end of the galaxy," Jen Sar observed dryly.

"I . . . Her education; I'd have to remove her from her team just when she's coming to understand consensus. She'd miss—"

"I do not for a moment believe," he interrupted, "that Professor Kamele Waitley would find the oversight of her minor daughter's education inconvenient in the least. Surely the school will provide a curriculum, exercises, reading lists, self-tests."

"I—"

"Kamele . . ." He extended a hand and put it over hers. "Think! This solves—many problems. It preserves custom, removes Theo from peril, and expands both your base and hers. Sub-chair Waitley *of course* accompanies the forensic team on its mission. *Of course* she has her daughter, the precocious and alarming Theo, at her side. It is mete. Theo is, after all, expected to follow her mother's path. Such a trip, with its insights into collegial collaboration and the ethics of scholarship, must be invaluable to her education."

He did make it sound a like a tenured opportunity, Kamele thought. She sat back, delicately slipping her hand out from beneath his.

"Speaking of expanding bases," she murmured pointedly, and had the rare opportunity of seeing him chagrined.

"Your pardon." He inclined his head briefly, then looked into her eyes. "Over-enthusiasm aside, it does answer many difficulties."

She sipped her wine, considering. "It seems to," she said slowly. "But when we come home—Jen Sar, she'd be odder than ever! And an absence will give the Safety Office time to write a recommendation. Without me here to deny it—"

"Yes—exactly so. Which is why you will be canny and schedule her *Gigneri* immediately you are both returned."

Kamele stared at him. A sister's understanding, indeed! she thought, anger sparking.

"She's too young!" she snapped. "If I won't drug my daughter for expedience, what makes you think that I'll push her into a—"

"Allow me to be utterly sympathetic to your concern," he interrupted. He pulled out his mumu and tapped the screen.

"I put my time to profit while awaiting your return," he said. "And I find that—you may contrive."

"Excuse me?"

"There's a loophole," he explained, putting the mumu on the table before her, pointing at the screen. "Look."

"As recently as fifty years ago, the *Gigneri* and the First Pair were distinct as rites of passage. First, one is entrusted with the full tale of one's genes. Then, when one has had a bit of time to adjust and to—expand one's base—one fully participates in a celebration of joy, as a new and potent adult." He sat back. "*Much* more rational than piling every shock and discovery into one event."

Kamele listened to him with one ear while she read his précis.

"You might remember that I told you of my mother's best friend," she murmured, most of her mind on reading. "She came from Alpensward, where they kept to the older ways." She looked up, eyes bright. "She was a secondmother to me, and I miss her still."

"I remember." Jen Sar smiled. "What better tribute to her memory than to induct your daughter into adulthood as she would have wished?"

Kamele nodded, chewing her lip, then handed the mumu back to him. "Send me the cites, if you will."

"Of course." He touched a quick series of keys. "Done."

"Thank you." She reached for another cracker and some cheese.

"When will the committee depart?" Jen Sar asked.

Kamele sighed. "We need to get Hafley's approval, the dean's approval, the directors' approval, then the Bursar's office—you know the procedure. We could have something in two days—or by the end of the semester."

He nodded, looking thoughtful.

"I believe, then, that we must address my topic." He gave her a wry look. "I do know that it is late, but I must plead necessity."

Necessity, as Kamele had learned, was not invoked lightly. For Jen Sar to do so must signal an overwhelming concern.

She nodded, and held out her cup. "Pour, then speak."

He poured, going so far as to refresh his own cup, though the wine must be even more dreadful for him, Kamele thought, than for her. He did not, however, immediately speak, but sat for some few moments, his hands curled 'round his cup, staring into the unsatisfactory depths.

Kamele sipped, and recruited herself to patience.

At last, he looked up.

"Theo has given me what I believe to be the round tale of her last few encounters with the Safety Office," he said slowly. "In addition, this evening I took the liberty of administering a few very small tests of physical reaction." He paused, looking at her.

Kamele nodded for him to continue.

"Based on Theo's report and my own tests, I believe her to be . . . quite near to that point we had discussed previously, where all of her powers align. In my view of the matter, it would be . . . tragic for the Safety Office to be allowed to interfere at this juncture. I therefore proposed to Theo, and now to you, that she enroll in a dance class."

"A—dance class," Kamele repeated, blinking at him. Had she drunk *that* much wine, she wondered? But, no; Jen Sar's points were often oblique. "Please explain."

"Gladly. Dance is a marriage of mind, body, and— soul, if you will. Taking such a class will demonstrate to the Safety Office that you are seeking to treat Theo's 'agility problems.' Indeed, dance is a well-documented therapy for clumsiness and certain so-called 'physical limitations.'"

"It is," Kamele noted, "mid-term. And I'm afraid, my friend, that I am not acquainted with anyone in Dance."

"But I am," Jen Sar said, not altogether surprisingly. "I have this evening been in communication with Visiting Expert of Dance Professor Noni, who tells me that she has room for a novice in her Practical Dance class, and will be pleased to send the student's mother the necessary card."

Kamele shook her head. Jen Sar *did* meddle, though usually not so blatantly as this. He must, she thought, be very worried.

"If Professor Noni will still agree to include Theo in her class after she is informed of the . . . uncertainty of her continued attendance," she said slowly, "I'll be pleased to receive the card and to approve the change in my daughter's academic schedule."

"I will relay that message to her." He picked up his mumu, tapped a rapid message, thumbed *send,* and slipped the device away.

"Thank you, Jen Sar," Kamele said, and smiled when he looked up. "It's late," she added.

"... and neither propriety nor our current circumstances allows me to remain for what is left of the night," he finished lightly, and slid to his feet. "I believe I may repair to my office and get some work done. Do you think you will have the matter with the Chapelia settled by the time I leave the Wall ... later today?"

"Yes; I'll take care of it first thing," she promised, slipping off her stool and walking with him to the door. "Was Theo—very alarmed?"

"Curious, rather. Though ..." He paused and turned to face her. "I fear that I have made a misstep. She now knows that it's possible to turn off the emitter."

"Oh," Kamele said, feeling slightly giddy, "no!"

"I trust it will take her a few days at least to puzzle out the method."

"A few days—" She looked at him helplessly, then giggled.

"Well," she said. "It ought to keep her out of trouble." She giggled again and shook her head.

"Indeed it ought," Jen Sar said solemnly, and touched her cheek, very briefly.

"Good-night, Kamele. Sleep well."

# SIXTEEN

. . . . . . . . . . . . . . . .

*Retrospection on an Introduction*
*Number Twelve Leafydale Place*
*Greensward-by-Efraim*
*Delgado*

KAMELE SPUN ON HER TOES IN THE CENTER OF THE common room, looking down into the floor mosaic. Leaves, and birds, and cunning furred animals moved beneath her feet.

She laughed as Jen Sar came into the room, wine glasses in hand. "I thought you said *small*."

He lifted an eyebrow and looked about, as if just discovering his environment.

"Small," he said, stepping forward and offering her a glass, "is a relative term. The house I grew up in was larger." He looked about again, and bowed gently. "Many times larger, in fact." He sipped wine. "Of course, it enclosed the clan entire."

Liad, Kamele thought, raising her own glass, was certainly a strange place, with an abundance of odd customs. She would have gladly heard more of those customs, but Jen Sar was disinclined to talk much about the world he had left. Kamele theorized some disagreement with the directors of his kin group, which had resulted in his taking up the role of traveling scholar, until nomination to the Gallowglass Chair brought him to Delgado.

"Can you see the stars from your garden?" she teased him.

"I can and I do," he answered with a gravity that was belied by the quirk of a brow. "Shall I show you?"

She hesitated, belatedly covering her hesitation with another sip of wine. "That would be lovely," she murmured, "but the stars rise late, don't they? I need to be back to the Wall before—"

"Yes, of course." He hitched a hip onto the arm of the couch and looked about him, glass held casually in long, clever fingers, the silver ring a sly gleam against his golden skin.

Kamele bit her lip and walked over to sit on the couch near his perch. He looked down at her, smiling, and her stomach tightened.

Her friendship with Jen Sar Kiladi had grown deeper over the last two semesters; the pleasure she took in his company as surprising as it was satisfying. But Ella was right, she acknowledged. Satisfying as it was, it was time to alter their relationship, or cut the association entirely. People were beginning to talk, the more so since Jen Sar had declined Professor Skilings' offer. She'd heard from Skilings' assistant, who had been working, forgotten, in the next room when the offer was made, that Jen Sar had professed himself honored, obliged, and desolated not to be able to accommodate her.

Skilings had not been pleased. No one had *ever* turned her down, not, so rumor went, since she'd moved to Topthree. Mortified, she had looked about her for a reason for Jen Sar's refusal—and her eye had inevitably fallen on Associate Professor Kamele Waitley, who spent a great deal of time in the company of a very senior scholar. And, as Ella so reasonably pointed out, Kamele could not afford to have Skilings as an enemy.

It would be best for everyone, Ella said, for Kamele to end the friendship.

Ella, Kamele reminded herself, liked pretty men.

"Jen Sar . . ." she began, sounding breathless to herself.

He lifted an eyebrow. "Yes, my friend?"

"I . . . that is . . ." Her voice failed her entirely, and she looked away, biting her lip. It wasn't as if she was inexperienced! She'd had two previous *onagrata,* not counting her *Gigneri* pairing—and here she was acting like a green girl, stumbling over her first offer!

"Kamele?" Jen Sar's deep voice carried concern. "Are you well?"

"Yes, I—yes." She leaned forward and awkwardly put the wine glass on the side table with a bit of a clatter, then turned to face him, looking up into his sharp, unhandsome face. She took a breath.

"Jen Sar," she said firmly, her hands clasped tightly in her lap. "It would be . . . an honor to accept you as *onagrata.*"

Both eyebrows rose, his lips parted—and then there was that moment of arrested movement that had become familiar to her, and the odd feeling that Jen Sar had . . . stepped away . . . from himself.

Abruptly, he smiled, a sweet, open expression she had never before seen from him. He leaned forward and put his glass next to hers on the table.

"*Tra'sia, cha'leken!*" he said gladly, and bent down to kiss her on the mouth.

Strictly speaking, she should have initiated the kiss, but Kamele found she didn't mind that he had taken the lead. Indeed, it was some time before she could speak, and some little while more until she cared to.

"What did you say?" she asked eventually, her cheek snuggled against his shoulder. "Before you . . . kissed me?"

Jen Sar sighed lightly, ruffling her hair.

"A Liaden—expression of joy," he murmured, sounding . . . chagrined.

Kamele laughed, and reached for him again.

# SEVENTEEN

. . . . . . . . . . . . . . . . . . . .

*Leisure and Recreation Studies: Practical Dance*
*Professor Stephen M. Richardson Secondary School*
*University of Delgado*

DANCE WAS...UNEXPECTEDLY INTERESTING.

She'd had to swap out of the multi-Team free study session, which meant having to do more of her solo work after school, but, Theo acknowledged, that wasn't exactly a burden, since she was grounded, anyway.

But dance...it was like math, and lace making, and scavage, all together; and it was *almost like* the patterns she saw in her head. Better even than that, she thought as she stripped out of her Team coveralls and pulled on the clingy leggings and stretchy sleeveless shirt, once everybody in the class had the pattern down, they all did *what* they were supposed to do, *when* they were supposed to do it, and nobody got hurt, or fell, or bumped into anybody else.

Not even her. Theo Waitley, the clumsiest kid in Fourth Form.

She grabbed the bit of lace out of her bag, slammed

the locker and headed for the dance floor. Bek was already there, propped up on an elbow and doing lazy leg lifts. She dropped cross-legged to the floor next to him.

"Hey, Theo." He gave her a friendly nod, like he always did. Bek had been in class since the beginning of the term, and he was *good*; one demo was all he ever needed to pick up a dance move. She wouldn't have blamed him for being annoyed that Professor Noni had teamed him with the new kid. Instead, he actually seemed *happy* to have her as a partner.

"What've you got there?" he asked, sitting up in a boneless move that reminded her of Father.

"This?" She held the lacy web outstretched on her fingertips. "It's a dance."

"Really." He leaned forward, gray eyes slightly narrowed as he traced the connections. "I'm not sure I see—oh! It's the new *suwello* module we started last time! I can see the wave..." He extended a careful finger and traced the line. "And here's where we all spin out into a circle..." Bek sat back, grinning, and running his fingers through his heavy yellow hair. "That's pretty smart. How'd you think of it?"

"Well..." Theo bit her lip. "I make lace for a—for something to do with my hands. And I was thinking about how dancing was like math *and* like making lace, so I—what's wrong?"

Bek was staring at her. "*Dance* is like *math*," he repeated, and shook his head. "What an idea!"

"But it is!" Theo said, surprised, and then looked at him closely. "You're joking, aren't you?"

"No, I'm not joking," he assured her. "Dance is *an escape* from math!"

"But you're so good at it! Dance, I mean."

"That's because," Bek said patiently, "dance is nothing like math." He put his hand over his heart. "Two repeats and four remedials in Fractal Trigonometry. I'm not wrong about this, Theo."

"What is it, then?" she demanded. "If it's not math?"

Bek looked surprised. "A conversation," he said, reasonably. "What else?"

"A—"

"Well, well!" Professor Noni's high and somewhat unpleasant voice cut across Theo's response. "I don't know whether to be delighted or horrified to hear that the argument between theory and art continues unabated. The heat death of the universe will doubtless find them arguing still." She clapped her hands. "Everyone up! Stretches! Sequence Five!"

"Ms. Waitley, stand forward, if you please," Professor Noni said. "I need your assistance in a demonstration."

Theo blinked. Professor Noni always called on Bek and on Lida—the class's lead students—to assist during demos. To call on the newest student—*I've only had eight classes!* Theo thought, her fingers tightening on the bit of lace.

"Go on, Theo. You'll do great." Bek leaned over and worked the lace free. "I'll hold this for you."

"I am *waiting*, Ms. Waitley."

"Yes, ma'am!" Theo took a deep breath and stepped forward. She met Professor Noni's eyes and consciously straightened her shoulders.

The dance professor's lips bent in one of her chilly smiles. "A good stance from which to begin almost anything," she said. "Now, Ms. Waitley, what I want you to do is...answer me."

Theo blinked. "*Answer* you, ma'am?"

"Precisely. Dance, as Mr. Tehruda has expressed it, might be seen as a conversation. I will make a 'statement' and you will answer me, whereupon I will reply, and so on, until our conversation is, by mutual agreement, completed." She inclined her head.

"Or, to put it another way; I will propose a equation, you will refine it, and we will collaborate until we have achieved agreement. Now. Attend me."

Theo watched worriedly as Professor Noni moved her left foot forward, back-extending her right leg, and raised her right arm until it was a straight line from her shoulder, hand bent at a right angle, fingers pointing toward the ceiling. And that was a completely familiar move; nothing other than the opening move in Stretch Sequence Three. Theo relaxed into the second move in the sequence, dropping back on the right leg, stretching the left in front, bringing her left arm up to join the right.

Professor Noni moved into the third phrase, Theo answered with the fourth, and Professor Noni responded, a little more quickly. The room and the small noises made by her classmates as they watched faded from Theo's attention, as she concentrated on the moves—statement, answer, statement, response. At some point they left the familiar stretches; at some point, they sped up. Theo barely noticed, her mind's eye filled with the pattern they made as it *would become,* while her body responded to the pattern as it *was now.*

They moved, describing circles and squares; they approached, retreated, sidestepped, and the conversation went on, and on...

Professor Noni spun on a toe and lunged. Theo leapt, spinning—and suddenly the pattern in her head and the pattern of the dance diverged. All during the dance they had maintained a distance of between six and eight steps, and now—

Now, they were going to be too far apart!

Theo twisted, lunging in an attempt to mend the error, while the pattern in her head shattered and flew apart. Professor Noni skipped to one side, spun lightly and came to rest, feet flat and hands folded. Theo staggered and went down hard on one knee.

"Enough!" The dance instructor raised her hand. She was, Theo saw, breathing hard, and visibly sweating. Now that she was noticing, she was sweaty, too, and taking deep breaths.

"Tell me, Ms. Waitley—why did you correct your statement?"

"I'd... miscalculated," Theo gasped. "We'd been dancing at the same distance, and suddenly we were going to be farther apart..."

"I see. And yet it is... a natural human interaction—to come together, to part, to meet again." Professor Noni paused, then nodded. "Despite that last... miscalculation—I am impressed, Ms. Waitley. A very interesting conversation, indeed!"

The second bell on the session sounded then, startlingly loud. The professor looked out at the rest of the class, sitting so still they hardly seemed to be breathing. Bek's grin was so wide Theo thought his face must hurt.

"We break for an eighth," Professor Noni said. "Be ready to dance the *suwello* when you return, students."

❋     ❋     ❋

Dancing the *suwello* really woke you up, Theo thought, as she finished sealing her coveralls. She felt—she felt like she was—like she was *smooth*; like all her muscles were moving in sync. And *that* was an . . . interesting thought. She paused with her dance clothes in her hand, staring down into the depths of her bag, thinking.

Did her muscles usually feel like they weren't working together? No, she decided after a moment; mostly she felt like she was . . . *stiff*, and so afraid of tripping somebody else up, that—

"'Bye, Theo!" Lida called, interrupting her ruminations.

She looked up as the older girl and her two friends moved past on their way to the door.

"'Bye," she said, giving the three of them a nod and a smile. "Looking forward to next time."

Jinny—the tallest—grinned. "Me, too! The *suwello* sure does sharpen you up!"

The three of them laughed and hurried by. Theo blinked at the dance clothes still in her hand, quickly stuffed them in her bag, sealed it, and headed for the exit, moving quick and smooth.

Bek was lounging against the wall across from the dressing room. Theo grinned. When he wasn't dancing, Bek looked lazy and boneless, like an especially spoiled cat. Like a cat, though, once he started to move, it was with precision and strength.

Like now. He straightened out his lean and swung in beside her, matching steps like they'd practiced the whole thing.

"Hey, Theo, where do you go now?"

"Home," she said, feeling a little of the spring drop out of her step. "Over in Quad Eight."

"Mind if I come with you part of the way? I've got a tutorial over in Merton."

She looked at him from beneath her lashes. "Fractal Trig?"

"Oh, no!" Bek said cheerfully. "I'm out of Fractal Trig. My mentor got me a 'change into Consumer Math. I started mid-mester, so I've got to do the make-ups, that's all."

They came to the belt station and went up the ramp, walking light and quick, and stepped onto the belt still in sync, without even the breath of a boggle. Theo sighed in pure pleasure.

"You going to the Saltation on Venta?"

"To what?"

Bek blinked. "The Saltation. Started I don't know how long ago. All us dancers get together and—dance. There's freeform, and competitions, and—you'd like it, Theo."

She looked at him doubtfully.

"I don't know," she said slowly. "I wouldn't know anybody, and I'm not really a dancer—I mean, I just started, and I don't know any of the dances, really."

"You're a natural!" he told her, eyes sparkling. "And today—Professor Noni was testing you—you know that, don't you? And she said she was *impressed*. I don't think I've ever heard her say that to anybody before."

"But you—"

"I've been taking dance whenever I had a free-study since I was a littlie," Bek interrupted. "But you, you just came in cold, and picked up the moves really fast. You're already better than Jinny, and she's been taking dance as long as I have!"

Theo laughed.

"What's funny?"

"You are—no, I am!" She shook her head, and laughed again. "Bek, I've got at least a thousand notes in my file saying that I'm physically challenged. I bump into people and trip over things that aren't there."

"Really?" He shrugged. "Looks like dance is just what you need, then." He took a breath. "So," he said, speaking a little too quick; "I'll be going to the Saltation."

Theo looked at him, seeing the tinge of pink along his cheeks. Her stomach tightened. Bek *wanted* her to go—as his partner? He'd said there were competitions. But he was being polite, giving her a hint, and hoping she'd ask him . . .

"I—" she cleared her throat. "I have to ask my mother," she admitted, feeling like a littlie, herself. She met Bek's eyes and felt her mouth twist into a half-smile. "I'm grounded for the rest of the 'mester, except for school and teamplay and . . . some appointments."

Bek smiled. "Tell her it's for extra cred."

"Is it?"

"Well—Professor Noni comes sometimes."

"I'll ask Kamele," Theo said, suddenly decisive. "If—if she okays it, I'd . . . I'd like you to come with me, Bek."

His smile got wider, and his cheeks got pinker. "I'd like that. A lot." He looked around. "My stop's coming up. Text me, Theo, Okay?"

"Okay," she agreed, her stomach still tight and her head feeling light. "G'night, Bek!"

"'Night!" He swung off the belt and jogged down the ramp.

Theo looked down at her feet—and smiled.

# EIGHTEEN

• • • • • • • • • • • • • • • • • •

*University of Delgado*
*Faculty Residence Wall*
*Quadrant Eight, Building Two*

KAMELE HAD A MEETING. AGAIN.

Theo sighed. She was still feeling...sharp...from dance—and she wanted to talk to Kamele about the Saltation. Maybe it *would* be good for her to go, she thought. It would show the Safety Office that she was taking her responsibilities to society seriously. And if she and Bek won a competition, then wouldn't that show them that she was getting better?

She'd put the argument to Kamele that way. If she ever came home.

Theo shoved her mumu into its pocket, and danced a few *suwello* steps on her way down the hall. In the kitchen, she drew a soy cheese sandwich and a cup of juice from the kaf and carried them back to her room.

Coyster was curled up in the center of the rug, more or less, snoring with his tail over his nose. Theo grinned and sat down at her desk. She had a response paper to write for Advertence and some math problems to finish up.

After that, she thought, touching the keys lightly, she'd have another go at finding the turn-off code for her mumu. That project had gotten so frustrating that she'd put it aside, to "let it grow some leaves," as Father said. She realized now that she'd started with the wrong set of assumptions. She'd expected it to be *easy*—and maybe it was, once you figured out the trick. But figuring it out—that *had* to be hard. If it wasn't, then everybody would turn their mumus off, and the Simple at the gate wouldn't have been fooled at all.

There was another suspicious circumstance, Theo thought darkly. Even though they'd had several Oktavi dinners together since the Simple called her name, Father hadn't once asked her about her progress with her mumu, though he must've known she'd try to find out how to turn it off.

Of course, she hadn't mentioned it, either. She was going to figure it out herself, and not ask Father for help.

Not that he was likely to tell her.

"Solos first," she said aloud, scrolling through what she'd already written while she had a bite of her sandwich. Father would say that it was disrespectful of the food to concentrate on work while one ate.

On the other hand, she thought, going back to double-check a secondary cite, Father had probably never tasted soy cheese out of the kaf.

The cite checked. Good. Halfway through Social Engineering, she'd been struck with the conviction that she'd flubbed it—or misunderstood the content.

She put the sandwich back on its plate and began to type.

She was sipping juice and rereading her response, tweaking words and patching sentences, when a flicker of green tickled her peripheral vision. Frowning, she looked down at the bottom left corner of the screen, and the dark green Serpent of Knowledge.

Chewing her lip, Theo considered the icon. None of the rest of the Team had gotten a mystery assignment; she'd asked. She'd even gone back through Professor Wilit's public class notes, and there was no mention of solo assignments made on the date the Serpent icon had first showed up on her screen.

All that being so, and after giving it some careful thought, Theo had deleted the icon.

And now it was back, pulsating gently while it waited for her attention.

Well, she thought, it could just wait, that was what. She had other things in queue before it.

Determinedly, she turned her attention back to her response paper, finished the editing and saved it before opening her math solos.

Despite Lesset's repeated claims during their commute between classes, the problems weren't hard. In fact, Theo thought, as she double-checked her work, they'd been kind of boring. Sighing, she closed her math space.

The Serpent icon was still there at the corner of the main screen. Waiting. Theo stuck her tongue out at it. Pulling her mumu from her pocket, she dropped to the rug next to Coyster, who stretched out of his curl, and relaxed bonelessly, licking his nose, all without opening his eyes.

Theo tapped her mumu on and called up the advanced diagnostic. The one thing she had figured out, before she'd gotten too angry to think, was how to circumvent the self-test program. Which hadn't been particularly easy to do. If she'd been even a little advertent, that would have told her that the rest of the problem was going to be tricky.

"The thing is," she told Coyster, "that the *trigger* has to be something simple—on and off. Because, if you're *never* on the grid, somebody'll notice. So it needs to be fast, so you can go off-line immediately in an emergency—and come back just as fast. Or faster."

Coyster yawned. Noisily.

"You just feel that way because *you* don't have a collar that tells everybody where you are all the time. Think if you were a dog."

Coyster opened one eye, glared at her pointedly, and closed it.

"Sorry." Theo turned her attention back to the mumu.

The key *had* to be in the advanced diagnostic, she told herself for the eighty-eighth time. She tapped the toolbox open and sat frowning at her choices:

**ISOBIOS**
**Grid Calibration**
**Schedule**
**Unitize**
**Cloud Absorb**

None of the sub-routines was helpfully labeled *Turn off ID emission*. In fact, there was no mention of the ID-shouter at all, though every kid knew that their mother could track them through their mumu. You only had to be where you weren't supposed to be *once*, for that lesson to stick.

Frowning, Theo touched *Schedule*, even though she knew the list of sub-routines by heart. *Schedule a self-test, schedule a back-up, schedule a grid calibration*. Grumbling to herself, she chose *schedule a self-test* and glared down at the next set of choices: *diagnostic* or *complete*?

"Chaos-driven, nidjit programs..." Theo muttered— and froze. She'd been through this screen dozens of times. Why was it only now that she wondered what exactly a *complete* self-test was?

Cautiously, she made her choice.

Her mumu emitted a strident, drawn-out beep. Coyster flicked an ear and put his paw over his nose. On the screen, words appeared, limned in orange.

*This diagnostic will thoroughly test every resident system. Several functions may be unavailable or taken off-line during diagnosis. These include any function that requires syncing with the local Cloud or Grid. Voice messaging will remain unaffected.*

Theo held her breath.

*Do you wish to continue? Yes/No*

She touched *yes*.

The next screen was a configuration chart. She could, Theo quickly learned, instruct her mumu to conduct up to sixteen consecutive test sessions. She could also dedicate a key combination to initiate testing from outside of the diagnostic program, though she was warned to choose a nonintuitive combination, so that a test session would not begin in error.

"I found it," Theo breathed to Coyster, who greeted

this information with no visible sign of awe, joy—or even consciousness.

She thought for a moment, staring at the mumu's keypad and thinking about combinations that were easy to code, but that she wouldn't likely hit by accident. Finally, and deliberately, she keyed in the trigger combo. After further consideration, she set the loop to nine consecutive checks, reasoning that she could hit the hot keys again, if she needed more time off-grid.

Needed for *what* was a question she had been studiously not asking herself, even as she had pursued the answer to the puzzle. Instead, she reminded herself that the Simple at the door would have taken her under study if Father hadn't been prepared. Being prepared was very close to *thinking ahead,* and it seemed to her that an advertent scholar—which Father demonstrably was—ought always to be prepared.

"I should test it," she said, holding the mumu in her hand. It wouldn't be *thinking ahead* if she just assumed it was going to work. In fact, it would be *wishful thinking,* which was almost as bad as making excuses.

"How?" she asked, putting the mumu on Coyster's side. His skin rippled in protest, and he flicked his ears, but he didn't bother to open his eyes.

Obviously, she didn't want to just vanish off the grid; even she could see that would be reckless. She might, she guessed, tell Kamele what she'd done and ask for her help, in the spirit of scholarly exploration.

On second thought, that wasn't such a good idea. Theo plucked the mumu off of Coyster and held it in her hand, staring down into the screen. She'd wait until Oktavi, she thought, and ask Father to check her.

That was fair. In a sense, she'd gotten the assignment from him.

It wasn't the best solution—she wanted to test her work *right now,* and Oktavi was *days* away. On the other hand, it would have to do; and anyway, it wasn't like she planned on *actually using* it; it was only a precaution. In the meantime, she had more than enough to keep her busy—worrying about the Review Board for one, and why they'd asked for an extension to decide her case. Kamele seemed to think that the extended time for additional discovery and deliberation was good news. Theo—or, at least, her stomach—thought otherwise.

She could also, she told herself firmly, think about dance, work on her lace, and do extra-credit solos.

And, if she got bored, she could see about scrubbing the Serpent icon and the program that generated it from her school book.

As a matter of fact, she had an idea about that.

She rolled to her feet and approached the desk. The Serpent of Knowledge was still down in the left hand corner, still pulsing, oh-so-patiently waiting for her attention.

Sighing, Theo slid into the chair and tapped the icon. Once.

A menu bar appeared in the center of her screen.

- **Theory, Annotated**
- **Safety Office History, Delgado University**
- **Surveillance History, Delgado**
- **Map, Interior**
- **Map, Exterior**
- **Timetable, Real Time**
- **Algorithm**

Theo blinked.

Whatever it was, the Serpent had done exactly what she'd asked it to do, and more thoroughly than any search program she'd ever used. She bit her lip, one hand fisted on her knee, the other hovering over the selection key.

*There isn't,* she thought, *any assignment.*

On the other hand, she *was* interested in the information. So what if there wasn't an assignment? Information for its own sake was—

"Theo?" Kamele's voice echoed down the hallway. "I'm home! I hope you're hungry!"

"Admin has okayed the trip," Kamele said, sounding tired and relieved and anxious all at once. At least she was eating, Theo thought, helping herself to another slice of spice bread with veggie-paste stuffing. 'Course, it was hard to turn down spice bread.

"When will you be leaving?" Theo asked, trying to remember where Melchiza was, exactly, with reference to Delgado.

"The in-time to make the next outgoing liner—call it two days," Kamele murmured, and Theo put her bread down, staring.

"That's, um . . . really soon," she managed.

Kamele nodded. "It is. We're very fortunate that *Vashtara* is due in at the station, and has room for passengers."

Theo chewed her lip. "How long—how long will you be gone?" She'd stayed with Lesset for a day or two at a time when Kamele and Father had gone on short trips, just like Lesset had stayed with her when her mother went away.

At least twice, Theo had stayed with Aunt Ella in her cluttered apartment, while Kamele and Father traveled.

"The return trip may be a day or two sooner or later, depending on transition links. I thing we ought to assume most of two hundred days."

Theo sat back on the stool, a gone feeling in her stomach.

"Close your mouth, Theo. You look like one of Jen Sar's prize fish." Kamele had a bite of spice bread.

"You're going to be gone—" *I'll miss you!* Theo thought, and blinked her eyes to clear a sudden start of tears. She cleared her throat, and tried to sound calm and matter-of-fact. "I guess I'll be staying with Aunt Ella, then."

"Oh, no." Kamele shook her head and reached for her cup. "You'll be coming with me."

Theo gasped.

"Coming—to Melchiza?" she repeated. "I can't go to Melchiza!"

Kamele looked up. "Of course you can. Tomorrow, you'll file for solo studies from your teachers; I've already transmitted my authorization. I have an info packet from *Vashtara,* which I'll send along to you; they include guidelines for what and how to pack. Your immunizations are up-to-date, but they'll screen us on-station, anyway." She paused, looking at Theo consideringly. "Coyster will need to go live with Professor Kiladi. I'm afraid cats aren't allowed on cruise ships."

She was going to strangle, Theo thought, around the buzzing in her ears. Her chest was tight and she was suddenly very sorry that she'd eaten quite so much spice bread.

"But, I can't! Not for—what about dance? There's a freeform that I wanted to dance in on Venta, Bek— What about the Review Board? I—why can't *I* stay with Father, too?"

"Because you're not a cat," Kamele said crisply. "Really, Theo. You're behaving as if this were a punishment instead of an opportunity to learn."

"I don't," Theo said breathlessly, "*want* to learn."

That was stupid. She knew it the second the words tumbled out of her mouth. But of course, it was too late to call them back.

Kamele shook her head. "The situation is quite settled, Theo. Whining isn't going to change it. I must say, however, that I'd never expected to hear my daughter say that she doesn't *want* to learn."

Theo bit her lip. "Kamele—"

Her mother raised a hand. "It's a shock, I know. Very sudden. Unfortunately, there's nothing to be done. I suggest that you sleep on it."

# NINETEEN

· · · · · · · · · · · · · · · · ·

*Number Twelve Leafydale Place*
*Greensward-by-Efraim*
*Delgado*

THE ARTICLE WAS FINISHED, POLISHED, AND ON ITS WAY
to the journal that had commissioned it; all of the mid-
term student papers had been perused, marked up, and
returned to their authors, who would hopefully learn
*something* from his comments. He had finished reading
his entire backlog of journals, and was now reclined in
his chair, one ear on the audio from the Orbital Traffic
Scanner, and both eyes closed.

"Truly," he murmured to Mandrin, who was napping in her usual spot on the desk, "it's nothing short
of amazing what one can accomplish when one is
unencumbered by child and mistress."

Mandrin vouchsafed no reply to this observation, if
indeed she heard him. Indolent creatures, cats.

Well.

"*Scallion,*" the OTS crackled around the permanently
irritated voice of the second shift master on Delgado

Station. "If your vee isn't adjusted by my next refresh, that's a megadex fine."

"Ain't nothing the matter with our vee, Station Master, 'cept a big, griefen cruise ship in the way."

"If you wanna pay the fine, *Scallion,* that's—"

"This is *Vashtara,* out of Ibenvue." The new voice was crisp, no-nonsense and bore a heavy accent that was neither Liaden nor Standard Terran. "I infer that it is we who have muddled the station master's calculations. It is suggested that the pilot of the ship *Scallion* bring the vessel to a slightly tangential course which retains the precious vee, perhaps on the propitious heading oh-two-seven, oh-four-seven, oh-eight-seven. This heading will avoid holing the *big, griefen cruise ship,* which will please me perhaps even more than it will please *Scallion.*"

There was a pause, while pilot and station master likely did their math, then the rather subdued voice of *Scallion*'s pilot. "That's good to do it. Station Master?"

The sigh was audible even through the static. "Adopt and amend course, *Scallion.*"

Jen Sar Kiladi shifted in his chair, lazily considering the exchange. The pilot of the *Vashtara* had been . . . marginally within her *melant'i.* That she had broadcast the amended course, rather than beaming a private suggestion to the station master hinted at deeper tensions between cruise ship and station. He frowned slightly. Ibenvue, was it? He had lately been reading some interesting news out of—

From downstairs . . . a sound.

The man in the chair opened his eyes and came silently to his feet. On the corner of the desk, Mandrin had raised her head, ears pricked, staring at the doorway.

The sound came again, stealthily. The sound of the garden door. Being closed.

Silent, he glided across the revolving star fields, plucking the Gallowglass cane from its place near the door as he passed through. He paused in the shadow at the top of the stairs, the stick held cross-body at waist level, fingers curved 'round the grip.

Quiet footsteps came from below, and the sound of soft, irregular breathing. He took a breath himself, deep and deliberate—and waited.

On Delgado, a handgun was unlikely. On Delgado, let it be known, sneaking into a house uninvited was all but unheard of. Which meant that he might in a moment face someone desperate to the point of foolhardiness.

Or a professional. He wondered, briefly, if he were any longer the equal of a professional.

The footsteps passed from carpet to wood—and did not strike the tuned board. He let the point of the stick go, free hand flashing out to the switch as Mandrin rushed past him, taking the stairs in one long leap. The hall light flared from dim to brilliant. At the bottom of the flight, a thin figure with pale, wind-knotted hair threw an unsteady hand up to shield her eyes.

"Ow," she said. And, then, as Mandrin hurled herself against canvas-clad knees. "Hey."

At the top of the stairs, he took a careful breath, and if he leaned a moment on the cane, it was not... only... to be certain that the blade was well-seated.

"Good evening, Theo," he said—*Calmly*, he cautioned himself; *the child's half-frantic already*. "To what do I owe the pleasure of this unexpected visit?"

She blinked up at him, dark eyes wide and cheeks

reddened with cold. "I have to talk to you," she said, her voice wobbling, though he thought it was adrenaline, rather than fright. "I—Necessity, Father."

He sighed quietly, and inclined his head.

"An appeal to necessity must of course be honored," he acknowledged gravely. "However, as survival is also an imperative, I must ask if your mother knows that you are here."

Theo blinked up at him. "No," her voice voice wavered. She cleared her throat and repeated, more strongly. "No, I came on my own decision."

"I see."

He descended the stairs, taking care to move slowly. When he reached the bottom of the flight, he touched her cheek gently, finding it chill, indeed.

"I will make tea, I think, while you go into the common room and call your mother. Please tell her that I will bring you home, discreetly, when you and I have finished our business, and that you are quite unharmed." He raised an eyebrow and made a show of scanning her hectic person. "You *are* quite unharmed, are you not, Theo?"

She gulped. "Yes, sir."

"Good." He nodded toward the common room. "Call your mother."

· · · ·❋· · · ·

"You're *where*?" Kamele sounded more shocked than angry. Theo wished she knew whether that was a good thing or not. "Why?"

*Okay,* she thought, tucking her left hand under her right arm. *Should've expected that.* She took a breath. "Necessity," she said firmly.

Silence. Theo bit her lip. Necessity was—Kamele *knew* that you didn't fib about necessity. Not to Father. But whether she would want to know more, right now, and how to answer her if she did—

"Very well," Kamele said. She was starting to sound mad, now, Theo noted unhappily. "I will expect a full explanation when you get home."

"Now you must tell me, Theo," Father said, handing her a cup of tea, "precisely how you arrived here. Not, I trust, the late bus again?"

She pulled her legs up under her and cuddled into the corner of the double chair. It was funny, now that she was starting to get warm, she was shivering.

"No-o," she said as Father settled back into his chair. "I . . . used a Skoot."

"Ah." He sipped tea, meditatively. Theo did the same, smiling at the notes of orange and elmoni—and smiled again when Mandrin jumped up and curled without preamble against her.

"I feel compelled to mention," Father murmured, stretching his legs out before him and crossing them at the ankles, "that the Skoots do call in."

"I know *that*," Theo said, though she hadn't until she'd asked the Serpent icon.

"Indeed," he said politely. "Therefore, you intended to be caught out?"

"No," she said, looking down to stroke Mandrin. She looked up and met his eyes. "I ran it on manual."

One eyebrow rose. "Forgive me, Theo. The fact that you've had training on the Skoots momentarily slipped my mind."

"Well, I haven't," she blurted. "And I did have a

couple seconds where I thought maybe I'd made a mistake. But then—it was easy."

There was a small pause while he sipped his tea. "Just so," he murmured. "Easy."

There was another small silence while they both addressed their cups, then Father spoke again.

"I apprehend that you have mastered the puzzle of turning off your mumu's ID emissions. But I do wonder about the Eyes."

She looked down, watching her hand slide along Mandrin's glossy fur. "I—I found a map of unwatched exits and streets," she said, which wasn't *exactly* a fib.

"Fascinating," Father murmured. "One wonders— forgive the prying ways of an elderly professor!—one does wonder, however, where you ... found ... this map."

It was never a good idea to try to slide a fib—even a half-fib—past Father. Theo sighed and looked up, reluctantly.

"I have a ... research program on my school book," she said slowly. "It found what I needed."

"Well! What a delightfully useful program, to be sure! You must show it to me when we return you to your mother's arms. But, where have my wits gone begging? Here I am wasting your time with pleasantries, when you have pled necessity! Please, unburden yourself."

Here it was. Theo nodded and sipped her tea, trying to settle her suddenly unsettled stomach, then sat holding the empty cup in her hand for the count of one, two, three ...

She looked up and met dark, inquisitive eyes.

"Kamele's research trip has been approved by Admin," she said, having told him about the application for this over an Oktavi dinner. He nodded.

"Right. They're leaving in two days, and—she wants me to go with her."

Her voice quavered a little, and she shrunk against the chair. Someday, she thought, she'd learn how to keep her voice reasonable and calm, no matter what she was feeling.

"This is certainly excellent news for your mother," Father said, "but I fail to see how it warrants a desperate midnight escape to my door." He raised an eyebrow, eyes stern. "Much less an appeal to necessity."

Theo's stomach was suddenly even more unsettled. Father usually understood so quickly—but, she reminded herself, he hadn't been living with them day-to-day. He'd probably forgotten all about the Review Board.

"I have to stay here—on Delgado," she said, forcing herself to speak slowly, like she was giving an oral report. "The Review Board called for an extension, and if we go to Melchiza, then we won't be here when they announce their findings."

Father nodded, and moved his hand slightly, signaling her to continue.

"If they decide that I'm a Danger to Society—" *Which*, she added silently, *they would*. Why should they be different than the rest of the world? "We won't be able to appeal the decision, if we're traveling. When we come home—if there's a DtS in my file, the Safeties won't have to ask for permission to give me any drug they think will keep me from hurting anybody else."

She took a deep breath.

"So, if I leave Delgado *now*, I'm putting myself—and Kamele—in a position of peril."

Father sat very still in his chair, gazing intently at the toes of his slippers. Theo gulped and put her hand flat on Mandrin's side, trying to take comfort from the vibration of the cat's purrs against her palm.

"I see," Father said, and looked up. "Plainly, you have thought this situation through, and plainly, given the facts you have marshaled, you have cause for concern." He paused, then inclined his head.

"Did your mother share with you the probable length of your voyage?"

"Two hundred days."

"As few as that? And yet—even if your worst-case scenario should come about, two hundred days is sufficient to produce a radical, positive change in your abilities. You are on record with the Safety Office as attempting to address the issues that concern it. There is no reason that you cannot—and every reason that you should—continue exercising and dance during your time off-planet. If you are seized by the Safety Office upon your return, you and your mother would be justified in calling for a secondary review to determine if, in fact, you have overcome the difficulties noted in your file."

Theo thought about that. "Do you think," she asked, her voice sounding almost as small as she felt, "that I *will* have overcome the difficulties noted in my file, Father?"

He smiled. "Are you still enjoying dance as much as you were when last we spoke of it?"

"Even more!"

"Then I believe that there is a better than good chance that you will be able to demonstrate great improvement to the Safety Office, should it come to that." He considered her gravely.

"Have we dealt adequately with your necessity?"

Theo thought about it, and finally nodded. "Yes, sir."

"Excellent." He stood and placed his cup on the side table before holding his hand down to her. "It is time I took you home. With only two days until departure you doubtless have an errand-packed day before you. It may be beneficial to have an hour or two of sleep to support you."

Theo sighed, and looked up at him. "Kamele says Coyster needs to come—to come home."

"I will be pleased to have him, of course," Father said gently.

Theo blinked sudden, silly tears away, shifted her legs and reached up to take Father's hand. His fingers were warm, the ring he always wore slick against her skin. She paused, and turned his hand over, looking down at the intricate twists of silver. It was an old ring—when she'd been a littlie, she'd thought it was at least as old as Father himself. It was so much a part of him that she had never thought to wonder at it, or even ask the question.

"Where did you get your ring?"

There was a small sound, almost as if Father had caught his breath.

Theo looked up, but he was smiling in that fond, gentle way he sometimes did, and squeezed her fingers.

"I had it from my grandmother," he said softly, and pulled her to her feet. "Come along, now, child. Let us not subject your mother to any more anxiety than necessity demands."

She followed him out of the room, marking how lightly he moved—like Bek, or Lida, or—

"Do you dance, Father?" she asked.

He laughed as he moved across the kitchen. "The social climate of Liad made dance a necessity, child. Come along, now." He opened the door onto the star-washed garden.

"The Skoot!" she cried suddenly, remembering.

"I will take care of the Skoot," he said repressively. "For tonight, however, we shall ride in the luxury of my car, and you—" he extended his hand to touch her cheek—"you will attempt to stay awake. Recall that I will want a demonstration of that useful program of yours when you get home."

· · · ·✳· · · ·

"I've . . . never seen anything like it," Kamele murmured, staring down at Theo's school book. After conducting a brief demo, the owner of the 'book had yawned herself off to bed, leaving bemused adults in her wake. The fact that she *was* merely bemused rather than horrified, Kamele thought, must be an indication that she was becoming hardened to the impossible.

"Yet you must own that it is quite amusing." Jen Sar murmured, and she laughed.

"Amusing is one word." She rubbed her eyes.

"Indeed, and a number of others do suggest themselves." His fingers hovered above the icon, but he did not touch it. "I would welcome a chance to study that 'research wire' in greater depth."

Kamele considered him. "Why?"

"It's an oddity," he said, and looked up, flashing her one of his less-real smiles. "And one must of course be interested in any new oddity."

"Of course," she said politely, and added, with a

surety born of long association with him, "but there's another reason."

Another dandle of long fingers just above the icon. "Well, if you will have it, I wonder how much of an ... accident the assignment of this particular apartment was."

"Housing never has *accidents*," Kamele told him— and blinked, recalling. "This was Flandin's apartment."

"So it was. And that wire is not standard." His glance this time was serious. "One must wonder—is the fact that it remains here beyond Professor Flandin's departure a sign of intent, or merely sloppiness?"

*At least,* Kamele thought, *one must wonder such an outrageous thing if one were Jen Sar.* She covered a yawn and looked down at the screen, frowning at the patient glowing Serpent. It did also bear recalling, she told herself, that Jen Sar's suspicions were very often correct.

"You're assuming that this ... program, and the non-standard wire are linked," she pointed out.

Jen Sar inclined his head. "Indeed. And I may be entirely in error." Another smile, this one rather more genuine. "You only feed my desire to inspect that wire, you know."

Kamele shook her head. "Well, if you must inspect it, you'll have to appeal to Ella. For lack of a better plan, I'm going to drop it in her lap."

"An excellent idea," Jen Sar said surprisingly. "Well, then." He stood, gathering his cane to him. "It is dreadfully late, my friend. Allow me to bid you good-day, safe journey, and prosperous scholarship."

Kamele felt her eyes sting. "Thank you, Jen Sar," she said softly.

She walked with him to the front hall. Coyster was curled atop the table, palpably asleep.

"Now, that's fortuitous," Jen Sar murmured. He bent and deftly swept the cat up, tucking him firmly beneath one arm. "I'll just have this young rascal off, before he arranges to pack himself again."

Kamele laughed once more. He looked up, black eyes glinting. On impulse, she bent, and kissed him on the cheek.

"Hah," he said softly, and his smile this time was tender.

"Take good care, my dear." Kamele murmured, and opened the door to let him go.

# TWENTY

. . . . . . . . . . . . . . .

### Vashtara
### *First Class Dining Room*

SENIOR SCOUT CHO SIG'RADIA STRODE TOWARD DINNER with her mind more than half occupied with the report she was composing. Gone ahead of her, likely by the somewhat improper use of the crew corridors, was her immediate second on this mission, Trainee yo'Vala. She shrugged Terran-style to herself as she moved along the public promenade toward the dining hall; soon enough the trainee would discover that courtesy of ship varied considerably. That crew on *this* ship respected a pilot's jacket—was good to know. That the trainee had the happy gift of making friends was—well for the trainee.

For this portion of the trip, Scout sig'Radia had herself eschewed pilot leathers, wishing some relief from what had been a tedious, if necessary, chore of inspecting and certifying a new flight school. Too, she traveled at the expense of Ibenvue's planetary government on this newest of its cruise-passenger ships, a touching show of faith that she felt, in Balance, ought to be rewarded by a similar exhibition of discretion. That this reciprocity of good manners also allowed her the opportunity to explore the ship as if a mere tourist was—a bonus.

The school now, the certification of which had been so very important to Ibenvue's self-declared pacifistic and newly outward-looking government. Quite an *interesting* school, with the capability of producing... quite a number... of pilots. She had certified it, of course—how could she not? The school employed two Terran master pilots as trainers, either capable of approving a pilot's skill—and signing the all-important license. It was said—many times said, by the escort she and yo'Vala had been provided with—that Ibenvue's school sought to train pilots who would train pilots, thus bringing the homeworld fully into galactic commerce, and for this laudable goal both Terran Guild and Scout approvals had been sought.

An interesting venture, to be sure, this expected export of pilot-teachers. Match it against the investment of a staggering portion of Ibenvue's Gross Planetary Product in the acquisition of large, easily convertible "luxury" ships—such as the gracious *Vashtara*—and an enhanced military—necessary of course for the protection of both pilots and of ships, and one had a situation which... bore scrutiny. Perhaps even close scrutiny, and by those who were not put boldly forth as a Scout Inspector Specialist. Which suggestion she had made, very strongly, in her report.

Well, she told herself, as she approached the junction with the hospitality module, best to put the report and thoughts of the report aside for the next while and instead partake of those diversions created by one's fellow passengers. This being, by reason of a lack of handwritten invitations from the captain, an informal meal, tables were formed from random groups of hopeful diners, and the luck of the draw often provided amusement, and not infrequently, useful information.

From the corridor opposite came a sudden din, closely followed by its authors, the same small handful of academics she had briefly encountered yesterday.

That meeting had produced something akin to amusement, for the loudest of the group had mistaken her for a tour-aide and demanded her assistance. Professora, perhaps an attending bedmate or two, and a female halfling trailing, quiet and large-eyed, behind, all expectantly waiting for her to solve the universe in one quick answer. Well, except for the halfling, whose attention had been claimed by a pair of buskers, autopipes at volume, and donation dish well over the docking line.

The solving requested of Cho had been simple enough—she had simply pointed to the nearby help terminal. The buskers, alas, had not fared so well. A crewman, directed by a flutter of the dock steward's fingers, bore down upon them, snarling what Cho had taken by tone to be an insult in the local dialect. Scooping up the bowl, he'd thrown it at the taller musician's head, after pocketing the few coins it had held.

The halfling had seen it all, so Cho thought, though by then she had been on her way up the ramp, surrounded by the noisy confusion of her elders.

The professorial group burst into the corridor ahead

of her, their talk filling the space with echoes. Cho took a deep breath in protest of the hubbub, and stood to one side, observing.

The first into the intersection was the halfling, skipping lightly through the change of the gravity field at the lock boundary as if she were born to such things. Behind her, one of the elders tripped, and bounced sharply against the wall. The halfling turned, one hand extended—

"Theo, please don't . . ." a woman's fine voice said, perfectly audible beneath the elder's loud exclamations. The halfling—Theo—spun deftly on one toe, removing herself from danger as the elder staggered, colliding with the other side of the passage. She barely kept her feet, her lamentations increasing in volume and degree, her uninformed actions elevating her rapidly toward a risk to passengers and to ship.

This, Cho thought, would not do.

Moving away from her watching place, she brought up her brightest meet-the-Terrans smile, and called out with calm good cheer, "Yes, these grav-interfaces can be quite shocking, can they not? That is why these yellow-and-green stripes line the walls—to warn of the coming field differential."

Now she was among them, pleased to see that they slowed in response to her tone and her posture of relaxed goodwill. With luck, the rest would avoid a repeat of the loud woman's misadventure.

Alas, that woman, rather than sensibly awaiting rescue, had wallowed into a turn and now blundered back across the divide, smacking the wall for a third time. She would, Cho thought dispassionately, have bruises on the morrow, which would have been well enough, had there been any remotest possibility that she would have also learned something.

"My stomach..." the clumsy woman moaned, clinging to the smooth wall and closing her eyes tight. "Why must we cross this chasm for every meal?"

A younger and considerably fitter woman moved toward the now-stable sufferer, her posture somewhat stiff, but well-enough for a grounder approaching a change of gravity.

"Chair, we needn't come to the dining room, after all," she said, her voice coolly matter-of-fact. "Our meals can be brought to us, if we like..."

"Chair" seemed to consider this point; at least her vocal agitation subsided. The cool-voiced woman turned slightly and directed a half-bow to Cho.

"Ma'am, you appear to travel comfortably. Do you take all of your meals on-board in public, I wonder?"

Cho gave the bow back, pleased to meet good intent with courtesy.

"I tend to do so, traveler, unless duty keeps me at my desk. Much of my joy in travel comes from the people." This was perfectly true, and something she often said. If certain travelers therefore assumed that they were the cause of joy—what harm done?

"Then you *are* an experienced traveler?" The woman's voice was trained—perhaps, Cho thought, she was a singer, or a teller of tales. She appeared not only sharp and alert, but also seemed to be one who had perhaps dealt closely with Liadens. The careful inflection, and the deliberate structure of a yes-no query was very nearly a challenge.

Cho laughed out loud, in fellowship more than amusement, and inclined her head.

"Travel is my life, I warrant! I do not willingly stay long on any world. It is not, you understand, that I dislike worlds, but that I prefer space."

Her interlocutor smiled, perhaps in shared fellowship, and several others of the group laughed softly, as people will who have recognized humor without entirely catching the joke. Beneath these sounds, Cho detected another, and glanced aside to discover the ignored halfling—winsome Theo—amusing herself with the gravity nexus. She leaned playfully forward, allowing the field to keep her upright, pale hair flowing—

"Theo, surely that's not safe!" Chair snapped. From Theo's blink and the stiffening of the woman with the storyteller's voice, Cho surmised that this input was both out-of-bounds and unwelcome.

"But I'm not having a problem, Professor Hafley," Theo said, holding her arms out at her sides, as if she were a bird gliding down a placid breeze. "It's like leaning into a wind!"

The thin young face was almost impish with the joy of her play and it took Cho's best effort not to laugh.

"Certainly leaning into the wind isn't safe!" Chair— but no, Cho corrected her thought—*Professor Hafley*— snapped. "You'll fall flat on your face when it changes direction!"

"Chair," the woman who knew Liadens murmured; "I think Theo has demonstrated that she's not in danger—"

"Even if she isn't, she's making me queasy! In my day, junior scholars stood up straight, kept still and displayed a proper respect for their elders in learning!"

"Orkan," the prettiest of the group's two males spoke up suddenly, his voice plaintive. "It's time for our seating, and I, for one, am hungry."

Cho's stomach quite agreed with the need for food; and the pretty one's complaint seemed to carry weight with Professor Hafley, who turned with heavy-footed care to face her nemesis once more. Moving quickly, Cho dodged past, waving Theo to her side with a wink.

"Youngling, if you'll favor me, we may walk ahead and claim a table for the group."

Theo glanced over her shoulder, but apparently whoever held her in care gave permission, for she came along willingly; and if she skipped a little in the lighter gravity of the access hall, who, thought Cho, could blame her?

· · · ·⚙· · · ·

They'd claimed the last full table—or rather, the woman with the short gray hair had, calmly telling the steward that, "the rest of our party comes at leisure, while we two madcaps raced before."

The tables in the dining hall were round, which Professor Crowley said neatly solved many potential problems of precedence and protocol. That it didn't solve *all* problems of precedence Theo had learned only at breakfast, when she had mistakenly taken the chair at Kamele's right. That chair also being to the left of Clyburn's *onagrata,* it was, so he had informed her—and the rest of the dining hall—*his*. Mere children were to stand respectfully aside until the adults were seated, and then quietly take the chair that had been left for them.

"Favor me, child," the gray-haired woman murmured; "and sit at my right. I am desolated to perceive a lack of mine apprentice, derelict in his duty to keep me upon my mettle."

The tone was suspiciously close to Father's over-serious voice. Theo looked into the woman's polite face, catching the faintest twinkle in the brown eyes.

"I'll gladly do that, ma'am," she said carefully. "But what if your apprentice comes—later?"

"Why then, he shall sit at *your* right to observe such technique as you will display, and to bask in my displeasure at a survivable distance."

Theo laughed as she took the chair the woman indicated. "We didn't do introductions," she said. "I'm Theo Waitley."

"I greet you, Theo Waitley," her seat-mate replied, with a heavy nod—almost a seated bow, Theo thought. "My name is . . . Cho sig'Radia."

Theo copied the nod. "I greet you, Cho sig'Radia," she said.

Her companion smiled—a smile quite different from the smile she had worn at the intersection lobby. As if, Theo thought, the other smile had been . . . deliberate, somehow . . .

The sudden babble of familiar voices disrupted these musings. Theo turned to see the rest of their group at the steward's station.

"The remainder of our party joins us! How delightful, to be sure!" Cho sig'Radia exclaimed cheerily.

Theo glanced at her, and saw the *other* smile in place, too bright and too obvious, and then the others arrived, conducted by the steward. He held the chair for Professor Hafley and saw her safely seated with her napkin on her lap before leaving them in search of their waiter.

"Theo Waitley and I have introduced ourselves, as we had overlooked this nicety in the press of other matters. I immediately seek to amend this affront to civilized behavior by making the group aware that I am Cho sig'Radia."

There was a pause, so long that Theo began to worry that Professor Hafley was still upset enough to be rude. Across the table, Kamele frowned, which probably meant she was worried, too.

Finally, Professor Hafley produced a stiff smile, with no trace of liking or pleasure in it. "Cho sig'Radia, I am History of Education Chair Orkan Hafley," she said formally.

"Professor Hafley," Cho murmured, inclining her head.

Theo relaxed as Kamele introduced herself, "History of Education Sub-chair Kamele Waitley," she murmured, and raised her eyebrows in Theo's direction. "Mother of Theo Waitley."

"Ah, is it so? Allow me to compliment you upon your most charming offspring."

Kamele laughed softly. "You are too kind," she answered, and the introductions moved on.

"Emeritus Professor Crowley; Emeritus Professor Able; Clyburn Tang..." Theo let the introductions slide past her ear, watching Cho sig'Radia as she acknowledged each. The smile, she thought, like the earnestly polite expression Father showed to strangers, was a kind of mask. Like it was...amped up, unmissable, the emotional equivalent of speaking slowly and distinctly.

"Behold, the lost is found!" Cho exclaimed and rose from her chair, hand sweeping out to show them the boy with the rumpled hair and the leather jacket who approached their table.

"To the Delgado scholars I am pleased to present Trainee Win Ton yo'Vala, who has taken the not-so-short route to dinner."

The trainee bowed to the table, while the fingers of his left hand danced a pattern in the direction of Cho sig'Radia.

"Delgado scholars, I greet you," he said, his accent tickling the inside of Theo's ear. "Captain, I am at your feet. You were, as always, correct."

"Flatterer!" Cho reseated herself and waved him toward the seat next to Theo. "Comport yourself with courtesy, I pray you. When we are at leisure, I will entertain reasons why you should not be spaced."

"Ma'am." He bowed again, fingers quiet now, and moved smoothly 'round the table to Theo's side. Cho turned her attention once more to the scholars, and he leaned close to whisper, "Have pity on me, I beg you."

Theo turned her head, looking directly into a pair of merry brown eyes. She smiled at him without meaning to.

"What do you want?"

"Only to live out my allotted span," he said, smiling back. "Depend upon it, she will grill me on the names and occupations of everyone sitting to dinner, and if I do not have them . . ." He sighed, not convincingly. "Why, then, it's the airlock for me." He bent his head, and sent her a glance from beneath reddish eyelashes. "Without a suit."

Theo bit her lip so she wouldn't laugh, and shook her head. "Cho sig'Radia said I was to keep her on her mettle, since you weren't here."

"Look at her," he returned. "Have you ever beheld

a woman more mettlesome? Were she any sharper, she would be a danger to herself."

Theo's rescue this time came in the shape of their waiter, who approached bearing a tray full of beakers.

"What's that?" she wondered.

Beside her Win Ton yo'Vala laughed softly. "Oho. Perhaps we might trade, Sweet Mystery."

She looked at him. "Trade?"

"Of a certainty. We each hold knowledge which the other lacks. Commerce may therefore go forth." He paused as beakers arrived before them.

"Here," he said; "I will show my earnest. This..." He touched the pale green glass with a light finger. "This, Sweet Mystery, is chilled vegetable broth. It is meant to prepare the palate for the delights to come. One sips it directly from the container."

A quick glance showed Cho and Kamele and Professor Crowley lifting their beakers as described, hesitantly copied by others of their party.

Theo glanced back to Win Ton. "My name isn't 'Sweet Mystery,'" she told him, picking her beaker up carefully. "It's Theo. Theo Waitley."

Win Ton's smile widened and he leaned closer to touch his glass to hers. "So," he said conspiratorially, "the trading begins."

By the time the plates bearing what Win Ton assured her was the "main course" arrived, he was in the possession of the names and positions of each of the Delgado party, and Theo had learned how to "address" three different "befores"—one cold, one tepid, one hot—and the uses of the various utensils provided at her place.

This was much better than breakfast, she thought, as she tried to imitate Win Ton's use of the tongs. At breakfast, the scholars had discussed their project, leaving her Clyburn for company. Since he considered himself above talking to children, except to issue directions, that meant she'd spent the meal trying to figure out a conversation she clearly wasn't meant to understand, and wishing she was back home.

As near as she could figure it in her head, it would be about time for Advertency. She'd wondered how Lesset had done with the last solo—which turned out to be a bad idea, because that made her eyes sting, and she *wasn't* going to cry in front of the whole Research Team; and *especially* not in front of Clyburn. Happily, the waiter had come to tell them that their table was needed for the second meal-shift before Theo scandalized everybody by pulling out her mumu and calling up a game.

She tasted a bit of what Win Ton said was poached Siclarian Walking Mushrooms, catching her breath at the unexpected burst of hot spiciness, and reached for her water glass.

With two strangers at the table, the scholars had to be polite, and to converse on topics comprehensible to everybody. Surprisingly, it was Emeritus Professor Crowley who carried the bulk of the conversation with Cho sig'Radia, admitting to her supposition that their destination was Melchiza.

Questioned regarding their purpose, he had tipped his head, ironically, Theo thought, and murmured, "We are to perform a literature search, ma'am. Quite tedious and scholarly. And yourself? Can we hope to have the pleasure of your company all the way to Melchiza?"

"Your hopes are fulfilled," she assured him with one of her real smiles. "We have business on the station there, my disgraceful apprentice and I."

"What business?" Theo asked Win Ton, as Clyburn— too long ignored—began a rambling commentary on the clothes worn by passengers at other tables.

"We are assigned to retrieve a ship," he said, matter-of-factly, and sent her a sharp glance.

"You sigh, sweet Theo! Is it possible to hope that you will miss me?"

"How could I miss you when I've hardly met you?" she asked prosaically. "But—'assigned to retrieve a ship' sounds so much more interesting than 'stuck at boarding school, studying'!"

"One may acquire a fondness rapidly, don't you find? As for study, there will be a wealth of that on my side, as well, I assure you! No one who travels with my captain is safe." He smiled. "Perhaps I will lose credit with you, but I confess that not a few of the lessons available to passengers of this ship tempt me. History, drama, the science of star travel, lectures on the arts and culture of the ports we approach . . ."

She blinked at him. "You make it sound like fun!"

He laughed. "And so it is fun! Shall I prove my point?"

"How?" she asked doubtfully.

"Meet me tomorrow at fifth gong in the morning lounge. They call it 'Breakfast All Year' because someone is always on a schedule where breakfast is the meal they need. From there we two shall visit the daily lecture at the Pet Library. Tomorrow is to be 'Introduction to Norbears,' if I recall correctly."

"What's a norbear?" she asked, and his smile became mischievous.

"Behold," he murmured, "an opportunity to learn. "Have we a bargain, then?"

"My tutoring should be over by fifth gong . . ." she said slowly, doing the time conversion in her head. Professor Able said they'd get used to ship's time quickly, but for now, her body still thought it was on Delgado.

"Send me a message via ship's web if circumstances overtake you. I am Passenger Nine-nine seven, six four-four. Otherwise, we shall test my proposition, eh?"

"All right . . ." Theo said, and then smiled. "Passenger ninety-nine, seventy-six, forty-four. I hope I can make it."

"I hope you can make it, too."

"In fact, no," Cho sig'Radia was saying to Clyburn, "the truth is that the attire you so admire three tables over is not worn by the least of those seated, but the first. I have been away from fashion this while, and so may be in error. However, he appears to be wearing the very latest from Rombert's, and would be welcome in any of the finest halls on Liad dressed thus. Alas, here he is—a bit too grand. Perhaps he thought to sit with the captain."

Clyburn didn't like to be corrected. He drew a breath to answer—and was quelled by a look from Chair Hafley, which warmed Theo toward her slightly, and mumbled his way into silence.

"It *is* difficult when traveling," Win Ton said into the small quiet that followed this, "to correctly read clothing and position." He paused and looked about, saw that he had the attention of the table and continued.

"The—you will forgive me, that I have no proper word in your tongue—the *melant'i* of those around one can only sometimes be determined by dress, or lack of it, when one travels. I have had cause..." He looked toward Cho, his cheeks darkening slightly. "On this very trip, I myself had cause to be surprised at a meal. A man dressed all in white, with the smell of spice and oil about him, and perhaps, too, a dash of sauce upon a sleeve, came to our table...I thought him a...servant, perhaps a worker in the kitchens. Rather he...wore the ring!"

Here he paused, fingers rippling, as if he were handing something past Theo to the woman on her other side—

"Rather," Cho sig'Radia said, taking up the tale, "he was Zed ter'Janpok, Clan Tangier. Tangier Himself, you will apprehend, whom one values as an old friend, come to visit." She paused to sip from her glass. "Mind you, the impulsive young apprentice had not entirely mis-observed, for my good friend is a chef of the first water, and so, indeed, a *kitchen worker*." She cocked an ironic eyebrow downtable. Professor Crowley and Kamele laughed in appreciation, echoed by the others.

"And now, unless I mis-observe myself—yes! It is our servers, with dessert!"

"Do candied dromisain leaves with sour sauce not please you, Sweet Mystery? You might call for a sorbet, instead, you know."

Theo blinked, her face heating. She'd dozed off, like a kid kept up past her bedtime.

"Stop calling me that!" she whispered fiercely. "It's stupid."

There was a small pause. A glance at Win Ton's face showed him suddenly serious, his lips pressed tight.

"I'm sorry." Impulsively, she reached out and put her fingers on his leather sleeve. "I'm—I'm not on ship time yet, and I'm falling asleep. And I miss my cat, and Fa— Professor Kiladi. But none of that's your fault, and I shouldn't have yelled at you."

"Ah." His mouth softened and he inclined his head. "It is forgotten. And it is my fault, I think, a little. You had told me your name." He frowned down at his plate and put the spoon carefully aside.

"In truth, the sauce is somewhat too sour for my taste," he said, and tipped his head, his eyes bright again. "Tell me about your cat."

There was a note of...wistfulness in his voice.

"Do you have a cat, too?" Theo asked.

Win Ton moved his hand in a sharp gesture, like he was tossing something away. "I, a cat? Never think it. My delm dislikes the creatures and refuses to have them in clan house or garden. So you must tell me: What is it like to have your own cat?"

"Well," she said slowly. "Sometimes, it's a lot of trouble..."

· · · · ❖ · · · ·

The conversation grew more interesting with dessert, which Cho welcomed—and welcomed again, as the beautiful Clyburn was effectively silenced by the ebb and flow of discussion. Truly, a vapid individual. On the other hand, his lady seemed pleased with his secret charms, and that of course must be what counted.

The senior traveler Crowley was sharp and quiet at once, and the Sub-chair Kamele Waitley—ostensibly second to her Chair!—was both sharper and quieter.

Interesting *melant'i* play it was to see the discussion moved about at apparent random, where the Chair was sometimes at a loss, while the Emeriti appeared very much interested in the opinions and the process of the Sub-chair's thoughts. That this was not lost upon Chair Hafley was also apparent, and promised more adjustment of *melant'i* in future. It was to be hoped that the elder scholar would be wise, though Cho thought that she would be...otherwise.

Too, perhaps young Theo's presence could not be dismissed simply as a doting mother's whim. There was little of the doting parent in Kamele Waitley. And how convenient, to have another of one's house as extra ears, in what was surely a situation fraught with tension.

The halflings had kept good company, to the benefit of both. Their present topic...Cho spared them an ear, and hid her sigh inside a sip of wine. Cats! The gods send that there would be no opportunity for the boy to adopt a cat before she handed him off to other trainers.

"But it's the old 'unlimited energy' canard, brought to a new face!"

That was Crowley, taking fire from what was apparently a favorite topic. "We in education know—I can prepare cites if you like!"

But there, the youngest of them was nodding off in the midst of a recitation of the wonders of her personal cat, her dessert uneaten, spoon drooping in her hand.

Cho glanced aside, meaning to draw the mother's eye, but the sharp and formidable Kamele had seen, and was already in motion, pushing back from the table with a smile all around.

"Scholars, apprise me in the the morning if you solve this. I'm afraid Theo and I are not yet in sync with the ship's clock. Perhaps tomorrow evening we'll be more in tune."

"I wonder if I may suggest," Cho murmured for Kamele's ear alone as Win Ton helped Theo to her feet and deftly rearranged the chairs to clear her path, "that your daughter join some of the lectures and events offered to passengers. I know she will have lessons—as does my scamp of an apprentice—but with a table full of educators to draw upon it ought not be difficult to assign value to something far more—interactive—than rote read-and-repeat..."

Kamele gave her a sharp glance, and Cho produced a small bow for a mother's consideration.

"It must be admitted," she said, more quietly still, "that Win Ton has asked Theo to accompany him to a lecture at the Pet Library. If you are able to allow it, I would own myself in your debt, for the boy needs to practice his Terran against a native speaker."

"Ah." Kamele smiled as she put her hand on her daughter's shoulder and turned her toward the entry. "I think I can allow that."

The two departed. Win Ton reseated himself, and Cho returned her attention to the remaining scholars, who had taken up a debate of the educational opportunities available on-board. Cho smiled and leaned back in her chair, pleased that the politics of unlimited energy had been, for the moment, put away.

# TWENTY-ONE

. . . . . . . . . . . . . . . . . . . . . . .

Vashtara
*EdRec Level*
*Pet Library*

THEO JUMPED OUT OF THE ELEVATOR AT THE EDREC
Level following the blue lines marked "Education" to
the right, while most of her fellow passengers went
left, pacing the glittery orange sparkles to "Recreation."

She'd looked Breakfast All Year and the Pet Library
up on the shipmap, then scanned the info-page for
the library.

Sadly, there were no cats listed in the Pet Census,
though the entry did say that the kind and number of
creatures on inventory was subject to change. She'd
been about to look up norbears when the Tutor in
her traveling school book noticed that she'd finished
the math solo it had set her to, *and* the self-test,
and called her attention to the next lesson in series.
That one had been a little harder, and the Tutor had
insisted that she finish the self-test for it, too.

"I'll be late for an appointment," she told it, half of her mind on the self-test.

*Skillset remediation: Time Management,* the Tutor noted.

"I manage my time just fine!" Theo said hotly, her fingers continuing to work out the problem while she spared a glare at the dialog box. She'd heard that the AIs in the traveling 'books were old, but nobody had mentioned cranky. Just her luck to draw one with a disciplinarian streak.

*Had you moved on immediately to the next lesson, you would have completed your work early,* the Tutor answered. *Instead, you chose to do unauthorized research, and wait for a prompt.*

A prompt that the Tutor, Theo suspected darkly, had put off providing until it knew she'd have to rush to finish. She stuck her tongue out at the dialogue box, and filed the answer to the last problem with a tap that was harder than it needed to be.

There was a long moment when nothing happened at all, then the Tutor's dialog box flashed green.

*Self-test satisfactory,* it allowed—grudgingly, Theo thought. *The student may undertake mother-approved social project. Next lesson is chemical theory, at eighth gong.*

Theo tapped the "recess" button as she came out of her seat. The door had closed behind her by the time the screen blanked.

Even with the Tutor's nidjit delay, Theo thought she'd have plenty of time to get to Breakfast All Day. Unfortunately, she had reckoned without the sheer size of the ship.

While it was very true that the belt to the 'vator

bank serving the EdRec Level was directly across the
Retail Concourse, that area was far larger than the
shipmap had led her to expect. Nor had she counted
on the other impediments in her path.

The belts—the few that were in service—moved
slow, and none of the other passengers seemed to be
in a hurry. They ambled from one side of the main
promenade to the other, peering into shop windows,
playing with the auto-vend units, stopping dead in
the center of the walkway to talk to each other...

She'd never seen so many adults with nothing to
do—and so inadvertent in doing it!

At long last, the 'vator bank came into view. She
slid in between leisurely closing doors, last one in, and
very shortly first one out, remembering to walk-not-
run, though surely it was all right to walk fast when
you were going to be late for an appointment....

Walking fast, Theo outstripped the eight passengers who had turned to follow the Ed lines with her.
Directly ahead an ID shimmered above a store front,
resolving, as she came closer, to a graphic of a large
yellow cup with steam rising from it. The cup faded,
replaced by the words, "Breakfast All Year."

A subdued and genteel gong sounded down the
corridor, counting five.

"Chaos!" Theo did run the last few steps across the
hall, dodging the cluster of chatting adults blocking
the entrance—and froze just inside, stomach sinking.
*I'll never find him in this!* she thought dismally.

Hundreds of glossy dark tables and chairs stretched
away and up three curved, bright yellow walls. It
might, Theo thought, have been meant to create the
illusion of being inside of a coffee cup.

Inside of a full-to-overflowing coffee cup.

She strained high on her toes, scanning the room without much hope. The restaurant was so crowded that one boy with reddish brown hair and a black jacket wasn't going to stand out—

"There you are—and prompt, as well!" His voice was so close that she jumped. She took a breath and settled slowly flat-footed before turning her head to look at him.

"Late, you mean," she said.

"Arrived directly on the fifth gong," he retorted. "I insist that this is on time—and well done, indeed, if you navigated the public halls. You might think yourself at Festival, with so many dawdlers and pleasure-seekers blocking the ways!"

"But you—come by the . . . private halls," Theo said, remembering his arrival last night—and Cho sig'Radia's apparent displeasure with his chosen route.

He laughed softly. "Never think it! Today, my captain has decreed that I am to go as a passenger-guest upon this vessel and thus sample humility."

She eyed him. The jacket he'd worn last night was gone, though he was dressed neatly enough in a brown vest over a shirt like pale sunshine, and dark trousers.

"You were kind of late for dinner," she commented.

"Kind of, I was," he agreed, then brought the tips of his fingers sharply against his temple.

"Bah! In addition to my lack of humility, I have no manners, and even less address! First, I must beg your forgiveness. This place is never so full, being in an unpopular hall of an unpopular level. The manager must have noticed this, as well, for what should there be this morning on the public band but a discussion of this little-known treasure of our ship—" He flicked his fingers at the crowded interior. "With this result."

"You couldn't have known," Theo said. "I am glad you saw me, though..."

He smiled. "But how could I overlook you, Theo Waitley?"

"A lot of people do," she told him seriously.

"It becomes apparent, then, that a lot of people," Win Ton announced, turning toward the entrance, "are a fool. I suggest that we continue our conversation as we walk, if we are to arrive at the lecture on time."

"Oh!" She turned with him. The noisy group blocking the doorway had grown—waiting for tables, Theo thought. Win Ton threaded his way effortlessly through the blockade. Following, Theo wondered if he would teach her how to do that.

"Are the private halls less crowded?" she asked, once they were able to walk side-by-side.

Win Ton glanced at her, looking down, she realized, but not such a long way down. She was used to being the shortest one in every group, but it was pleasant not to be so *much* shorter than her companion.

"For some," he said slowly, "there are private halls—and only at some times. Most usually, they are less crowded and more direct, being less concerned with—" He swept his arm out in a grand gesture that seemed to include *Vashtara's* entire interior—"the art of space." He grinned at her. "Or the enticement of tourists."

Whatever, Theo thought, the "art of space" was. Still, she liked to hear him talk; he had a nice voice, and his accent was...interesting. Rounded and...flowy, like he'd buffed all the sharp edges off his words.

"Did your jacket let you get into the back hallways?" she asked, which gained her another glance from beneath long, reddish lashes.

"In some measure," Win Ton said slowly, "the jacket allowed me into the private ways. Be aware, though, my friend, that the jacket is both a burden and a joy, as my piloting instructor was somewhat over-fond of telling us."

Theo blinked. "What—" she began, but Win Ton was angling toward a wall mounted with a dozen or more screens, each showing a different animal.

"The Pet Library!" he exclaimed. "*Now* we shall see wonders, Theo Waitley!"

. . . . ⚙ . . . .

In light of her long service to the Liaden Scouts, as well as her position in a clan that had given many to a similar service, it would not be wrong to suppose that Cho sig'Radia had a lamentable tendency to . . . meddle in matters that did not, perhaps, fall directly within her duty.

Indeed it could with some accuracy be said that the Liaden Scouts as an entity stood as the galaxy's premier meddler—witness her most recent assignment.

Despite which, one did not wish to unnecessarily disturb the peace of chance-met strangers, nor meddle too nearly—or at all!—in a collegial situation fraught with nuance one could not hope to master within the space of one brief seating.

And, yet . . .

Unless matters Melchizan had altered considerably since her last briefing session, there was perhaps more peril attending the scholarly group's so-dry and tedious search of literature than might be realized.

One would dislike, Cho thought, rising from her desk and running her fingers through her short hair, to find that the lack of a word in the right ear had placed innocents in the way of danger.

One would dislike that, extremely.

· · · · ❖ · · · ·

"Many base creatures adopt a social order," the lecturer said, in his abrupt, disapproving way. Theo couldn't figure out if he disapproved of his audience in general, of the cranky littlie who had several times announced that he wanted to "see bears *now!*" in particular, or if it was the subject of his lecture that he found annoying. Disapproving or not, though, he did have a number of interesting facts about norbears to impart, for which Theo was willing to forgive his uncordial lecturing style.

"Norbears are highly socialized creatures. Typically, a family group will rally around a chieftain, and claim a certain territory as their own. When the family group grows too large for the chosen territory to comfortably support, a secondary chieftain will arise, and lead a portion of the group to another territory, where they will settle and live, until force of numbers triggers the rise of a tertiary chieftain who in his turn leads a sub-group to a new territory."

The lecturer paused. In this small silence, the fidgety littlie sighed, and asked his mother in a loud whisper to make that man be quiet.

"Norbears have few natural enemies," the lecturer resumed, carefully. "However, their natural habitat is unregulated and quite wild. Fluctuations in the avail-ability of food are common, and, as base creatures will do, the norbears have produced a biologic coping mechanism. When food is scarce, fewer cubs are birthed. Strangely, it has been noted that domesticated groups, such as we have here on *Vashtara*, adapt themselves to their artificial but far safer conditions by also birthing fewer cubs."

He looked out over the audience.

"In just a moment, those of you who wish the opportunity may follow our pet librarian, Mr. Rogen, to the norbears' enclosure. Before you go, however, I would like to speak a little about expectations.

"As I have said, norbears are natural empaths. However, they are also base creatures. If you expect intelligence, or cognition, you will be disappointed."

Another pause, and then a glance to the back of the room.

"Mr. Rogen. If you would take over, please?"

· · · ❊ · · ·

The cafe on the atrium deck was, in Cho sig'Radia's experience, underused. It had perhaps been the intention of the designers that it be a quiet place for contemplative study, or for sweet privacy of other sorts. Certainly, the tables tucked well into the embrace of fragrant foliage, and the numbers of flowering vines artfully scaling the walls spoke of a certain thoughtfulness in the matter.

That the designers had designed poorly—well, no. The place was very pleasant, for those who valued solitude. Woe to the designers that not many, at least, of this passenger complement, desired solitude.

Cho herself was more often to be found on the Promenade Level when she was at leisure, sitting at a small table with a glass of wine to hand, and a keen eye on those who passed her by in their pursuit of pleasure. It was a pure marvel, how much people told of themselves by the simple acts of walking and talking. Her work, however, she engaged in the privacy of her cabin, venturing out when she had need of stimulation, or to beguile herself with observations and guesses while serious business sorted itself out in her backbrain.

Her quarters were quiet, despite the proximity of the young apprentice, who for all his youth addressed his studies with a serious intensity that might alarm a fond senior, if she had not also detected a similar intensity in his...less weighty...activities.

There were some, however, whose quarters were perhaps not so convivial as her own, and whose work might best be pursued away from the possibility of busy eyes.

It was just such a one that Cho sought now, moving casually down the wending pathways. Conscious of her mission, she made a special effort to brush up against leaves and to tread firmly upon the rare fallen stick. There was no need to startle as well as surprise.

Aha! She had not guessed wrongly! There, boldly framed in scarlet blossoms, her screen open before her, pot and cup to hand, sat Kamele Waitley. Yet, having run her quarry to ground, Cho hesitated, not wishing to add herself to the list of prying eyes, inconvenient questions, and interruption of duty.

A moment's study of the scholar at work failed to entirely reassure her. The screen was extended, yet it seemed that Kamele Waitley gazed beyond it, her face soft, her eyes unfocused. She made, Cho owned, a charming picture thus, with fawn brown hair wisping out of the knot in which she sought to confine it, and curling bewitchingly along her pale cheek. Indeed, she looked not so much like a scholar at study, or an administrator at her regulations, as she seemed a woman considering some pleasurable, but regrettably distant, item. Perhaps she thought of a favored companion; or of a particular garden-nook, of which the surrounding artful greenery was but a thin charade.

Cho dropped back a step, bestirring neither leaf nor branch, unwilling to disturb such contemplative delights. The woman at the table blinked, her eyes sharpening as she turned her head.

Discovered! How embarrassing, to be sure.

Cho stepped forward immediately, swept the bow between equals, and straightened, remembering to smile.

"Good shift, Sub-chair Waitley," she said. "Pray forgive the interruption. I do not," she added, with perfect truth, "often find an acquaintance here."

· · · ·❄· · · ·

"Remember what Mr. Chorli told you, now," the pet librarian cautioned. "Norbears are natural empaths. Each one can hear a slightly different—let's call it 'music.' What you'll want to do is let them make the approach, don't rush them or show any fear. These are domestic animals; they won't hurt you." There was a slight pause while Mr. Rogen—an extremely fit man with yellow tipped black hair who Theo thought looked more like a Leisure and Recreation instructor than a librarian—gazed at the six people who had decided to brave a visit to the norbears.

The area—room was far too quaint a word for the airy and multicolored space they stood in—flowed into distinct ecological sections differentiated by lighting, color, and floor covering, as well as by the vegetation visible in the interiors of those sections.

"Twelve!" Win Ton said, approvingly.

Theo looked around her—Oh! There were twelve eco-sections. He had quick eyes!

Between the sections and the public were portals of varying transparencies and shades. Their group stood in front of one with nearly clear door. Through it, the interior's inviting greens and blues appeared ragged.

"It could be that one or even two of you won't be approached," Mr. Rogen continued. "That only means that an animal able to hear your particular music isn't present in the group.

"So, with all that said . . ." he slid opened the gate to the eco-section, and waved them through.

Theo quickly slipped 'round the edge of the enclosure and went down on one knee with her back against a thicket of skinny boughs. The floor didn't merely look ragged, it *was* ragged—and unexpectedly soft and springy. A closer inspection showed that it was made of vines and lichens, all woven together to form a comfortable, crinkly habitat.

The norbears—nine plump, rough-furred mammals—were on the far side of the enclosure, some half-buried in the floor-stuff, some lolling about on top, all seeming oblivious to the presence of humans in their space, going about what the lecture had told them was typical norbear business—eating, wrestling, grooming, and sleeping.

Except, Theo thought, watching them with a critical

eye, there wasn't much sleeping going on. Oh, there were roly-poly recumbent bodies nestled into the vines, eyes closed while rounded ears twitched and pivoted, tracking soft footsteps—or maybe listening to the new songs, measuring each against some secret norbear standard.

Which was remarkably catlike behavior for creatures that looked so very different from cats...

Suddenly, there was a flurry, a rustle of vegetation, and one of the norbears was on the move, rocking from side to side as she made her way across the enclosure, straight for the little boy with red hair who'd been so cranky during the lecture.

*But, that's not catlike at all,* Theo thought. There was no mystery about the approach, no measuring glance over one shoulder, no sitting down to groom—no *suspense*. Instead, the norbear bumbled merrily onward until she had run her round head practically into the boy's knee. The littlie gave a shout of laughter, and promptly sat down in the blue-green expanse, gathering his new friend into his arms.

As if that had been a signal, the rest of the norbears were suddenly moving, fairly charging the gathered humans. Theo was bumped by a white norbear with a brown spot on her spine. She reached down to pet her, and discovered that the rough-looking pelt wasn't rough at all, but plush against her skin, while—

"She's purring!" she exclaimed, glancing over to Win Ton, comfortably cross-legged on the woven floor, a black norbear snuggled against his hip.

He placed his hand gently against the charcoal fur and smiled.

"Is this catlike, then?" he asked, softly, as his friend

suddenly sat up on her hind legs and grabbed his sleeve with a tiny hand.

"Not quite," Theo said. "The resonance is—it's like I'm hearing half the sound inside my head!"

"Ah. Perhaps that is the so-called 'natural empathy' at work?"

"You mean, since they can't hear on—on every frequency..."

"Precisely! It may be reciprocal. In fact, it *must* be reciprocal. Is it not the same with the *cha'dramliz*—ah, your pardon! I mean to say—" He blinked and sent her a wry glance. "Your pardon again, Theo Waitley. I find that I do not know what I mean, speaking in Terran."

"Maybe if you describe—" Theo began, and blinked, interrupted by the sudden arrival of a second, much skinnier—maybe younger?—norbear, who charged up her knee, grabbed onto the front of her sweater with tiny hands and climbed until she had gained the height of Theo's shoulder, where she sat up on her back legs, one hand clutching Theo's hair to keep from rolling over and down.

The shoulder-sitter was purring, too, and the interweaving of the two "sounds" inside her head was— energizing.

She laughed as the first norbear, not to be outdone, despite the fact that she was considerably more portly, grabbed onto Theo's pants leg, and began to haul herself up, hand over hand. Laughing again, Theo scooped the creature into her lap, and cuddled her. The norbear relaxed against her, purrs intensifying. Theo shivered pleasurably, and looked around the enclosure.

The littlie was rolling in the vines with his norbear, squealing with laughter. Two of the adults were sitting down, norbears at cuddle and grins on their faces. The oldest of their group was standing, his back against the wall, norbear on his shoulder, furry cheek pressed against his ear. The man's eyes were closed and he was smiling.

Mr. Rogen stood off to one side of it all, hands behind his back, face expressionless; the only one of their group not visited by a norbear.

"Have some manners!" Win Ton exclaimed from beside her, over a sudden frantic sound of claws scrabbling against cloth. "It's hardly my fault you were lost in dreams!" He extended his hand and raised it slowly, a ginger colored norbear no bigger than his hand curled down on his palm, ears quivering.

"There," he murmured. "No need to be distraught..."

The sounds in her head increased again, like she was maybe hearing Win Ton's norbears, too. She wondered, if she listened closely, if she'd be able to tell which purr belonged to each norbear. Theo closed her eyes for a moment, the better to concentrate—and jerked as the librarian called out.

"That concludes our lecture for the day! The norbears are available to passengers in cycle every shipday, please consult the Library's schedule for exact times! Now, please rise, and place your animal gently on the leaves. There may be a moment of dislocation as the empathic bond is—they have very little range—Yes. And please now leave the enclosure."

Theo put her norbears on the green-tangle with a pang made sharper by the skinny shoulder sitter wrapping tiny fingers around the base of her thumb, as if pleading with her not to go. Win Ton was standing, though, and the rest of the group was filing through the gate, the little boy still giggling softly to himself.

"I've got to go," Theo whispered to the skinny norbear. "I'll come back and visit—promise!"

She forced herself to pull her hand back, stand up, and follow the rest of the group out of the enclosure.

· · · ※ · · ·

Kamele smiled and inclined her head easily, neither scrambling to stand and bow in return, nor ignoring the courtesy offered. She had not, Cho thought, been simply given a rule, for there was a naturalness to the gesture that mere rule-learning could never attain. Rather, it was the gesture of someone who had learned by proximity, over time, until the easy courtesy was part of her social repertoire.

"I came down to do some work," Kamele said, "but I think that work has done with me." She moved her hand, showing Cho the empty chair across from her. "Please, won't you join me? The coffee is quite good."

"Ah." Cho slid into the offered chair. "The tea is also entirely drinkable, as I have had occasion to discover. Also, there is a small cheesecake—small in size, but large in delight. May I order one to share, and more coffee for yourself?"

The blue eyes sharpened on her. Cho kept her face as innocent as may be, displaying restrained pleasure at this chance meeting. She was, as most Liadens were, all praise to the lessons of the homeworld culture, very good at schooling her expressions. And yet there was a moment, fleeting but poignant, in which she was convinced that Kamele Waitley had pierced her small veil of deceit.

Whatever discoveries the professor may have made, she decided not to remark upon them. The moment passed, and Kamele Waitley once more inclined her head.

"A sweet shared with an ally would be very pleasant, I thank you."

Hah. Now, *that*, Cho thought, had more of the feel of received information, as opposed to practical understanding. Still, even scholars might hold truce over table.

Cho touched the discreet button set into the tabletop and entrusted her order to the smiling young person who shortly arrived at their alcove. By the time Kamele Waitley had folded her screen away, the server was returned, bearing a tray with two pots, two cups, the single sweet and the utensils with which to address it. These were deftly set out with a murmured wish that the diners enjoy, and they were once again in private.

Kamele poured coffee. Cho poured tea, looking up to see what the other would do—and delighted to find that she took but a single sip from her cup before placing it gently on the tabletop, her eyes steady on Cho's face.

Here indeed was a fully capable woman, Cho thought, admiringly, and stifled a sigh at the memory of the person to whom she sat second.

Well.

Cho took the ritual sip and likewise put her cup aside, returning Kamele Waitley's regard.

"At our shared meal last evening, the so-delightful Professor Crowley allowed me to know that the scholars of Delgado travel to Melchiza, there to undertake a search of literatures."

"That's right," the other woman said, a small line appearing between delicate brows. "We checked the Advisories available to us and found no warnings of . . . danger more than would await any traveler, ignorant of local custom."

Gods, the woman was quick! Cho inclined her head.

"The Advisories are . . . adequate for most travelers. Melchiza values its tourists even more than it values its trade. What concerns me is this search which your team would undertake. For Melchiza holds its intellectual treasures close, and does not easily share."

Kamele Waitley's face smoothed. Almost, she smiled. "I thank you for your concern," she said softly. "But we go as scholars to scholars, with an identical regard for the treasures of the intellect. That common bond will, I think, bridge our differences." She reached for her cup and raised it, apparently of the opinion that the meat of their interaction was consumed. "We've been in contact with the curator of the items we wish to examine, and she's been everything that's obliging and scholarly."

Well, and perhaps not so quick, after all. Cho picked up her cup. But no, she chided herself, as she savored the truly excellent ship's blend—that was unkind, and likely also untrue. Kamele Waitley thought in terms of her team's mission, and those arrangements that scholars made between scholars. Of those other influences upon her mission which were yet outside of it—of those things, she was ignorant. And how not?

"It is," she said softly, "doubtless exactly as you say. Certainly, there are those ports where I would scarce dare set foot, except for the surety of meeting a like mind."

She would, Cho thought, consider a bit more, and weigh whether the warning repeated, and more strongly, might cause more harm than good. There was time. And it might, after all, be true that the scholars would stand sheltered within the shadow of their kin in research and never catch of glimpse of the more...peculiar...aspects of Melchizan culture.

In the meanwhile, she smiled and nodded at the untouched sweet between them.

"Please, let us enjoy this together." She picked up the spoon that had been set by her hand, and saw with a breath of relief that Kamele Waitley also picked up hers. She had not offended. That was well. One did not like the notion of offending Kamele Waitley.

. . . . ❁ . . . .

Theo's head was buzzing, like she still heard the norbears purring there; and she felt—charged with 'way too much energy, and if she didn't do something to channel it, or contain it, then—

"I need to make lace!" she exclaimed, feet jittering against the deck as they walked away from the pet library.

"And to think that they are merely domestic norbears!" Win Ton's voice sounded like her head felt, bright and full of unexpected edges. "How might we have fared, faced with—what?" He looked down at her, brown eyes glittering. "You need to make—*lace*?" She hadn't realized he was so close; she could feel the excitement jumping back and forth between the two of them, arcing, like electricity...

"No," she said, and forced herself to stop, to keep both feet firmly on the deck and both arms at her sides. She closed her eyes, forcing herself to think through the buzz. When she had the thought firm, she looked up at Win Ton, who was standing forcibly still, not even a hand's breadth away.

"I *don't* want to make lace," she said, speaking slowly and clearly. "I want to dance."

He grinned. "Now that may indeed be the tonic that cures us! Hold a beat." He spun rapidly on a heel, arm shooting out and up, pointing at the sign that flashed and spangled across the wide hallway.

*Arcade.*

Like everything else on *Vashtara*, the arcade was too big and too ornate; certainly it was too noisy. Theo followed Win Ton through the sliding gates and was nearly overwhelmed by the racket. Such a blast of sound and distracting lights would never have been allowed on Delgado; it couldn't be either safe or secure to have so many *things* going on at once!

On the other hand, with the norbear buzz still in her head and the feeling she had, the *will to dance* so strong, the noise seemed to echo and . . . almost . . . satisfy some craving she hadn't 'til this minute known she'd had.

Win Ton had a plan, so she kept his shoulder close to hers as he slipped deeper into the noise and the crowd.

He paused, and she thought he'd found it . . . but maybe he was watching the woman with the stupidly tiny skirt walk by—as were half the people on deck it seemed like. *Pffft* . . . she didn't move half as well as Win Ton himself . . . but then his gaze traveled on. He jerked his head, like he was pointing with his chin.

"There! Will that satisfy you, Theo Waitley?" There was a note of—of *challenge*—in his voice. She looked in the direction he'd pointed.

*There* was a trio of platforms, one barely above floor level and swathed in a pulsing green light. The next level, up a ramp to the right, was bathed in a lurid red light with a double pulse. The third platform was higher still, glowing with a blue-silver nimbus, a dozen smaller overhead highlights reflecting off its glittering hardware.

The beat from the first platform was plain and simple; it was occupied by three adults, trying to do something . . .

Win Ton leaned comfortably into her shoulder, murmuring so softly that she had to practically put her ear against his lips to hear him.

"I said, Theo, that we need not start on the base platform if you don't wish to. It only goes up to level nine."

The three adults, Theo saw suddenly, were *dancing*—sort of—in a semi-coordinated kind of way, each following a pattern that was projected in Tri-D in front of them. The image showed them where to place their feet next, with hints for tempo and hand location . . . and they weren't all that good at it. There were . . . scores they must be, at the top of the Tri-D, points for doing things right. It looked like the three dancers were being corrected quite a bit by the machine; though they'd managed to make it to level three. The man in the center . . . he wasn't too bad, she decided, watching him catch the beat with his hips and start to move a bit more easily.

"Have you danced this way before?" Win Ton asked.

She shook her head *no*. The guy in the center had it now—he was really moving with the beat...

"I've never used one," she said to Win Ton, "but I see how it works."

"There is room on the second platform," he said, his breath tickling her ear, "if you can give over gawking..."

The beat and the movement and the patterns on the Tri-D were sort of mesmerizing, and watching people was good...but she felt there'd been something else he thought was funny in that phrase. She turned her head so that she could see him, and caught a look on his face like—well, like Father's, when he thought something was *interesting*.

"Will you dance with me, Theo Waitley?" Win Ton asked, his accent making the words into something exotic and exciting.

"Yes," she said, like her stomach didn't feel suddenly odd. Her fingers were tingling with energy, and her feet kept shifting against the floor, feeling out the beat.

Win Ton smiled, brilliant, and offered his hand. She took it as they skirted the first-level adults, and arrived at the red-bathed platform. Here were two younger dancers, on the first and third of the level's four dance pads. The music was louder, and Theo saw Win Ton's free hand move as if he was saying something to her...

"What?" she asked, leaning in, because...

"I said," he said against her ear, "that this machine goes up to level eighteen, though these tourists are hardly more skilled than the first level people, and surely not worthy of us. Up with you, she who dances, up!"

Theo tried to give him a quieting glance, but he

was already on the ramp, heading for the third level, and there was nothing she could do but follow him.

The silver platform was more than a tall head's height above the common floor, and a fair number of people were watching the two dancers on the leftmost pads.

The scores for both dancers were rising steadily, the right one more rapidly than the left. Forcing herself to concentrate, Theo watched them, noting that the nearer dancer's eyes were half-closed, as if he was barely watching the pattern while his body wove from move to move. His partner, on the other hand, was staring intently at the pattern, every motion deliberate.

Theo leaned against Win Ton's shoulder and put her mouth next to his ear. "That's not very fair," she murmured. "The man on the right is—is a dancer, and the other one isn't!"

It seemed that Win Ton shivered, but it was probably only the norbear buzz and the excitement of the lights and the noise. He moved his hand in a gesture that was almost dancelike, then bent to speak into her ear.

"You may be right. Still, the one on the left is making a good effort. Effort should count for something, should it not?"

There was question underneath the question—she heard it without understanding what it was—and then was distracted as the dancer on the right abruptly stumbled and stepped off the pad. Laughing and shrugging, he pulled his serious friend away, and they descended the ramp, heads together, and their arms around each other's waists.

"There," Win Ton said with satisfaction. "We have it to ourselves, Sweet Mystery...please choose your pad." He glanced at her with a smile almost as glittery as the silver lights. "First one to give up buys lunch."

"I'm really clumsy, you know!" Theo said seriously, taking the pad all the way on the left. "And I haven't really had that many dance lessons."

Win Ton bowed. "Fairly said. I will therefore pay for the dance, as you will be paying for lunch."

He waved his key card at the panel, the lights came up, the beat started, and the pattern formed on the screen before them.

Theo put her foot forward. Challenge or not, she still wanted to dance.

· · · ·❋· · · ·

They were both sweating, involved, unaware, sharing a moment of movement alone among many.

Kamele stood transfixed, watching along with dozens of others as the dancers on the high platform laughed at each other. Theo stuck her tongue out at something her partner said, her hand moving in flippant motion to the beat that was gone, waiting for the next round on the machine, entranced.

On the level below three young men were dancing hard . . . each had aspired to the higher level and had given up after a dance or two; the pair on the top hardly noticed their arrival—or their departure.

"How much longer?" Kamele asked faintly.

"They have finished level thirty-five," Cho sig'Radia said, with really remarkable calm, "my apprentice and your daughter. The game has only one more to offer—it is called 'The Overdrive Level.'"

Kamele shook her head extravagantly. "Overdrive? I must tell Ella about this!"

A woman, resplendent in a gold and red Arcade uniform, paused at Kamele's side and smiled up at the two silver-limned dancers. "They're the best we've had so far this trip," she said, sounding for all the worlds like a fond mother. "Even the really good dancers hardly get past level thirty." She nodded impartially at Kamele and Cho and passed on into the crowd.

Above them, the music started again, the pads lit and the dancers began to move, step-step-twist, the scores flickering on the machine's face insisting that they were evenly matched in skill.

They were so very closely matched...Kamele looked to her companion. "How old is Win Ton?"

The Liaden moved her shoulders. "A matter of some sixteen Standards, add or remove a handful of days."

"But he is—a pilot," Kamele insisted, as the dancers pirouetted above.

"Indeed, he is a very able pilot." Cho smiled. "Mind you, he has mastered Jump, and so has earned the jacket, but he has more yet to learn."

"I...see."

Her attention drifted upward again, to the pair now marching in time, knees high, elbows pumping. Kamele felt a sudden doubt, and looked 'round to her companion.

"He's not *letting her* match his score, is he?"

Cho laughed then.

"Kamele Waitley, as enchanting as your daughter may be, I think young Win Ton has not the 'let her win' wit in his head." She paused, apparently weighing the efforts of the pair on the high platform, then looked back, smiling.

"No," she said, almost too softly to be heard under the whistles, claps and encouragement shouted by the watchers on the arcade floor. "Assuredly, he is not *letting her* keep up."

· · · · ❁ · · · ·

"You almost missed that last, Theo Waitley!"

She laughed and stuck her tongue out—"Was I the one who almost fell on his face because of a simple waltz step?"

"A trick move! Who on Liad learns waltzes from Terra? I say again, a trick move."

She moved her hand, mimicking the motion he seemed to use for the more ironic flavors of "no."

"All right, and what was that *thing* that made you laugh, if you please?"

Win Ton laughed again, ruefully this time. "It is a preliminary move, taught in classes of marriage lore—and more than *that,* I will not say, though you pull my hair out by the roots!"

She snorted, her hand still carrying the beat of the last round. "Oh, and you've been married?"

He sent a glance to the far ceiling, his fingers snapping lightly.

"Nay, I was not, though I might have been, had the captain not accepted me as her apprentice. So, you see, I am doomed, whichever foot I stand upon."

Theo laughed again. He used that as an excuse to step up to the board, fingers hovering above the selection for the next level.

"Are you ready, Sweet Mystery?"

"I am if you are," she answered.

"Bold heart." He smacked the start plate with his toe. "Go!"

✳        ✳        ✳

The music poured through her, mixing with the norbear hum, filling up her senses. She was aware of the music, the patterns, and of Win Ton, matching her step-for-step on the pad next to hers.

Together, they tore through the first section of the level, and then hit a complex series of moves seemingly a repeat of a much earlier level, as if the game-programmer was toying with them. Surely they weren't going to regress?

There! The tempo picked up again, and now the music moved into something her dancing instructor called contrapuntal dysrhythmia, with the point being that the dance moves were not in sync with the music.

Theo laughed and dared a glance at Win Ton, who saw her look and made a silly face. She laughed again, caught the next footwork and saw that, too, was being silly.

And then she...

Almost fell over.

The music—just stopped. The platform shook with a weird rumbling. Lights flashed. Buzzers went off. The Tri-D screen showed a senseless pattern, twirling wildly. Glittery streamers fell from somewhere, tangling in her hair, cluttering the dance pad, and drifting in the air from the blowers.

She spun, careful of her footing among the fallen streamers, and stared at Win Ton, who was stubbornly kicking at the start plate.

"What happened?"

He flung his hands out, eloquent of frustration. "We have beaten the machine, you and I! There are no more levels to dance."

Theo *fuffed* hair out of her face.

"It *can't* be over. I still have dance left!"

Win Ton laughed again, and suddenly pointed over the edge of the platform.

"I fear we may have danced past lessons. There stand my captain and your mother, and I very much fear it is going to go badly with us."

She *fuffed* her hair out of her face again, saw her mother waving at her to come down.

"Kick it again," she said to Win Ton. "Maybe it'll start if we both kick it!"

· · · · ✸ · · · ·

"We scarcely had a workout at all!" Win Ton said to Cho sig'Radia across the table the four of them had claimed at Breakfast All Year.

Kamele sipped her coffee, trying to hide her amusement. That the boy *had* had a workout was all too obvious. Disregarding the fact that he and Theo were both still sweat-dampened and in high color, they had between them consumed a so-called "nuncheon plate" advertised to feed four, and were making short work of the follow-on sweets tray. Theo had eaten with a delicate voracity that had frankly amazed, letting the boy do the talking, except for a few early comments regarding norbears.

"Yet you advanced to the overdrive level," Cho pointed out. "It seemed from the floor, young Win Ton, that you and your partner ended the game in the top first percentile of players—"

"It does not advance to the challenge level!" Win Ton interrupted, and Theo paused with her third—or possibly fourth—petit pastry halfway to her mouth to blink at him.

"I thought we *were* at the challenge level!" she exclaimed.

"No, sweet dancer—a proper machine, such as the one I am accustomed to from—" a quick glance at Cho "—from school, has several levels yet above where we found ourselves, which allow for free form, and other variations."

He sounded, Kamele thought, genuinely aggrieved, and despite herself she chuckled.

Three pair of eyes came to rest on her face, which was—disconcerting, but she had brought it on herself.

"I'm sorry," she said to Win Ton, who had probably thought she was laughing at him. "I'm reminded of—of a dear friend of mine who makes similar complaints about the equipment we have at home." She sipped her coffee, marking how the boy's gaze never faltered. "His answer is usually to... *correct* ... the poor performance into something he finds more reasonable."

Win Ton's face grew thoughtful.

"I will ask my apprentice," Cho sig'Radia said, with emphasis, "to recall that he is a guest and a passenger upon this vessel."

He turned to her. "But, Captain—"

She raised a hand. "Spare the poor device, my child; it is a game only, and never meant to withstand a full testing."

"But—"

"It wasn't a test," Theo interrupted. "We were just trying to work off the—the buzz from the norbears!" She looked at Cho seriously. "And it was just what we needed. Making lace wouldn't have done *at all*!"

There was a small silence during which, Kamele

strongly suspected, Cho sig'Radia struggled courageously with her emotions.

"Ah," she said at last, inclining her head. "You must tell me more about this lace making, if you would, young Theo. I have, as you may understand, some interest in strategies for bleeding excess energy."

# TWENTY-TWO

. . . . . . . . . . . . . . . . . . . .

Vashtara
*EdRec Level*
*Library*

**WIN TON REALLY CALLED THAT ONE!** **THEO THOUGHT AS**
she moved out of the lecture hall. Hindsight clearly
showed that she should've gone with him to the
"Antique Recipe Workshop."

*Pffft.* If *she* was ever a teacher she was going to
lecture better than Mr. Chorli. He hadn't been very
good with the norbear presentation and he'd been
even *worse* with "All The Languages of Space." Not
only didn't he speak anything but what he called "pure
Terran," he used some kind of promptomatic on his
speakeasy display so all he had to do was read ahead
a few seconds to sound like he knew his subject. She
could get better than that off any classroom channel
at home any hour of the day. Worse than *all* of that,
though—he hadn't taken questions.

Not that he probably *knew* anything about non-
verbal languages.

Well, she'd just have to download the extra study packet off of the Library site when she got back to the stateroom. She was at liberty until six bells, though she was supposed to meet Win Ton in front of the Arcade after their respective lectures were over.

"All the Languages of Space" had ended some minutes short of its advertised time frame, which she guessed was just as well. It did, however, mean that she had a little bit of time to make good on a promise.

She glanced around her, located the pointer, and was shortly in the Pet Library, the norbears' eco-section before her, status light glowing a cheery yellow for *accepting visitors*.

Theo smiled. She'd just look in and see if anybody was awake. Carefully, she eased the gate open and slipped inside the eco-space.

If she hadn't known better, she would have said that the enclosure was empty; a first glance showed only the ragged vegetation, the sticklike shrubbery, and a little pool of gently flowing water. It was quiet, too; the only noise she heard for three heartbeats was a sort of soft under-mumble, which was probably the pump powering the pool.

Three or four careful steps into the space, Theo sank to her knees on the crinkly floor.

"Hey," she called softly. "Anybody home? I promised I'd come back."

Nothing moved. Theo sighed. She'd thought she'd at least see the little norbear who had seemed so sad when she'd left, before. Still, she reminded herself, naps were pretty serious for cats—and probably for norbears, too. Just because the Pet Librarian decided they were receiving visitors didn't mean that the norbears agreed.

She shifted slightly on her knees, waking a rustle.

"Maybe next time," she said, gently, and began to rise.

Somebody... sneezed, tiny and delicate.

She froze.

The vegetation rustled, and a pair of round ears hove into view, quivering.

Theo held her breath as the rest of the norbear became visible, sneezed again, then bumbled into action, charging across the crinkly floor at full norbear throttle.

She laughed and held her hand down. The skinny one who had wanted her to stay barreled straight onto her palm. Carefully, she brought the little creature to her shoulder, already hearing the buzz inside her head, and feeling a warm pulse of pleasure. The norbear was glad she had come back. Theo was glad she had come back. She sighed as the tiny fingers gripped her hair, the audible part of the purr tickling her ear.

"I can't stay long," she said, keeping her voice soft so as not to wake any of the other norbears. "But I didn't want you to think I'd forgotten you."

Her palm tickled, like she was holding fur, and the feeling of warm well-being increased. Theo smiled.

"You didn't forget me, either. That makes me feel good. I'll come back again, if you want me to, but I'm going to have to go in a couple minutes to meet Win Ton."

The purring quickened; the feeling of half-sleepy comfort shifting into a kind of bouncy inquisitiveness. Maybe, Theo thought, the norbear was describing Win

Ton, as he was perceived by norbears. The tempo changed again, brightening; Theo felt a sparkle of energy, and breathed a laugh.

"Oh, no, you don't," she said, reaching up and schooching the norbear from her shoulder to her hand. "The last time we were here, you gave us so much energy we had to dance it off. We beat the machine and now Captain Cho says we can't dance it anymore!"

The purring took on a quizzical tone.

"Well . . . she said we'd be making a display of ourselves. But Win Ton says he's got something that's even better than dancing, which is why I'm supposed to meet him."

She put the norbear gently down on the floor-stuff, and shivered pleasurably when the little creature once again wrapped her fingers around the base of Theo's thumb.

"I'll visit you again," she said; "promise. But next time, you need to wake up quicker!"

The norbear flicked her ears, rubbed her head against Theo's fingertips and let go, settling back on her hind legs.

Theo rose, not without a pang, and let herself out of the eco-section. When she looked back through the transparent door, she could still see the norbear, sitting tall, watching her.

Theo left the Pet Library, walking with the light, quick stride she'd learned from Win Ton. It wasn't quite like dancing; in fact, it was like math. *A lot* like math, where the rest of the objects and pedestrians in an area three strides ahead and to either side of you were points. And it was your job to navigate through the space created by those points. Frowning, she wondered how she'd explain it to Bek. Maybe she'd just have to show him.

She passed one of the 'vator banks as the doors opened and what looked like a whole secondary school was disgorged. The crowd swept 'round her, walking quickly, voices raised in a confusion of language and dialect—not one of them, Theo thought, spitefully— "pure Terran." In fact, it *did* look like a secondary school, she saw: There were some adults mixed in, but mostly the crowd was made up of kids her age or a little older, wearing sweaters in what must be their Team colors. They sorted themselves as they streamed past, yellow sweaters finding other yellows; magentas grouping together; blues swirling 'round each other like water.

She increased her pace, but they soon outstripped her, hurrying past the Arcade, toward the retail areas beyond.

Theo slowed and let them go. She was supposed to meet Win Ton in front of the Arcade; it was no sense running a race when she was almost there, and not at all late, despite her visit with the norbear.

From behind her came the sound of rapid footsteps—maybe some of the kids had gotten separated from their group, Theo thought, and swung toward the wall, so she wouldn't impede them. That would be anti-social.

Behind her, the rushing footsteps slowed considerably, and a boy spoke softly—though still loud enough for her to hear.

"Hey, hey, Jumbo. There she is! That cute Liaden girl you were faunching after—she's right there. I told you she wouldn't be able to stay away. People get addicted to that dance thing. And her boyfriend's not with her!"

Theo scanned the crowd ahead, looking for the "Liaden girl." The rushing Teams had mostly been Terran, she thought, though she hadn't seen everybody, and it would've been hard to pick a specifically Liaden girl out of the crowd. How would you tell? Even Father, who, as he had assured her gravely, stood every inch a Liaden, sometimes startled inadvertent people, who just assumed that he was Terran.

People, Theo thought, weren't generally very advertent.

The Arcade was in sight, and there was Win Ton, in his jacket today and and—but, no! That person's hair was more red and less brown than Win Ton's hair, though he was wearing a similar jacket. He was shoulder-to-shoulder with a black-haired woman, both of them on the alert for someone, by the way they stood.

"Catch her before she goes in the Arcade!" another boy—maybe Jumbo?—cried.

The footsteps quickened again, scuffling in haste, and suddenly her view of the Arcade and the interesting people before it was blocked by a group of three young men in tight black pants and glittery, open-necked shirts. They looked faintly familiar—maybe she'd seen them in one of the shopping malls, or at lunch; but she was certain she'd never spoken to any of them.

The tallest of the three, which put him 'way taller than her, stood slightly forward, blocking her way, and smiled like he expected her to recognize him. He had a square face, made squarer by the fact that he'd slicked his hair back so it was flat to his head. Two blue stripes were painted from the outside corners of his eyes to the tips of his ears and he had an earring that matched his glittery shirt dangling in his left ear.

She'd seen him *some*where, Theo thought, glancing over his shoulder at his friends, who seemed to be having a hard time not laughing.

"Mamzel," the tallest boy said abruptly, his voice sounding breathless, "may I offer you congratulations on a great dance? I've never seen a girl dance so well before."

*Oh.* The captain had explained that they might expect people seeking them out to congratulate them on "beating" the dance machine.

"It is to be a wonder, young Theo; some people will wish to share your glory by speaking of it to you. There are those who will admire the performance even of the sullen young apprentice, though he owns himself barely tested." Captain Cho had paused to look pointedly at Win Ton before continuing, "This is yet another reason to refrain from repeating such a display of virtuosity. Rest, both, upon your accomplishments; be gracious to those who seek you out—and find some other avenue for excess energy."

Theo gave the boy before her a smile and a nod.

"Thank you," she managed, trying to sound gracious; "we had a lot of fun."

Again, she looked beyond him, hoping for Win Ton, but seeing only the friends of her admirer, and feeling—feeling more nervous than gracious.

She moved two steps to the right, but one of the friends matched the move, so that she couldn't leave, unless she wanted to duck around him and look like a kid.

"I was wondering..." said the tall youth. He bowed a silly, off-centered bow, like he was fragile, or didn't know how to stand on his feet. His friends tried to follow suit and looked even sillier. "Would you care to join us for a dance on level two or three?"

Theo took a breath. *This isn't*, she reminded herself, *the late bus from Nonactown. This is an open hallway. Lots of people can see you, right here, right now. There's no way they can cover up all those eyes.*

Another breath, and she gave the tall boy Father's nodding half-bow, because Captain Cho had *said* "gracious."

"I'm honored," she managed, "but I don't—I'm not sure it would be fair. I'm—"

The leader's smile dropped away into a hard, angry line. He leaned forward, looming over her, and interrupted loudly.

"Not *fair* to dance with us? Are you that good, do you think? Grizzat's bones, I've heard Liadens are stuck up, but—"

Theo dropped back a half-step, sliding into a move from the *Suwello,* which spun her sideways to the tallest boy. The one who had blocked her had dropped back, but whether that was because he didn't want to be part of the argument, or he wanted to give his friend space, Theo couldn't tell—and didn't care. His absence created an opening. She could dance to the left, spin right and—

"Boyfriend!" came sotto voce from the friend on the left, barely ahead of another, familiar, and welcome voice.

"I'd measure 'not fair' as a polite enough *no*," Win Ton said, with a certain bland emphasis. He paused at her side and set his shoulder against hers. "Liaden or otherwise. As our dancer was waiting for me, as I feel certain she was about—Oh, Pilots!"

He bowed, pretty as a dance move, to the left of the three boys, where the red-headed person she'd almost mistaken for Win Ton and his companion came.

"Pilot, well met," the woman said. She returned his bow precisely, the black hair curving over her shoulder showing highlights of blue.

The three boys suddenly went back a step, then another.

"Win Ton!" her teammate cried, with a grin. "We were told we might find you and your fair partner here!" The bow he swept was full of flourish, and aimed, Theo saw with a blink, at her. "Star Dancer, allow me to be honored beyond my powers of expression!"

"If only it were so!" the woman added.

Theo giggled. The red-haired man straightened, fingers flickering with rapid purpose.

"Precisely," Win Ton answered, and turned his head toward the visibly nervous boys.

"Young sirs, our party has found us, and we are wanted elsewhere," he said crisply. "The very best of good luck to you, in your crusade to conquer Level Two."

"Well, there wasn't really a *problem*," Theo said half-huffily as they strode toward and through a grav-change spot. None of her companions commented on it, so she didn't either. Of course, none of her companions had commented on the boys who had wanted to dance, either. But Theo...her stomach was still unsettled, though really, she told herself for the fourth time, there hadn't been any *danger*.

"They just wanted me to dance with them," she said, "and I was trying to say that it wouldn't be fair to start a dance when I was expecting a friend and would have to leave. But he misunderstood what I said, and he wouldn't let me finish..."

Win Ton looked beyond her to the other members of their party, a hand sign directing them and her left at the next intersection. The gravity changed there, too, lightening.

"You spoke nothing but truth, Theo," Win Ton said. "Indeed, you might have stopped in good conscience with 'not fair.' Those three will never be pilots—nor dancers. It is therefore nothing more than the duty of one who is a most exquisite dancer to protect them from harmful ambition."

Theo glanced at him, and took a deliberate breath, trying to let the last of the upset feeling go.

"You're right," she said. "It's nothing that needs to go to Delm Korval."

Win Ton blinked, eyes widening.

"Certainly not," he agreed. He touched his tongue to his lips, then looked past her, speaking to Cordrey, the red-haired man, and his friend Phobai.

"Hear me, Pilots, we went shoulder to shoulder to Level thirty-six, and might have gone to Level fifty, had the machine not been burdened with a governor. Those clumsy halflings could have learned *nothing* from dancing with Theo! You could see that they wanted only to be admired!"

"Your eyesight that bad, Pilot?" Cordrey asked, giving Theo a grin and a wink. "Looked to me like what they really wanted to do was admire Theo, all to themselves."

Win Ton did an odd little shrug-and-bow on the move. "Point taken," he admitted. "Ah, we'll want my pass here."

He dropped one step behind Theo and took two long steps to Cordrey's side, a key card appearing between his fingers as they approached the gate across the hall. Phobai shifted her position so now she was walking next to Theo.

"Still feeling a little fizzy, aren't you?" the black-haired woman asked.

Theo bit her lip, and nodded.

"Thought so. Those guys weren't anything you couldn't handle, even if we hadn't happened along. The fizz, though, that'll be good for what we're on course for."

Ahead of them, the gate snapped open, and Win Ton waved them through.

"Quickly, friends! Now..."

He moved ahead of their little party, Cordrey at his heels. Phobai stayed with Theo, walking as close as a mother.

"What—course are we on?" Theo asked. Phobai smiled, slow and lazy.

"You'll like it," she said, which wasn't an answer at all. "Not far now, I don't think."

"Fourteen," Win Ton said to Cordrey; "though fourteen-b, I'm told, is the actual entrance we wish to use."

They walked on, quiet and companionable. Theo felt a comfortable bounce to her step that wasn't just the light gravity. It did feel good to stretch her legs, and the . . . fizz . . . that Phobai had noticed seemed to have given her something like a norbear buzz.

A double-doorway was coming up on the left, gold-colored numerals blazoned Theo-high on the wall, accompanied by the legend, "Captain's Ballroom."

They strode on another two dozen steps, to the much more modest door labeled "14-B."

"Now!" said Win Ton, brandishing the key once more. He looked to Theo, his eyes sparkling. "*Now*, we can be private! "

· · · ·✻· · · ·

"Why did you come back?" Chair Hafley's voice was not as calm as she wished it to be; the tension was in the over-careful enunciation.

Kamele raised her coffee cup and sipped, savoring the bright, acidic taste. It was very good coffee; the sort to be enjoyed in pleasant solitude or shared with an old and dear friend.

Unhappily, there was instead of either solitude or a friend, Orkan Hafley.

Kamele placed her cup gently onto the saucer and met the Chair's hard blue gaze. She could plead ignorance, but there was nothing to gain, really, from pretending not to understand the question.

"It was time," she said calmly, "to come back."

"Oh, it was *time*!" Hafley's laugh was harsh. "What I don't understand, Kamele, is why you waited *so long*. The Liaden bed-toy performed his function well. You had years ago gotten your introductions to the high scholars and ingratiated yourself into their regard. A well-enough plan, aptly executed, and nothing more than a canny scholar with an eye to her future—and her daughter's!—might put in motion. Though the Liaden wasn't quite well-placed enough to get you into the Tower, was he?"

"I believe that Professor Kiladi is well-thought-of at the Administrative levels," Kamele said, carefully now.

"I'm certain that *he* is," Hafley said, with heavy sarcasm, "but are *you*?" She plucked a pink sponge cake flower from the pastry tray on the table between them and disposed of it in one bite.

"You are not thought of by Admin at all!" she said, answering her own question somewhat stickily. "And that was not very forward-looking. If you wish to solidify your position, you'll need Admin behind you. Unless," she continued, giving Kamele a speculative look, "unless *that* is the reason you've come back? The Liaden is getting long in the tooth, and I daresay he isn't as ... satisfactory ... as he might once have been. A rising young Administrator, however ... Parlay the position you gained from the old man, and, of course, your own worth as a full professor and a woman at the height of her powers. Yes, that might well open the Tower to you. A young man warms the bed nicely, if I may offer the benefit of my experience—and so eager to be led! It will be quite a change for you."

Kamele thought about her coffee, but did not reach for it. Her anger was gaining on her puzzlement—and Hafley *must not* see her hand shake.

"It's kind of you to say, Chair," she said, keeping her voice calm. "One does like to know that one's planning is appropriate."

"Appropriate," Hafley agreed, reaching for the pot and pouring herself more coffee. She did not offer to warm Kamele's cup.

"Appropriate," she said again, as if the word had savor, "but so time-consuming. Had you not lingered so long outside the Wall, this plan might have served you better. As it is, I believe I may save you some time—and perhaps some effort."

"You . . . intrigue me," Kamele said honestly.

"Of course I do; you are a woman of ambition. Now, how if I were to offer you entree to highest levels of the Tower, immediately upon our return to Delgado? Of course you may still wish to secure that warm and eager-to-please ornament to your sagacity. But! Your choice need not then be constrained by a job title."

She didn't care if her hands shook or not, Kamele thought; she needed coffee.

The cup was tepid now; she drank it anyway. A memory rose: Jen Sar's first polite sip of the coffee she had made for the two of them to share: a special blend, purchased for the occasion. By the measuring glance he'd given the satiny dark beverage, he'd been braced for staff-room coffee, and it had been liquid bliss to see his eyebrows rise in surprise, and his lips soften into a smile when he lowered the cup.

"I wonder, Chair," Kamele said, putting her cup down and reaching for the pot. Her hands were quite steady, after all. What a surprise. "I wonder what you mean to say?"

Hafley laughed and chose another sweet cake from the tray. "Why, only that I can forward your ambition, Scholar. All you need do is ally yourself with me, and to support my purpose."

. . . . ✸ . . . .

Phobai took off her jacket and tossed it into a far corner.

"It might be tall enough," she said, tilting a measuring eye toward the ceiling; "if we're careful!"

"Oh, we'll be careful, we will," Cordrey said, stripping out of his jacket and dropping it casually next to hers.

Theo looked up, and shook her head. "I don't think I can jump that high, even if the gravity shifts and I dance real hard!"

Cordrey laughed, and leapt straight up, arm over head, fingers extended. He might, Theo thought, have been trying to touch the ceiling. If so, he missed by several hand-lengths, and dropped lightly to the floor.

"See?" he said to Phobai. "Careful."

He went off to the side and began tapping at the walls, his ear close. At a little distance, Win Ton was paying serious attention to the floor, scuffing at some spots, tapping at others.

Curious, Theo looked down, surprised to find that the surface was like the Scavage court—elastic and slick. She bounced experimentally on her toes, pleased at the give. Maybe she could touch the ceiling, after all.

"Hey, Theo."

She turned to face Phobai, who had taken off her jersey, to reveal a sleeveless stretchy shirt that looked like a dance top. She lifted her arms, swept her hair up, gave it a twist and pinned it into a smooth knot at the back of her neck. Theo felt a pang, lost when the pilot smiled at her.

"You might want to take off that sweater. Things are likely to get warm."

"Oh!" Theo looked down at herself, disconcerted by

the long sleeves, so comfortable for most of the ship's tourist areas—and not comfortable at all for dancing.

She sighed and looked back to Phobai. "I'm afraid I didn't bring any dance clothes."

"You're among friends," Phobai said, smiling. She leaned forward and brushed Theo's hair off her forehead. "If you need to get comfortable, we'll understand."

"Phobai!" Cordrey called from across the room. "Listen to this, will you?"

No one had asked her to do anything, so Theo walked out into the center of the floor, and began Stretch Sequence Three from dance class. The sequence ended with a jump, and she surprised herself—maybe she could touch the ceiling after all!

She landed light, gasping a laugh, and glanced around her. Phobai and Cordrey were down-room, their heads together over a section of wall.

Well. She danced a step, another; heard Professor Noni's high voice chanting the time in her head— "One, *two*, three; *one*, two three; one, two, three, *four*!"—swayed, her arms moving in pattern across her chest and belly, the steps unrolling, as her hands came up, pushing air . . .

As she spun into the last sentence, and there was Win Ton, moving with her, his steps a flowing reflection of hers. They came to rest on the final *four*, and she heard him say, softly. "Again, one, *two* . . ."

She stepped into the dance again, delighted as they moved, each the perfect reflection of the other. The module flowing around them like water.

*Four.*

Theo came to rest, hands folded before her.

Win Ton spun to the left, hands describing the dimensions of an invisible ball—and stopped, flat-footed and abruptly graceless, as he realized that he danced alone.

"Shall we not continue?" His voice was wistful.

"I . . . don't know any more," she said, feeling more than a little wistful herself. "Professor Noni was going to teach us the next module, but my mother took me out of school to travel with her." Funny, she thought, how she wasn't so sure that was a bad thing, anymore. "I—could *you* teach me the next part? Bek says I catch new steps quicker than anyone he's seen, and he's been dancing since he was a littlie."

Win Ton was seen to take a breath.

"I can and I will teach you the next part, Theo Waitley," he said, sounding stern, and much older. "Your instructor should be—to leave a student with only the first four moves of the most basic self-defense? How can this—"

"Wait!" She threw her hands up; they settled into the pushing-air gesture, left hand slightly ahead of the right. Win Ton shifted, his weight going to his right leg—then stood down, somehow, as if he retracted a motion he'd made in his head and stored it away for some future moment.

"Caught between dreams and called to waken from both!" he exclaimed, bringing his hands to belt-level, palms facing Theo, fingers spread wide. "For what am I to wait, Sweet Mystery?"

"You said, self-defense," she stammered, lowering her hands to her side. "But—that's just a dance routine we were learning. It's called the *Suwello*."

"Ah," he said, sounding very much like Father in

that monosyllable. "Yes, in some places where self-defense is frowned upon . . . *menfri'at* may be taught as the *Suwello*."

He looked about. Theo followed his gaze, finding Cordrey and Phobai dancing the *Suwello* some distance down the room. Their tempo was quicker than Professor Noni had taught—so quick that it almost looked like the soft, air-pushing hand-motions were . . . strikes, and some of the footwork—surely Phobai hadn't meant to *kick* at her partner, like that!

"Pilots?" Win Ton called. "*Menfri'at* some other day!"

Cordrey spun in a move that looked related to the one Win Ton had left unfinished, his hands twisting toward Phobai's shoulder.

"Pilots, tell the tale, pray!"

Cordrey ducked, and stopped moving, his arms straight down at his side. Phobai did the same, neatly. They turned together as if continuing the dance and jogged forward, moving with that economy of motion that Win Ton and Captain Cho displayed, as if the whole ship and everyone in it were part of the same dance. The same way that Father moved, she realized, though it was hard to see because of the cane . . .

"The walls are strong enough for light bounces," Cordrey said upon his and Phobai's arrival, "but not for us, I fear. We don't want to risk tearing the fabric, or damaging the wiring behind some of the panels."

"We are well warned then," said Win Ton. He jammed his foot hard at the floor, his boot squealing against the slick stuff. "The floor requires footwear, but is well enough for dives if need be, if you tuck skin."

"Warned!" said both the pilots in unison, now nearly as close to her as Win Ton.

"Warned for what?" Theo asked.

Phobai chuckled. "Just warned, and kind we are to do so."

Theo blinked at her, before Win Ton claimed her attention with a wave of his hand—just a wave, not the deliberate motion he used at Captain Cho, or the pilots.

"Admit it, Theo," he said, "you have been warned about the walls, the ceiling has been mentioned, and you have now heard of the floors."

She laughed, not informed at all.

"Yes," she agreed. "I heard it so I guess I'm warned!"

"Good." He reached inside his jacket. "We are going to teach you something that will change your life, Theo Waitley," he said, and his voice was serious, indeed.

She sputtered a laugh, but the two pilots nodded gravely.

Win Ton pulled his hand out of his jacket.

"Let's move!" Phobai yelled, and backed rapidly away, while Cordrey turned and ran up-room.

Win Ton spun, throwing . . . something underhanded to Phobai, who caught it, and flashed it toward Cordrey . . . who threw it quite hard toward Win Ton. It was a ball, Theo thought, but it didn't arc right, it danced and shimmied as it flew, then made a sudden, illogical dive, which Win Ton managed to intercept just above his foot.

He straightened, holding his captive high, and cried, "Pause!"

Turning, he displayed the object to Theo. It *was* . . . sort of a ball, she saw, globular rather than round, sporting every color of the rainbow and a few Theo thought it had made up on the spot.

"Sixty-four sides, none the same color," Win Ton said softly, leaning forward to let her get a good look at it, but keeping a firm hold. "This, Sweet Mystery, is a bowli ball. It is bad form to permit it to touch the ground. It should only cease motion by mutual agreement. Play most generally begins slowly and builds, and I believe you will discover it a most exquisite dance."

He leaned closer and placed the bowli ball in her hand, closing her fingers over it. She felt a purring, almost like a norbear, and felt the device move against her fingers, as if it was trying to get free.

Win Ton leaned closer still, as if, Theo thought, her face heating—as if he were going to kiss her!

Instead, he whispered into her ear.

"Call pause, if you need to stop or to be left out of the circle. The ball is the thing, and all of us wish you to do well. Once the game starts, there is no quarter, without a call of *pause* or *halt*. Because this is a game between friends, and you new-come to the play, you may drop a ball thrice before you are required to bow out." He stepped back and grinned, eyes sparkling. "This is the challenge level, Theo."

He backed away quickly, then, waving his hand in a broad motion that included including the pilots and himself.

"No quarter, Theo! Throw as you will—pilot's choice!"

# TWENTY-THREE

. . . . . . . . . . . . . . . . . . . . . . . . .

*History of Education Department*
*Oriel College of Humanities*
*University of Delgado*

ELLA BEN SUZAN LEANED BACK IN HER CHAIR AND
rubbed her hands over her face as if the friction
would order her tumbling thoughts. It did not, she told
herself forcefully, bear considering by what unsubtle
means Kamele had secured concessions from Admin.
Far better to dwell on the happy outcome—Ella
named TempChair of EdHist, Hafley forced to lend
her countenance to the Research Team, and Emeritus
Professor Beltaire attached to EdHist as an archival
advisor.

True, these things had not come without price.
There was, for instance, the annoying but easily led
Jon Fu elevated to TempSubChair, not to mention
the disordered nerves of the department as a whole.
Bad enough to have discovered and dismissed Flandin.
Ten times worse, to find that Flandin might only be
the crumbling edge of a very steep cliff.

Ella leaned back in her chair and sipped staff-room coffee. For a wonder, she had no meetings scheduled until tomorrow morning, and nothing on her extensive to-do list that couldn't wait for ten hours. It might not be the worst thing she could do, to go home and get some sleep.

She put the coffee cup on top of one of the small piles of hard copy and reached for her 'book. Sleep would be—

The buzzer rang.

Ella closed her eyes. "Enter," she snapped.

The door mechanism rasped. She opened her eyes and immediately wished she hadn't.

"Ella." Jen Sar Kiladi bowed gently over his cane. "I hope I find you well."

"You find me exhausted, overworked, and impatient," she told him bluntly. She was always blunt with Jen Sar, but he never returned the favor.

"Then you will enjoy a quiet moment of conversation with an old friend," he answered, and sat in the empty visitor's chair, folding his hands over the knob of the Gallowglass cane.

Ella sighed, and did not give voice to her thought that it would be a good thing indeed, were an old friend present. There was no reason to escalate plain speaking to rudeness—and it wouldn't rid her of the man one heartbeat sooner than he intended to go.

"May I request the consideration of a *short* conversation?" she asked, reaching for her cup.

"I will contrive to be as brief as possible," he murmured, black eyes glinting. "To come immediately to the point, then: I have inspected the suspect wire in Professor Waitley's apartment—a task for which you gave me leave. That inspection led me in time to the offices of Information Systems, where Technician Singh was gracious enough to give me a tour of the facilities, including a site map for the 'old wire.'"

Ella frowned at him. "*Old* wire?"

"So it is known to the Techs. It would seem—again, briefly—that in some sections of the Wall, apartments had been provided with a research protocol which pre-dates the current Concierge system. That system provided a research AI which was more free-ranging than the Concierge, and which shortly produced a wealth of inconveniences that Technician Singh was pleased to recount to me in detail. In the interests of brevity, I shall not enumerate them."

"Thank you," Ella said, with real gratitude. "If I understand what you've said, then it seems as if Theo...accidentally invoked the former system, and downloaded the old program to her 'book."

"I also entertained this comforting thought. Alas, Technician Singh assures me that the previous AI was not merely taken off-line, but fragmented. Each fragment was then isolated and erased."

She stared at him. "As 'inconvenient' as that?"

"According to the tale told out by Technician Singh, it did seem to interpret its duties with a broad brush," Jen Sar said. He paused, his gaze directed to the floor, perhaps contemplating the wages of mischief, then looked back to her with a ripple of his shoulders.

"This episode was finished many years ago. Any number of Wall residences have 'old wire' in them, supposedly capped, but Technician Singh did not pale noticeably at the suggestion that some wires may have escaped this fate. She allowed me to know that anyone who accidentally jacked into the 'old wire' would receive only dead air."

"Theo certainly got something more than dead air!"

"So she did. I fear that I may not have been ... quite forthright with Technician Singh regarding my sudden interest in these matters."

"Of course you weren't." Ella sighed, finished her now-cold coffee, and threw the cup at the recycler.

She missed. Naturally.

"So, we didn't learn anything from this little excursion of yours."

"On the contrary, I think we learned a great deal," Jen Sar answered.

"We still don't know where the AI on Theo's old school book came from."

"Did I not say? It came through the wire marked 'research' in Theo's room."

"But InfoSystems says the AI was deprogrammed!"

"Indeed. We have thereby learned that the Serpent of Knowledge AI is not under the control of Delgado University Information Systems. All that remains for us is to discover who does control it."

She eyed him. "That's all, is it? Well! Since it's so simple, we'll just put that puzzle aside for Kamele's return. Something a little different for her to—"

"This must be solved," Jen Sar interrupted sternly, "*before* Kamele returns."

Jen Sar never interrupted, and he was much too good an actor to allow sternness to glare through the cordial mask he habitually wore. If it had been Monit Appletorn in the chair opposite her, Ella might have put this sudden display down to overreactive male sensibilities. Jen Sar Kiladi, however—

Ella blinked, as suddenly it fell into place, all of it, with a *snap* so loud she was certain the man across from her heard it.

"She *didn't* put you aside!" she exclaimed.

Jen Sar tipped his head. "May I not display even the least concern for the woman who permitted me to share so many years of her life?"

"Dissembling gains you nothing," Ella told him, leaning forward in excitement as the whole scheme rolled out before her mind's eye. "Kamele knew there was something off-key about Flandin's departure—or, I should say, Hafley's handling of the matter. We talked about it, she and I, and then... She had to seem strong—she had to *be* unencumbered by her politically unhandy relationship with the honored Gallowglass Chair. But she *never released you*! Who looked for the notice in *The Faq*? The act of moving back to the Wall with her daughter at her side—it said everything!"

She collapsed into her chair-back, suddenly exhausted. *Kamele,* she thought, *life with this man has changed you more than I knew.*

Jen Sar raised an eyebrow. "You choose the oddest moments to be perceptive."

Surprised into a laugh, Ella struggled to sit upright. "Honesty, for once!"

The second eyebrow joined the first. "When have I lied to you, Ella?"

"When have you told anyone a straight story?" she countered, and laughed again. "Chaos! No wonder she refused poor Monit quite so sharply, poor man."

He tipped his head, lips parting; Ella raised her hand.

"No, don't say it—I agree completely! Tell me instead what you intend to do."

"I intend," he said quietly, "to find the origin of that Serpent AI. Once I have done that, I will know what needs to be done next."

That was a sensible course, Ella admitted, and nodded approvingly at him. "Kamele was right, then. This is something much larger than a few adjusted cites."

Jen Sar moved his shoulders and stood. "No one is right until we have proof," he said austerely, and bowed. "Good evening, Ella."

· · · ·❖· · · ·

Alone at last in her stateroom, Kamele tapped up her 'book and opened a file, but she had no concentration for her work. 'Round and 'round the refrain echoed inside her head, "I was right! Hafley *is* in it! I was right!"

She had accepted the Chair's offer, of course; how else would she obtain proof of intent to harm the university, its faculty and students?

Kamele relaxed deliberately into her chair, closed her eyes and concentrated on breathing. She would make notes, she decided, lay out her thoughts and her concerns, exactly as she would do when opening any other line of research. In fact, it would be best to think of this as research—field research.

She so concentrated on this task that she barely heard Theo come in, or the sound of the 'fresher being engaged.

# TWENTY-FOUR

. . . . . . . . . . . . . . . . . . . . . . . . .

Vashtara
*Gallaria Level*
*Passenger Lounge*

THE CONSUMERS' LOUNGE ON THE GALLARIA LEVEL had become Theo's favorite place to meet Win Ton. It was, usually, quiet, even when, like now, there was a quartet playing music up front; the chairs and sofas were comfortable, and there didn't seem to be any rules about how long you could stay without being visited by a staff member worried that you might not be having a good time.

It was also equidistant from their three usual destinations—Ballroom 14-B, Private Studio Blue Three, and the Pet Library.

Just now, she was sitting cross-legged on the soft blue sofa next to the potted lemon tree. Her attention was mostly on the pattern she was trying to capture in lace. The sofa was easy to see from two of the three entrances, so even if she got too concentrated, Win Ton wouldn't miss her.

A shadow flickered over her busy fingers, and she looked up, blinking, from her needle.

"Win—" she began, and blinked again, because the friendly shadow didn't belong to Win Ton after all, but to Captain Cho.

"Ah," the woman bowed her head a shade too gravely, putting Theo forcefully in mind of Father. "I am desolate to have disappointed you."

Theo shook her hair back from her face, and grinned.

"But, you haven't disappointed me. I was expecting Win Ton, but I'm glad to see you!"

Captain Cho smiled—her real smile, not the too-bright one—and bowed softly. "Sweetly said, Theo Waitley. Truly, you honor me." She straightened and used her chin to point to the couch. "May I join you?"

"Please," Theo said formally. "I'll be glad of your company." She hesitated, then added, "I will need to go in a few minutes. Win Ton—"

"Ah, yes, the amiable and opportunistic young apprentice. As it happens, I have need of a word with him." Captain Cho sat next to Theo, and leaned slightly forward to study the pattern in progress.

"Is this the lace-making of which you spoke—which channels excess energy? May I see?"

"It's not finished," Theo cautioned, holding it out between careful fingers.

Cho studied it for three long heartbeats, tracing the lines with her eyes.

"I feel that I am acquainted with this pattern," she said, leaning back into the sofa's mannerly embrace. "Yet, where I might have encountered it eludes me just now."

"Well, it isn't finished," Theo said again, frowning

down at the incomplete work. "And I don't think I've got this bit here exactly right . . ." She traced the questionable connections with her finger. "That's why I wanted to make the pattern." She held it out again, spread wide between her fingers.

"It's part of a dance," she said. "The—"

"It is the eighth *menfri'at* module," Captain Cho said suddenly. "Yes, I do see it, now—and you are correct. There is—not an error, I think, but rather a questionable variation in that transition phrase. It does not seem . . . entirely at ease with the intent of the next statement."

"That's it!" Theo exclaimed. "I put in an extra stitch—a kink. But if I smooth that out, then the rest of the line will play out awfully . . . fast."

"Indeed," Cho said softly. "The eighth module teaches us commitment to purpose. Have we come so far, only to falter? Surely not." She extended a finger and traced the kinked line. "It is the final meshing of commitment and skill which produces this speed of which you speak. Where there is certainty, there is no need to hesitate."

Theo nodded, thinking about the *Suwello—menfri'at*. It was true that the modules she had been learning from Win Ton produced a statement of—of expertise, something like—how strange! She paused, staring down at the lacework in her hands, seeing Father's Look inside her head.

"Theo?" Captain Cho murmured. "Is there something amiss?"

She shook herself, and looked up with a grin. "No, I just—made a connection, I guess you'd say." She chuckled. "Kamele says that a true scholar never stops learning, not that I'm a true scholar, really..." She looked down again and shook her head. *Well, she thought, she'd just have to pick out the kinked bit. That wouldn't be so bad, really...*

"Was it your mother who taught you this lace-making?" Cho asked.

Theo shook her head. "No, that was Fa— Professor Kiladi." She glanced up beneath her lashes at her companion. "He was Kamele's *onagrata* for—well, for all my life, really. When I was a littlie, I had some *excess energy issues*—that's what the school report said. And...Professor Kiladi, he showed me how making lace could help me...stop fizzing, sort of, and think."

"He seems a wise person, Professor Kiladi."

There was an emphasis on Father's name that drew Theo's gaze upward.

"Do you know him?" she asked. Cho was the sort of person that Father would find *interesting*, she thought. "He's very famous in his field—cultural genetics. Students come from all over the galaxy to study with him."

"A great teacher spans worlds," Cho said; it sounded like she was quoting something. "Alas, I doubt that I have met him, though it would surely be an honor. It is merely the name—quite an *old* name—which caught my ear."

"It is? I didn't know that." The unpicking wasn't being easy. Theo chewed her lip. "I guess it never came up," she said slowly. "Kamele did say that his...family had a call on him, even though he's been away all this time—studying, you know, and then teaching."

"Indeed, one's clan does have a call upon one, down the whole length of one's life. Those of us who are fortunate—among whom I count myself—find the burden easy to bear. Others, of course..." She let the sentence drift off, watching Theo slowly unravel her handwork.

"Who is it," she asked softly, "who is teaching you *menfri'at*?"

"Win Ton—and sometimes Phobai," Theo answered. There! She'd worked back past the kink. Now, she could do it right. She looked up to find Captain Cho watching her, as if she expected a fuller answer.

"It is pilot lore, of a kind, did they tell you that?"

Theo frowned, puzzled. "Well, but I'd already been taught the first four modules. Win Ton... thought I should learn more, if I knew that much."

"Ah. And Pilot Murchinson?"

Theo blinked, then remembered the name stitched on the left breast of Phobai's uniform.

"She says that I knew just enough to be a danger, but not enough to be dangerous."

Captain Cho laughed. "Indeed! Practical to the core, Pilot Murchinson, and a treasure for all of it!" There was a small pause, then, "Do you not agree, Trainee yo'Vala?"

Theo looked up as Win Ton approached their sofa, his hands moving in those purposeful gestures, his eyes on the captain's face.

"Indeed, Pilot Phobai is a marvel and a wonder," he said. "Good shift to you, Theo. I pray you will excuse my lateness."

"I've had good company," she said, smiling up at him. "And I was early." Captain Cho moved her hand, perhaps an answer to whatever Win Ton had told her.

"I wish someone would teach me that," Theo said, and felt her face heat. She was pretty sure that she wasn't supposed to notice—

Win Ton looked to Cho, who sighed even as she rose.

"I will discuss it with your mother," she said. "If you will excuse me, young Theo, I require the attention of my apprentice—briefly, so I swear!"

Cho swept her hand out—sternly, Theo thought. Apparently Win Ton thought so, too, because his mouth went straight like it did when he was being extra serious. He bowed slightly, and followed his captain away.

At first glance, it seemed that the discussion between Captain Cho and Win Ton was mannerly and relaxed. They sat together on the red sofa, at their ease against the pillows, chatting casually.

Their hands—that was something else again.

Fingers danced with—energy. Maybe, Theo thought, watching out of the side of her eye—maybe even anger. And there was more than one meaningful glance in her direction. Theo sighed. She'd begun to form the opinion that Cho *liked* her, but—was the captain angry that Win Ton was spending so much of his time with her?

Not that everything in the universe was about her, of course, as Kamele and Father were quick to assure her, in their variously annoying ways, whenever she began taking things "too personally." In their opinions.

The lace was relaxing, and after awhile she settled into the pattern quite nicely, still with the odd glance toward the side. In the front of the room the quartet had bowed, nodded, and placed their instruments on stands. She hadn't heard if they were finished or merely taking a break, her attention having been toward the lace first and Cho and her assistant second, barely leaving room for...ah, here he came now.

"Did I get you in trouble, Win Ton?"

She'd surprised him; his eyes widened just a bit.

"Captain Cho wasn't happy," she ventured...

He glanced aside, but Cho was already on her way out of the lounge, gray head held high. Win Ton sighed, and looked back to her, moving his hand, carefully, toward the sofa.

"May I at least sit before we begin interrogations?"

She *had* gotten him in trouble. Theo bit her lip and patted the cushion beside her, courteously folding her work.

Win Ton extended his hand. "May I see? My captain would have me understand that this work of yours is something out of the common way."

"This?" She laughed and unfolded the piece, stretching it on her fingers so they could both see it. Now, she thought, pleased, it looked *right*.

Like Cho before him, Win Ton leaned close to inspect the lace, then leaned back against the cushion.

"I see—the eighth module, plain as plain. Do you often...record things thus?"

"Sometimes," she said. "It helps me to really understand spatial things—my fingers are smarter than I am!"

She'd meant it for a joke, but Win Ton didn't laugh. He only nodded and looked serious.

"Of this other thing, and insofar as it concerns you, Theo Waitley, yes, my captain is unhappy with me. I fear that I must offer you an apology, for I was full of my own enthusiasms, and yours, and did not think to ask Kamele Waitley if her daughter might take part in bowli ball. I barely told *you* that we would be doing more than some light and fashionable dance. My captain reminds me that bowli ball is not considered fashionable in many quarters, and that those who play bowli ball are not always regarded as fit company. Too, and as you know, from time to time one might take abrasions, bruises or worse away from a match."

Having taken some bruises herself, not to mention picking up a little floor-burn on her elbows—none which had been major enough to report to Kamele—Theo nodded.

"Yes." Win Ton sighed once more. "As my captain now requires me to inform your mother of this recreation that we have been sharing, and its peculiar dangers, it may be that I will get *you* in . . . trouble."

Theo thought about that. "So—you're sorry?"

Win Ton failed to stifle his laughter.

"May I ask that you not volunteer this to your mother or to my captain?"

"Volunteer what?"

"What I am about to say."

"That depends on if it passes muster, huh?"

He snorted.

"Yes. But then to the point. I *am sorry* that I acted without first requesting clearance from your mother. I am very pleased that you have been able to participate in our games."

Theo smiled, relieved. "I'm glad—oh!" Relief turned to dismay. "Does Captain Cho say that we can't play bowli ball any more?"

Win Ton reached out and put his hand on her knee, his face serious.

"That is for your mother to say, is it not?"

Of course it was for Kamele to say, Theo thought grumpily; mothers had the right to make those decisions for their *minor children*.

"So fierce a glare, Sweet Mystery! What are you thinking, I wonder?"

She looked up at him. "I was thinking I can't wait to be grown up so nobody else has the right to make my decisions for me," she said.

Win Ton laughed, and came to his feet, stretching, the scrape on his left wrist from a particularly vigorous retrieval during their last match almost glowing.

"As my captain is clear on the point that my mission is not one brooking much delay, I wonder if you know where we, or at least I, may find Kamele Waitley at this hour?"

· · · ·✴· · · ·

She was, Kamele thought, coming to value Professor Emeritus Vaughn Crowley. He had a sharp eye, a sharper ear, and an intellect keen enough to parse those things he observed. That he brought his concerns regarding Chair Hafley's timetable for the literature search to Kamele, ought, she thought, flatter her. Instead, it only made the knot in her stomach tighter. There had-been a dangerous moment when she thought to confide in him, to reveal that Hafley believed her bought. The moment passed, and Crowley left their meeting unenlightened as to Kamele's double role—which was, doubtless, wisdom.

The encounter had left her shaken and with an appreciation of the gravity of her undertaking. Deceit was *hard*, and yet here was Hafley, scheming to deceive the administration and faculty of Delgado University, and seeming none the worse for the subterfuge.

*You're too honest,* she told herself, as the intersection with their "home" hallway approached. *Surely honesty was a virtue in a scholar? It was what she had always believed.* But, there, Hafley wasn't renowned as a scholar, was she?

She rounded the corner, careful to stay close to edge in case of traffic, and there, tapping on the door to their stateroom was Theo, Win Ton yo'Vala standing quite close behind her.

"Not here, I guess," Theo said, slipping her key out of her pocket. "Let's—"

The knot in Kamele's stomach tightened more, making her regret the coffee she'd drunk in Crowley's company. She stretched her legs. Win Ton looked up, put his hand on Theo's sleeve...

"Are you looking for me, Daughter?" Kamele asked.

# TWENTY-FIVE

. . . . . . . . . . . . . . . . . . . . . . .

*Number Twelve Leafydale Place*
*Greensward-by-Efraim*
*Delgado*

A WARM BREEZE WANDERED THE GARDEN, STROKING the new leaves with fingers full of promise. Overhead, the stars stretched in a glittering tapestry, made finite by the spill of light from Efraim and the Wall.

Jen Sar Kiladi reclined upon a bench that would later in the season be hidden by a fragrant tumble of westaria vines; one soft-shoed foot on the stone seat, one braced against the ground. His head was on the cold arm rest; and his eyes on the stars. His thoughts, however, were elsewhere.

*Theo was not the target,* Aelliana said, her voice quiet inside his head.

"I consider it unlikely. What we must consider is if *Kamele* is the target."

There was silence for a time, save for the flirtatious rustling of the leaves. He did not have the sense that she had withdrawn, however; merely that she was considering the matter. As he was.

*No,* she said eventually. *It would require conjoined efforts from Housing and Info Systems—and how yet would they know which room she would choose as her own? There are too many hands, and too much left to chance.*

"Chance," he murmured. "Are they so slovenly, do you think, Aelliana? Or are they—" He stopped and sat up so suddenly last season's vines clattered around him.

*What is it?*

"What if it is not sloven chance, but bright cunning? Recall that Technician Singh told us 'old wire' was woven all through the elder apartments. Why confine the Serpent to one apartment?"

*If, indeed, it could be confined.*

"Precisely."

*But how to prove it?*

He smiled. "We ask an expert, of course."

· · · ✳ · · ·

"You needn't wonder if I'm in, Theo," Kamele said sharply. "I've just returned from a meeting."

*Right,* Theo thought, *another meeting.* And not a good one, either, judging by her mother's tone and the set of her shoulders. Kamele being in a bad mood wasn't going to make Win Ton's apology any easier, but it was obviously too late to go away and come back later.

Kamele looked past her, pointedly.

"Trainee yo'Vala, how good of you to escort Theo."

The words were polite, but spoken in that too-sharp tone. Chair Hafley, Theo thought, must've been at the meeting. Maybe Clyburn, too. Out of the side of her eye, she saw Win Ton bow, slow, as if he wanted to convey some special meaning.

"Professor Waitley, I enjoy Theo's company, and... appreciate her kindness in permitting me to attend her—your pardon!"

The last phrase held a note of surprised excitement. Theo turned, her eye following his, but—really, there was nothing to see except the seam where the stateroom door sealed against the floor. Or—

Win Ton went to one knee, his hand going inside his jacket.

"Please," he said, with a glance up to her face; "mark where this goes, if it escapes me."

He produced a clear tubular container, thumbed the lid off as it came into view.

"What do you have?"

Theo jumped. Kamele was at her side, peering with her at the edge of the door. Win Ton's back and head were mostly in their way but there was something brownish, very nearly the colors of the floor, moving—scuttling—up the frame...

With a practiced air, Win Ton suddenly flicked at the scuttling something with the lid and pressed it down on the tube.

"I am not certain what I have, Professor Waitley," he said, rising easily to his feet. "Here."

He showed them the tube: within was an insect... or maybe not.

"If you see any more of these, would you please point them out?"

Theo frowned, staring at the thing in the tube. "It doesn't look quite right, does it? I've seen lots of bugs but this one . . . it isn't really an ant, or a beetle." She touched the tube gently. "It looks hurt or something."

Kamele leaned in, her shoulder against Theo's, looking closely at the tube.

"It also seems to be changing color," she commented, and at least she didn't sound snappish any more.

Win Ton glanced at the tube with its transforming burden, and inclined his head.

"Perhaps," he said softly, "we should take it out of the hall. Theo, do you see any more?"

She looked around the door seal, to the ceiling, along the edging that ran the length of the hall . . .

"I don't see any," she said, "but I don't think I would've seen that one. You've got quick eyes!"

"As you do," he returned. "And now that you have seen one, you will know what you are looking at, if you should see another."

Kamele approached the door, key out, and paused a moment to do her own visual check.

"It seems that it was acting alone," she said ironically.

"Good," Win Ton answered seriously.

Kamele used her key, and waved them into the stateroom.


"Should we report an infestation to the ship?" Kamele asked, staring at the tube, "Or does that require multiple sightings?"

Win Ton glanced away from tube, and looked directly into her face.

"If I had found this elsewhere, simply sitting or walking randomly on a wall or table . . . it might have been a curiosity. I would still likely have . . . taken it for a specimen, since they are rarely seen. However, finding it . . . working, as indeed it may still be working, I am made far more curious. An infestation . . . that would be an extreme. As to reporting it—"

He held the tube out to her.

"Look closely, Professor Waitley. Theo has very good reactions. Very good."

*Amazing Theo*, Kamele thought as she received the tube, which was lighter than she'd expected. She held it up to her face.

The . . . insect was about the length of a finger joint, and it was testing the tube's seal. Thwarted, it turned and . . . ran! . . . toward the opposite side. Stopped precipitously by the end of the tube, the insect tried to climb the slippery stuff . . .

"It appears to be autonomous action, does it not?" Win Ton's voice was so soft that it barely pierced her attention mist. "For all we know it is recording, what we say, or what it sees of us. Or it may need to establish a location before it can transmit."

She looked up at him. "You're saying this is a construct? A . . ." She groped for the proper word—"A *spying device*?"

"So it would seem to me. I will show it to my captain and gain the benefit of her knowledge of such things. In the meanwhile, perhaps we should let it rest." He reached into his jacket again and withdrew a small bag. It shimmered as he flicked it open, as if it had silver woven among the threads.

"What're you carrying in there," Theo asked, "a laboratory?"

Win Ton laughed gently as he slipped the tube into the bag and sealed it.

"I am carrying a sampling kit, Sweet Theo, which

I am required to do at all times by my captain, since I failed to carry one when I should have on another occasion. I am also carrying this..." He tucked the tube away, produced a bowli ball, and handed to Theo, "...which we shall wish to discuss shortly, and some ration bars, and candy, which I always do."

"Why," Kamele said slowly, "would it be *here*?"

"Maybe it got lost," Theo said.

"Perhaps it did, as Theo suggests, become lost," Win Ton answered seriously. "Or perhaps it was meant to be here. It may, after all, be a ship's tool, though if that were so, we must surely have seen others."

"Well." Kamele sighed. "I'll be interested in learning what you find out about it."

He bowed. "Certainly."

Kamele took a deep breath and smiled at the two of them. "As fascinating as this episode has been, I gather that it was not the reason I am afforded a visit to my stateroom."

"No, ma'am, it is not," the Liaden agreed, bowing again. "My captain instructs me that I should...be offering apologies." He glanced at Theo, a friendly, even a warm glance.

Kamele felt her stomach tighten all over again, and held onto her smile.

"In that case," she said brightly, "perhaps we should sit down."

. . . ∗ . . .

*Do you think it will lie?* Aelliana asked.

"Perhaps it will," he answered, pouring a glass of wine. "Certainly, it has demonstrated some craft. We shall see."

# TWENTY-SIX

· · · · · · · · · · · · · · · · · · · · · ·

Vashtara
*Mauve Level*
*Stateroom*

KAMELE SAT OVER *THERE* IN THE BIG CHAIR, WHILE
Theo and Win Ton sat together over *here,* on the
sofa. The feeling that she was a guest in her own
stateroom warred with the feeling that she and
Win Ton were on one team and Kamele was on
an opposing team. Which was just silly, Theo told
herself, fidgeting with the bowli ball. It rolled from
one hand to the other, unsteadily, its erratic motion
drawing her mother's eye.

Cheeks hot, Theo brought the ball under control, pressing it firmly onto her thigh. The internals
vibrated against her restraining palm, like Coyster,
purring. Theo blinked.

Coyster would have taken just this moment to
stretch and yawn before curling around in her lap.
She took a breath, pressing harder on the ball, feeling the vibration in her bones. There. She'd hold

319

the ball like it was Coyster. That would make her feel . . . less strange.

Win Ton cleared his throat. "Professor Waitley," he said formally, "I wish to make known to you the certain activities that Theo and I have enjoyed together." He paused, like he did when he was trying to find an exact match between the Liaden word he knew and the Terran word that—usually—didn't exist.

Kamele's mouth straightened slightly, which meant that she was concerned, but trying not to interrupt.

Win Ton's pause was too long for her though, and she leaned forward—carefully, Theo thought, her fingers pressed tightly together.

"Could you continue? You have my attention."

Seated as he was, Win Ton bowed.

"Yes," he said; and again, "Yes, of course, Professor. The circumstance . . . my captain has pointed out to me that, according to the customs of her homeworld, Theo has yet to attain her majority. Since I have become accustomed to Theo's company, and to her common sense, my captain feared that I was perhaps presuming . . ."

He paused again, his careful search for words leaving a pause into which Kamele leaned, so alert she seemed to quiver.

"My captain's concern," Win Ton began again—"and mine now that I am acquainted with my error, is that I may have presumed too much about Theo's . . . autonomy."

He paused again, and sent a glance to Theo. Since she wasn't sure what point he was making, and she didn't think she'd fool anybody by trying to look autonomous, she looked down, where the silly ball, rather than the silly cat, sat on her lap. The thought made her want to laugh, and she struggled to stay serious, gripping the ball as if in fact she were wrestling a cantankerous feline.

"Autonomy." Kamele repeated carefully, and she, too, sent a glance at Theo. "Indeed, I've found Theo to be showing distinct signs of autonomy, not to say levity."

Theo looked up, mirth startled away. Kamele waved a careless hand in her direction.

"Please," she said to Win Ton, "let's not permit Theo's mirth or her toy to interfere with your disclosure."

*This isn't good,* Theo thought rapidly. It was never a good sign when Kamele started talking like Father.

"In fact, "Win Ton answered slowly, "My . . . disclosure—an excellent usage, which I shall remember!—my disclosure is very nearly *about* Theo's toy."

Abruptly, he stood, surprising Theo and, judging by the way she sat straight up, surprising Kamele, too.

"As you know, we conquered the dance machine on our first attempt. Theo has a—a very mature approach to the dance, intuitive, one may say. That she was . . . amazed to discover herself so very apt a dancer was enlightening. Self-discovery is a good thing."

"Self-discovery is often a good thing," Kamele said after a moment. She glanced at Theo, who tried to keep her face calm. It wasn't comfortable being talked about like she wasn't there. She looked at Win Ton in order to avoid her mother's gaze.

"After our run, my captain forbade us to dance further at the Arcade, and, truly, the machine is so easily beaten that we would very soon have lost patience with it. However, there was still the question of energy, and exercise and, and comradeship. I therefore located several convivial acquaintances on-board, and we discovered an opportunity to continue with the theme of . . . mature self-discovery. I will also say enjoyment of discovery, for Theo so enjoys a challenge."

Theo felt her shoulders relaxing and realized that she was petting the bowli ball, in small, quiet motions. Her mother glanced at her again, and this time Theo met her eye.

"So," Kamele said to Win Ton, though she continued to look at Theo. "You arranged for a . . . mature challenge for Theo."

Win Ton bowed lightly, danced one pace toward the door, one pace back.

"Yes, exactly!" he exclaimed. "The pilots, you must understand, were known to me. We found a private room, and—Theo is such a joy to challenge. I knew all this, but in my enthusiasm, I fear that I did not fully explain to Theo what we would be about, nor did I ask your permission beforehand . . ."

Kamele leaned slowly back into her chair, her hands finding each other, her fingers locking together, interleaved. What scared Theo was that Kamele's face was nearly blank, and she was staring at her hands rather than at either of them.

"I see," Kamele said quietly, but Win Ton was now following his course with some vigor, pacing energetically in the small space, and using his hands for emphasis.

"And thus, with a room, and partners, and a willing novice, I'm afraid we introduced Theo to a game many never play, a game many lack the urges and reflexes for. Knowing how physically apt Theo is, it never occurred to me that I ought to ask permission from her parent for her to play bowli ball. So I ask, Professor Waitley, that you please hold Theo blameless, and lay it all to me . . . ."

Theo saw her mother's face go from blank to . . . confused.

"Wait," she said; "if you please. I understand you to say that you and your friends found a private room so that you might play *bowli ball* with my daughter?"

Theo picked up the not-cat from her lap and tossed it in the air, very gently, to illustrate the phrase "bowli ball."

The motion caught Kamele's eye, so Theo tossed it higher, whereupon the ball took it upon itself to perform a mid-air detour of several hand-widths. Theo snatched it down and wrestled it guiltily to her lap.

"One of these!" she explained.

In wonder, rather than enlightenment, Kamele said, "I see. Bowli ball."

"Yes!" Win Ton said enthusiastically. He plucked the ball away from Theo, carefully cuddling it into quiet before placing it into Kamele's hands.

"It is a complex game, Professor Waitley," he went on with energy; "requiring physical dexterity, concentration, mature thoughtfulness, luck . . . it is a favorite game of pilots because of these things!"

Experimentally, Kamele tossed the ball from hand to hand, barely managing to keep it under her control.

She shook her head, and tried it again, using less energy and across less distance, really just rolling it from one palm to the other.

"What a strange idea," she murmured. "Why should you need permission for Theo to play a simple game of ball?"

"Well, it isn't so simple!" Theo broke in, indignant. "The ball goes every which way and you've got to be ready for it, and you've got to see where it gets thrown and how it's rotating and which spiral is next and..."

Win Ton caught Theo's eye with a motion of his hands, and she subsided, hoping that she hadn't just gotten him in more trouble with Captain Cho.

"Professor, some call bowli ball a game of wit and physics. That might suffice if it were played on a snug lawn among...office workers, let us say. But, with pilots, the game can become quite challenging. This is what I forgot, and why I should have asked your permission for Theo to play."

He paused, glanced at Theo, and faced Kamele directly.

"It is not unknown for those playing the game to accept a broken shoulder in order to return a pass, to sprain an ankle on an interception-and-launch, to... forget harm in order to follow the flow and make the connection. Truly, it is a game for pilots."

Kamele held the ball in one hand, turning it this way and that way, studying it, as if she had never seen something so gaudy and irregular in her life. Suddenly, with no warning, and without preamble, she threw the ball at Theo. Hard.

Theo was already in motion. Her hands leapt up and out, she shifted her balance on the sofa, leaned left to absorb the spin...

*Slap!* was the sound the ball made when she caught it, and it took an effort of will not to continue the momentum and...

Win Ton spun, centering himself, left hand rising, facing forward, right hand coming down, in case...

"Not here," he cautioned, sounding remarkably calm, but by then Theo had the ball stopped, stable, and purring on her knee.

In the big chair, Kamele was laughing, her eyes closed, the bridge of her nose pinched between fore-finger and thumb, while she shook her head.

· · ·✦· · ·

Professor Jen Sar Kiladi leaned discreetly against one of the extremely rare stone walls within the Wall, sipping tea from her own cup. On the wall were metal-lic plaques commemorating events and people from the early days of the Wall; some few pre-dated the Wall itself and had been brought from the remains of the original, burnt-out campus.

The wall being just inside Open Cafeteria Three meant it was one of the few areas where one might expect to see all levels of students and all levels of faculty intermingled. True, faculty did not always take their meals here, most preferring the private lounges, or, by necessity, a corner of their desk, but it was writ-ten that they *ought* to take a meal here every ten-day.

He watched. Quietly, he watched, his cane tucked behind him as if in support—but actually to disguise it from those many eyes he wished not to notice it at the moment.

By tradition, a full professor might sit anywhere. A department head, dean, or Board member could do the same and claim some minor precedence...

That, of course, was the start of hierarchical shenani-gans, for the corollary was that students or those lower on the food chain must not join a table claimed by a full professor without permission or invite. Associate professors and other instructional types had a leg up, of course, and it was considered bad form for a professor to sit at a table with others in order to claim it and so dismiss them to less exalted company.

Jen Sar Kiladi had the honor of being a full professor and, in effect, his own department head. *He* could sit anywhere.

Yet, he stood, out of the way and deliberately unobtrusive, counting tables.

*There* was the north wall. Seventeen tables in from it, three aisles in from the East, there ought to be...why yes. There *was* a ceramic clad column there, and against it, a table being scrupulously cleaned by a member of support staff. How gratifying.

Jen Sar sipped some more tea, waiting.

The schematic provided by the Serpent AI had been fascinating in the extreme, precisely overlaying as it did the "old wire" map Tech Singh had shown him. A simple query to the Concierge netted the names attached to those addresses, which had made for interesting reading over breakfast. Two names in particular caught his fancy, and he whiled away an entire pot of tea over the question of which he ought to attempt first.

In the end, it had come down to expediency. As exhilarating as a contest of wits might prove, yet it might keep him overlong—and he was mindful of his mother's advice to him, given so very long ago: "Do not play with your food, my child. Be careful, take all the time you need to be certain, but when you are at the final stage, act quickly, and never hesitate."

Therefore, and not without a certain pang, he turned his attention to less satisfying quarry.

The chimes of seven-bells-none rang through the hall

and were echoed from countless 'books and mumus, prompting some to snatch up their belongings and rush off, others to change tables, and still others to approach the food line.

Those for whom he had waited so patiently walked past him without noticing, though that was scarcely their blame; he did not, after all, *wish* to be noticed. They had heads bent together, as if communing, a sweet, domestic picture, surely. Wrapt in themselves, they marched on, heedless of any in their path, their goal apparent.

There was a small wait, as staff finished cleaning the table, and relinquished it with a nod very nearly a bow.

That was interesting. Perhaps he'd need to include support staff in his next round of fact-checking. He knew the schedule; identifying an individual ought not be too difficult...

His quarry... piled books and a sweater on the table, thus claiming it for themselves, and wandered away toward the food line.

Professor Kiladi smiled, and moved toward the north wall, using the column as a shield, and handily arrived at the pleasantly private table.

No one being seated, he took the extremely comfortable chair at the head of the table, laying his cane to the left, where it would block the two chairs on that side.

Mug at hand, he was all smiles, and everything that was convivial when they returned, bearing plates and mugs.

"Lystra Mason—well met. And young Roni, of course. What a delightful seating this is! Please, you must join me!"

# TWENTY-SEVEN

. . . . . . . . . . . . . . . . . . . . . . . .

Vashtara
*Mauve Level*
*Stateroom*

THEO WAS ASLEEP IN HER BED, THE NIGHT WALL SHIELD-
ing her from the rest of the room. Kamele was still
curled into in the chair, in theory reviewing her notes;
in fact reviewing the conversation with Win Ton yo'Vala.

*Truly, a pilot's game,* the boy insisted in memory.
And, again, *Theo so enjoys a challenge.* The young
woman described by the young man was a veritable
paragon—bold, courageous, and able. How was she to
find Theo—clumsy, uncertain Theo, with warning notes
in her file—in this changeling?

"Children grow up," she murmured. "They leave
their mothers and become mothers themselves."

And yet, to grow at such an...odd tangent...

*You can't say that you weren't warned,* Kamele
told herself. For, indeed, she had been warned. She
remembered telling Jen Sar that she had chosen to
have a child, in itself a...small...oddity...

\*　　　\*　　　\*

There. It was said. All that was left was to hear what he said in response.

Kamele closed her eyes and sipped coffee. Fresh-roast it was, and fresh-ground from a bag of blue beans Jen Sar had brought back from one of his fishing trips. It was an aromatic blend, whispering hints of chocolate and sweetberries.

"A child in the house is a joy." That was what he said, gently and respectfully. Kamele felt her shoulders relax. She smiled and opened her eyes.

Across the little stone table, Jen Sar's answering smile was slightly awry. He glanced down into his cup as if he wished the coffee were . . . something stronger, then looked into her eyes.

"I am aware," he said, and his voice now was . . . careful, "of the custom on Delgado. One decides for oneself when the time is proper to . . . invest . . . in a child. The custom upon my homeworld is . . . somewhat different. I ask, therefore, if the child . . . partakes of my gene-set."

She frowned at him, and set her cup down. He raised a hand, the twisted silver ring he never took off winking at her from his smallest finger.

"Please. I know that I should not ask—indeed, that I have no right to know! It is, however, not merely vulgar curiosity that moves me to break with custom."

Kamele went cold. Jen Sar leaned forward and put his hand over hers where it lay next to her cup.

"I am beyond clumsy," he said wryly. "Kamele, I'm not ill! Surely there were tests done, certifications made—whoever you chose! But there is something you should know, if you've gotten a child of me."

He tipped his head, face earnest; his hand was warm on hers, his fingers braceleting her wrist, a comfort.

Surely, she thought, there was room here for custom to meet halfway. Jen Sar was an intelligent man, and . . . usually tolerant of Delgado ways. That he asked this of all questions, signaled, she thought, a strong cultural imperative.

Kamele took a breath, opened her mouth to tell him—and closed it, unable to force the words out.

"This is idiotic," she muttered, turning her head to look out over the dusky garden. Her words danced back to her on the little breeze and she gasped, her eyes flashing back to his face. "I didn't mean—" she began . . .

But Jen Sar, as usual, seemed to know exactly what she'd meant.

"The burden of custom is not lightly put aside," he said. "As we have both now demonstrated. Perhaps a simple 'no,' if the child is none of mine?"

That was certainly fair enough. Kamele met his eyes. And said nothing.

"Hah." He smiled, ruefully, she thought. "So, then, the thing that you must know is that . . . those of my Line, as is said on Liad—siblings, cousins, parents—tend to have . . . very quick physical reflexes. Many, indeed, become star-pilots. Since many of us also have a . . . certain facility . . . in mathematics, and as Liad depends upon its trade, this is not too odd a life-path."

He paused, watching her face. Kamele nodded to show she was following him, and after a moment he continued.

"Here on Delgado, where the trade is in knowledge, there are few pilots, and, perhaps, very little understanding of those whose genetic heritage is predisposed toward quickness."

She frowned slightly. "My daughter wouldn't *have* to be a pilot, after all..."

"Indeed she would not," he soothed her. "However, until she has grown into her body and learned to... control...her reflexes, she may produce some...unexpected results." He shook his head. "I do not wish you to be uninformed—or unprepared. So I must confess that the raising of a child who partakes of these genes is...sometimes a challenge to those who are themselves very much of the Line."

Kamele smiled. "I think adults always find children a challenge," she said. "The more so with our own children."

On the chair in the stateroom of a starship, Kamele stirred, and ran her fingers through her hair. *Fairly warned,* she thought again; *who could blame Jen Sar, if she had been too ignorant to understand what he said?* And truly, she could have chosen another donor. It was on her head, that she had wanted *his* child; a whimsy that Ella had done her best to talk her out of.

From behind the night wall came a mutter and rustle of covers. Kamele raised her head, but Theo subsided, perhaps to dream of bowli ball, or of pilots.

# TWENTY-EIGHT

. . . . . . . . . . . . . . . . . . . . . . . . . . .

Vashtara
*Dining Hall Lobby*

HE FEARED HIS REPUTATION WOULD NEVER MAKE A recover.

*Well,* Aelliana said tartly, *if you will make it a habit to meet questionable people in public...*

"Precisely! Though I contend it a habit we both treasure of old."

*I knew no questionable people until I met you.*

"Can that be true? But, fear not! Today is the day that I redeem myself in your eyes."

*Will she tell you?*

"One can only hope. I fear that Lystra has concluded that my interest lies in Roni's direction, so you see, the stakes are high!"

Inside his head, Aelliana laughed.

. . . * . . .

It had become their custom to gather in the antechamber of the dining room. From there, they would claim a table for themselves and talk over the events of the day, reaffirming themselves as colleagues and a team.

Quite often, Chair Hafley and her *onagrata* were late to the gathering, rushing in breathless from casino, shopping, or other pleasurable activity. It seemed that the Chair considered the journey something of a honey-trip for herself and Clyburn; it was seldom that he was not sporting some new, and often provocative, costume, or an added bit of jewel-glitter to some portion of his person.

Kamele raised a hand to cover her yawn. Her sleep had been . . . unsettled of late; it seemed the more time that wore on without a sign from Hafley that *now* was the hour in which she demanded Kamele's promised support, the more uneasily that false promise sat upon her heart. Yet, what else could she have done? If, as she believed, Hafley was but part of some . . . conspiracy to discredit Delgado University, then surely Kamele needed to be in her confidence? If only the woman would say more! But, no, she apparently pursued her pleasures without the least thought of future perfidies.

And there was doubtless, Kamele thought wearily, a lesson to be learned there.

Another yawn; and a sense of someone at her elbow. She turned, and a young woman in the livery of the ship's wait staff smiled at her.

"A cup of coffee while you wait for the rest of your party, Professor?" she asked.

Kamele returned the smile and nodded.

"A cup of coffee would be most welcome, thank you," she said, and the girl glided away to make it so.

Watching her go, Kamele shook her head. It was,

she thought, far too easy to become accustomed to being served. Perhaps on Melchiza they would be allowed to lift a hand to help themselves. Otherwise, they would arrive home quite ruined.

The coffee arrived; she received it, and sipped, sighing in pleasure.

Eyes narrowed, she sipped again, just as Professors Crowley and Able rounded the corner. They nodded as they joined her, Professor Able waving the server over and bespeaking two more cups of coffee.

"I may be ruined for staff-room coffee," Crowley said, receiving his cup. "One would think that a man of my years would be above these petty pleasures."

Their weeks together having given her a fine understanding of Crowley's humor, Kamele smiled at him.

"It is very good coffee," she answered. "And as scholars are we not enjoined to open ourselves to experience and study the moment?"

"Indeed, an excellent point! A moment, if you will; I must study my cup."

He proceeded to sample his beverage.

"Is Theo not with you this evening?" Professor Able asked.

"She and Win Ton yo'Vala are attending the buffet and seminar offered by the Visitors' League."

"There's a well-mannered lad," Able said. "Not a scholar, of course, but thoughtful, in his way. So *kind* of your daughter, Kamele, to escort him to these broadening events."

Professor Able had an edge to her, and a circumspect way of prying into matters that did not concern her that harked back to an earlier day. Kamele smiled and replied only that she felt that Win Ton was a perfectly conformable young man, and well-supervised by his captain.

"It may be that the Visitors' League will provide Theo with the chance to mingle with other students of her own age." That was Crowley, looking up from his cup. "They seek, so the senior advisor I spoke with over lunch assured me, to be both inclusive and diverse. They also seek recruits, which the advisor did not say, but which was implicit in her description of the League and its purpose."

"What is its purpose?" Able wondered, holding her cup daintily on the tips of her fingers.

"Scholarship, of a sort, though the method is unique. The group arrives upon a planet—with a connection in place, of course—and explores that world. Group membership is drawn from worlds previously visited. The goal, as much as there is one, is to visit or be resident on all worlds which speak or understand Terran, and which have humanity in common. I am told that this particular tour has been on-going for seventeen Standards, and will on its twentieth anniversary quadricate."

"Quadricate?" Kamele asked, suspecting one of his more obscure jokes.

Crowley gave her a nod, as if rewarding her percipience. "Yes, a play on the inner Terran. What it means is that the group will split teachers, advisors and travelers into four, staying most of a Standard on the host planet while each develops plans and destinations of their own."

"Surely, they must settle sometime," Able commented.

"Some do—many do, so my luncheon companion said. It is expected that they will lose and add members, though it is also true that some stay with the group for many years, first as students, and then as advisors."

"An odd scholarship," Able said, and looked again to Kamele. "I don't wish to pry into a mother's domain, but I wonder if you have considered what Theo will be about on Melchiza. Our work is plain before us, but it seems as if there will be very little to occupy her, beyond her school work. While opportunity for study is of course always welcome, it often appears less so to the young—and especially after a journey so crowded with excitement."

"There is a Transit School," Kamele said, keeping her voice moderate. As she had said, this was none of Able's business. On the other hand, the two elder members of the forensic team had taken to regarding Theo somewhat in the light of a granddaughter, and were correspondingly free with their advice to Theo's mother.

A familiar racket brought her head up as Chair Hafley and her *onagrata* bustled importantly into the area. Kamele blinked. As was his habit, Clyburn was dressed to display his winsome figure—in fact, this evening's costume of sleeveless black shirt so tight his pectoral muscles were clearly defined, and billowing sheer pantaloons cuffed tight at the ankles, was rather restrained. Chair Hafley, who usually contented herself with sensible coveralls, was wearing an iridescent red sweater cut low over her bosom and a bright blue skirt that brushed the deck plates.

"So," Able said, turning away from this onrushing spectacle. "You'll be contacting the Transit School for Theo?"

"Why, there's no reason for her to do so!" Hafley cried, pausing in her rush toward the dining room. "Kamele, you must allow Clyburn to arrange everything for Theo; his mother is well-placed in Administration and has many contacts in the Transit School."

Kamele blinked, looking from Hafley to Clyburn. Clyburn smirked and bowed his shining head. "I would be pleased to be of service, Kamele," he said, actually sounding sincere.

"Thank you, Clyburn," she said, trying to match sincerity with sincerity. "But as I was just about to say to Professor Able, I've already taken care of Theo's registration." She turned to Able. "It is a boarding school, which Theo objects to, but, as you say, our team's hours may be long and irregular."

"It is best for young scholars to have regularity in their studies and their sleep," Crowley said, too pointedly, in Kamele's opinion. "Sub-chair Waitley has looked ahead and planned for the best outcome—for everyone."

"Well . . ." Hafley glanced at Clyburn, as if she expected him to be disappointed by not being obligated to register someone else's daughter for school. "That seems well in hand," the Chair finished, and nodded briskly.

"If the assembled scholarly lights will excuse us, we are invited to dine with the captain! Come, Clyburn." She moved off, her skirt rustling against the floor, her *onagrata* one step behind her.

Kamele, Able, and Crowley turned as one to watch them go.

Hafley spoke briefly to the room manager, who bowed, and waved them into the dining room.

It was . . . some moments before Kamele caught her breath. The rudeness of this woman! The—

"Well." She looked to her colleagues. "If you are so

minded, I know an unhurried and secluded restaurant where we might find a pleasant meal."

"That sounds," said Crowley, "like an excellent plan."

Able, her lips tight, merely nodded.

. . . . . ⁂ . . . .

Over the last while, the threesome who met for breakfast at the table by the column, had generated . . . curiosity. Certainly, it was not, viewed with certain facts in mind, an unlikely threesome: the mother, her nubile and soon to be available daughter, the elderly professor recently put aside, in pursuit of—ah, but there the curious were doubtless divided, though the mother believed she knew his mind.

"Roni, fetch Professor Kiladi some of those maize buttons he likes so much," the mother instructed her daughter. She glanced to the elderly professor.

"Maize buttons will be very welcome," he said with a smile, "and perhaps some cheddar spread, or creamily, with them."

The daughter had taken to wearing other than the usual school coveralls to their breakfasts. A charitable observer might allow them to be "special outfits." He supposed that he ought to feel honored, that his gray hairs inspired such flights of . . . creativity. Instead, he worried that the child would contract a chill. Then, too, there was the subject of . . . subtlety—but where was she to learn that merely exposing skin did not make one interesting? Certainly not from her mother, nor, to judge from the glances of the would-be gallants about the room, from her peer-group.

Roni stood, to all eyes eager to serve, and bowed, allowing him an unimpeded, if blessedly brief glimpse of her assets. Turning, she walked toward the line, her progress somewhat slowed by the hip motion she was attempting to perfect.

Jen Sar, his eyes on the retreating form, sighed. Not a dancer, that child.

Lystra heard the sigh, as he had meant her to, and leaned close, placing a daring hand upon his sleeve.

"Come, now, Jen Sar, admit that you don't meet us here only to *look* at my Roni."

Well, and that was bold enough to terrify. He lifted an eyebrow.

"A man of my years is surely allowed the privilege of admiring the scenery?"

"Indeed he is!" Lystra said warmly, and leaned back in her chair, a coy smile at the corner of her mouth. "One must be so careful," she said, picking up her coffee cup, "when one has charge of a girl so *eager* for her *Gigneri*. The first-pair is so very important, don't you think so, Jen Sar?"

"I agree. Indeed, I have long deplored the custom of first-pairing couples near in age. It may seem a kindness, I allow, but in truth it becomes at best a comedy of error, and at worst does honest damage. An older, experienced partner, who is able to teach and to be patient; that is the best choice for a first pairing. Especially if, as you say, the girl is eager for adulthood."

She laughed and leaned toward him slightly. "Now, I'll make a confession to you," she said playfully. "My mother was very much of your mind with regard to the first-pair, and I was, like Roni, very eager to embrace adulthood. There was a boy in my form . . . but she would have none of it! Before the event, I was—a little—disappointed, but after! Ah, then I saw mother's wisdom for what it was."

"I am gratified to find my opinion validated," he said, and inclined his head. "In fact, Lystra, you do stand guardian over that which interests me nearly. Perhaps we might speak . . . alone . . . after breakfast."

She smiled again. "Yes, let's do that," she said, and here came the eager child herself, seeming in imminent danger of losing the laden tray to the floor.

"Ah," he said, leaning forward to clear a place on the table, and lending a guiding hand to its safe descent. "My thanks, Roni. Please, you must both partake."

# TWENTY-NINE

. . . . . . . . . . . . . . . . . . . . . . . .

Vashtara
*Atrium Lounge*

CHO SIG'RADIA ARRIVED WITH DESSERT, A CIRCUMSTANCE that both failed to surprise, and pleased, Kamele. She had grown used to the Liaden woman's penchant for simply appearing, and, besides, she was good company.

Professor Crowley appeared to share this opinion. He welcomed Cho cheerfully, and pushed over to make room for her on the bench next to him.

"My thanks," she said, with a gentle bow and a smile. She seated herself, and laughed when their server appeared with a pot of tea.

"I come here too often, I see," she said. "But it is so pleasant an aspect." She poured tea, and looked across the table to Kamele.

"In fact, I know that we share a fondness for this venue, and so I came here, hoping to find you."

Kamele smiled. "It's been taken care of," she said, guessing the other's intent—"and very eloquently."

"So he has also reported," Cho said. "But it was

another, though closely related, reason that I sought you out. To find the others of the search team—that is fortuitous, for I have something also to say to all, if you will grant me time."

She was assured by Crowley—who must, Kamele thought, surely be smitten—that their time was hers.

"A generous gift, of which I am in no wise worthy." Cho sipped her tea, put the cup down and curled her hands 'round it. Leaning forward slightly, she caught Kamele's eye.

"The captain of this vessel sees an opportunity to permit a reserve officer to train by offering to train Win Ton. It is perhaps not necessary to say that this is an offer which . . . ought not to be turned down, and which will, indeed, benefit my charge a great deal." She inclined her head, very slightly. "These new duties will regrettably place him on a divergent shift, and severely curtail his time at liberty for the remainder of our voyage. I regret the disappointment that the loss of his companionship must cause your daughter, and I would make amends."

"There's no reason, surely, to make amends?" Kamele said. "It sounds a wonderful opportunity for Win Ton and I'm sure Theo will be happy for him."

"Well she might be, for she is a generous child. However, I feel that we come into a situation of precarious Balance, and I would not have such a thing between us. I therefore ask if you would allow me to teach Theo the rudiments of finger-talk. She was quick enough to spot Win Ton conversing thus with those other pilots whom she has met in his company, and on the occasion of our last meeting expressed a desire to learn the language. It is something that I will gladly teach her, with your agreement."

"But, surely, your own work . . ."

Cho moved a hand; if her fingers conveyed anything other than a casual dismissal of her own work, Kamele could not read it.

"It is a minor thing. I will be joining Win Ton on the altered shift, but I have the leisure of making my day a bit longer. I may, therefore, enjoy an evening cup of tea while Theo breaks her fast. Thus, she will wake eager with study before her, and I will have a quiet unwinding before sleep." She tipped her head. "I had taught finger-talk at Scout Academy; it will be . . . comforting to teach it again, and to a willing scholar."

"If you're sure, then—I'm grateful," Kamele said, thinking suddenly of Jen Sar's fluid hand-gestures. If this . . . finger-talk was something known to pilots, perhaps, like bowli ball, it was something that would benefit Theo.

"I am certain—and I insist that it is I who am grateful," Cho said with a smile. She sipped her tea and looked 'round the table.

"Now, for the patient search team, I would say, and say plainly—Melchiza, despite contacts and assurances, is perhaps not such a place as Delgado. There have been changes of late, in government structure, in alliances aggressively sought, and in . . . other matters somewhat worrisome to those whose job it is to worry about such things."

"Have you been . . . endangered on Melchiza?" Able asked.

Cho laughed. "Not I, Scholar. Melchiza values pilot-kind, and if they admire us so much that they seek to keep us with them—well, that is a trap that cannot close." She looked to Kamele, to Crowley, back to Able.

"Understand me, you are accustomed, perhaps, to the watchfulness of those whose mandate is to wish you well—to the oversight of those who hold your safety high. On Melchiza, there is also oversight, but your safety is not by necessity the first interest of the watchers. Be careful, Scholars. Trust no one. Produce a contingency plan, if your contact fails you. Above all, follow the rules—of which there are a number, and which *Vashtara* will shortly make known to you. If someone threatens you, believe them, and act accordingly, without hesitation."

There was a moment of silence at the table, then Crowley laughed.

"You make it sound the veriest frontier!" he said, and raised his hand. "We appreciate your warning, Captain sig'Radia, but you must know—not all of us are native to Delgado. Why, in my student days, I raised some ports so rough, it was a wonder that anyone survived them. We will be watchful."

He glanced 'round the table. Able nodded curtly. Kamele felt it necessary to add something more.

"You're correct, however, that we should make a contingency plan, in case things go awry. I believe that none of us have thought of that, and I appreciate the reminder."

It seemed that Cho hesitated before she inclined her head.

"It is my joy to serve, Scholars," she said quietly, and sipped her tea.

· · · ❖ · · ·

He settled himself in the visitor's chair while Lystra bustled behind the desk, doubtless intending to make him squirm, a little. Such was the pitch of his ardor that he was able to quickly become its master, and look about himself.

Unlike Ella's office, or Kamele's, or, to be perfectly fair, his own, Lystra Mason's office was tidy to the point of painfulness, with scarcely a pin out of place. There were no piles of hard copy, or scatter of infoslips on the desk's gleaming surface. Indeed, there was nothing on the desk at all until Lystra dared to risk its finish by placing her 'book upon it.

Likewise, the walls, which in his office were over-burdened with gene maps, language maps, population dispersal rates, and any number of other items useful to his position, here were perfectly bare, perfectly white. Simple, one might say.

Lystra was settled, her hands folded primly atop the gleaming desk top, eyes sharp and acquisitive.

"Now, Jen Sar," she said crisply, "I think you know that there are certain considerations a mother wishes to see adorn her daughter's *Gigneri*. What are you willing to bring to Roni?" She smiled at him. "While we agree that there's value attending an older man in a first-pair, I think we may also agree that the experience of conducting a new-woman into adulthood might balance that value neatly. You have position, contacts, fame, and I expect that you earn a tidy annual bonus. There's a good deal there to work with, and I'll tell you frankly that I think we may reach an accommodation. I hope, very much, that we'll reach an accommodation. However, I wouldn't want you to think that your position is assured. I have received expressions of interest from several very worthy senior scholars, and a query from the Administration Tower itself."

"Ah." He leaned back in his chair, his hands folded over the top of his cane. "I am afraid that you misunderstand me, Lystra. I have no interest in your daughter's *Gigneri*."

She blinked, momentarily at a stand, then laughed. "You will have your joke, won't you?" she said, gaiety forced. "Come now, Jen Sar, you said yourself that you were interested—"

"I said that you stand guardian over something that interests me nearly," he interrupted, keeping his voice pleasant and equitable. He met her eyes.

"The Serpent AI, Lystra."

She paled, but rallied immediately.

"I don't have any idea what you're talking about."

He shook his head. "That won't do; you know it won't do, and so do I. The best plan—the *simplest* plan, by far—is to give me the name of your contact and pass me up the line. I will immediately cease to be your problem, Roni may continue to widen her circle of admirers, and the future may roll out as it will."

She took a breath. "I hardly understand you, Jen Sar! You seem to be accusing me of conspiring with the Simples!"

He smiled at her, gently, as if she were a backward student who had against even her own expectation produced a correct answer.

"Precisely. That is exactly my point."

"Well, it may be your point, and your fantasy, you and this Serpent, but it has nothing to do—"

"No, please," he interrupted again. "You will only tire yourself, and I will have what I came for in the end. Let us deal as adults—as colleagues. Now, I will give you something, to buy your trust: I know that you have access to a Serpent AI. I asked it for a map of those facilities within the Wall to which it has access and an activities log. You have been . . . quite an avid user, and not all in pursuit of the plan, eh?" He held up his hand and gave her a friendly look. "Who could blame you? Not I. To have so powerful a search tool in hand—well! You see the use to which I put mine."

She remained silent, white to the lips, her hands knotted 'round each other on the glossy desk top.

"Yes, well. I do confess to some other snooping—so indelicate, but what can one expect of a Liaden, who hails not only from outside the Wall, but from well off-planet? Outsiders . . . Quite the opposite of your family, for instance, which has kept firm ties with the Chapelia. It was your mother—or perhaps an aunt?—who sat on the Liaison Committee for thirty years, advancing Simple goals to the Administration."

Lystra licked her lips. "My aunt. But—"

"Forgive me, but did it not seem to you that this plan—the AI, the altering of records, the stealth—did it not seem to you that this was no simple plan? It reeks of complexity! Surely, the Chapelia might wish to burn the library and destroy complexity wholesale— that was a simple and straightforward plan, and if it failed once, who is to say that it must fail twice? But to sow lies and misinformation, that is not simple. It hints, indeed, of plans made by those to whom Delgado—Chapelia, university, scholars and nonacs alike—are but counters in a much larger game. A game that keeps its main board well off-world."

She gaped at him.

"The name of your contact," he prompted gently. "Come, now, Lystra, there is always the chance that I will forget who sent me to her. The memories of old men are notoriously frail."

The silence stretched. Inside his head, he felt Aelliana stir, her interest lying so nearly next to his that he could scarcely tell out her from him.

"Chapelia have no names," Lystra Mason said softly. She looked down as if the task of unknotting her hands required all of her attention. "I will write the symbol for you."

# THIRTY

· · · · · · · · · · ·

Vashtara
*Breakfast All Year*

KAMELE HAD A BREAKFAST MEETING. AN *EARLY* BREAK-
fast meeting. Theo, who had a breakfast meeting of
her own, though hers, she thought crankily, was at a
*normal* hour, did a couple of self-tests on her school
book, then slipped the mem-stick out of her pocket
and slotted it into the stateroom's conneck.

Win Ton's letter came up onto the screen, letters
bright and crisp. She'd answered it, of course, just as
soon as she'd received it, but he hadn't written again.
Which just meant, she'd assured herself, that he was
just as busy as he'd expected to be.

*Dear Sweet Mystery,*

*It appears circumstances and opportunities con-
spire to place us on opposing schedules. It is just
as well; your destination shows it to nearly share
the ship's schedule you are familiar with, which is
probably not an accident. My new schedule will*

*put me in sync with the shift schedules expect-
able when we arrive to retrieve the waiting ship.
Accident or not, this change also puts within grasp
one of my goals, which has been to be Officer in
Charge of a ship so large there need be a lost-
and-found not only for objects but for persons.*

*Do not fear! My Captain promises me I will
be Officer In Charge for no more than a dozen
beats at mid-shift while back-up pilots change
seats and test boards; I feel it likely if they know
I am the one sitting oversight the changeover
will happen in three beats!"*

*I intend to see you before our orbits diverge;
you have helped make what might have been an
ordinary transit into a memorable passage indeed.*

*I remain your humble servant, and, I very
dearly hope, your friend,*

*Win Ton yo'Vala*

Sighing, she pulled the mem-stick from the conneck and tapped random reload. One of the stupid
"How to behave on Melchiza," info-spots popped up
on the vid.

"Remember!" the narrator chirped annoyingly.
"Anyone wearing a blue shirt or a blue arm band may
require you to halt, state your business, produce your
ID, and prove you have sufficient credits in the form
of cash to buy food for yourself for three days. You
may not carry another adult person's ID for them,
and cash on your person will not be considered as
available to another member of your party. Public
displays of affection are forbidden on Melchiza, with
detention and fines for all infractions. All public areas

are subject to monitoring by camera, radar, and visual inspectors; infractions will be dealt with as discovered."

"Yah, yah, yah . . ." she said to the screen, and punched "random" again. They were *days* out from Melchiza yet, and the entertainment bands were flooded with these stupid mercials. She wondered if she should write a new one; certainly, she knew the key points: Don't touch anything or anyone; don't be where you aren't supposed to be; always listen to anything blue; and always carry cash. Maybe Public Communications would pay her, so she could buy some clothes to replace the ones she couldn't wear on Melchiza, because they were blue . . .

She turned her back on the vid, slipping the memstick with Win Ton's letter on in into her pocket. Then she put on her *blue* sweater and left for her meeting with Captain Cho.

. . . . ❖ . . . .

The three of them had formed their own subcommittee, its task to develop a contingency plan. That the group did not include, and its existence was consistently not mentioned to, Chair Hafley was something they did not discuss. *Which means,* Kamele told herself, as she sipped her coffee, *that you are now affiliated with* two *secret organizations.*

"We are agreed, then," Able said, pushing the remains of her fruit platter to one side, where it was immediately whisked away by their efficient waiter. "If Professor Dochayn is unable to deliver what she has promised, we will proceed upon our own recognizance and petition the administration of the Treasure House in the form set forth in this document." She tapped the reader set in the center of the table.

"The procedures set forth are lengthy," Crowley said, "and our time on Melchiza limited. Fortunately, study shows that a good deal of the paperwork portion may be completed ahead of time. I propose to complete as much as can be done, in the ardent hope that we will not be called upon to produce it."

"That's a good plan," Kamele said. "Certainly, the political climate on Melchiza seems . . . stern. We wouldn't want to place Professor Beltaire's colleague in an untenable situation."

"I wonder," Crowley said, his voice more than usually careful, "if we ought not also procure open departure tickets for each of our party."

Kamele straightened, glancing to Able. A shrug was what she received from that party, so she addressed Crowley.

"That would be a significant expense, I think? What would be the justification?"

Crowley glanced down at his empty plate before meeting Kamele's eyes.

"You will recall that I told our charming Captain Cho that I had traveled some rough ports in my youth. Sometimes, regrettably, one is forced to—not to put too fine a point on it—one is forced to run. Sometimes, one is detained beyond the departure time of one's primary transport. I would hope that the authorities on Melchiza, while stern, are not *petty*, but I would not wish to strand one of our party."

Kamele considered him. Something—perhaps it was the utter seriousness of his face—convinced her that this was not theory for Professor Crowley, but something that had happened to him. Or to someone he had traveled with.

*Which would be more terrible*, she wondered, *to be left behind, or to leave a colleague?*

"I'll look into the options and costs," she said. Able nodded without comment.

"Thank you," Crowley said seriously.

· · · ·⚙· · · ·

Breakfast All Year was surprisingly crowded. After the initial rush of popularity, it had slid off everybody's must-do list, and gotten quiet enough to have lessons in.

This morning, or—if you were on Captain Cho's shift, this evening—the place was crowded with merrymakers, making the trip to their usual back table an adventure in dance.

Captain Cho was ahead of her, like she most usually was, seated and with tea to hand.

*Appears me*, Theo motioned even before she caught her tutor's eye; *timely, hungry.*

Cho's fingers flickered, almost too fast to read, though Theo knew the basic signs by now.

*Food appears rapidly, fine usual welcome*, was the response, as near as Theo caught it; *table held against noise rushers; good crew recalls schedule ours! Sit faster!*

The last was a warning as well as a command. A man in yellow tights had darted in from the crowded table to the left, apparently intent upon removing the "extra" chair from under Cho's nose.

Theo lunged, hand out, fingers firm on the chair back.

"I'm sitting there, thanks," she told the man, who gave her a one-sided grin and darted away in search of other quarry.

Cho smiled widely, her fingers saying something Theo couldn't quite read. She felt like she had the emphasis and mood...but...

A loud clapping broke out behind her as she sat, and a large person with a large bottle in her hand and a crowning blob of yellow hair on her head waved the crowd quiet.

"Four down and only fifteen more bars to hit before deadline! Next is Deck Five's Low End, which is opening...right now! Allie, Allie in free!"

There were cheers and hoots and hugs all around, as fully three quarters of the partyers exited in one fell swoop,

Theo's voice said "Geesh!" while her hands indicated *Batch bad noise bad connected head computers, gone is good...*

*Moment,* came the response, *two pilots leave also look.*

Theo glanced up, saw the pair, one wearing a leather jacket and the other in what looked like exercise clothes, mumbling at each other by hand as they reluctantly followed the crowd.

Their fingers were moving, but the signs weren't as clear or as broad as Cho's, leaving Theo more confused than enlightened.

*Big plan better do us us need good long something double roll talky bright skin*

Theo heard Cho make a sound perilously close to a snicker, and her fingers snapped out *query?*

Her tutor tipped her head as if she were congratulating Theo, her fingers forming *out-duty shop talk...* the rest squashed into meaninglessness as a palm came up and out, the signal that they should stop talking.

"Breakfast, mamzelle?" Their waiter this morning was a slender man with quiet eyes. Theo gave her order, out loud, of course, her fingers dancing the words as she spoke them.

"Allow me to counsel you to still your fingers when you speak," Cho said, after they were alone. "There may seem to be no harm in it; indeed, it may at first reinforce learning. However, it may quickly become a . . . difficult habit, and troublesome to break."

Theo guiltily curled her fingers into her palms. "I'm sorry, ma'am."

"Pah! I am a Scout. As such, I study survival in all its faces. Many find that a Scout's level of caution is far beyond what is useful in their own lives. Still, I would be less than a true teacher, did I not advise you thus."

Theo considered that. "We're taught advertency, at school," she said slowly. "Scholars need to be cautious, too."

"Indeed they do," Cho said seriously, pouring more tea into her cup.

Theo's cereal arrived. She smiled at the waiter, and thanked him, and turned her head to watch him bus the table beside them, balancing five cups and an unfinished tray of pastry with effortless grace.

"And so," said Cho suddenly, pulling Theo's eyes to her.

"What have we learned thus far, my student? Aside from the fact that one cannot read hand-talk while in full admiration of a view?"

Cho had her hands wrapped comfortably around her cup. Theo, her face warm, placed her fingers firmly against the table, and answered by voice.

"May I ask a question, first?"

Cho inclined her head.

"That man—our waiter—he's a pilot, isn't he?"

Cho lifted her head, her casual glance at the departing figure sharpening abruptly.

"Indeed," she said finally, "he may be. But what makes you ask?"

Theo shrugged, and sipped her tea, concerned that what she was about to say wasn't really very smart. Even so, there wasn't any way not to answer, now that she'd brought the question up.

"I think I see pilots," she said, meeting Captain Cho's eyes. It sounded as silly as she'd feared, but Cho only looked interested.

"Oh, indeed? Is there anyone else, besides myself?"

"Not that . . . now that he's gone." Theo leaned forward, fingers pressing the table hard. "But, I can look at people walking, or sometimes even standing, and tell if they're pilots. Now that I know what I'm seeing—Win Ton has it, you do, the man who left now . . . the pilots chasing the party . . . the pilots I play bowli ball with."

"Hah!" said Cho, taking a sip. "It," she repeated, and poured more tea into her cup.

Theo forced herself to pick up her spoon and address her breakfast. It was good; soy-oats with apple bits . . .

"It may well be that you are able to see, as you say, 'it,'" Cho said eventually. "Some have eyes that see more than others, after all."

Theo looked up. "But—I couldn't see it before!"

Cho inclined her head.

"I venture to predict that there are very few pilots among your classmates," she said. "And Delgado is not such a world as one sees pilots upon every walkway."

"I guess most of my teachers aren't pilots," Theo agreed, "and there's no piloting school on Delgado—" She looked up, hope sudden and hot—"is there?"

Cho shook her head, emphasizing the denial with a firm finger-spelt, *not*.

Theo sighed, and took a spoonful of her cereal. It tasted a little flat, suddenly. Maybe, she thought, it was getting cold. She pushed it aside and wrapped her hands around her tea cup.

"You asked what I had learned," she said slowly. "Besides the signs themselves, I've learned that hand-talk is . . . fun, but that you can't say everything in it."

"Do you think so, indeed? It is true that hand-talk developed for speed and clarity in . . . radical environments. A survival tool, you see? Still, pilots are inventive, and there are some who discuss philosophy in it, and those who use it to—"

"Philosophy?"

"Assuredly. In this ship's public library archives you may find, in translation or transliteration, a copy of *The Dialogs of the Hospice.* Two rescued pilots were for some years among a sect forbidding writing and speech. They thus held lengthy debates in hand-talk. After a second rescue, this to a civilized world, they transcribed their discussions, verbatim as it were. Do not think that hand-talk is so limited. And, of course, the more used among friends or associates, the more it becomes personal."

Theo thought about that.

"So everyone who hand-talks has their own accent?"

"Yes, that is a good way to see it. Terran pilots will have a different accent from Liaden pilots, and a Scout may bear yet a third accent. However, we may all speak together in an emergency, for the basic signs are held in common."

"And this," Theo asked, striving to reproduce the sign Cho had flashed in the aftermath of the chair rescue. "This means . . . ?"

"Ah!"

Cho repeated the sign. It came with overtones of *extrafine best ready complete perfection,* and a ghostly finger-snap at the very end.

"This is a phrase mostly in use among Scouts. To speak it, we would say *binjali.* Consider it to mean . . . well, it can mean *ready* or *excellent* or *all things are fine and good.*"

"So, that's a Liaden word? *Binjali*?" Theo smiled, liking the feel of the word in her mouth. She tried again to wrap her fingers around it, and found that felt good, too.

"No," Cho said slowly. "Many Liadens will not know this word, which has only accidentally become a Scout word and thus slithered into hand-talk." She smiled. "I had said that pilots are inventive, did I not? Scouts are trebly so—and that may serve you as a warning!"

Theo laughed, her fingers moving, it seemed of their own will.

*Captain,* she signed, *this spaceship voyage binjali!*

# THIRTY-ONE

· · · · · · · · · · · · · · · · · · · ·

Vashtara
*Breakfast All Year*


"...BACK-UP?" AELLIANA INQUIRED. CREDIT WHERE credit was earned, her tone was no more acid than was necessary to carry the point.

"Suggestions?" he countered, slouching into his chair and closing his eyes. "Who shall we risk? Ella, charged with guarding Kamele's back? The Dean of Oriel? The Bursar?"

*Monit Appletorn,* his lifemate stated.

He opened his eyes, staring startled at the ceiling. "What an...*interesting*...suggestion."

· · · ❋ · · ·

She was packed. All of her blue clothes were in a special bag provided by *Vashtara,* which would be stored in a locker on Melchiza Station. The claim-ticket was sealed safely in the innermost pocket of her travel-case; her school book was asleep and tucked into a protected sleeve.

Melchiza-cash—thin rectangles of blue plaslin woven with data-thread, the denomination of each bill stamped in white—she had in several places. The mandated three-days-eating-money was in the inside pocket of the new red jacket Kamele had bought her when she realized that Theo's jacket and all her thickest sweaters were blue. The rest of her Melchiza money, her cred from home, and the mem-stick with Win Ton's letter on it, she had in a flat pouch that hung around her neck by an unbreakable cord. She'd bought the pouches during the same shopping trip that had produced the red jacket—one for her and one for Kamele.

Kamele had looked . . . kind of funny when she opened the bag, but she'd only said, "How foresightful, Theo. Thank you."

She sealed her bag and pulled it out into the main part of their stateroom. Kamele was curled on the big chair, her attention on her book.

"I'm going down for my lesson with Captain Cho," Theo said, adding silently *for my last lesson with Captain Cho.*

Her mother looked up and gave her an abstracted smile. "Good. Please give her my warmest regards, Theo. It was a pleasure to travel with her."

Throat tight, she nodded, and turned away.

The public halls were crowded, even over-crowded, as if everyone on the ship had thought of something that they needed to buy before Melchiza and were resolved to visit every shop on-board until they found it. By contrast, Breakfast All Year was very nearly empty. A man and a woman sat with their heads together in a booth in a corner of the room; a threesome she vaguely recognized as being attached to the Visitors' League were sitting on stools at the counter.

Captain Cho was at their usual table, but that was all that was usual. Theo stopped in amazement, staring at the formal tea service, the dainty cakes, small breads, and cheeses...

Cho's fingers rippled like water.

*No alarm—(smooth face!) budget mine!*

Right, that lesson was on-going with the finger-talk, though Theo was pretty sure she'd never manage to perfect the smooth, uninformative expression that Cho considered polite for everyday use.

*Please sit*, Cho motioned now. *Feast celebrate joint learning.*

*Parting?* Theo asked, her hands giving the word more energy than she had intended.

"Those who part," Cho said aloud, "may anticipate the joy of reunion. Sit, child. I wish to mark in this small way the pleasure you have brought to me, as a student, and as a fellow traveler. Truly, this journey would have been much duller without your companionship."

Theo felt her eyes sting. She blinked, and bowed— one of Father's brief, crisp bows that could mean anything from "thank you" to "your point," and slid into the chair opposite.

"Excellent." Cho poured tea for them both, raised her cup and sipped. Theo followed suit, and put the cup down, and looked up, wondering what—

"If you will excuse me," her tutor said briskly. "I will return in good time." With that, she rose and was away, leaving Theo to contemplate the plates of goodies, none of which she felt hungry enough to eat.

"Sweet Mystery, may I join you?"

She gasped, spinning in her chair. Win Ton inclined his head, his smile looking, not *quite* certain. He was wearing his leather jacket—his *pilot's jacket*, she corrected herself—and his hair was rumpled, like he'd just pulled off a hat . . .

Her fingers were more eloquent than her voice, or maybe it was that she was smiling so hard there wasn't room for any words.

*Welcome well met sit be at ease.*

"Thank you," he murmured. He sat next to her, his smile not so tentative anymore, in fact looking positively joyous.

"Theo, I'm so very glad to see you. I received your note, and treasure it. Duty has been stern, for of course, once I was on-roster this and that little thing could be found to occupy my time. I have been hoping to match schedules . . . However, that is last shift! I have just now overseen the docking of the ship carrying the Melchiza pilot to us, and therefore have, as even my shift boss admits, earned a break."

"Officer In Charge?" Theo asked, peering at the name tag affixed to his collar.

"So they say. May I share tea?"

She blushed, her fingers dancing, *pleasure friend sharing*.

Remembering Cho's deliberate motions as she had poured, Theo strove to match them. Maybe she did, maybe she didn't, but at least she didn't spill the tea, and Win Ton took his cup with a serious, "My thanks to you."

He sipped, and she did, each putting their cup on the table with care.

*Goes well lessons query,* he offered. *Mine good.* Theo watched his face as well as his hands as Win Ton signed, seeing him offer emphasis as well as concentration.

*Binjali,* she returned, and he laughed.

"*Binjali?*" he said aloud. "Excellent! You've been among pilots, then!"

Theo made her eyes very wide, the way Father did when he was pretending to not to know what you were talking about.

"Isn't Captain Cho a pilot?" she asked.

He grinned and inclined his head, fingers accepting her *true point.*

"She is that, a pilot," he murmured. "She also is very careful of her language at all times. I think the captain approves of you."

Win Ton sipped delicately at his tea, judiciously eyeing the cheese plate before making a graceful swoop with his right hand and nodding his thanks to Theo.

"Captain Cho," she began, "provides..."

"Assuredly, she does, but she would not be if she did not approve of you. If she did not approve of you, I would not be permitted to sit here now, for it is certain that she barely approves of me."

Theo scanned his face, but all she could see was bland politeness.

"Is that true?" she asked.

*Joke* his fingers told her, while he answered dryly, "It is the fashion, I believe, to disapprove of one's apprentice."

She grinned and took some cheese for herself, suddenly hungry, after all.

"Time flies, my shift boss swears," Win Ton murmured. "And I fear that I must find him correct in this, as in so much else that he has taught me. So, quickly, before I squander all to no purpose—there are two topics I must press for..."

His hands motioned *with your permission only*, and Theo answered *continue* without really thinking about it, then interrupted herself.

"I'm surprised Cho has been gone so long..."

"It has been some time," he agreed; "but she must be, else she would be party to a conversation which is not hers and which is...of a nature perhaps not entirely covered by the Code."

"She's hiding while we talk?" Theo blinked. "Isn't that silly?"

He bowed, very lightly.

"'Silly' is among the more difficult of Terran words to translate," he said gently. "Let us say, rather, that, in Liaden terms, her absence is a nice balance of courtesy and esteem."

"Then we should get on with it," Theo said, "before her tea gets cold."

*Very good* his hands signaled, while he bit his lip.

"First then," he said when he had recovered his composure, "I will repeat myself and say I have been pleased to make your acquaintance, and to have been permitted to spend time with you. And while it is...statistically and logistically unlikely that we shall meet again, I..."

Theo felt herself go bland, nearly blank.

"Theo?"

She was quiet a moment; the blank feeling went away, and suddenly her head was filled with whizzing thoughts, and a dreadful understanding that he could be right.

For some reason, her eyes were wet.

"That's hard..." she managed, voice wobbling.

Win Ton paused, watching her, his hands fluttering *true true true*. After a moment, he gathered himself and went on.

"This accident of our meeting is, I think, a fine accident. The odds of our meeting again—as an accident—those are not good. It is perhaps this bit of pilot lore which my captain required me to learn best on this part of our journey. The necessities of the Scouts and those of my clan being only slightly less aligned with each other than the necessities of Delgado with either, and none of them aligned with the necessities of Kamele Waitley—Theo, we dare not depend upon accident if we wish at some future time to be—or not to be!—in the same place."

He paused—his searching-for-a-word pause—then rushed on.

"The problems are complex. Simply said, my clan has no interest in me or my affairs until it is time for me to marry. The Scouts, being of the opinion that only clan and life-debts have call upon me greater than their own, thus do not pass on any communications save their own. This means that the only address I have which may be permanent for someone in your condition is one that..."

"My condition?" Theo hadn't realized she was going to speak; it seemed as if Win Ton was babbling. As if he were *nervous*—but of *her*?

"Yes," he said, quickly recovering from the break in thought. "Yes, your condition. The condition of a student on the verge of becoming her own person, yet tied still by necessity to a world for which she is not best fit."

The look he gave her was nearly a glare, while his hands motioned, *permission to continue?*

Theo felt her cheeks warm, muttered, "Sorry..." as her fingers agreed, *continue now.*

"Yes." Win Ton sipped his tea, carefully, Theo thought.

"Given your condition," he said, more moderately, "I propose to share with you my Pilots Guild address, which will be stable for the next seven Standards and likely the seven Standards after that, and the seven after that. It is the only address I might consider permanent, for even if the Scouts cast me aside as unworthy I cannot imagine being other than a pilot."

His fingers, flickered—not hand-talk, but rather a motion to his pocket and then an extension to her.

Held between the first two fingers of his right hand was a card, light gray in color. She took it, the paper rough against her fingertips, and looked down.

His name was rendered in shiny black letters in Trade beneath what she assumed was his name in Liaden; there were also numbers and letters but they were hard to read...

She sniffed through her tears, looked into his face. "I so wanted to see you before I left," she said, her voice wobbling, "and now I'm a wreck because you're here!"

He sighed and spoke softly, "I have training as a Liaden, which indeed is fearful training, else I might weep as well. You see, *this* is why my captain is presently standing where she and I can both pretend that I cannot see her, waiting patiently for me to leave!"

Theo laughed shakily, sniffed, and wiped her eyes.

"When you are someplace," Win Ton continued, "where you feel the reply address will be good for some while, if you feel that you would like me to know about your doings, or that you wish to know about mine, use this address."

He paused for a sip of tea; Theo slipped the card into the pocket with her Melchiza three-day money. Later, she'd put it in the pouch she wore around her neck.

Win Ton cleared his throat. "It might be that you are away to further schooling; it may be that you have partnered or wed—or that you have determined to become a dance champion! Whatever you wish, I will be pleased to have your news. If it becomes clear that we are, as pilots say, ships passing in the night, then you need only destroy the card. Do you understand these conditions? Will you abide by them?"

She nodded, her hands assuring him, *is fine check is clear check will comply check* and she was able to smile without having to wipe tears from the corner of her mouth.

There was a loud buzz. Win Ton said the word she figured for his version of "Chaos!" and snatched a ship comm from his pocket. A glance at the screen and he was on his feet.

"Theo, I must run! A gift for you, my friend, use it wisely! Also—advice: never buy a bowli ball on a cruise ship!"

His hand came out of his jacket again and he placed a package wrapped in red spangled paper in her hands, his fingers lingering on hers a moment.

Then he was gone.

Cho settled into her chair while Theo unwrapped the package, silently calling for a fresh pot of tea. She warmed both cups while Theo read the warning on the package, indicating with a nod that the third cup could be taken away.

"This clearly states," Theo said, "that this is for sale to pilots only!"

"Ah," said Cho, waving a fluid hand toward the open box. "Conditions are met, are they not? The apprentice is a pilot of some skill. I confess that I overhead his parting advice to you and I must allow it to be wisdom. To have purchased such a thing at the Crew's Store...Well. Necessity."

Theo unfolded the enclosed rule book. "The stochastic reverberation tuned-molecule core makes long range accuracy problematical. Never throw, kick, or launch your stochastic reflection device in the direction of a person or fragile object..."

She looked up at Captain Cho, who was patiently sipping her tea.

"Never throw it at a person? But..."

"Pilots, as you will likely come to see, have their own small jokes."

"Never use this equipment in a closed environment. Avoid handling with damp hands or in uncertain footing..."

She sighed, felt her fingers moving and thought to pay attention to what they were saying: *never never never careful danger pilot use only not a toy not for competition avoid deep knife cuts...*

She laughed slightly, and looked up.

"Thank you, Captain Cho."

The Liaden woman smiled slightly. "You are welcome, Theo Waitley. Now, I mark that time passes and that we shall soon be under docking rule. It happens that I, too, have something to place into your hand."

She reached into a slip pocket on her belt, and extended her hand as Win Ton had, a card held between the first and second finger.

Theo took it, her fingers delighting in the smooth feel of the creamy paper.

"More properly, that is for the pilot who trained you. If you will hand deliver this to that pilot . . . I would be appreciative."

Theo looked down at the card curiously. The front bore a graphic of a ship and a planet, with what she guessed were Liaden words written beneath. On the back, in neatly lettered Terran was: *Captain Cho sig'Radia, Piloting Liaison.*

That was followed by a series of letters and numbers, much like Win Ton's Pilots Guild address.

"My address with the Scouts is there, as well as— but the pilot will know."

Theo looked up, confusion and dismay threatening to invite the silly tears again.

"But *you're* the pilot who trained me," she protested. "Or—Win Ton or Phobai—Cordrey! I don't *know* any other pilots!"

"Ah," Cho said, sounding infuriatingly like Father. "Perhaps it will come to you. In the meanwhile . . ." She inclined her head. "It is time that we part, my student. Go well, dance joyously, and number your friends with care."

# THIRTY-TWO

· · · · · · · · · · · · · · · ·

*Melchiza*
*City of Treasures*

THEY WERE MET IN THE EGRESS LOUNGE BY THEIR officially assigned Melchizan Chaperon. According to the handouts, they weren't supposed to stir outside their hotel room or other quarters without their Chaperon. Visitors caught roaming around on their own faced the usual litany of Melchizan penalties: fine, imprisonment, or immediate expulsion from the planet.

Their particular Chaperon was tall and thin with droopy yellow mustaches that made his long face look even longer. He had pale brown eyes and big knobby hands in which he held a data screen and a sheaf of brightly colored cards.

"Greeting! Greeting, sir, professor, professora, mamzelle! I am Gidis Arkov, your assigned guide and protector. All questions are for me; I stand between you and all harm. I am the keeper of the schedule, I carry copies of your bona fides next to my heart—" He lifted the data screen—"Consider that I am your elder brother; any problem or concern you may have during your time on Melchiza, bring to me and I will make all smooth for you.

"Now!" he continued briskly, "we have the bus just here, with the driver waiting. Before we board, however, we must be insuring that your identification is in order." He slipped the data screen into the side pocket of his bright orange jacket, which was not, Theo thought critically, next to his heart, unless biology on Melchiza was very strange.

He glanced down at the cards in his hand, and looked up, scanning their faces earnestly. "Which is Farancy Able?"

Professor Able stood forward. "I am, Chaperon Arkov."

He smiled, his mustaches lifting. "Please, I am your elder brother, eh? Gidis is what you may call me. Now, this." He extended the purple card to her. "This is very important. You must at all times have it visible. Attach it to your coat and surrender it to no one, excepting anyone of Security." He looked 'round at all of them.

"You have read that Security will wear blue. In general and most usually, this is so. Sadly, there are rogues, not so many in the City of Treasures as elsewhere, but! Please be observant. If it seems to you that the person wearing blue is not behaving as a security person ought to do, you may politely ask to see identification. A legitimate security person will not take this amiss. A rogue will bluster and seek to bully. If this should happen, that a rogue seeks to separate you from your identification—*do not acquiesce*. Refuse, become loud and create a commotion.

The rogue will—often—run. If they do not run fast enough, Security, having heard your commotion, will catch the impostor." Gidis smiled. "It is a very bad thing to pretend to be Security on Melchiza.

"So, Farancy Able, please affix this firmly to your coat so that all may see it. Know where it is at all times. Sleep with it, eh?" He laughed, and looked down at the next card.

"Vaughn Crowley."

Professor Crowley stood forward and took another purple card, subjecting it to a moment of study before pressing it against the breast of his jacket.

"Yes, excellent." Gidis smiled and looked down to the next.

"Orkan Hafley." The chair silently held out her hand, and slapped the identification card against her dull green sweater, where it adhered somewhat crookedly.

Gidis lifted the last purple card with a smile and held it out to Kamele with a little bow. "Kamele Waitley, yes? Please, do as your companions before you."

The next card was white. Gidis bowed again, without the smile. "Sir," he said.

Clyburn nodded and pressed the card against his elaborately fringed jacket.

The last card was pink.

"Mamzelle," Gidis said, handing it to Theo. "You will be vigilant, eh? The rule for you, it changes, only a little. The people who have the right to ask for your card are Security and your teacher. *Your teacher* only, yes? If another teacher wishes to peruse your information, he must apply to your teacher, who will, if he considers the request reasonable, ask you to surrender the card to him. If you are confused about this rule, you will please ask your teacher. All of this is plain and clear?"

*Does he think I'm a littlie?* Theo wondered grumpily, but she remembered that the rule-book listed pretty serious penalties for arguing with a Chaperon, and while immediately being deprived of the Chaperon's services wouldn't matter to her, since she was going to be locked up at boarding school, it would matter a lot to Kamele and the research team.

"Everything's clear," she said to Gidis, and pressed the pink tag against the shoulder of her red jacket.

"Excellent. Now! The schedule for the rest of this day. First, we board the bus and transport the mamzelle to school. There will at the school be a short moment for mamzelle's mother to speak with the teacher. The bus then takes us to the hotel. Dinner has been ordered in, as the scholars will wish to rest in their apartment. The sir has of course, been cleared for visiting." He nodded, then spun on a heel. "Follow me, please!"

Theo moved at once, Kamele right with her, both of them following Gidis down the room toward the doors. The others hesitated for a long moment, as if they thought there'd been a mistake, then hurried to catch up, their feet noisy against the 'crete floor.

"Visiting?" Theo heard Professor Able say. "Oh, of course! Your mother, is it not, who is placed high in Admin?"

"Precisely!" Chair Hafley took the question to herself. "As it happens, Clyburn's mother and sister live on Melchiza. Of course he must visit them! I insisted upon it."

"Certainly, one must pay one's respects to one's

mother," Professor Crowley said, but in the tone of voice Theo noticed he used when he was saying something else instead.

"Oh, no doubt," Professor Able agreed. "I simply hadn't known that Clyburn was native to Melchiza."

Chair Hafley sniffed. "Why do you think I insisted that he accompany us?" she demanded. "A local guide will be invaluable to us!"

Except, Theo thought, Clyburn was going to visit his mother and the team had an assigned Chaperon, so how was he going to be any help? She looked at Kamele, who was biting her bottom lip, apparently listening just as hard as Theo was to the conversation to the rear.

"How long will the research take?" Theo asked.

Kamele glanced at her, blue eyes dancing. Her voice, however, was grave. "Professor Crowley estimated anywhere between four and seven local days, depending on the accessibility of the records, and how many hours per day we're allowed inside the Treasure House archives."

"So, if Clyburn is going to go visit—"

"Yes," Kamele murmured, cutting her off. "I think it's safe to conclude that Chair Hafley brought Clyburn so that he might have the treat of visiting his mother." She gave Theo a sideways glance. "It shows well of her, that she treats her *onagrata* with kindness," she added.

Theo sighed. She knew from Life Class that a woman who was responsible for an *onagrata* should take pains to let him know that he was valued, and to give him those little gifts and treats that were so important to the male ego. It was just that Professor Hafley treated Clyburn like he was . . . learning challenged, which, despite the fact that she didn't like him, Theo was pretty sure he wasn't. In Theo's opinion, it took real observational skills to be as snarky as Clyburn.

Ahead of them, Gidis waved open the doors. Before them was a short, canopied walk, with a long, orange car pulled across the far end.

"The bus!" he called, moving to one side of the walk and making shooing motions with one hand to hurry them along.

Kamele and Theo walked on, Theo turning her head, attention caught by a flicker of what might have been sense . . .

Yes, there it was again, woven between the nonsense waving and posturing, a phrase she almost recognized, but it couldn't be *all is in readiness*.

Could it?

"Theo," Kamele called from the bus door, "do you want to sit in the front or the back?"

Theo turned as Clyburn detached himself from their group, mincing in his fancy boots, clearly heading for another vehicle at the far end of the drive.

"Where's he going?" she asked loudly. "He doesn't have a Chaperon!"

"Hist! Hist, mamzelle! The sir is not a visitor! He is a returning son of Melchiza. Such require no Guides."

"Really, Theo!" Chair Hafley added, as she stepped past on her way to their bus. "If you spent as much time minding your own business as you spend monitoring others, you'd be in Four Team One, instead of Three!"

"Theo?" Kamele called again.

Ears burning, Theo turned back toward the bus.

"Why are you telling me these bizarre things?" Monit Appletorn kept his face averted, most of his attention seemingly centered on the screen of his mumu.

Jen Sar Kiladi tipped his head to one side, and considered the other man's profile. Strong bones, and a stubborn chin, dark hair beginning to recede from a high forehead. There was a tightness in the tiny muscles around the eyes that perhaps spoke of more interest in bizarre topics than he wished to have seen.

He had not been offered a seat, which was only Balance, as he had arrived unannounced and all but forced himself into Appletorn's office. If he had called ahead and made more seemly arrangements to meet, perhaps the good scholar might have found time to move a pile of hard copy from one of the overburdened chairs. One did wonder, however, where his students sat when they came to solicit the scholar's advice.

Jen Sar flexed his fingers where they were folded atop his cane, and shifted his weight slightly. Appletorn reluctantly turned his face until it could be said that he was giving his guest due attention.

"I am telling you these things," Jen Sar said, keeping his voice gentle, "because you live in one of the compromised apartments. In theory, you have access to this rogue AI. Should this situation be discovered, your scholarship, your conclusions, and your standing as a Scholar Expert all are cast into doubt." He bowed slightly, as if in sympathy. "The work of a lifetime, tarnished by mere proximity."

"I think you overstate the case," Appletorn said, doubtless meaning to sound assured. "My work is

well-known; certainly the earliest monographs predate
the arrival of this . . . *rogue AI*, as you care to style it."

"Is that so? I have myself no firm date for the onset
of the infection." Jen Sar murmured. Appletorn's face
paled. "But, no! Doubtless you are correct. You have
not always lived in that apartment; your earliest work
would, in fact, escape doubt . . . as long as your former
residence was free of the old wire."

The other man closed his eyes. When, at the count
of twelve there was no further response forthcoming,
Jen Sar set the next hook.

"Come, we both know that these things can be
managed. The trick is to be in control of the information and its revelation, rather than allowing it to
be discovered impromptu and subjected to dismaying
interpretations by persons ignorant of the actual facts."

"I have never used this 'old wire,'" Appletorn
said, which was . . . perhaps . . . true. "This rogue AI is
unknown to me. I am, therefore, not in its logs, nor
listed among its users."

"Ah. That, you see, is the genius of the program.
Asked, it helpfully provided a map of those places
to which it potentially has access. A second request,
this to our own Concierge, produced the names of
those currently residing in the compromised apartments." He smiled, sympathetically. "It is so difficult
to prove a negative."

Another lengthy silence was the reward of sympathy,
and at last a sigh.

"You say that you have the means to contain this
malignancy and shut it down at the source."

Jen Sar *tsk'd* lightly. "I say that I have a pointer
to a person. In all truth, this is likeliest to be an

intermediate contact. As to finishing quietly—perhaps not. I do not despair of *quickly*, however, granted able and advertent assistance. And surely we shall emerge both politically stronger for our defense of Delgadan scholarship, and more able to control the flow of information to the ignorant."

Monit Appletorn was not a fool; the tension in his face and shoulders was ample evidence that he understood the stakes. It remained only to see if he was ruled by fear, or by *melant'i*.

"I'll do it," Appletorn said, and nodded toward the nearest chair. "Pitch that stuff on the floor and tell me what you plan."

· · · ❖ · · ·

"Waitley?" a tall stout woman with a pink band around her left bicep shouted from the bottom of the ramp.

"Yes, ma'am." Theo went carefully down the ramp, pulling her case behind her.

"I'm Instructor Tathery. You're on my roster. Class is over for the day and you're a little late for supper. I'll show you to your room; the kitchen's already been told to send up a tray when you arrive." She looked over Theo's head.

"You'll be Professor Waitley?" she asked.

"Theo's mother," Kamele agreed coming off the end of the ramp to stand next to Theo. She held her hand out. "I'm very pleased to meet you, Instructor Tathery."

The bigger woman blinked, then took the offered hand, Kamele's fingers vanishing inside the large grasp. "A pleasure, Professor," she said gruffly.

"I don't mind talking while we walk," Kamele said, after her hand was returned and the other woman hadn't said anything else.

"Yes, well . . ." Instructor Tathery looked up the ramp, to where Gidis stood in the doorway of the bus.

"I'm not a Government Chaperon," the big woman finally produced. Kamele looked puzzled, but Theo suddenly understood.

"You can't go anywhere on Melchiza without a Chaperon," she said. "And if Gidis comes with us, then the rest of the team will be without a Chaperon."

Kamele sighed and shook her head. "I am not acclimated as yet," she said ruefully, and looked to the instructor. "I apologize for having placed you in an uncomfortable position and thank you for your patience. What I wish to say can certainly be said here, though I would have liked to see Theo's room and the learning areas."

"It is suggested, Professor Waitley," Gidis said from his position on the high ground, "that you speak quickly. The schedule—we must not fall behind."

"Maybe on your way back, ma'am," Instructor Tathery said, "you and the rest of your party would like a tour of the facilities."

"That would be very pleasant," Kamele said, keeping her eyes on the instructor's face; not even acknowledging Gidis by a glance. "I only wanted to explain—because I know custom varies from world to world—that, according to the custom of our homeworld, Delgado, Theo is yet a minor child, under the care of her mother. We wish to preserve our customs as nearly as possible while visiting Melchiza." She paused, but Instructor Tathery didn't say anything.

"If you will call me," Kamele said, "should there be any difficulty, or misunderstanding, and before any remediation is applied, that would satisfy our customs."

"I understand." There was a pause. "I'll do the best I'm able, Professor, as far as the customs of Melchiza allow."

Theo expected Kamele to argue, or press for a firmer agreement. Instead, her mother nodded gravely.

"Thank you," she said. "I appreciate your care of my daughter."

"The schedule, Professor Waitley!" Gidis called from the top of the ramp.

He might as well have been on Delgado for all the attention Kamele gave him. She turned, opening her arms. Theo stepped into her hug, leaning her forehead against her mother's shoulder.

"You have everything?" Kamele asked quietly.

"Everything" in this case, Theo knew was more than her school book, her clothes and her ID. It also included the emergency backup ticket that she was to use without prejudice, as Professor Crowley had it, if she felt her safety was compromised. Theo was pretty sure that undertaking a starship voyage to a place she'd never heard of would compromise her safety more than anything she could imagine happening at school, but he and Kamele had looked so serious, she hadn't bothered to argue. The ticket was in the secure pouch hanging 'round her neck by its string.

"Yes ma'am," she said now, her nose filled with the scent of Kamele's hair, feeling her mother's arms around her, strong and firm. She raised her head and looked into serious blue eyes.

"Be *careful*, Kamele," she said impulsively.

Her mother smiled. "I will be as careful as I can and still pursue my duty," she said. Her arms tightened slightly and they exchanged one of their rare kisses before Kamele stepped back, ruffling Theo's hair, like she was a littlie.

"Learn well, Daughter!" she said, loud enough for Gidis to hear at the top of the ramp.

"Keep well, Mother," Theo answered. "I'll—see you soon."

"You'd better go," Instructor Tathery said, low voice. "It'll be points off for the driver and the Guide if they're late on the schedule."

"Professor Waitley!" Gidis sounded somewhere between angry and anxious.

"Coming," Kamele called, and ran lightly up the ramp.

Gidis stepped back to let her in, the door closed and Theo gulped, eyes stinging.

"All right, Theo Waitley," Instructor Tathery said. "Let's get you settled and some dinner in you. Tonight's study work will be on the comdeck. Breakfast at four bells, and a map of the school..."

· · · ·❊· · · ·

"We are agreed, then?" Jen Sar Kiladi asked Monit Appletorn.

The long scholar leaned back in his chair and ran his hands over his hair, staring at the ceiling. Finally, he sighed.

"We're agreed," he said, meeting Jen Sar's eyes. "When do you propose to move?"

"Tomorrow, if your schedule can accommodate me." Jen Sar said. "The weather is predicted to be very fine."

• • • ❄ • • •

The Treasure House Hotel had provided them with a suite—four private rooms around a common parlor-and-kitchen combination. In Kamele's room, the single wide bed served to remind her that she was—alone. No daughter tucked into an alcove bed, or showering in the 'fresher. No lover leaning on his elbow under the sheets, watching her with a half-smile on his interesting, unbeautiful face. No one, in fact, to testify to her existence, should she suddenly vanish from this place.

She took a shower, trying to take pleasure in the luxurious soaps and lotions provided by the hotel. Alas, her depression was not so easily vanquished; rather than relaxing her, the shower seemed only to soften her resolve, so that all of her doubts ambushed her the moment she slipped into the bed and waved the room lights out.

What kind of mother was she, she asked herself, breath coming short against the heavy darkness, to leave her minor daughter in the care of strangers? How could she simply have turned her back and gotten back on the bus, not knowing the conditions of her child's welfare? A mother had her duties, and Theo—

Theo, she thought deliberately, had demonstrated an . . . astonishing level of self-sufficiency aboard the *Vashtara,* as befit a young woman who was soon to accept the responsibilities of adulthood.

But a mother's duty—

In the chill embrace of the wide bed, Kamele closed her eyes and took a deep breath—and another, keeping her attention focused on the mere act of breathing.

An old lesson, this one, learned from her first singing instructor: *Breathe, and when your foolish panic has passed, affirm yourself!*

Another breath, deep and calming. Another. Her muscles were warming now, and she could smell the subtle aroma of the bath lotion, clinging softly to her skin.

Another breath, and she was calm, drifting on the edge of wakefulness.

"I am," she whispered, "a scholar of Delgado."

Another breath, and she slipped over the edge, into sleep.

# THIRTY-THREE

. . . . . . . . . . . . . . . . . . . . . . . .

*Melchiza*
*City of Treasures*

THE INFORMATIONAL VIDS DID NOTHING TO PREPARE
one for the reality of the Melchiza House of Treasures.
While much of the building was of course underground;
the above-ground portion dwarfed its festive and
fragile attendant buildings, a hulking 'crete block,
with neither finesse nor grace about it. It seemed,
Kamele thought, to be daring the heavens to deliver
the meteor strike that the Melchizan government
insisted it would withstand.

And then, there were the doors. The outer doors
were guarded by a dozen stern-faced individuals in
blue coats, gold laces shining in the faintly roseate light
of Melchiza's dawn; sidearms very obvious. The team
was required to pass through a checkpoint, surrender
their badges, state their names, their occupation and
their planet of origin into the recorder, and submit
to a retinal scan.

Badges returned, they were reunited with their

387

Chaperon, who led them inside, across a forbidding metal lobby unsoftened by sculpture, tapestry, or other art, to an equally forbidding metal desk, behind which a woman in yet another of the ornate blue-and-gold coats awaited them, frown in place.

She took their badges, scanned and returned them before asking their business.

"We are here at the invitation of Professor Dochayn to do a literature comparison of the Beltaire Collection," Kamele said, keeping her voice smooth and pleasant. Beside her, she felt Chair Hafley stiffen slightly, but if she was offended by Kamele overstepping herself, she did not choose to pursue the matter.

"I have your names on my roster," the security woman said crisply; "and your badges are in order. Your Chaperon may guide you to the next station."

*Well*, Kamele thought, *that wasn't difficult at all, really.*

"Thank you," she said, but the woman had apparently already forgotten them, her eyes returning to the bright bank of busy instruments at her right hand.

Kamele gathered Gidis with a glance, and he skittered ahead of them, clutching his notebook, staring down into its screen with such concentration that Kamele feared he would trip and do himself an injury. Of course, there was nothing to trip over—there were no uneven tiles, or unruly rug-fringe marring the metal floor—though they were approaching a door with the inevitable blue-coated individual standing before it.

Once again, they surrendered their badges, saw them scanned and received them back. The security man opened the door and Gidis dashed across the threshold, the forensic team following at a slightly more sedate pace, careful of their footing on the metal surface.

They had been admitted to an antechamber, where a blue-coated security person sat behind a desk, quietly observing his bank of instruments. He scanned their badges and gave his permission for them to proceed.

· · · ❖ · · ·

There were two dozen kids in Class TS3N, slightly more boys than girls, and ages ranging from Monti, two Standard Years Theo's junior, to Yzel, three Standard Years older.

Instructor Tathery was the teacher for the class, which was . . . odd. Who could be an expert in all subjects? Still, Theo thought, it would be interesting to see how it went. She sat down at the desk with her name on it, and touched the keypad to wake up the computer.

Yzel acted as teacher's aide, wandering the room while the class did a math warm-up, and answering questions. He was good, Theo thought, patient and quiet. He paused behind her chair while she was working out a particularly cumbersome word problem, but he didn't intervene or offer to help. When she found the derive, he moved off, soft-footed, and she felt like she'd been given approval.

After math was culture. Everybody sat in a circle and told the group about an important holiday on their homeworld. Theo talked about Founder's Day, which was pretty tame compared to Monti's Sun Fete, and downright boring put against Ave-Su's Loki's Night.

Culture moved seamlessly into history, Instructor Tathery leading a discussion of political alliance.

"Political alliance is expediency, ma'am," Yzel argued. "It would be better to cultivate an ignorance of history in the cause of choosing allies."

"Not only that, history lies!" the boy with black and gold striped hair called, speaking out of rotation.

Instructor Tathery didn't reprimand him, or give him a down. She just waved a broad hand at him, in an almost casual invitation to continue.

"How does history lie, Dalin?"

"The—the, Yzel was talking about expediency. It's expedient for the history-makers on some planets to write untrue things down and file them in their libraries, in order to block competition or to serve old grudges. It's coward's warfare, my First-Father says, and those who traffic in lies ought to be held to a warrior's accounting!"

"But," Theo protested, "on Delgado, scholars research events. If there hasn't been any research done—or, if the research that has been done is suspect for some reason, a scholar will travel to the place, talk to the people who were there—primary sources, they're called—to find out the facts of the event, as well as the causes, and write an impartial account, so that everyone is informed. Then, if two former enemies want to pursue an alliance—like Yzel says, of expediency—they have the facts of the last matter before them, to learn from, so they don't make the same mistakes again."

"Oh, really? My First-Father says that—"

"This is a very interesting discussion," Instructor Tathery broke in. "Rather than try to compress it into the time we have left for history, let's plan on using our open period tomorrow for an in-depth exploration. I want each of you to come prepared with an argument for or against the manipulation of history, with examples. Now, everybody up! It's time to move around, people!"

· · · ·✳· · · ·

They had begun their pilgrimage at dawn. It was now past lunchtime, as they were passed through another metal door, and stepped into yet another antechamber with a desk, the inevitable blue-coated security person, and another; a woman wearing a red coat, a pale blue knot nattily adorning her buttonhole, who leapt to her feet as the team crossed the threshold and bustled forward.

"You must be the Delgadan Search Team!" she said, bringing her hands together briskly in what she may have thought was the open book salute. "I am Jeyanzi Pikelmin, Third Director of the Treasure House. The Beltaire Collection falls under my administration."

"Thank goodness!" Hafley cried, stepping forward. "I don't hide from you, Director, that I am exhausted! We have been walking for *hours*! If there could be someplace for me—for us—to sit down and perhaps have a bit of lunch, that would be most welcome!"

"Also," Professor Crowley interposed smoothly, "if a message might be sent to Professor Dochayn, who is our sponsor to the collection, that would be most welcome as well, Director. The team had been under the impression that she was planning to meet us and conduct us personally to the archives."

"Ah, but that is why you see me here, Scholars! You must accept my apologies, Professor Dochayn was granted a fellowship at the premier archival center on our sister planet of Ibenvue."

"Really?" Crowley murmured. "She said nothing of this in our correspondence."

"Indeed, indeed! The honor came upon her unaware, the announcement so late that she thought another had been chosen. Just between us, sir, I would say that another had been chosen, who had then been obliged to turn it down. These things happen, of course, and in this case it was to Dochayn's benefit. Off she went to Ibenvue, with scarcely a day to pack and see to her affairs here. The department is still a little hectic, as support staff scramble to divide her work between them. If you know her, sir, you know that she was always in the midst, sleeves rolled up, notebook in hand."

"Indeed," Crowley said politely.

"I'd hardly think the Museum would let her go on such short notice," Professor Able said, "with such a workload and no second to take up the work in her absence."

"The Treasure House would scarcely put itself between one of our most valued scholars and so noteworthy an honor. What she will learn on Ibenvue, she will bring back to us here, while teaching Ibenvue in her turn. When she returns, the Treasure House will benefit from this synergy. Truly, we would be shortsighted with regard to our own greater good, did we refuse to allow such migrations. Temporary interruptions can be dealt with. But come!" She turned her smile and her attention to Chair Hafley.

"I apologize for the inconvenience to which we have subjected you this morning. It will be my pleasure to provide a place to rest and a meal. Please, follow me."

Hafley turned to walk with the Director, leaving

the other three to follow. Kamele glanced to Crowley and to Able, and raised her hand, as if to make sure that her badge was securely affixed, and touched her finger to her collar in the exact location where Director Pikelmin wore her dainty blue knot.

Crowley inclined his head, and Able, advertent scholars, both.

Kamele inclined her head and followed Hafley down a short hallway to a conference room, where four chairs had been set around a square table.

"Please, be seated," Director Pikelmin said. "Catering will be here momentarily.

"Excellent," said Hafley, taking a chair. "Kamele, sit here, at my right."

Stomach tight, Kamele took the seat at Hafley's right.

"Delicious!" Hafley proclaimed. "Better than anything *Vashtara* served, even at the captain's own table!"

"I will tell the catering manager that you approve of his efforts," Director Pikelmin said, bowing slightly.

It was, Kamele admitted, very good coffee, the foodstuffs certainly equal to that served in the atrium cafe aboard *Vashtara*.

"Sit with us," Able invited, "and have a cup of your excellent coffee."

"Thank you," the director said, "but I lunched earlier."

She straightened, suddenly appearing several inches taller. Kamele observed this with interest, having seen Jen Sar perform the same illusion innumerable times. Its success depended almost entirely upon attitude, as Jen Sar, at least, was always upright in his posture. Director Pikelmin seemed to have been slumping just a bit, and only now allowed her full height to be seen. Which was, in Kamele's opinion, cheating.

"Now that we have perhaps made some small amends for your inconvenience of the morning, Scholars, I think we must talk of your reason for visiting our delightful planet. I believe that I learn from Dochayn's files that your purpose is to compare copies of the Beltaire papers held by Delgado University's library with the originals, held in our archives. Is this correct?"

"That is most wonderfully correct," Crowley answered. "I carry, in addition, not supposing that it should be needed, a letter from Professor Beltaire, granting us unlimited access to her family's archive."

"Certainly, it is wise to be prepared for all possible unpleasantness, so that one may be agreeably surprised when the way is smoother than anticipated," the director said with a smile. "Professor Beltaire's foresight—and your own, sir!—are appreciated, but the letter is not necessary."

"What I wish to offer is an . . . option which our own Professor Dochayn appears not to have mentioned to your team. Since the archives are our own and we are very familiar with their contents and the system under which they are filed, why not spend an hour or two with Dochayn's research assistants, outlining precisely what it is that you want, and leave all in our hands? You may take a well-deserved vacation, tour our splendid city, make the trip to Tampere Falls—spend a night, or two, in the lodge behind the falls. When you return, rested and content, your information will be waiting for you."

"That's a very . . . interesting offer," Crowley said, looking 'round the table.

"No!" Hafley said, astonishingly. She glared at Crowley. "It's not *interesting*, Emeritus Professor, it's—generous to a fault! This is what it means, to be part of the community of scholars! We may live on different worlds, abide by different cultures, but we all inhabit the universe of the mind." She smiled at Director Pikelmin. "We can do nothing else but accept. Isn't that correct, Sub-Chair?"

*This*, Kamele thought, *this is what I agreed to, when I said that I would stand her ally.* The other members of the team were looking to her, waiting for her response. She swallowed, finished what was left of her coffee, and put the cup carefully into its saucer.

"Actually," she said, pleased to hear that her voice was perfectly composed, "though the offer is generous in the extreme, we cannot accept. It is our duty, as Scholars of Delgado, to do our own research. We cannot ask our sisters in scholarship to prove our point for us. The request we made of Professor Dochayn was for access to the archives. Professor Beltaire's letter of permission also grants us this—access to the archives." She met Director Pikelmin's cool eyes.

"Your offer is well-meant," she said, "but we must pursue our own course in this."

"I think so, as well," said Crowley.

Able nodded. "Let's finish what we came here to do."

"Scholars!" Hafley cried. "We have all been teachers. Surely we can give Professor Dochayn's trained assistants instructions regarding our needs. There's no reason to weary ourselves, to learn the filing system in use, to risk muddling the archive's records..."

"I have been a scholar for seventy Standard Years," Crowley interrupted. "I have pursued source documents into hovels, where the texts were left exposed to humidity, radiation, and other damaging elements; where the notion of a filing system was to simply stack all those with matching covers in a certain corner of the room. I take offense at the statement that I would be unable to decipher the civilized and sophisticated archival system in use at this facility. The insinuation that I would somehow, in my base male ignorance, *muddle the files* I consider beneath reply."

"Professor Crowley—"

"I agree with Professor Waitley," Able interrupted the Chair. "Delgado didn't become the watchword for careful scholarship because Delgadan scholars let others do their research. We hold ourselves to scholarly rigor; it is our pride and our duty. Students come to us from the far reaches of the galaxy because we do not stint ourselves, nor take the easy path. We have our task before us; let us continue."

*Not a consensus*, Kamele thought, *but a majority. So be it*. Hafley, however, was opening her mouth, apparently to argue or cajole further.

"The scholars perhaps are not entirely informed on the conditions of research in the archives," Director Pikelmin said smoothly. "Dochayn would hardly have thought to mention it; she was here at all hours, herself. As you can see, we have an immense facility to maintain and protect here. What this means in terms of visiting scholars and research teams is that they may, at the invitation of a resident archivist—which your team has of course obtained—visit the relevant archive. However, checking large groups of foreign scholars in and out puts an unacceptable burden on our security personnel. That is why all visiting researchers are required to stay within the archives until they have either completed their work, or they have overstayed their welcome."

*Theo*, Kamele thought, calm inside the suddenly cool room.

"How long," she asked, "are visiting researchers welcome?"

Director Pikelmin smiled. "One local week, Professor."

"I see." Kamele glanced around the table, seeing agreement on two faces. "Since time is so short, I suggest that we begin immediately, if the director can find someone able to lead us *directly* to the archives."

"I will myself lead you, Professor Waitley, if you must go. I should mention that conditions are perhaps not what you are accustomed to. The apartments are very small, and the food provided—alas!—not by our most excellent catering department but by a cafeteria vending service."

Kamele did not laugh, though she did glance down at her empty coffee cup.

"Those conditions are acceptable," she said, and looked 'round the table. "Scholars?"

"Acceptable," Able said.

"More than acceptable," Crowley said. "I wonder, however, if someone—perhaps our excellent Chaperon, Gidis Arkov—could be dispatched to bring our cases to us. We came, you understand, prepared to do our research, not to take up residence."

Jeyanzi Pikelmin pressed her lips together.

"If it's against the rules," Able said, dryly, "then think nothing of it. We'll manage. I assume that there is a sink?"

The director looked to Hafley, who threw up her hands.

"We have a consensus, or so it would appear! I thank you for your attempt to make our work easier."

"Then you will also be staying in the archives, Chair Hafley?" the director asked.

"It would seem that I have no choice."

"Of course." She bowed slightly to the room at large. "Licensed Chaperon Gidis Arkov will fetch the scholars' cases to the archive. You will understand that this may take some amount of time, it being an extra burden upon him. Melchiza is, however, famous for its hospitality. We would not wish to leave a guest in discomfort."

Kamele nodded.

"That's settled, then," she said briskly, and rose, smiling brightly at the woman in her red coat and blue knot. "Director Pikelmin, let me thank you again for a most delicious meal! It's time for this research team to embrace its purpose, dreary as that might seem to some. I believe you said that you would be able to guide us . . . ?"

"Yes, Professor Waitley," the director said gently. "I will myself escort you."

. . . ✹ . . .

Movement was freeform; you were supposed to stretch and move around, so Ave-Su said, to get the blood back up to your brain. Theo staked out a piece of floor toward the back of the big room and danced a few phrases of *menfri'at*. The voices and heavy steps of her teammates fell out of her awareness before she completed the first phrase. Closing her eyes, she

imagined Win Ton moving with her, which was easy
since he danced so quiet—like there was a cushion
of air between the soles of his boots and whatever
mundane surface the rest of the population had to
deal with. Captain Cho moved like that, too, and
sometimes Father...

She stopped in mid-phrase, her eyes springing open
to behold her classmates, standing quite still, watching
*her*, like they'd never seen anybody dance before. And
coming forward was Instructor Tathery, eyes wide in
a face that seemed a little paler than it had been.

"Everybody awake?" she called out to the room in
general, and the rest of the class turned toward her.
"Good! We're due at the media center!"

· · · · ❋ · · · ·

"All communication devices must be checked at this
station," Jeyanzi Pikelmin said. "They will be returned
to you when you depart our facility."

Kamele considered the woman. "My minor daughter
is enrolled at the Transit School. The custom upon
Delgado is that a mother must always have available
to her the means to supervise and interact with her
child."

Director Pikelmin inclined her head gently. "Delgado's customs are well-known to me, Professor Waitley,
and I honor them, on those occasions when I am on
Delgado. This discussion is taking place upon Melchiza,
however, and here we have our own customs. Your
child is under the supervision of the instructor of her
class; you may rest easy." She looked up, eyes gleaming.

"If Delgadan custom must overrule Melchizan,
then I suggest to you that it is not too late to allow

experienced Treasure House staff to take the burden of your task out of your hands."

Kamele took a breath. To be . . . incarcerated, incommunicado, for the length of a thorough search—which Able had calculated at no less than four Delgadan days, and possibly as long as seven—with her child among strangers. It was—what if something happened?

*I should have,* she thought, *closed my eyes and ignored the signs, stopped myself from adding up the inconsistencies. Remained in Jen Sar's house, where everything was comfortable and my daughter was protected.*

Yet—Was that how a Scholar of Delgado comported herself? Could she have lived with herself, had she turned her head? And Theo—what lesson would her daughter have taken from such an act of cowardice?

"Professor Waitley?"

She looked around to her colleagues, to Hafley, smirking at the director's side, and bowed slightly. It seemed to her that she heard Jen Sar murmur quietly in her ear, *Necessity.*

"The Treasure House," she said composedly, "is to be commended for the care it lavishes upon those valuables that come into its keeping." She stepped to the desk and slipped her mumu from her pocket. The guard slapped a pressure-seal on it, and used her chin to point. "Fingerprints, please, Scholar."

Kamele pressed her fingers to the seal and stepped back, making room for Crowley, who already had his mumu out.

When it came Hafley's turn, she slid the mumu across the desk as if it were a toy. The guard picked up the seal, looked down—and looked up.

"This device is activated," she said.

"Again?" Hafley *tsked*, leaned forward and tapped the power-down key. "I really must get a new one; this habit of spontaneously powering up is very tiresome."

The guard shrugged, sealed the device and Hafley pressed her fingers down.

"There, now!" she said, turning around and smiling broadly. "Kamele, I believe you are, as always, correct! We *ought* to do our own research, and we should be able to make great strides, four scholars with no children beneath foot. Not that Theo is ever anything but a delight, of course, but she is quite, quite safe where she is."

# THIRTY-FOUR

. . . . . . . . . . . . . . . . . . . . . . .

*Delgado*
*Efraim Agricultural Zone*

"HAVE WE ARRIVED?" MONIT APPLETORN ASKED FAINTLY from the passenger's seat.

Jen Sar Kiladi touched the car's power switch. The prediction for a cloudless, lucent day perfect for driving had been correct, and he had, perhaps, indulged himself. He sent a sidelong glance to the other man. Appletorn's face was decidedly pale, his eyes squeezed shut so tightly that he must surely soon give himself a headache.

"I believe that we have arrived, yes," Jen Sar said, keeping his voice soft not only from respect of that incipient headache, but also because he had noted the location of three Eye-like objects, placed with intent to conceal among the trees and other growing things.

Appletorn took a rather shaky breath, and opened his eyes. Ascertaining that the car was, indeed, at rest, he cast his attention wider, taking in the pleasant aspect of the courtyard, the simple stone walk leading to the simple wooden door, set flush to the simple wooden walls.

"We are at the Chapelia's primary circle?" Appletorn asked, his voice likewise low.

"To the best of my knowledge and belief," Jen Sar assured him.

Appletorn cleared his throat. "I ask, not because I doubt your abilities, sir, but because there are two decidedly complex monitoring devices concealed in this . . . garden. Surely the Chapelia, who advocate and pursue simplicity in all things . . ."

"The Chapelia harness complexity when it suits them," Jen Sar murmured, pleased in his companion. To have immediately seen two of the concealed spy-eyes in what must surely be a bewildering profusion of leaf and branch, while one's emotions were yet in turmoil, demonstrated observational skills of a high order. But, there, Appletorn's area was advertence. Perhaps he would be useful here, after all.

"Well!" he said brightly, releasing the door locks and easing out of his seat. "Having arrived, let us go forth!"

He retrieved his cane from the boot while Appletorn extricated himself from the seat's embrace, locked the doors, and held the clicker out.

Appletorn stared. "What is that?"

"An extra key, in case it should be needed."

"Keep it," the other said shortly. "I could not, in the direst emergency imaginable, steer that . . . device."

"It's really quite simple," Jen Sar told him. "Only use the sticks to point it, and the pedal to accelerate. When you hit something, the town constables will be summoned to take you into custody, where you will be safe from any pursuit."

Appletorn glared at him. "I thank you, but—no."

"As you like," Jen Sar said agreeably, and slipped the spare away.

There was a simple bell hanging by the door, with a string hanging from its striker. Jen Sar used the head of his cane to strike a sweet single note, then set the ferrule against stone walkway, and composed himself to wait.

"Ring again," Appletorn said after a few minutes had passed. "They may not have heard."

"But to ring again would be to betray complexity," Jen Sar pointed out. "Surely, in the fullness of time, a single summons will find a single—ah."

The door opened, silent on well-oiled hinges, to reveal one of the Chapelia in her simple gray robes, face swathed in simple gray cloth, plain black lenses covering her eyes, a cowl over her naked head.

Jen Sar inclined his head, very slightly. "One comes," he stated.

The lenses glinted as the doorkeeper moved her head.

"Two come, Seeker."

"One comes," Jen Sar repeated, "seeking a rare simplicity." He raised his hand, drawing the sign Lystra Mason had given him in the air between himself and the doorkeeper.

There was a long pause, doubtless as the doorkeeper had recourse to her quicklink. Jen Sar recruited himself to patience, his eyes on the shrouded face. The robes and other shrouding of course hid any minute muscle tension attending the sub-vocalization, and he allowed himself to marvel anew at the range of complexity necessary to support a simple life.

"Two come," the doorkeeper declared, and turned her shrouded face once more to Appletorn. "Do you seek, also?"

"I seek to study this one's actions," Appletorn said serenely; "in order to see if they might Teach."

An excellent answer, that, and with the advantage of being true.

The Chapelia inclined her head and stood away from the door.

"Enter."

· · · ·❊· · · ·

According to the opening credits, the vid was a dramatization of an ancient Melchizan folktale. The plot revolved around a pair of sibs—girl and boy—who had fallen joint heirs to an estate in the mountains. There were a number of people attached to the estate, by something called *grunkild*. The sister got right to work team-building, learning names, families and what everybody's job was. Her brother had brought three members of his home-team with him; they each picked out three people from the *grunkild* people, claimed a wing of the big house for themselves and proceeded to ignore the sister's efforts.

Theo shifted in her seat. Except for the Melchizan social structures, this was a familiar story—very much like those told to littlies at home. What was going to happen now was that an emergency would arise, the arrogant brother and his isolationist group would get into trouble, and the team-builder would save their bacon. Then, after the emergency was over, the brother would ask to be brought into the team.

Sure enough, the emergency was not long in coming,

though its nature was ... unexpected. Instead of bad weather, or an equipment failure, or an attempt to discredit one of the group's scholarship, it was actual physical danger that they faced.

A group of bandits came down out of the mountains with the winter winds, and attacked the estate. Why they didn't just ask for help wasn't explained. Theo guessed it made a better story to just have them ride in and start catapulting rocks and ice against the estate's walls.

The sister went to her team and asked them what should be done, seeking consensus, but the team members were afraid of the bandits and hid. Lacking consensus, the sister went to her room to study the problem.

In the meantime, the brother, who had held himself away from the team, and his few friends, came around behind the *bandits'* position, and used firearms to frighten them away.

And that, the narrator said, demonstrated why a leader must always keep himself aloof and vigilant for his people.

Theo sat up straight in her seat, cold with shock. That wasn't right!

The lights came up. She shook herself, and looked around to see if anyone else was as horrified as she felt.

Dalin was sitting to her right, eyes half-closed. Possibly he was asleep. On the left, Ave-Su was combing her fingers through her hair, her expression decidedly bored.

Theo took a breath. "That—" she began and started as Instructor Tathery called from the back of the room.

"All right, students! Back to the classroom, please, and form a talk-circle. Another class is scheduled for the room!"

Theo got up, feeling strangely shaky, like she'd made a dive during a bowli ball match, and had missed the ball. But! There was going to be a discussion. That was good. Clearly, the story had been told wrong for a reason. Maybe it was to—

A hand landed on her shoulder. She looked up; Instructor Tathery smiled at her tightly and jerked her head to one side.

"Come with me, Theo."

"Yes, ma'am," she said automatically, following the big woman out into the hall, and to the right, instead of to the left, which was the way back to the classroom.

"Is there a problem, ma'am?" she asked.

The instructor looked down at her. "Just an administration error, Theo. You're in the wrong class."

She frowned. "The wrong class? But my mother—"

"Yes, yes!" the instructor interrupted. "But she might not have considered, ah, *how important* dance is to Melchiza. You'll fit in much better with—Ah, here we are!"

She waved Theo to an office on the right, where a man wearing a plain blue shirt and dark slacks stood, ignoring several comfortable chairs, his feet flat and stance ready, as if he were waiting for his dance partner—no, Theo corrected herself, remembering what Win Ton had taught her—his *sparring* partner to arrive. He was not as tall as Instructor Tathery, nor as substantial, but Theo felt herself respond to his presence. She stopped, dropping into the ready mode, as Phobai called it; feet flat, knees flexed, hands at rest—and looked up into his face.

He had a hook nose, thin lips, and very, very blue eyes. The lips smiled. The eyes didn't.

"I . . . see," he said and nodded to her, deliberately, almost like one of Father's bows.

"I am Pilot-Instructor Arman. You may address me as Pilot. It is obvious, Pilot Waitley, that you have been misassigned. That error has been rectified, and you will now enter my class."

Theo frowned into those cold eyes. "My mother expects me to be in Instructor Tathery's class," she said. "They had a protocol agreement."

"So Instructor Tathery informs me. I have relieved her of her promise to your mother and taken the burden to myself." He looked over her head. "Thank you, Instructor. You did right."

"Thank you, sir." The woman's voice was not quite steady. She cleared her throat. "Theo, your belongings will be shifted to your new room. Pilot Arman will direct you."

"Indeed, the pilot may look to me for all things," the man said, and gave a nod of dismissal. "Your class needs you, Instructor."

"Yes," she said, suddenly reluctant, as a new voice called out.

"Instructor Tathery?"

Theo spun, keeping Pilot Arman on her left, half-facing this new intruder.

A boy not much older than she was held out a piece of hard copy to the woman. "Student reassignment, Instructor," he said cheerfully.

"Reassignment?" She frowned as she took the hard copy—and frowned again as she glanced down.

The messenger departed, whistling. Instructor Tathery turned back, paper upheld.

"Theo Waitley," she said.

Pilot Arman extended a hand. "I will take care of it," he said coolly. "Theo Waitley has been transferred into my class. If you should receive any other administrative orders regarding her, please send them to me. Thank you, Instructor."

"Sir," she whispered, and fled.

Theo stood where she was, unwilling to relax, uncertain what she should do next. This man was Security, but—*who* was he? She didn't doubt his claim of being a pilot; in fact, he was more...blatantly so...than any other pilot she knew. His stance was not only ready, it was aggressive.

"Do I disquiet you, Pilot Waitley?" Her new instructor had broken the security seal on the message, glanced at it briefly, refolded it and slipped it into his shirt pocket.

"Pilot Waitley?" he said. "There is a question in play."

"Yes, sir," she said, and forced herself to meet those very blue eyes. "You look like you're ready to begin dancing."

"I see. With whom have you been dancing, Pilot?"

Theo cleared her throat. "Friends from the *Vashtara*. I'm not a pilot, sir."

"Plainly, you have not gone far in your coursework, however, we Melchizans value pilots, even those just beginning flight, and we accord them the respect which is their due. You have been transferred to the pilots' section at Instructor Tathery's request. I have reviewed the classroom record of your dance and agree that you do not belong among...shall we say *the passengers*? Your performance in mathematics is low, but not unreasonably so. You will be assigned a tutor and remedial work." He took a breath, and...relaxed in a move very nearly a dance in itself. Abruptly, he was only a man in a blue shirt, preparing to walk on.

Theo felt her muscles loosen, like she had somehow internalized the pattern of relaxation she had just seen. She took a step back and shook her hands, fingers pointing loosely at the floor, releasing the energy she had drawn.

"Very good." Pilot Arman smiled, coolly, and nodded toward the door. "Come with me, please, Pilot."

They walked down the empty corridor briskly, but without haste. Pilot Arman wasn't interested in talking to her, and Theo was just as happy to pursue her own thoughts.

Captain Cho had tried to warn her, she thought. This is what came of learning *pilot lore*: people just naturally assumed you were a pilot, even if all you knew were a couple dance moves, or a couple words in hand-talk.

"Step over here for a moment, if you please, Pilot. This will interest you, I think." Instructor Arman said suddenly, guiding her to an observation window like the one into Instructor Tathery's classroom. Theo sighed. That classroom was already starting to feel far away and long ago.

"Tell me what you see, please."

Pilot Arman's voice brought her thoughts back to the present. She looked through the window. Two long rows of students sat at their computers, their faces soft and very nearly expressionless. It took Theo a moment to realize that they were working, and not all of them napping at their screens; their movements were deliberate and slow.

"I see a classroom full of...students," Theo said.

She was cold, her stomach tight. She cleared her throat. "I think the teacher needs to call an exercise break; they look pretty sleepy."

"Yes, they do, don't they? That is, for your information, the Parole Class, where those students who have been deemed disruptive or, as we say here, dangerous, are kept. Of course, they are sedated; we have limited staff here, and cannot afford an incident among the children of our visitors."

She swallowed and looked up at him. "Why are you showing me this?"

He smiled his cool smile, and put his fingers against his shirt pocket. The paper inside crackled slightly.

"This is a student transfer memorandum. Theo Waitley was, it says, incorrectly placed and must be moved immediately to the Parole Class."

Theo shook her head. "I'm not dangerous," she said, but her voice sounded breathless.

Pilot-Instructor Arman laughed. "Of course you are dangerous, Pilot."

Her shoulders were tense. If she ran, she thought, where would she go? She was fast, but there were cameras . . .

"I'm not going in there," she heard someone say, flat and hard.

"Be at ease, Pilot. You are not going in there. The bookkeeping for this rests safely in my hand. This display is for your interest and information only. Please, walk with me again; you'll be eager to meet the other pilots."

Carefully, she turned and walked with him, keeping an extra arm's length between them.

"The sedation," she said, after they had gone a few steps in silence. "Is it perfectly safe?"

"Sedation that you administer is always perfectly safe, Pilot," her new instructor said calmly. Three steps further along, he spoke again.

"We have a thing that we say, Pilot, in such circumstances as you find yourself. It is . . . advice, and also an expression of . . . comradeship."

"What . . ." Theo cleared her throat. "What is it?"

"Watch your back."

# THIRTY-FIVE

. . . . . . . . . . . . . . . . . . . .

*Efraim Agricultural Zone*

THE HOUSE WAS SIMPLE TO THE POINT OF DULLNESS. Each room they passed through was the twin of the room they had just quit, identical down to the grain of the floor.

At the fifth room, their guide paused and turned to them, black lenses flashing briefly.

"The study of simplicity is not lightly undertaken, nor easily put aside," she stated, which was right out of the *Book of Plain Thought*.

Still, Jen Sar thought, critically, she might have done worse. Had he not himself been engaged in the study of simplicity for many years? Granted, in his case, he thought of the study more in the light of self-defense, but surely the basic thesis was sound.

"One wishes to continue," he said, meeting the opaque glance calmly.

"One's purpose is constant," Appletorn added, which made for oddly comforting hearing.

The Chapelia turned, her robes whispering to the floor, and walked on.

. . . . . ❊ . . . .

"What is this, Pilot Waitley?" Instructor Arman demanded.

Theo sighed. She'd come into class in the middle of Practical Repair—and a good thing, too.

According to Jeren, who was lead on the project, the team's repair project was styled a janci-wagon; he promised to let her ride it, once they had it working again. Since Theo was the smallest, she got to do the close-in, under-carriage work, while Jeren, who was considerably larger, but knew what needed done, watched on the remote and guided her through the steps. She'd just identified the crushed bus link, and was getting her guide splice into position to chomp in a new one. If she had to leave it *now*, she'd lose whole minutes of nasty, tight fiddling . . .

"Pilot?" The pilot-instructor sounded . . . irritated.

"*Theo* . . ." Jeren breathed.

Right. Grumbling to herself, she twisted and peered out from beneath the low-lift. Pilot Arman stood some dozen steps away, and he was holding . . .

"A bowli ball," she answered, and suddenly frowned, slamming the hatch to as she rolled out from under the lift and came to her feet. "*My* bowli ball. That was in my luggage!"

Pilot Arman looked down his beaked nose at her, blue eyes mocking.

"And that is where it was found, in your luggage. Everything that enters this wing is inspected by Security. The potential risk to pilots, if we did not, is unacceptable."

Theo took a breath, trying to cool the anger tingling at her fingertips and along her nerves.

"You know that a bowli ball's no risk to pilots," she said, and held out her hand. "It's mine. Give it back."

"Yet you would have had me believe earlier that you are no pilot," he said, holding the ball—her gift from Win Ton!—negligently in his hand, like it was someone else's dishes that he was carrying to the disposal.

Her eyes stung, and she swallowed. It would be worse, she thought, to cry in front of this man than to lose her temper. Though it wouldn't be smart to lose her temper, either.

"That's my bowli ball," she said again, her voice sounding clipped, like Kamele's did when *she* was trying not to lose her temper. "It was given to me by—by a good friend, and I—I'd like it back. Please."

Pilot Arman tipped his head to one side, as if considering whether she'd asked politely enough.

"I understand," he said at last. "Catch."

He threw the ball, hard, straight at the floor. It twisted, gyros screaming, reversed itself, and shot to the left. Theo jumped, got a hand on it, and spun, cuddling the ball against her side. She hit the floor lightly, spinning, and came to rest in one of Phobai's favorite *menfri'at* positions, facing Pilot Arman.

He smiled at her and raised his hands, fingers flicking *careful, no threat, stand down* at her, the signs as hard as pebbles.

"I see that the bowli ball is, indeed, yours, Pilot."

Theo took a breath, though she didn't relax. "It is, and I intend to keep it," she said flatly.

"Of course," he answered, as if it had never been in doubt. "You carry it by right; you know that it is not a toy. That is well. Now." He held out his hand. "Your badge, if you please."

He wore the blue shirt, and he was her instructor.

*Win-win,* thought Theo, around a chill of dread. She stepped forward, detached the pink badge, and held it out to him.

He received it with a slight nod, and slipped it away into his shirt pocket.

"This," he said, producing a green badge like Jeren wore, "will identify you to all as a pilot. As with the other, you will wear it at all times, and surrender it only to Security, to myself, or to a senior pilot. Am I clear?"

Theo nodded, and pressed the new badge into place. "Yes, sir."

"Excellent. You may resume your work."

· · · ·⚙· · · ·

The sixth room was not a precise duplicate of all the other rooms they had passed through previously, nor was the person behind the desk indistinguishable from every other Chapelia he had ever beheld. Startlingly, her face was free of bindings, showing velvet brown skin stretched tight over strong bones. The black lenses lay to hand, on the desk by her mumu. Her eyes were pale blue, rich as silver against that dark skin.

She shook her head as he and Appletorn crossed the threshold, the door closed behind them by their soft-footed guide.

"The University of Delgado sends us a brace of *men,*" she said, and her voice was the voice of all Chapelia, sexless and atonal.

"Indeed, no," Jen Sar told her, approaching the desk nearly. "We came on our own judgment."

"Is that meant to reassure me?"

"Is reassurance simple?" Appletorn asked, coming to stand beside Jen Sar.

"One who is truly simple requires no reassurances," Jen Sar answered, "for to doubt is to embrace complexity."

"Neither of you is simple," the Chapelia behind the desk stated. "Nor have you come seeking *a rare simplicity*."

Jen Sar lifted an eyebrow. "You might have turned us away at the door," he pointed out, "if our reasons were inadequate."

"Your reason was directly out of the Second Book." She frowned. "Of course, I must see you, or compromise the simplicity of the doorkeeper."

"Ah," said Jen Sar, who had indeed chosen his response for just that reason.

Her frown deepened. "State your case, simply."

"Indeed, indeed." He bowed, palm pushing his cane firmly against the floor. "We come to ask a simple question: Are the Chapelia involved with the Serpent AI which has infected scholarship within the Wall?"

Silence for the space of three heartbeats.

"That is no simple question," she said.

"It's a very simple question," Appletorn said, surprisingly. "Complexity arises in the answer. I have another question, simpler than that which my colleague poses."

She opened her silver eyes wide. "Ask this very simple question, then."

"Gladly," Appletorn said. "Are the Chapelia willing to starve?"

•  •  •  •  ✷  •  •  •  •

"Here we are, Scholars, the Beltaire archive."

Kamele looked about the thin, dank hallway which marked the end of their several descents. Three elevators, the third one an express with but this one destination, so the Research Team was informed. Kamele felt certain that they were in the original treasure house, buried far below the planet's surface.

At the far end of the hall was a door. Director Pikelmin used her key-card and pushed it open, standing courteously aside to allow the scholars to precede her.

A broad-shouldered man in the blue shirt of Security stood behind the counter to the immediate left of the doorway. The rest of the walls were lined with stasis cabinets, their doors opaqued in defense of even the low, UV-free lighting.

"Director," the man behind the counter said as she came forward.

"Solmin. These are the scholars from Delgado invited by Professor Dochayn. Scholars, this is Solmin, Professor Dochayn's aide. You may place yourselves wholly into his hands."

*What choice do we have?* Kamele thought, *having made our choice.*

"Solmin," she said, stepping forward, since Hafley did not. "I am Kamele Waitley, these are Professors Orkan Hafley, Farancy Able, and Vaughn Crowley. We are sorry to have missed Professor Dochayn, and will do our best not to disrupt your schedule."

"In fact," Crowley took up. "You will find us quite self-sufficient. A tour of the archive should suffice us; we are all experienced researchers. I wager that you'll hardly know we're here."

Solmin exchanged a glance with Director Pikelmin.

"Scholars," she said, flashing the bright smile that Kamele was beginning to distrust, "we stand now within the archives. In order to minimize any potential damage to the records, some of which are quite fragile, we ask that researchers submit a list of those volumes that they wish to study. Again, in order to minimize damage to the archive, we stipulate that each book may only be drawn once, for a period of no more than three intervals. Once a book has been examined and returned to the archive, it may not be drawn again. I am sure you understand our position. Such records are priceless and we are sworn to protect them as best as we are able."

"Of course." Kamele looked to her team. Crowley was calm; Able serious. Hafley was smiling to herself, as if at a particularly amusing private joke.

"As it happens," Crowley said, reaching inside his jacket. "I have here a list prepared by Professor Beltaire herself." He placed a standard data-key and a sheet of hard copy on the counter.

"Professor Beltaire has been very busy on research team's behalf," Director Pikelmin observed. "I wonder that she did not come herself."

"Professor Beltaire felt that her years precluded such a long journey," Able said glibly.

"I see," the director said. She glanced at the hard copy list, and then back to the assembled professors. "And yet Professor Beltaire is some years younger, is she not, than . . . Professor Crowley?"

Crowley shrugged. "It is not my business to inquire into the ages of my colleagues," he commented. "Speaking for myself, I'm afraid that it pleased all of my teachers and mentors to note that I was somewhat young for my age."

Director Pikelmin took a breath, her shoulders rising, and Kamele stepped forward, drawing the other woman's eyes.

"Since we have so little time available to us," she said. "I wonder if we might be shown to our quarters and to the study room while Research Assistant Solmin begins to pull the texts listed. The research team would like to get down to work at once."

Director Pikelmin pressed her lips together, then abruptly nodded. "As you say, Professor, time is short. Solmin, the professors are your primary concern while they are with us. Professors, please follow me. You'll find everything to hand. The dormitory is just a step down the hall, and scarcely more from the study area."

· · · ·✶· · · ·

"Starve? The Wall consumes; it produces nothing."

"In fact, the scholars of the Wall produce much that is of use to the world and the Chapelia. For instance, crop-plants that have been optimized for growing conditions on Delgado. Our numbers, which are a source of insult to the Chapelia, insure that Delgado remains on several important trade and passenger ship lines. We produce, also, an ideal of scholarly integrity that is unparalleled throughout the galaxy. The phrase, 'as sound as a Scholar of Delgado' has currency on a dozen worlds, and the assurance that not only Delgadan scholars, *but their research* is sound drives students to seek us, which in turn drives the prosperity of the entire world."

"Interesting." The woman behind the desk turned her cool silver eyes to her other petitioner.

"Have you anything to add to this litany of virtue?"

Jen Sar smiled. "In fact, my colleague has been both precise and comprehensive. It is only left me to mention that, should it begin to seem simple that two male scholars be made to vanish—an aerial map of this house and attendant satellite images, as well as certain pictures of yourself, will be published widely if we do not return to our associate within the wall by the first bell of the new day."

"Pictures of myself?"

"I assume so, though I will grant that the image quality is poor. The person you are meeting with was wearing a disruption field. While this did confuse the image, it also caused the station's cameras to take note of her more closely, and therefore tag the records." He bowed, not quite ironically. "Once again, we are shown the value of simplicity. Had your contact merely taken her chances with the surveillance devices, she would not have called attention to herself, nor to you."

"This is fabrication."

"Alas, it is not, though I admit you have no reason to believe me. My theory, which is complex, is that you were approached by an agent from off-world, who purposed to show you a way to attain that simplicity which the Chapelia hold as ideal. The Chapelia, after all, had once sought to destroy the university and burn the library in their quest to turn complexity aside. They did not succeed, but I allow it to be a simple solution. This new solution—do not *burn* the library, but make the information it contains suspect. The result will be the same, in time. Students will fail of arriving, scholars will leave in search of funds and opportunity for research elsewhere, the university will dwindle. Perhaps it will even fail. Simplicity returns, and the Chapelia are strong once more."

"That does seem," she agreed, "a simple plan."

He smiled at her. "Except for the part where the world is cut off from trade and from custom. Not all of those outside the Wall are Chapelia. Indeed, Chapelia are but fifteen percent of the world population. How will you handle riots?"

"There is no reason why there should be riots. A return to simplicity—"

"You must," Appletorn interrupted, "study history. Indeed, you *must* study—my assertions, and those of Professor Kiladi, are easily checked. It may be that the Chapelia have not acted...wisely. Or it may be that they have acted with sagacity. If they have acted without study...then it is less likely that their actions are...uniformly wise."

The symbol-bearer closed her silver eyes.

"What," she asked, "do you want?"

"The name of your compatriot inside the Wall," Jen Sar said.

"Why would I need a compatriot inside the Wall?"

He shook his head. "To give you access to the technical facility, and to mask what predations the AI might produce." He turned to Appletorn.

"Your point is well-made. We must allow the symbol-bearer time for study."

Appletorn nodded. "I could not, in conscience, ask her to make a decision based only upon what we have told her. She must inform herself."

"I agree." Jen Sar looked back to the Chapelia

sitting behind her desk. "I would ask, if you find that your research leads to an altered conclusion, that you contact me with the name of your associate."

"If I reach an altered conclusion," the symbol-bearer said, picking the black eye wear off of her desk, and rising, "I will consider that course." She slid the lenses over her eyes, and stared at them blackly. "Good-day, Scholars."

· · · · ⚙ · · · ·

The visiting scholars' dormitory consisted of the bunk room, and a common area in which a kaf unit, disposal, two tables and eight chairs fit like the pieces of a puzzle.

"It reminds me of my student days," Able commented, lowering and raising the privacy curtains around one of the beds. "Only roomier."

Kamele smiled, remembering the dorm room she had shared with Ella and two other women at the start of their academic careers. Four bunks, four desks, a table, kaf and disposal crammed into a room two-thirds the size of the common room, with a shared 'fresher down the hall.

"Perhaps we can set up a table and have a few rounds of ping-pong after the evening meal," Crowley said, as he inspected the kaf. "Kamele, such a shame that your daughter isn't with us; I know how she enjoys soy noodles."

"We'll just have to make up for her absence with our own enthusiasm," Kamele said. From the corner of her eye, she saw Orkan Hafley smile, and shivered slightly, as if in a sudden breeze.

"If you have inspected sufficiently for the moment,

Scholars," Director Pikelmin said from the doorway, "I will guide you to the study room."

They followed her a few dozen paces down the thin hall, and into yet another comfortless space, this one containing two rows of four utilitarian plastic desks, each backed by a forbidding plastic chair. The light from overhead was bright enough that the furniture cast sharp shadows onto the hard white floor. Along the right side of the room were two movable shelves, one marked "Incoming," the other "Outgoing." The ambient temperature was slightly less than comfortably cool.

"Well," Crowley said. "No distractions to scholarship here."

Kamele turned to Jeyanzi Pikelmin, who was leaning in the doorway. "How will we communicate with Solmin?" she asked. "I don't see an intercom..."

"You may input the titles you wish to have brought to you into that datapad—" Pikelmin nodded at the wall-mounted screen. Solmin will come in every interval to deliver requested texts and to take away those texts you have finished with; you may communicate with him then."

"I see," Kamele looked around her, her stomach tight. The elder scholars had chosen desks side-by-side, and were seating themselves, pulling pens and datapads from their pockets. Hafley hesitated, then walked to the back of the room, claiming a desk in the second row, nearest the movable shelves.

Kamele took a breath. *Necessity,* she told herself, and she smiled at Jeyanzi Pikelmin. "I think this will do splendidly," she said.

# THIRTY-SIX

. . . . . . . . . . . . . . . . . . .

*Melchiza*
*Transit School*

THEO HAD ALWAYS LIKED MATH, NOT THE LEAST BECAUSE
she was good at it, disposing in mere minutes problem-
sets that Lesset claimed had taken her hours to derive.
She had always considered that math was easy—and it
had been.

Delgado math, that was.

The math taught in the Piloting Section of the
Transit School was another matter altogether. She
was not only behind the class's work, but her general
scores were . . . low.

Theo wasn't used to having low scores. It was one
thing to be physically challenged, and quite another
to be . . . stupid.

True to his word, Pilot Arman had assigned her
to a tutor, who drilled her in what she called "the
basics" until Theo's shirt was damp with sweat. She'd
been given self-paced modules, to which she devoted
herself, taking the datapad with her everywhere, while

427

her lace needle and thread languished at the bottom of her bag. Occasionally, she would blink out of a haze of temporal fractions to glance at the calendar, and wonder how Kamele was, and if the research was going well.

Running to class after a working breakfast, she was bemused to realize that she had been at school for three local days. It seemed as though she'd been taking pilot classes for half a 'mester at least. Part of that was the fact Melchiza's day was longer than Delgado's, which meant a longer school-day.

The other part was that there was so much to learn! Not just needing to catch up on math, but the mechanics class—not *theory* of mechanics, either! They were actually building and repairing devices; reminding her of pleasant hours spent in the garage with Father, handing him tools, and watching him tinker. He would tell her what he was doing and why, not as a lesson, really, and sometimes ask her help in setting a screw or reattaching a wire. She'd apparently learned more from those informal sessions than she had realized; Gayl said she'd already brought the team repair-bay average up by a dozen points.

She hurried across the room to her team's square and slid into her seat just as the bell blared the beginning of the school day. Jeren, Gayl, and Moxi were already in place.

"Hey, Theo," Gayl said. Jeren nodded.

Moxi, the lower half of his face hidden by an embroidered half-veil, turned his head slightly. Moxi was in Cleansing, Jeren had told her, preparing for his *ianota*, which sounded to Theo like a *Gigneri*. He was only allowed to speak to his teacher, his father, and his *nya*—sort of like a mentor, Theo guessed. Gayl said that, usually, boys from Ecbatana didn't travel during Cleansing; *she* speculated that there had been an emergency in Moxi's family, but of course nobody could ask him.

Theo touched her computer screen, timing in just under the wire and not a heartbeat before Pilot-Instructor Arman strolled into the room accompanied by a short woman wearing a blue shirt and a frown.

"Uh-oh," Gayl muttered.

"What?" Theo whispered.

"Physical dynamics exhibit. I shouldn't have eaten breakfast!"

"Physical dynamics" was *menfri'at*. The piloting class had *menfri'at* practice twice each day. Despite that, Theo's teammates weren't particularly skilled, and most sessions left her missing Win Ton and Phobai, though she'd have welcomed any of the pilots she'd danced with on *Vashtara*.

"Pilots arise!" Pilot Arman called, and everybody leapt to their feet, facing front, hands at their sides.

Theo stood between Gayl and Jeren. Usually, Pilot Arman would walk down the line of students—pilots— looking each one down from face to shoes, like he was inspecting them for design flaws, then he would return to the front of the room, call out a module number, and everyone would dance.

This morning, though, Pilot Arman didn't perform his usual inspection. He stood near the door, arms folded over his chest, while the blue-shirt walked forward, her frown growing more pronounced with every step.

She came to rest midway between Pilot Arman and the line of waiting pilots.

"From the left," she snapped. "Module Six."

The leftmost team came forward three steps and danced Module Six, not very well, Theo thought, but better than her team usually managed.

The blue-shirt nodded and called for the next team to stand forward, assigning them Module Three. They were better as a team, and one boy was pretty good. The woman pointed a finger at him when the dance was over, and he walked to the front of the room to stand next to Pilot Arman.

"Our turn," Jeren said, sounding as dejected as Moxi's shoulders looked.

Theo led the way out the floor, her head pleasurably full of something besides math. The four of them stood in a line, facing the woman in the blue shirt. Theo smiled as she relaxed into the ready position.

"Module Eight," said the frowning woman.

Theo flowed forward, arms rising together on the left side of her body, the back of the right hand reinforced by the palm of the left. She spun—and realized that she was too quick; the rest of her team was two beats behind her—Gayl nearly three.

Biting her lip, she slowed, and used the tempo-step Phobai had shown her, so they could catch her up and they'd be on the same—

"Pilot Waitley!" snapped Pilot Arman.

Theo let the move complete itself, centered herself and turned, suddenly and forcibly reminded of Gayl's comment about breakfast.

"Sir?" she asked, but it was the woman who answered her.

"Why did you amend your process?"

Theo swallowed, and met the woman's eyes. "I didn't want to over-dance my team," she said.

The woman looked to Arman, who sighed and shook his head.

"Theo Waitley," he said, "these pilots are not your crew, they are your study group. You have no obligation to them."

Theo stared. "They're my team," she repeated. "I—"

"Enough," the woman in the blue shirt directed. She pointed at Theo, who blinked, then hurried to the front of the room to stand next to Pilot Arman and the other dancer who had been pulled out of line.

The last team in line danced without distinction. The blue-shirted woman turned without a word and marched to the front of the room.

Pilot Arman nodded. "You two pilots will attend Inspector Vidige." He looked out over the room and raised his voice. "Pilots! Return to places and open to general self-test twenty-seven."

Theo stared at the frowning woman—Inspector Vidige. Was she going to be relocated again? she thought, stomach tightening even more. This woman wasn't even a teacher! What if she was taken outside of the school? What if—

"Attend me, please, pilots," Inspector Vidige said, her voice polite if not cordial. "We adjourn to another room within this building for a fuller testing of your abilities."

· · · · ❄ · · · ·

They fell almost too quickly into the work. During one of their meetings aboard *Vashtara,* Kamele, Able, and Crowley had divided Beltaire's list between them. Hafley was therefore assigned the chores of internal librarian and secondary fact verification—roles she accepted with surprising grace, and performed with a degree of astuteness.

The room they labored in was cold to the point of being a health hazard; they all wore multiple layers of clothing from the luggage that had appeared in the dorm room sometime during the second—or possibly the third—day. While periods of intense study such as this project demanded did tend to dim awareness of outer conditions, yet Kamele did from time to time wish for a hot cup of coffee to warm her.

That, of course, was quite impossible; Solmin would never permit the precious papers under his care to be put at risk of a coffee-spill. Kamele could sign herself out of the study room when Solmin came in on one of his scheduled pick-ups, but she would then have to time her return to his next visit, and an entire Melchizan hour was far too long to stand away from the work.

There was very little conversation; there would be time for synthesis and comparison during the return trip to Delgado. Kamele's own findings were disturbing enough, in the rare moments that she allowed herself to lose focus, that a recertification of the University of Delgado's central library, at the very least, seemed mandated. Considerations of the expense might have kept her awake, but her few hours of sleep were deep and dreamless.

And, yet, for all the work they accomplished here, they only verified what they had known: That certified copies of documents in the Delgado library had some-how been altered.

What they—what *she*—lacked even now was proof. *Suspicion* of conspiracy was not enough. Conversations were subject to interpretation, as were expectations. Jen Sar's phrase: "No one is right until there is proof," had used to infuriate her, and yet . . . she needed not only proof, but the names of those involved in what would seem to be a vast conspiracy.

Whenever she tried to count out the number of people necessary to wreak such havoc upon Delgado and Delgadan scholars, she caught up on the shoals of *who* and *why*? Who attacked historic documents? And why?

. . . ·⚙· . . .

"Very well, Pilots, who will be first to demonstrate their ability?"

Inspector Vidige frowned impartially at all eight of them. The other six had been waiting for them in this exercise area—three girls and three boys, each wearing a green badge and a wary expression. Behind them was a sight both familiar and unfamiliar. It was, Theo thought tentatively, a dance machine. Unlike the machine she and Win Ton had beat, it was only one level high, hulking and dark, where the other had been brightly lit and colorful. Theo felt a thrill. Maybe this was like the machine Win Ton had learned on, at his school? Maybe—

"Come, come!" Inspector Vidige said sharply. "Modesty flies no ship, Pilots! But, I am previous." She turned to Theo and the other student who had been chosen from her class—Robit Josin, he'd told her during their quick march down the hall—and pointed at the machine. "Have the newest additions to our group used one of these devices?"

"I've used one like it," Theo said, and Robit nodded in agreement.

"Me, too. An arcade game."

"And how well did you score, on this arcade game?" Robit shrugged. "I hit level thirty-two."

Inspector Vidige nodded and frowned at Theo.

"I—my friend and I danced through the overdrive level," she said. "My friend said it wasn't a true overdrive, though."

"Well, then. Do either of you wish to lead the group?"

Robit shrugged again. "If nobody else wants to go first, I'll break the ice," he said, and jerked his head at a thin girl with her blond hair pulled into a knot at the crown of her head. "Show me the controls, why not?"

"No reason," she answered and walked with him to the machine, the rest of the group trailing after, and Inspector Vidige behind them all.

"Now the rules," she said loudly, after the girl had finished showing Robit the on-switch and the selector buttons. "The pilot-at-dance may dance so long as he likes, until he makes a misstep. You may begin at any level you like and advance to any level you can. One misstep and you must dismount. The machine is set to enforce this. Am I understood, Pilot?"

"Yes, Pilot," Robit said.

"Begin at will."

Robit looked at the rest of the class, bit his lip and looked back to the controls. He looked nervous and Theo didn't blame him.

"Come along, Pilot! Surely you'd like a little exercise?" Inspector Vidige sounded mean, Theo thought, and she was *pushing*. A couple of the other students giggled, like they thought intimidation was funny.

Theo cleared her throat.

"Excuse me, Inspector Vidige," she said, stepping forward.

The blue-shirt frowned at her.

"Pilot Waitley. What is it?"

"I was just wondering if he wasn't going to pick a partner," Theo said. "I thought this was a team game."

Inspector Vidige was seen to sigh.

"What planet are you from, Pilot Waitley?"

Theo blinked. "Delgado."

The boy to her left sniggered, and the blond girl with the top-knot covered her face with her hand.

"Oh," somebody else further along the arc said, sotto-voce. *"Safety first."*

"No chit-chat!" snapped the blue-shirt. "Pilot Waitley. The responsibilities borne by a pilot in the commission of his duties, heavy as they sometimes may be, are borne by *him alone*. This is the reality of piloting and of pilots. Melchiza recognizes that the mating of skill and temperament that creates a pilot is rare, which is why we honor our pilots and grant them privilege beyond what is allowed ordinary citizens. To be a pilot is to be the final judge of weighty—by which I mean *life-and-death*—decisions.

"To return to the point of today's exercise—no, despite what you may have learned from your *friend*, this is not a team effort." She turned her head. "Pilot Josin, your colleagues are waiting."

"Yes, ma'am," Robit said, and kicked the start-switch.

❋　　❋　　❋

Robit danced three levels before he made a mistake and the machine froze, knocking him off-balance. He staggered, recovered, and dismounted warily, but really, Theo thought angrily, he could've fallen on his head! There was no reason that the machine had to stop so hard—the silly *game* she and Win Ton had beat had just rocked to a gentle rest when the set was over. If a *game* could do it—

The blond girl mounted the machine next, spun the dial without hesitation and began to dance. She might've been good, but she didn't give herself any chance to warm up, so it looked like she was always half-a-beat behind the projected pattern. Eighteen moves in, she tried to recover the lag, got her feet tangled and jumped clear with a yell when the machine locked.

She'd barely landed when a tall boy with a shaved head, his right ear a-jingle with gold rings, stepped up for his turn. He turned the dials deliberately, and dropped back to the dance pad, his eyes half closed; his movements exact, but lazy. Theo thought of Bek— and then she thought of the man on the machine at the Arcade, dancing half-asleep, as if the challenge was too small to take seriously.

The boy with the earrings danced through four levels by Theo's count—and probably could've gone further, if he'd been paying attention.

He turned the stagger generated by the machine's abrupt stop into a somersault, landing light on his feet.

There was a hesitation then, as if the rest of the pilots were weighing whether they could beat the record so far.

Theo shook her head and walked forward.

· · · ✳ · · ·

Kamele rubbed her eyes and looked at the shelf again. Surely, the fifth book in the diary set she was studying had been right here on the shelf, next to the fourth, which she had just placed in the outgoing cart? She knew she was tired—they were all tired by now, but—no, she decided, she must have been mistaken. It must have been the fifth book in another set, even now under study by one of the other team members.

Sighing, she picked up the next on her list and took it back to the study station.

· · · ✳ · · ·

Unlike the dance machine aboard *Vashtara,* this machine *wanted* you to lose, Theo thought. It would throw in sneaky little half-steps, and change tempo when neither made sense. It also had a sensor for how hard you hit the pad, which she'd realized just in time to avoid getting tossed off about four moves in.

She'd started at level fifteen, so she'd have a chance to warm up, and now she was cooking, like Phobai said. While she wasn't particularly having fun, she wasn't mad anymore, either. Her legs were beginning to get tired though, and she scanned the control board, looking for the stop switch. The pattern switched into a fast jig, and she gave up her search to attend to that, *fuffing* her hair out her face.

*What if there isn't a stop switch?* she wondered. *Do I have to flub a step to make it stop?*

The idea of flubbing a step on purpose made her feel cranky all over again. The machine switched to the next level—her eighth, unless she'd lost count—with a series of movements that didn't go together *at all*. By the time she'd negotiated those, she was seriously considering flubbing that step. She was so sweaty, her hair was stuck to her face, and there was a stitch burning along her right side. Maybe, she thought, it wouldn't be so bad. It wasn't as if she hadn't done better than—

There was a flash of pale blue light, and a soft tone. The pattern-screen went blank and the machine . . . gently rocked to stop.

Theo wiped her forehead on her sleeve and looked out over the exercise area. The girl with the top-knot was shaking her head, and Robit's mouth was frankly hanging open. Inspector Vidige cleared her throat.

"Thank you, Pilot Waitley," she said. "That was most instructive."

. . . . ❊ . . . .

Orkan Hafley was working at the carts, sorting the books the scholars had finished with onto the outgoing bin. Kamele watched as the Chair worked; she handled the volumes with respect, as any scholar would, making certain that they were arranged in short stacks, which were less likely to fall over, and using all of the shelves. When she finished with the outgoing shelf, she moved to the incoming shelf, straightening the tumbled volumes there, picking one up in her off-hand and continuing with her work. While Kamele watched, she stepped over to the outgoing cart and slipped the volume she had taken from the incoming into the back of a stack.

Kamele came to her feet so suddenly her chair tipped backward and clattered to the hard, white floor.

"How long has this been going on?" she cried.

Able jerked back in her seat, clearly disoriented. Crowley, showing commendable reflexes for a man of his years, leapt up, and caught Hafley's shoulder, effectively restraining her.

"You don't have permission to touch me!" Hafley snapped. Crowley ignored her, as he looked to Kamele.

"Treachery, Sub-Chair?" he asked quietly.

Kamele took a breath. "I fear so, Professor."

· · · ❋ · · ·

As it turned out, Inspector Vidige's Advance Class was Theo and Robit's new posting. They didn't have to change dorm rooms again—that was the good news. Theo still had math remediation—that was the bad news. That, and the fact that all of the other pilots in her class thought she'd deliberately shown up better at dance than they were, and she didn't have a chance to do any social engineering to smooth things over, because the Advance Class didn't sit by team; they sat solo.

It made for a long school-day, and, despite the extra load of math Inspector Vidige had off-loaded onto her datapad for her off-hours work, Theo was glad when the bell rang for the free period before supper.

"Hey, Safety First!"

Theo turned, frowning as the blond girl—Initha, her name was—swaggered forward, her thumbs hooked in her belt. Beside her came Fruma, skating a bowli ball from hand to hand, his eyes on Theo's face. The other members of the Advance Class, including Robit, were spreading out on either side of them.

"What do you want?" she asked Initha.

"Want to ask you a question," Fruma answered.

Theo looked to the right, and to the left. She stood at the center of ragged circle. Somehow, she didn't think that was good. She slipped the datapad into a pocket and shook out her hands.

"Ask it, then," she said.

"You know why there aren't any Delgadan pilots?" Initha, again.

"No, why?"

"Because," yelled Fruma, "it's too *dangerous*!"

He threw the bowli ball, and Theo jumped.

# THIRTY-SEVEN

. . . . . . . . . . . . . . . . . . . . . . . .

*Melchiza*
*City of Treasures*

"WELL. THERE YOU ARE." MONIT APPLETORN ALL BUT dropped his cup of coffee on the table as he slumped into the chair across from Jen Sar Kiladi. There were dark circles under his eyes and a general air of weariness about him.

"Here I am," that gentleman agreed, "and well. I hope I find you the same?"

"Seems to me that I found you," Appletorn grumbled, ignoring the question; "though it wasn't necessarily easy. How do you do it?"

Jen Sar raised an eyebrow. "Do what?"

"Vanish." He raised his cup and drank deeply. "I walked past this table twice, knowing you must be here, and my eye slid by you."

"Ah." Jen Sar moved his shoulders. "I am a short man, and you, if I may venture, are a tired man. Have you had word from our friend?"

Appletorn shook his head. "I wish I had; it would be easier to sleep."

"You don't find suspense a tonic for a restful night?" Jen Sar raised his mug and sipped tea.

"Perhaps you do!" Appletorn snapped.

"At the least, I am comforted by the observation that we both remain as yet unassassinated."

Appletorn shook his head, finished off his coffee and put the empty cup none-too-gently on the table. "How—" he began, and stopped.

Jen Sar tipped his head in polite inquiry. "Forgive me, you were about to say?"

The other man half-laughed. "I was about to ask how Kamele Waitley . . ." Again, he hesitated.

". . . tolerated me for so many years?" Jen Sar concluded, and smiled. "The only explanation can be that she is a great-hearted and patient lady."

Appletorn shook his head again and returned to the original topic, like a dog worrying at an old bone. "Do you think we will hear anything, or will they ignore us?"

"I admit that hope of contact is growing faint. If they do ignore us, we shall need to do something . . . dramatic."

"Taking your case directly to . . ." He glanced around them, but all the nearby tables were empty on this off-meal hour. ". . . directly to our friend—that wasn't dramatic?"

"It was necessary," Jen Sar said, worry sharpening his own voice. "Time becomes . . . an issue, as we discussed." He sighed. "This is what comes of giving one's opponent time for study."

"We could hardly have done otherwise," Appletorn protested.

Jen Sar sipped tea. They could, of course, have done very much otherwise, but threatening one of the high-level Chapelia was risky, to understate the case by a magnitude of ten, and likely would have gained them no more than they held now.

On the other hand, time *did* grow short. If Kamele arrived home bearing proof of tampering, as he had no doubt she would, she would become a target for the as-yet-nameless outworld agent.

Locating that agent and her compatriots on Delgado, counting them and rendering them powerless—he had taken that as his responsibility, only to find that he was not equal to the challenge.

An outworld agent would not be constrained by the mores of a Safe World. One such agent had already cost him—dearly.

It would not happen again.

· · · · ※ · · · ·

"What reason do you have to sabotage the work of this research team?" Kamele demanded.

Orkan Hafley gave an amused shrug. "My dear Kamele, you're overwrought. A simple error—"

"Not quite so simple," Able interrupted, raising her datapad. "There are three volumes here which are marked as having been ordered in. When they did not arrive I put it down to the ineptness of our research assistant, and there are other things, after all, on my list to console me."

"I have four," Crowley said, "in similar state. I blamed myself, for hastiness begets error."

"I have one," Kamele said, looking to Hafley. "You have been busy, Chair, but why?"

"Professor Crowley said it himself—haste begets error," Hafley said. "Furthermore, age contributes to a poor memory. All of us have been working long hours and sleeping very little. I'll admit that I made one error of placement—which Kamele recovered! All's well that ends well, with the agreement of my colleagues."

Kamele turned to Able.

"The volumes you thought you had requested," she said urgently. "Request them again."

"Certainly, Sub-Chair." She rose and walked over to the wall-mounted datapad.

"Kamele, really—"

"It has been apparent for some time," Crowley interrupted, "that this project has not enjoyed Chair Hafley's full support. My report to the Directors will reflect this, noting in particular her willingness to place this vital research into the hands of scholars unknown to us, either by reputation or by name. This incident will also be documented. I suspect that the Directors—"

"*I* suspect that the Directors will know how to take such a report," Hafley interrupted in her turn. "Elderly males are well-known to suffer moments of delusion. Had *I* the staffing of this team, we should have had Beltaire herself, whatever she may have pretended about her health. This project demanded the weight that only such an august and senior researcher could lend to it. Admin chose to override me, but they will not allow a report that is clearly nothing more than a work of spite to pass upward to the Directors."

"I—" Kamele begin, and went back a step when the older woman turned to her.

"You!" she said sternly, and shook her head. "I tried to groom you, Kamele, but you would not learn. You're

ambitious—a little *too* much so, may I say? What sort
of mother allows her desire to achieve prominence to
overrule her rightful concern for her daughter's safety?
Anything might happen at that school—Melchiza isn't a
Safe World, you know! Who can tell but that you might
find that she's been...harmed in some way; changed
out of recognition? But you counted the possible cost
to Theo too small to consider, and here you are, incommunicado, unable to protect your child—your most
important duty! Small wonder you're fabricating threats
out of thin air! The guilt, Kamele, that you must—"

"I have a notation on my request, Sub-Chair," Able
said from her position at the datapad.

Kamele took a breath. "What is it?" Her voice
was steady.

"It says those volumes are no longer available to us."

Kamele took another breath and met Hafley's hard
blue eyes.

"Not just one error, Chair Hafley," she said, and
turned to the remaining members of the team.

"Compare lists; see if there is a pattern to the volumes we weren't allowed to see. When Solmin comes
in next, we will ask him to escort Chair Hafley to the
dormitory and confine her there."

"Excellent," Crowley said. Able nodded.

"In the meantime," Kamele looked back to Hafley,
feeling the quiver of horror in her stomach. *Clyburn,*
she thought, *whose mother is high in Administration.
Who could have had Theo placed well in the Transit
School...*

"In the meantime," she repeated, and her voice was
breathless now. "I want to know what you've done to
my daughter."

· · · · ✾ · · ·

Theo extended her leg, carefully, and danced Module One in slow-time, like Phobai had shown her.

"Stretching's good for your muscles and your reactions," she'd said. "*Slow* stretching's good for bruises."

She sure did have bruises, though nothing as startling as Initha, who'd gotten herself a truly spectacular black eye when she'd misjudged the angle of bounce. All of them had contact burns, though only Fruma'd gotten anything broken. His hand, of course, and he'd been sent to the infirmary when Inspector Vidige broke up the game. The rest of them had been sent to clean up for dinner, without even a mention that they might've been playing a little too rough.

At lights out, Theo had been feeling a little stiff. At wake-up, she'd been feeling a *lot* stiff. She'd gotten carefully out of bed, done some basic stretches and hobbled down to breakfast, where she'd found the rest of the crew, just as stiff. Initha'd nodded her to a place across from her and then they'd walked to class together, settling carefully into their solo seats.

It was free study now, and standing was permitted. Theo figured that meant *menfri'at*, too, as long as she didn't get too energetic.

Not much chance of that.

She slid into Module Two, aware that someone was moving on her right. Turning her head, she saw Initha and, beyond her, Robit, and Stan, earrings chiming softly, as they all danced slow-time.

"Good idea," Initha said.

"Good game," Stan added.

"It was," Theo said, and flowed into the next step.

# THIRTY-EIGHT

· · · · · · · · · · · · · · · · · · · · · · · ·

*Melchiza*
*City of Treasures*

A COMPARISON OF THOSE VOLUMES THAT HAFLEY HAD returned before they'd been used seemed to indicate that she had been opportunistic in her sabotage, rather than deliberate.

Small comfort there.

Kamele's request that she be allowed to contact the Transit School had been denied by a stone-faced Solmin. He understood, he said, that the professor's daughter might stand at risk. He understood that a mother might feel concern—even grave concern. He could not, however, allow the professor to call, though she could of course travel to the Transit School in the company of her assigned Chaperon. If she chose to leave, she could not return to the archives for a period of one Melchizan year. Those were the rules. He was sorry, but he was certain that the professor understood.

Kamele understood.

"Perhaps Chaperon Gidis could be dispatched to the Transit School with a message?" she asked.

Solmin frowned. "I will inquire of Director Pikelmin," he said austerely.

"Thank you," Kamele said, around the needle of dread lodged in her heart. "I appreciate your effort."

But whatever effort Solmin did or did not put forth, it hardly mattered.

Scrutiny of the list of texts that remained unexamined, excepting those that Hafley had returned, revealed that the task was very nearly two-thirds completed. The reputable remaining members of the research team redoubled their own efforts, and inside of a day they were done.

• • • ❊ • • •

"Pilot Waitley."

Theo blinked out of her self-test and looked up into Inspector Vidige's frown.

"Inspector?"

"Please shut down here, Pilot, collect your belongings from your dorm and be at Entry Port Three in . . ." She glanced down at the note in her hand. ". . . in one-quarter interval."

"Yes, Inspector," Theo said, her fingers already busy with the shutdown sequence. She looked up again, decided that the frown didn't look *particularly* forbidding, and ventured a question.

"Where am I going, please, ma'am?"

"I'm informed that a bus will be arriving to take you to the Visitors' Center, Pilot." She raised her eyebrows, and said, with emphasis, "*Soon.*"

· · · ❋ · · ·

"Well, there you are, Clyburn!" Orkan Hafley settled into the seat next to her *onagrata* and patted his knee. "Did you have a pleasant visit with your mother?"

"We had more to talk about than I'd thought," Clyburn said as the rest of the team filed into the bus and chose seats. "Thank you, Orkan."

"You're very welcome, my dear. I'm glad I could do you this little kindness."

Kamele slid into a seat near the exit door, her shoulder against the window. Able, who had entered the bus behind her, hesitated as if she might chose the aisle seat. Kamele turned her head aside. Able moved on.

"And how did your business go?" Clyburn asked Hafley.

"It started well," she said. "Unfortunately, Kamele took it upon herself to accuse me of dishonesty, and Crowley of withholding my approval for the team's mandate—as if I would have put myself to the considerable inconvenience of traveling to Melchiza if I *disapproved*—but you know what old men are, dear! If you find me more rested than the majority of the team, it's because my generous colleagues evicted me from the study room for the last two days while they labored, and so I was able to catch up on my sleep."

"Professors, professora, sir!" Gidis called, leaping up the stairs into the passenger compartment. "Your business is well-concluded, eh? We go now, immediately, to take the mamzelle up from school. From there, we go by directest route to the Visitors' Center. I will guide you to the Departure Lounge and log you in with the desk there—my last task as your elder brother! Once you are logged, you may leave the lounge only as part of the group ascending to Melchiza Station. On-station, station rule applies until you are once again aboard valiant *Vashtara*, and safely on your way home to Delgado! Keep your badges with you. Listen to your elder brother! *Keep your badges with you* while you are in Melchizan space. Once you are aboard *Vashtara*, you may dispose of them. Are there questions?"

There were not.

"Good!" Gidis said. "We are all informed. In a moment, the driver engages the route. Our schedule is close, so there will be no time to tour the school facilities, as Professora Waitley had hoped. Perhaps upon your next visit to Melchiza, eh?" He leaned over Kamele's seat and grinned at her.

She managed a smile. "That would be pleasant," she said, and he spun away toward the driver's compartment.

"It seems odd that Kamele would have accused you of dishonesty." Clyburn's voice was loud in the absence of Gidis. "After all, she's sub-chair, subordinate to *you*, Orkan."

"Well! We must make her some allowance. She belatedly realized that she had some reason to be concerned about her daughter's safety. Naturally, she should have thought about that before rashly refusing—but there! It's no more than mother's nerves, I'm sure, and it will be found that Theo took no harm, and is returned to us calm and biddable."

*Calm and biddable,* thought Kamele, dry-mouthed. The bus lurched slightly and began to move. The

Treasure House fell rapidly behind them as Kamele stared at the window, seeing instead into memory.

She recalled Theo high over her head, dancing with Win Ton yo'Vala; Theo playing in the change-field on *Vashtara*; Theo, her hands busy with needle and thread; Jen Sar and Theo, dark head bent over light, reading a book together . . .

*Is this how a Scholar of Delgado behaves?* she asked herself, blinking damp eyes. *Does she put everything— even the life of her child—behind her scholarship? If Theo . . .*

But if Theo had taken harm, what could she do, beside gather her child close and take her safely home?

· · ·✦· · ·

"Pilot Waitley."

Theo stopped on the threshold of her dorm room, blinking at Pilot Arman and another man in a blue shirt.

"Sir?" she said experimentally. "I'm supposed to get down to Port Three, right now."

"Exactly," said Pilot Arman. "We are your escort."

"Please," the other man said. He stepped to one side, clearing her route, his fingers flickering a command to *Move quick! Ship waits for no one!*

She renewed her grip on her bag and moved, quickly, the two men falling in behind her.

"Why an escort?" she asked over her shoulder.

"A small demonstration," Pilot Arman answered as they rounded the corner and headed for the 'vator, "for the benefit of those who would endanger pilots."

Theo punched the call-button, and spun. "Am I . . . in danger?" she demanded.

The nameless blue shirt shook his head.

"As I said," Pilot Arman amplified, "a demonstration only."

Behind her the 'vator door *shusshhhed* open. Theo put herself into the rear corner, her bag in front of her. The two security men stood with their backs to her, one on each side of the door.

"There is one thing that we would like you to recall, Pilot Waitley," the nameless one said.

"What's that?"

"Only that Melchiza values pilots, as you saw. If you should wish to continue your education with us, and join the Melchizan Pilot Corps, you will find us most receptive. I'd advise you to retain your badge; it will make reapplication simpler, though of course you may use Pilot Arman and Inspector Vidige as references."

Theo felt her right eyebrow twitch upward. "How long is this offer good for?" she asked. "With all the students that must come through here, they're—the pilots aren't going to remember me for very long."

The 'vator came to a halt. The doors sighed open.

"Oh, we'll remember you," Pilot Arman said, stepping out into the hall. "Never doubt that."

· · · ❖ · · ·

The bus pulled into the ramp, slowing only slightly. It slowed again as it negotiated the turn designated as "To Entry Port Three," and almost immediately thereafter stopped.

The door slid open, and Kamele lurched to her feet.

"Stop!" yelled Gidis, snatching at her arm. "The schedule!"

Kamele ducked, flying down the ramp to the inhospitable 'crete platform. A blast of oil-tainted wind hit her as landed, stripping the pins out of her hair. She shook her head, hair whipping out of her eyes, and there, coming toward her—

A woman walked toward her, pale hair floating on the breeze, her steps firm and her shoulders level. There was a green tag affixed to her red jacket, and she pulled a bag behind her. Two men in blue shirts flanked her, following a respectful two steps to the rear.

"Theo?" Kamele whispered. Then, louder. "Theo!"

Maybe she ran the few steps to meet her; maybe her daughter ran, too. Kamele folded the thin body into her arms and rested her cheek against the warm hair.

"Theo," she whispered. "Are you *all right*?"

"I'm fine," Theo said, matter-of-fact. She took a step back and Kamele reluctantly let her go, searching her face—there was a scrape along her right cheek, but her eyes were steady and her attention sharp.

"Are *you* all right?" Theo asked. "You look—are you *crying*?"

"A little," Kamele admitted. "It's been—are you certain you're all right?"

"The pilot has taken no harm while she was under our care," the man with the beaked nose said. The side of his mouth twitched. "Except for what might be expected, from a particularly *vigorous* game of bowli ball."

"Pilot?" Kamele asked, just as Gidis pounded up to them.

"Professora!" the Chaperon cried. "Mamzelle! I beg you both—the schedule! There is no time—"

"There is time enough for the pilot's mother to assure herself that all is well," the beaked nose man said sternly.

Gidis blinked. "Pi—pilot?" he stammered, and stared at Theo, his mustaches drooping even more than usual.

"Forgive, sir, but the mamzelle was issued the pink badge."

"She was issued the pink badge in error," the other man said, and raised his hand. "Administration has since corrected itself." He nodded to Gidis. "It's good you came down, Chaperon. You will of course see to it that Pilot Waitley is accorded every courtesy while she is in your care."

"But of course—how else! I say to her from the first, I am your elder brother. I protect you and guard you. Leave all to me."

"That's well, then," Beak Nose said. He bowed to Kamele, stiffly, from the waist. "Professor Waitley, it's an honor to meet the pilot's mother."

"We'll clear the bus for quick routing," the other man said to Gidis. "Deliver the pilot safely, Chaperon."

"All of them—every one!" Gidis swore, and turned, snatching at Theo's bag. She stepped sideways, avoiding him easily.

"I'll take it," she said. She glanced at the two men. "Thank you, Pilot Arman . . . sir."

"Our pleasure, pilot."

. . . ❖ . . .

Kamele was *scared,* Theo thought, as they followed Gidis up the ramp and found their seat. Theo slung her bag into the overhead and looked around.

"Hi, Professor Able—Professor Crowley."

"Good afternoon, Theo," Professor Crowley said, and his voice sounded odd, like he wasn't sure if he ought to be laughing or crying.

"Theo," Professor Able said. "You're looking well."

"Isn't she?" cried Professor Hafley. "What did I tell you, Kamele! There was no reason at all to take such a foolish pet. The child's perfectly fine, if a little . . . grubby."

Theo turned to look at her, and surprised a glare on Clyburn's usually vacuous face.

"Somebody gave Theo a pilot's badge," he said, glare melting into a mocking grin. "Isn't that cute?"

· · · · 🏵 · · · ·

It was late. He'd taken to working late at his office in the Wall. The house, despite the efforts of the feline contingent, was a little too . . . quiet of late. A house ought to be occupied, if one bothered with such things at all, and if on occasion a full house seemed rather *too* full, well . . . that was why elderly housefathers maintained a private study with a door that locked.

"*Eidolon*, I better see some trim in velocity before you hit station-space." The perpetually annoyed voice of the station master issued from the Orbital Traffic Scanner he had installed in the tiny office. It made the place much more homelike, especially in the late hours.

Vashtara *will be casting off from Melchiza Station soon*, Aelliana offered from the largely empty property inside his skull.

"Indeed it will, and we no closer to having our bit finished with than we were at the beginning."

*You did speak with the Chapelia symbol-bearer,* she pointed out.

"Much good it did me, or Kamele," he groused, and shook his head. "I'll tell you what it is, Aelliana; I've gotten old."

*Not so very old,* she said quietly; *and you bear it for both of us.*

"Ill-temperedly he bears it, but bear it he does. Do you ever think, Aelliana, that we might have chosen another path to Balance?"

*We might have done, but see what we should have missed!*

He laughed.

"There is that aspect of the matter. Well."

He stood, stretching carefully, then moving a few light steps down the tiny room. By the time he had waltzed between the rowdy chairs to the door, he was feeling positively rejuvenated.

"I think we must accept that the symbol-bearer has decided that it would be far simpler to allow complexity to strangle upon its own woven strands. If we are to aid Kamele's cause, we must take the assault to the Tower ourselves."

*Have we a name?* Aelliana asked. *A direction?*

"There's the rub," he admitted, walking back to his desk.

"We must, I suppose, inquire of the Serpent. I had not done so previously for fear of showing our hand. However, the time may have come for desperate—"

A chime sounded, heartbreakingly pure against the chatter from the OTS.

*It's late,* Aelliana said, *for visitors.*

"It is, isn't it?"

Plucking the Gallowglass cane up from its lean against the wall, he crossed to the door.

He took a breath, feet firm, knees flexed—and tapped the plate.

The door slid open.

One of the Chapelia stood before him, at a guess, quite young. She was scarcely taller than he was.

"One answers," he said, keeping his voice soft despite his heart's abrupt, foolish racing.

"One is sent," the sexless one-voice replied. "The man who opens this door is to accompany this one to a place." She raised her hand and drew a sign in the air, recognizable as that belonging to the symbol-bearer he had spoken with.

"One understands and is ready to obey—" He sketched the sign in the air "—immediately."

*Backup?* Aelliana demanded, as he stepped out in the hall, the door to his office closing behind him.

At long last, the game was afoot.

# THIRTY-NINE

· · · · · · · · · · · · · · · · · · · · · · · · ·

*Melchiza Station*

"NOTHING TO DECLARE?"

"Bored" didn't begin to describe the attitude of the pre-boarding customs monitor. Theo couldn't exactly blame her, since her job was to watch the luggage go by her on a belt. She did touch some bags lightly with a wand; others, she didn't touch at all, but merely stared at the scans set into the table before her.

Some bags, she pulled off the belt and inspected minutely.

Kamele's bag went through without a question. She nodded at Theo and moved to the slideway to the boarding lounge as her luggage went elsewhere. Theo breathed a sigh of relief. They hadn't had a chance yet to talk in private, but she was glad to see that Kamele was calming down. She'd been jittery until the bus had gotten to the Visitors' Center, and had clutched Theo's hand tight while they waited in line for the shuttle. Now, though, it looked like Theo was going to get a little space to breathe.

"Shielding on this, sir?" the monitor asked Professor Crowley.

"Vacuum and particle safe," he admitted, raising his hands. "It's been with me since my first trip to high camp when I was an undergraduate. We..."

But the monitor was bored again. She used the wand, and passed the old bag on.

"Nothing to declare?"

A pause.

"*Nothing to declare,* Pilot?"

That tone more than the words grabbed Theo's attention—she hadn't realized that Professor Crowley's luggage was through already; she'd been so busy thinking about Kamele and what could've happened—and there was the Professor, already on the slideway.

"Nothing to declare," Theo assured the monitor.

The woman glanced down at her read-outs, stiffened and directed a frown at Theo.

"Please open."

Theo raised her glance to the ceiling and sighed.

"The job must get done," the woman said, almost daring a reply...

Theo worked the dual combo and opened the duffel, the woman spread it half open on the counter and wanded it. When the wand beeped she looked not at all startled, but reached into the neatly rolled and folded clothes, pushed aside the traveling school book in its protective envelope, and pulled out the bowli ball.

"That's mine," Theo began—

"Yes, Pilot, but it is not properly shielded." The monitor reached below the counter and pulled out a silver bag, which she passed to Theo. "If you please, Pilot."

Biting her lip, feeling the line growing long behind her, Theo slipped the ball into the bag and sealed it.

"Thank you," the monitor said. "Please close your bag."

She did so, hastily. The woman produced a green card like the one Theo wore on her jacket and slapped it on the duffel's side.

"The tag marks this out as a pilot's luggage," she said. "You may enter the passenger lounge at will. The Pilots' Lounge on level three is reserved for active pilots just in or out, and their guests, please don't strain the regs. Have a pleasant journey."

She turned aside and Theo hurried away, biting her lip.

"Anything to declare?" the monitor asked the next passenger.

"Kamele, I'd like to go for a walk," Theo said. "Just around the duty-free. I—"

Her mother glanced up from the datapad she'd been studying and looked around the lounge. It was, in Theo's opinion, a boring space, mostly full of chairs, infoscreens, and nervous people. Beyond it, the Concourse glittered; the stuff in the shops was 'way too expensive, she knew, just like on *Vashtara*, but it was interesting to look in the windows.

"I think we could both use a walk," Kamele said, slipping the 'pad away. "If you'd care for some company?"

Theo thought about being annoyed. Then she remembered how upset Kamele had been, and smiled.

"Company would be good," she said.

✳   ✳   ✳

They'd window-shopped half of one long side of the duty-free shops, taking their time, and pointing out especially absurd prices to each other. Theo's recollection had been wrong; the duty-free shops on Melchiza Station charged *even more* for everyday items than the shops aboard *Vashtara*.

She let Kamele get a window ahead of her while she lingered over a display of "athletic equipment," including foam-core boomerangs, ping-pong paddles, and—there! Nestled in back among a row of ordinary throwing spheres was a bowli ball. Theo tapped the window for more information, and gasped when the price came up.

Hastily, she tapped the pop-up away, and shook her head. It was a good thing Kamele didn't know how much the bowli ball had cost, or she'd have never let Theo keep it. 'Course, Kamele thought bowli balls were toys.

Shaking her head, Theo moved on, dancing aside as a woman in a leather jacket came out of the athletic equipment store.

"Sorry!" The woman said, shaking black hair out of her face.

"Phobai!" Theo cried gladly.

The pilot grinned. "Theo! Hey, look at that!" She extended a hand and stroked the green badge. "Fast work."

"They even call students 'pilot' at the Transit School," Theo said, face heating.

"No," Phobai said, "they only call *some* students pilot in the Transit School." She touched Theo's cheek lightly. "Get into a fight?"

"No, a bowli ball game."

"Hah! Did you drop it?"

"'Course not!"

Phobai laughed.

"Theo?" Kamele had noticed she was gone. Theo grabbed Phobai's hand and turned her around.

"Phobai, this is my mother, Kamele Waitley. Kamele, this is Phobai Murchinson, she's one of the pilots on *Vashtara*. We played bowli ball together and practiced dance—"

"And a fine dancer she is, your Theo!" Phobai said with a grin. She held out her hand and Kamele took it with a smile.

"I'm always glad to meet Theo's friends—and her teachers!" she said.

"Not a teacher; Theo was born knowing the moves. All I do is remind her." She turned to Theo. "Do you want in on bowli ball? Cordrey's on opposite shift this first leg, but we've got Len, Joadin, and Truitt for sure, and maybe Valince and Jorj. You're welcome to play."

"I'd like that," Theo said. "Text me the time and room?" She bit her lip, realizing that she should have asked before—but a glance to the side showed Kamele smiling softly.

"Sure," Phobai said to Theo. "Are you shopping? Let's walk together. I've got some other things to pick up before they call crew back."

The three of them turned and walked down the row of shops, Theo making sure that the walk-crowders didn't push Kamele. Phobai looked at her from beneath her black lashes.

"Taking up some extra space, aren't you?"

Theo blinked, remembering Initha's swagger.

"Am I?" she asked, stricken. "I just—"

"Nothing wrong with it," Phobai said quickly. "It's just a new look for you. You're right, too; in this crowd you've got to walk wide or get crushed! Here's my next stop, and then I've got to run for the gate." She smiled. "Professor Waitley, it was good to meet you. Theo—I'll see you soon!"

She vanished into a shop displaying three diaphanous articles—lingerie, Theo thought, though with a bewildering amount of laces and other fasteners—

"Let's walk over this way," Kamele said, interrupting any further study of the shop's display. "I'd like to check the departure times."

Theo shook her head, trying to get her hair out of her eyes. Something about the change in pressure in the glass airlocks, or maybe it was the change in air source. The breeze had been sudden and cold; likely it was used to help keep the grounder dirt and bugs someplace other than in the station's air supply.

Now that she could see again, she was faced with a wall of chronometers keeping a dozen times, just like on *Vashtara*, though Melchiza local time was displayed where *Vashtara* had displayed Standard Time.

Underneath the clocks were infoscreens displaying the names and departure/arrival times of incoming and outgoing ships. *Vashtara* was comfortably listed right next to Melchiza Station; the notes stating that it was still debarking passengers to other lounges. Phobai must've gotten off-ship as soon as it docked, Theo thought.

According to the 'screen, they'd be boarding around the time that Theo had gotten used to thinking of as lunch time. She reached to her jacket pocket, where her three days' eating money rode, and said a word she'd heard Win Ton mutter upon certain occasions.

"What is it?" Kamele asked, as ignorant of the meaning of the word as Theo was, and happily without the benefit of its use in context.

"I've still got the datapad with my math remedials!" She pulled it out of her pocket.

"We must return it," Kamele said briskly and looked around her. "There!" She pointed to a sign that said *Shuttles and Private*. "We'll give it to the shuttle captain; he can take it back to the Visitors' Center the next time he has a fare, and the Visitors' Center can send it back to the Transit School."

It certainly sounded like a good plan. Theo fell in beside Kamele.

The glitter and noise of the shopping district quickly disappeared. Also, the warmth. Theo was glad of her jacket and wished she'd brought an extra sweater. They passed a couple of people in coveralls with "Melchiza Station" stenciled on the breast, and a few pilots, leather jackets fastened close.

The corridor curved; and ahead of them were two more people. A male pilot, pulling luggage or last-minute stores, walking slowly with someone who was patently not a pilot. Her hair was slightly askew and she walked uncertainly, like she'd wandered into a change zone once and did not ever wish to repeat the experience.

The pilot had one hand around the woman's arm, urging her on. He wasn't wearing a leather jacket, but a fringed one, like—

Theo blinked.

*Clyburn isn't a pilot*! she thought, and looked again.

Gone were the mincing steps and swaying hips, traded in for a pilot's smooth stride.

"What are *they* doing *here*?" Kamele exclaimed, and rushed forward, her voice sharp.

"Orkan Hafley, there's a review board waiting for you on Delgado!"

Clyburn dropped Professor Hafley's arm and spun, pilot fast, green tag shining through the fringe. The expression on his face reminded Theo of Fruma, right before he had thrown the bowli ball at her.

"Go away, Kamele," he said, his hand going inside his jacket.

Theo jumped.

She landed between Clyburn and Kamele, her hands out in defensive mode, her feet set firm.

"Don't!" she snapped.

Clyburn blinked, his hand moved—

"Theo!" Kamele cried, putting a hand on her shoulder. Theo twisted, but her balance was destroyed—and Clyburn was running, and Professor Hafley with him, as best she could, suitcase clattering after.

"Stop!" Kamele cried.

Theo grabbed her arm. "Let them go!" she shouted.

Her mother turned and stared. "Let them go? Theo, Chair Hafley has committed an ethics violation that endangers the entire university. She must come up before the review—"

"He was going to—to throw something at you!" Theo interrupted. "He was going to hurt you!"

Kamele blinked. "Surely not," she said, but her voice was uncertain.

Theo sighed.

"Let's get back to the main hall," she said. "You need to talk to your team."

· · · ·✳· · · ·

.The child was admirably light of foot, and fleet, besides. Jen Sar followed at a distance, as an old man might, though he dared to pause only once, where the hall was straight for a length that gave him some hope of catching her again. He leaned lightly against the wall and reached into his pocket, bringing forth a silken handkerchief, which he touched to his temples and upper lip before letting it fall negligently to the floor in his haste to catch up his guide.

She kept scrupulously to the back halls and the service corridors. Possibly, the symbol-bearer had meant thereby to confuse him; possibly, it was the only route the child knew. In neither case did their direction elude him.

That their final destination must lie in the Administration Tower was certain; such a scheme as they had uncovered would need an administrator in it, and a librarian, too. He hardly thought it could be more than two, and then the secret would have to be sealed with fear as well as bribery.

His guide pushed the button to summon a lift, lenses glinting as she turned her head away.

Jen Sar sighed lightly. It would, of course, be most elegantly simple, to deliver him into the midst of the conspirators, and let them each make of the other what they might. The symbol-bearer being no fool, this was doubtless precisely her intention.

It would, he thought, be interesting to see how that played out.

# FORTY

· · · · · · · · · · ·

Vashtara
*Mauve Level*
*Stateroom*

"CHAOS DRIVEN NIDJIT," THEO MUTTERED, BENT OVER the datapad that hadn't gotten sent back to the Transit School, after all. She'd sent a message down to Pilot Arman via Melchiza Station's Public Comm, asking how she could return it.

The answer had arrived before she'd gotten back to the boarding lounge.

*Consider it a gift, Pilot, with my compliments. Arman.*

Which was great—or not, depending on the results of the most recent self-test.

"Why can't you figure this stuff out?" she asked herself, tapping the screen and glaring down at the latest troublesome set of equations.

Kamele, curled into the double-chair while she worked on the report about how the research team had managed to misplace Chair Hafley in transit, looked up, and murmured, "I'm sorry?"

Theo glanced up warily.

"Nothing, sorry. It's about this math."

"Math?" Kamele repeated. "You can't be doing math, again, can you?"

Theo pushed the datapad forward.

"Yes, I can. I'm behind."

Kamele rose.

"Let me see that. Why don't you go to the Atrium and ask them to give you one of those cheesecakes for us to share? The walk will sharpen you up!"

· · · ·✦· · · ·

"Here," his guide said abruptly. She pressed the plate and turned away before the door was wholly open, walking back the way they had come.

Jen Sar watched her round the corner of the hallway, then stepped through the door and into a foyer. Turning quickly, he tapped the manual override, and eased the door along its track until it was almost closed.

"That must be the Chapelia!" a woman's voice said sharply from the room beyond. "Come in, come in! You're late!"

Jen Sar took a breath, renewed his grip on his cane and walked forward.

Tandra Skilings—the other name he had recognized on the Serpent's list—saw him first; her reaction a mixture of anger and disbelief.

"Kiladi, what are you doing here? Leave at once!"

"Alas," he said softly, bowing as the others turned to stare at him. "I come in the place of the symbol-bearer, who I deduce has . . . decided on the part of simplicity."

"Who is that?" a woman he did not recognize

demanded. She wore a Director's coat, but she held herself more like a fighter than an academic. Her right hand was in the pocket of her jacket, a fact he observed with sorrow.

"I am Jen Sar Kiladi, Professor of Cultural Genetics," he said gently. "And you are, perhaps, the off-world agent responsible for alteration of certain library records? I hope that you may be; I had particularly wished to make your acquaintance."

The false director looked to Skilings, then to Sub-Chancellor Kylin, standing stiff with alarm at her right hand. "We've made significant progress; we cannot allow our efforts to be nullified by one elderly professor."

She pulled her hand out of her pocket. As he had suspected, she held a gun.

· · · ❖ · · ·

"Theo, how did this happen?"

Kamele was standing when she returned, datapad in hand.

"I'm a nidj?" Theo asked, putting the dainty box with its pretty blue bow on the table.

Kamele shook her head. "I used my override for your school book," she said. "It reports that your math scores are higher than average for your learning group. So much higher, in fact, that it has placed you in an accelerated learning program. This—" She shook the datapad, "shows me a list of failed self-tests, multiple re-tests and produces a statement that the student requires remediation."

"I'm a nidj," Theo said.

"Theo . . ." Kamele said dangerously. "If you have any insight into why there's such a wide gap in the results reported by these two programs, I would very much like to hear it."

"I think it's because that—" she touched the datapad Kamele still held, "is *piloting math.* Pilot Arman said my scores were low—and my tutor! She couldn't believe I'd never had any of this material. *She* said it was basic!" Theo smiled, mouth crooked. "At least I got to understand how Bek feels about math, in general. But, I had to catch up. It's just that it's being ..." She frowned, looking down at the sculpted mauve carpeting. ". . . a challenge."

There was a small pause. "Your friend Win Ton told me that you relish a challenge."

"Well, I do. I guess. But I like to feel like I'm making some *progress!*"

"I see." Kamele put the datapad next to the school book and went over to the hospitality unit. Silently, she drew a cup of coffee and a cup of tea and brought them over to the table.

"Sit," she said, placing the cups.

Theo sat. Hospitality tea was pretty good. Not as good as fresh-made, but drinkable. She wondered, idly, if the university could afford to upgrade the kafs in the Wall to hospitality units . . .

Kamele finished decanting the cheesecake. She handed Theo a fork and took the other for herself.

"Eat," she said. "It seems to me you've earned this."

Theo needed no more encouragement to enjoy cheesecake. Kamele, though, wasn't eating.

Theo put her fork down and looked at Kamele, seeing her fingers twitch, almost as if there were something she needed to say in hand-talk, or as if, as if her fingers wanted to shout out in song . . .

Kamele closed her eyes.

"Theo, I haven't been able to tell you...there hasn't really been enough time..."

Watching the hands again, hearing the nondirection in the voice, Theo realized what she did see: Kamele was nervous!

"Theo," Kamele started once more, moving both hands forward with a flick, like she was passing a ball so someone else could score....

"I want to tell you how proud I am of you," and now her voice was strong, her hands calm. "This trip has been so busy, and I've been too much involved in the things I need to do. Necessity. I was concerned—many times—that you were in over your head, and that I was."

She paused for a sip of her coffee. Theo waited, wondering what this had to do with failing math.

"This trip, you haven't acted like the—the person Marjene claimed you were, full of accidents and immaturity. You haven't been avoiding social situations. You've made friends. You've studied, you've grown so much. And I need to tell you, that I'm so very proud. I'm so pleased that Jen Sar suggested you come with me. You..."

Theo sat up straight, cheesecake forgotten.

"Father *what*?"

Theo felt her hands demanding *explain*, even as the words tumbled out of her mouth.

"Are you telling me that Father *wanted* me to come with you? It was *his* idea?"

Kamele nodded; for some reason she seemed amused.

"I was going to leave you with him, since Ella was...overcommitted. And asking anyone else: with the complications of Marjene, and the hearing—I needed someone secure. And, well..."

Here Kamele paused, hands showing a touch of that hesitation again.

"He was right, Theo. I couldn't leave you on Delgado—it was too *dangerous*. He told me that what you needed was to spread your wings."

"He told *me* local custom demanded that I go with my mother!"

They stared at each other. Both began to laugh at the same moment.

"Theo, you *know* Jen Sar always plays both sides against the middle!"

Theo nodded, recalling times that he'd made her think something was her idea when surely it was his...

She felt her fingers flicker, and looked down, catching a repeated refrain: *good plan, good plan, good plan.*

Kamele moved, visibly relaxing, her hands moving briskly, as if she swept crumbs off a table, or finished with an idea. She glanced at the room's chronometer, and stretched.

"Maybe you'd better check with Phobai Murchinson about the times for bowli ball," she said. "You're pushing too hard, Theo. Relax. Tomorrow, the next day, too—take some lectures. Pick a couple, and I'll join you. Take a few days off from math."

Theo looked hard into Kamele's face.

"But the scores..."

Kamele looked back, hard, and held up her hand, first finger extended.

"One," she said sternly. "As a teacher and a scholar I have noticed that, sometimes, the best one can do is to *not think* about a knotty problem. Brains need rest and diversion. More often than not, when the scholar returns to her vexing problem, the solution is obvious. Two."

She tipped her head to one side, like Coyster considering the merits of a new toy.

"This is the last time I expect to do this," she said slowly. "I am invoking Parental Override. You're on holiday. Go—do something else! Dance, turn somersaults in the hallway, but no more math, not today and not tomorrow. You're on holiday!"

· · · · ❊ · · · ·

Jen Sar leapt sideways, rolling, meaning to get under the furniture and stay there until—

"Wait!" Kylin shouted, grabbing the outworlder's arm. "What are you—we can't kill Kiladi!"

"Certainly we can, and must," the woman snapped, wrenching herself free. "And if the Chapelia have withdrawn their support—"

"Why should they?" Skilings demanded. "The new order will be advantageous to them."

"The new order?" Ella ben Suzan asked loudly. "The new order where the university is in tatters and knowledge is suspect?"

They strode into the room, Ella, Monit Appletorn, Emeritus Professor Beltaire, Technician Singh and five Safeties, restraints adorning their belts.

"What is the meaning of this?" Skilings demanded. "Since when can colleagues not enjoy the company—"

"Matter of public safety," Appletorn interrupted. "Suspicion of intent to harm scholarship."

"That," Professor Beltaire said in her voice that

sounded like a breeze moving over yellowed paper, "is a weapon, Safeties. Please act according to your training."

"And Jen Sar," Ella added. "You can come out from beneath the couch, now."

# FORTY-ONE

. . . . . . . . . . . . . . . . . . .

*Delgado*

THEO STEPPED FORWARD TO GRAB KAMELE'S CASE OFF the conveyor belt, which she managed without bumping into the woman with the inefficient, jabbing gestures, and no sense of balance. That woman grabbed too soon, knocking her bag off the belt and dragging it against the direction of its rollers, missing running over Theo's feet by no effort of her own. Theo shook her head, scanning up the belt for her bag, wincing when the ambient sound system cycled from music to the "Welcome to Delgado" message. She'd hardly been in the terminal half an hour and she already had that announcement by heart. If she heard it much more—and it was, she thought glumly, certain that she would—maybe it would just fade into background noise.

Maybe.

Somebody was too close to her left shoulder. Theo shifted and turned her head, finding one of the numerous terminal "helpers" practically in her pocket. This one was not quite as old as Professor Crowley, and portly, the lavender smock with "helper" blazoned across the front stretched too tight over his paunch.

"Confused, dear?" he asked with a smile. He pointed at the exit ramp, off to the left. "Now that you have your baggage, you need to clear the area so that others can find theirs. Would you like me to help you?"

She spotted her case, far up still, riding down the almost exact center of the belt. Theo settled herself like she would for a *menfri'at* lunge.

"No, thank you," she said, keeping one eye on the target. "My mother asked me to get her case while I was getting mine." *Because,* she added grumpily, *Kamele had to say "one last word" to Professor Crowley, like she was never going to see him again, or something.*

"Your mother sent you to get two heavy cases *all by yourself?*" The helper, whose name, stitched in red on the left shoulder of his shirt, was "Hieri," demanded, sounding absolutely horrified. Theo blinked.

"They're not heavy," she said, mildly, as her bag crept closer down the crowded belt.

"But you're alone," he insisted.

Her case was almost within snatching distance. Theo rose slowly to the balls of her feet, leaned over and snagged the handle, safely clearing the shoulder of a man so intent on rescuing his own luggage that she doubted he even noticed she was there.

"Be careful!" Hieri yelled, but by that time Theo had put the bag down and had hit the button to telescope the handle. She hooked the two bags together with the magtether, turned—

And found her way blocked by the still-indignant Hieri. She stopped, her body dropping into the first, centering, *menfri'at* form before she had a chance to think.

*Wait!* she told herself, deliberately relaxing. *He's only a busybody*.

"I'm not alone," she said carefully. "My mother's in the terminal. I'm supposed to meet her at the Soybean on the first level—" she made a show of looking over his head to the local-time-and-weather display—"right now."

Hieri took a breath so deep his paunch shuddered. "I," he said firmly, "will escort you."

She stared at him, then shrugged. "If you want to, then you need to step back so I can get my bags rolling."

Grimly, he did just that, and Theo stepped out briskly, bags in tow, Hieri puffing at her side.

"Leaving a child alone in the terminal is not safety conscious!" he wheezed.

Theo looked at him. "Do you mean the terminal's not safe?"

He colored and shook his head violently. "No! No, that's not what I mean *at all*. What I mean is that children wander off, get distracted. A mother should always be with her child in this sort of crowded and—and *unregulated* situation!"

"Oh." Theo thought about that as they went down the ramp to the first level. It seemed like the sort of thing Marjene might say—was it only six Standard months ago? She glanced at the infoboard as they passed, noting the date—and noting it again. Six months, indeed!

"I'm not a child," she said to Hieri, which wasn't much of a fib, since tomorrow was her birthday.

Hieri peered at her as if he suspected her of playing an elaborate joke on him. "Have you had your *Gigneri*?" he asked.

Theo's stomach sank.

"No," she admitted. "I haven't."

"Then you're a child, and your mother should take better care of you!" he said triumphantly, and slapped hasty fingers to his lips. "Not that your mother shouldn't take good care of you *after* you've had your *Gigneri*, of course. I only meant—"

"There she is," Theo interrupted, nodding toward Kamele, standing by the info pole to the right of the Soybean kiosk. "You can go help somebody else now."

"A proper escort," Hieri said, sounding like he was quoting out of the helper training manual, "finishes the job properly."

And so it was that Theo came up to Kamele, towing the two cases, and a puffing escort.

"Theo," Kamele said, looking at Hieri in mild astonishment. "Thank you for fetching those! Professor Crowley's friend met him just as they had arranged, so he's well on his—"

"Ma'am!" Hieri interrupted. Kamele raised her eyebrows, and suddenly extended her hand, her smile almost identical to Captain Cho's too-wide "public" smile.

"Helper, thank you for escorting my daughter! I do appreciate it." She let the smile fade a little as Hieri shook her hand, looking slightly bewildered.

"Have you a comment card?" she asked, and he nodded, eagerly producing the flat device from the pocket of his smock.

"Thank you." Kamele took it, tapped in a code,

and handed it back, still smiling. "I do *very much* appreciate your trouble," she said again.

"That's all right," Hieri said, blushing and nodding as he slipped the card back into his pocket. "Thank *you*." He cast a stern eye on Theo. "And you, young lady, don't you be afraid to ask for assistance from anybody wearing this shirt." He puffed his chest out proudly. "We're here to *help*!"

With that, he turned around and marched off, head swiveling back and forth, already looking for another victim.

Theo bit her lip and looked down at the floor.

"Well," said Kamele in her normal voice, "that was relatively painless."

Theo sputtered, and heard Kamele laugh, which made her laugh harder. The two of them were still laughing while they got Kamele's case transferred to her, and turned toward—

"Um, Kamele? The light rail station is that way." Theo pointed at the map displayed on the info terminal.

"So it is," her mother said agreeably, but she kept on walking toward the exits for the hotel, mall, and garage.

Theo shrugged and followed. After all, she thought grumpily, it wasn't like Kamele *had* to tell her anything.

The corridor to the mall branched off. Kamele kept walking. So, Theo thought, they were going to the hotel or to the garage. That was information, though she still wondered why.

The crowd had thinned somewhat, but there were still more than enough people around, dressed in bright holiday colors, walking noisily; calling back and forth to each other, the rollers on their luggage clacking across the seams in the floor tiles.

And in the midst of all the motion and noise—a spot of... invisibility.

Theo frowned, turning her head to track what her eye had passed over—

A pilot stood against the far wall, well out of the way of the busy rush of people, but perfectly apparent, if you happened to be looking for him. His hands were folded quietly atop his cane; his stance was balanced, but not quite... completely... relaxed.

He was watching Kamele, who was oblivious, turning her head this way and that, watching the crowd. He was being so *quiet*, Theo thought in sudden agony; Kamele was never going to see him! Not that Kamele was stupid, or inadvertent, but she wasn't a pilot, and—*Should I say something?* Theo thought frantically. But, if Father wanted them to—

Kamele paused. Chest tight, Theo looked at her face. She was smiling, and a quick glance showed that Father was smiling, too, as he cut across the stream of noisy passengers with such an unhurried, lithe grace that Theo wondered how she could ever have missed the obvious fact.

*The pilot who raised me.*

"Good afternoon," he said, and at last he included Theo in his smile.

"Father—" she said, meaning to tell him right then about Cho, and the card, and Melchiza, and *menfri'at,* and—but her throat got tight, and her eyes blurred and anyway Kamele was talking.

"Good afternoon, Jen Sar," she said. Theo thought she meant to sound composed, but her voice was shaking, just a little.

The three of them were an obstruction in the

flow of traffic, and while most people were advertent enough to avoid them, they really should start moving again, a point Father made by waving his cane gently and turning to walk with them. Theo moved to the right, so he was between them, and jumped when her bag was clipped by a man who swerved too late. He kept going without a word, apparently oblivious to the contact, even though his case was spinning on its rollers, trying to re-orient itself.

Theo struggled briefly with her own case, muttering the word she had heard Win Ton use under her breath, and got the wheels turned the right way.

"Travel is broadening, I hear," Father murmured, glancing at her with an ironic quirk to his near eyebrow.

Her face heated, but she met his eyes. "I learned lots of things," she said firmly.

"It could hardly have been otherwise. I shall hope to hear that the balance of your acquisitions are somewhat less ... organic ..."

Her lips parted.

"... in the fullness of time," he continued. "At present, I suggest that we make all haste to gain the garage, where by the greatest good fortune I happen to have a car waiting."

Theo eyed him. "We've got too much stuff to fit in your car."

"Do you think so? I had thought we might put the contents into the boot and leave the bags themselves for whoever might care to scavenge them."

"That might work," Theo allowed, dead-pan. "But what about passengers?"

Father pointed a walking half-bow at Kamele. "You

mother of course will ride in the passenger's seat, as befits her age and accomplishments."

"And me? In the boot with the dirty laundry?"

"Theo." He looked at her reproachfully. "You, of course, I would lash to the roof."

"That might work," Kamele said from his other side, in a tone that Theo recognized as a duplicate of her own.

"Not," she said to Kamele, across Father, "the way he drives."

"You're right," her mother said thoughtfully. "We'll stop in the mall and buy you a safety helmet."

Theo laughed, and Kamele did.

Father, meanwhile, solemnly used the tip of his cane to press the key for the elevator.

"What," Theo said, staring at the hulking vehicle that took up two whole spaces in the garage, made even taller by the light dome on its roof. It was painted an eye-scorching yellow that couldn't have missed being rated a Hazard by the Safeties, and had two broad black stripes down each side. "Is it?"

"Well you should ask," Father said, opening the boot. "Precisely, it is Andri Manderpon's vintage restored Sunlight Taxicab."

Kamele retracted the handle of her bag; he grabbed the swing-grip before she could, and gave her a small smile. "I agreed to a long list of conditions in order to borrow this vehicle from my good friend Andri, including a guarantee that I would not allow heavy objects to be thrown willy-nilly into the boot."

He swung the bag up and over into the gaping maw, settling it with the barest thump, then turned, one eyebrow raised slightly.

*I see you,* Theo signed the greeting one-handed, retracting the handle of her bag with the other.

Father bent and took hold of the strap, swinging Theo's case in to join Kamele's, and lowered the hatch gently.

"Your carriage awaits," he murmured, slipping his hand under Kamele's elbow and guiding her to the passenger side door. He opened it and bowed her inside. "Please fasten the straps. Another condition upon which my friend was adamant." He shut the door and turned, intercepting Theo as she reached for the latch to the back door.

"My hand alone," he murmured, popping the door. He inclined his head. "If you please, Theo. And do fasten the straps."

She shook her head. "I can't see you driving this."

"There are many things that you have not seen, child," he answered. "In, if you please."

She slipped into her seat, and he closed the door behind her. Mindful, she sealed the finicky straps as Father slid into the driver's seat, snapped his own restraints, and turned to Kamele.

"Where shall this humble driver be delighted to take you, Professor?"

Theo held her breath.

"I would be pleased," Kamele said serenely. "If you would take us home. I would like to have tea in the garden."

Theo gasped, and raised her hand to hide the grin. In the front seat, she saw Father's shoulders lose that tiny bit of tension they'd been carrying. He tipped his head.

"It is well, then?" he asked Kamele.

"As well as it can be, considering," she answered and shook her head. "There's a meeting with the Chancellor and the Directors tomorrow evening."

"Yes," Father said. "I have some bit of news regarding that, myself."

"Which we will talk about . . . later," Kamele said.

"Oh, indeed." He leaned forward to touch the starter button. The big car came to life, its motor quieter than Theo had expected, but decidedly louder than the-mannered purr of Father's car.

They moved out of the parking space and into the exit lane. Theo leaned back in her seat, thinking.

Father had come to meet them, and brought a car big enough to accommodate them and their luggage. He hadn't been sure, though, until Kamele . . . But—she must have sent him a text, or—

"Theo," Father's voice broke into her increasingly confused thoughts, "I must beg that you not believe everything you may hear of me."

She looked up and caught his eyes in the rear view mirror.

"What did you do?" she asked, genuinely curious.

Father laughed, and eased the big yellow taxi on to the parkway. "The young today," he said conversationally to Kamele, "have so little respect for their elders."

# FORTY-TWO

. . . . . . . . . . . . . . . . . . .

*Number Twelve Leafydale Place*
*Greensward-by-Efraim*
*Delgado*

"I CAN'T BELIEVE HOW BIG YOU'VE GOTTEN!" THEO exclaimed for maybe the fifth time.

Coyster yawned from his position in the center of her bed, and settled his chin on his paws.

She laughed and bent to her case again. "I know! I sound like five silly aunts! But it's really good to see you again!"

Her closet was still in the apartment in the Wall, of course, but she was unpacking anyway—the stuff from her bag would go into the chest of drawers just fine for now.

Her room was so big! Closing the drawer, she spun slowly on her heel, surveying unlimited space. The room was set to default—pale blue walls and darker floor—the old mobile spinning lazily in the breeze from the vent, and the row of ragged storybooks providing the only splashes of color. She could, she thought, put all her old pictures back up, pour the fish into the floor—make it all just like it had been, before.

Later.

Now, she went over to the bed and stretched out next to Coyster, her arms folded under her head, and her eyes half-slitted. She thought about calling Lesset, but didn't move. Beside her, Coyster began to knead, his purr punctuated by tiny popping sounds as his claws penetrated the quilt.

"I'm glad you're glad," she murmured, and the volume of his purrs increased.

They'd had tea and a cold luncheon in the garden, just the three of them, and they hadn't talked about the trip at all, but listened to Father ramble on about the cats, and the new plantings he'd made in the garden, and his fishing trip in the mountains near where Kamele's second-mother had been born—and it had been . . . relaxing.

*He was giving us time to get our planet-legs*, Theo thought drowsily. At some point Mandrin and Coyster had joined them. Mandrin jumped onto Father's lap, but Coyster sat on the grass directly in front of Theo, his back to her, and his ears swiveled 'round so that he could hear her slightest move.

"Oof!" Theo said, jackknifing as Coyster stepped firmly on her stomach. "You really *have* gotten big!" She squooshed him down flat on her chest, giggling when his whiskers tickled her throat.

Kamele had promised not to keep Father long, though, of course, they had to "talk." Theo sighed.

"I'm going to be fifteen years old tomorrow," she told Coyster. "Delgadan years," she added, just to be clear. Coyster puffered a purr and stretched his right front leg 'way out, so it was resting on her shoulder and his paw was in the air next to her ear.

She should write that to Win Ton—about being fifteen tomorrow. 'Course, he wouldn't get the letter for who knew how long, but she'd kind of gotten in the habit of writing to him on the way back—just things she'd seen that she thought he might think were interesting, or funny, or—

There was a tap at her door. Theo rolled, dumping Coyster unceremoniously onto the bed, and crossed the room to touch the plate.

The door slid away to reveal a smiling Kamele.

"Thank you, Theo," she said. "Jen Sar's waiting for you in his office."

"Father," she said from the threshold of the room, while her fingers signed deliberately, *Pilot*.

He watched her face, not her hands, his own occupied with rubbing Mandrin's ears.

"Theo. Come in, child."

"Thank you," she said. Why was he ignoring her? Was she wrong? But, no, she told herself as she slid into the chair next to his desk. She *wasn't* wrong.

"How do you find your room?" he asked, leaning back in his chair. Mandrin shook her head and jumped down, hitting the starry floor with a solid *thump*.

"It feels huge!" she answered, and her fingers moved again: *Pilot duty here is*.

His eyes on her face, Father shook his head slightly. "Theo, is there a reason that you are persisting in this?"

Maybe, she thought, heart sinking, maybe she *was* wrong. She met his eyes firmly, folding her hands tight on her lap.

"Yes," she said steadily, "there is. I have a card from a—a scout and a pilot, she told me to say—to be given to the pilot who trained me." She took a breath and forced herself to finish calmly. "And if that's not you, then I don't know who to give it to."

Silence, followed by an almost soundless sigh.

"I see," he said, his fingers flickering so neatly that she almost missed, *Duty accepted.*

Relief knifed through her. She bit her lip and fished Cho's card out of her safe pocket, where she'd kept it ever since Melchiza.

"Here."

He slipped it out of her fingers—so quick, so sure! Theo shook her head again, mentally chiding herself for having been so blind.

"Why didn't you *tell* me?" she demanded.

"Tell you what?" he returned absently, turning the card over.

"That you're a pilot. Does Kamele know?"

"Until now, it has not been pertinent to our relationship. Possibly she does, though it's conceivable that I have not been entirely clear. It is," he murmured, leaning over to slot the card into his computer, "so difficult to be certain in these matters."

"But why are you *here*?"

"To teach." His fingers flickered: *Quiet incoming.*

Theo bit her lip, watching the side of his face— which told her just about as much as it ever did. She came to her feet and moved to stand behind him so she could see the screen—which did her no good at all; it was filled with flowing lines of written Liaden.

"Do you read Liaden, Theo?"

"No," she said, sadly. "I was going to start learning, but I had to catch up my math, instead."

"A difficult choice, I allow. Well. Scout Captain sig'Radia proposes you to me as a young person of wit and promise, who has demonstrated both flexibility and strength of purpose. She therefore offers, if your mother agrees and she does not offend local custom, to stand as your sponsor."

"My sponsor," Theo repeated blankly. She leaned over his shoulder, glaring at the screen as if she could wring sense from the alien letters by sheer force of will. "My sponsor for *what*?"

"I note that the good captain does not include 'patience' in her list of your many excellencies," Father said dryly. "To continue. Captain sig'Radia, in her *melant'i* as Scout Pilot and Trainer, offers to sponsor you to Anlingdin Piloting Academy on Eylot."

Sponsor her! To a piloting academy! *I want it!* was her first thought. Her second, with a glance at the starfield spinning beneath the study floor to steady herself, was more sobering.

"What does that mean—sponsor?" she asked. "What's the—" A sudden thought of Win Ton, tapping his beaker against hers—"What's the trade?"

"Ah." Father leaned back in his chair and looked up into her face. "Travel is broadening, indeed."

"It's a fair question," she said, frowning at him.

He raised a hand, the old silver ring glinting on his finger. "Do not eat me! It is indeed a fair question, and well-asked." He nodded at the screen. "Captain sig'Radia offers a paid scholarship for the first three semesters—a full Standard year, you will apprehend. If, at the end of that time, you have not placed in the top thirty percent of your class, she will withdraw her support, without prejudice. There will be no debt to repay. If you thereafter wish to continue pilot training at your own expense, you may of course do so."

The top thirty percent? She couldn't remember a time when she hadn't been in the top five percent of her class!

"I'll do it," she said, stomach fluttering.

Father inclined his head. "You will, of course, need to bring your math scores up."

Theo's stomach lurched. How could she have forgotten?

Father reached across his desk and picked up the datapad, tapping in a quick sequence. "Instructor's override," he murmured and held the device out so that they could both contemplate the information displayed.

"These are," he murmured, "perfectly good—even quite good—math scores for someone destined for almost any life-path except that of pilot. Pilots hold ship and passengers in their hands. Their math must be nothing less than sublime." He paused.

"It is not," he continued a long moment later, in a carefully neutral tone, "a trade at which everyone excels—or a trade at which everyone *can* excel. It is . . . exciting. Exhilarating. Dangerous—in many ways—and it often weighs heavy, for lives are not light."

Theo looked at him doubtfully. "You sound like you—don't want me to try."

He raised an eyebrow. "Child, this choice rests with you."

She bit her lip. "*Did* you . . . work . . . as a pilot, Father?"

He might have sighed, very gently. "Yes."

"Was it—do you wish you hadn't?"

"Never in my blackest hour." He laughed softly. "What a poor advisor I am, to be sure!"

"No," she said seriously. "A bad advisor lies just to keep somebody safe." She took a breath, but, really, her mind had been made up the moment she had heard Captain Cho's offer.

"I want to go." she said firmly.

"Go where?" Kamele asked from the doorway.


"How long, then," Kamele said, "to bring up those math scores?"

Father moved his shoulders. "I can tutor her, if you like it. Or I might assist in choosing an appropriate self-study course . . ."

"*Would* you teach me?" Theo asked diffidently. It was late, and her head was heavy. As far as she was concerned, the decision was made, all that was left were details. Kamele, though, seemed to want every corner nailed down tonight.

They'd long since repaired to the common room, breaking once to rustle sandwiches, and again to brew a new pot of tea.

"I will," Father said, lifting an ironic eyebrow. "If you will endeavor to recall that you desired me to do so."

"I will," she promised him, and smiled when Coyster, asleep on her lap, rolled over on his head and yawned hugely. "Really."

"How long?" Kamele repeated her question.

Father moved his shoulders. "If she is an apt pupil, she may be ready to enter the lower class at Anlingdin by the end of Delgado's current semester."

Kamele nodded, eyes thoughtful, and sipped tea.

"Is Eylot a Liaden world?" she asked then, and Theo blinked. She hadn't even thought to ask that!

"Eylot is what is politely termed 'an outworld' by proper Liadens," Father said. "Roughly, there is parity between the Liaden and Terran populations."

"So I should learn Liaden, too," Theo broke in, "before I go."

"You may wish to make a beginning, yes," Father said. "It's never amiss to carry an extra language or six in one's pocket."

"Conservatively, then, Theo will remain on Delgado for at least six—local—months," Kamele said.

"I believe that a fair estimate, yes," Father murmured.

"Well, then." She rose. "If you will both excuse me for a moment..." She left the room at a brisk walk.

Theo yawned, belatedly raising a hand to cover her mouth. "Is there any more tea?" she asked.

"A bit," Father answered. "We have drunk epic amounts, but I believe to good effect."

Theo giggled sleepily. "Would you pour me some more tea, please, Father?"

"Certainly, Theo." He did so and handed her the cup.

Theo sipped. It was the bottom of the pot, tepid, and absolutely delicious. She closed her eyes to savor the astringent flavor—and opened them as Kamele's step sounded in the hall.

Her mother re-seated herself on the sofa next to Father, and put the slim packet tied with pink ribbon on her lap.

"Theo," she said, leaning slightly forward. "Today is your fifteenth birthday."

"Today?" Theo sat up straighter, and looked over

her shoulder at the clock. "You mean tomor—" But it was, so the clock told her, past midnight. She looked back to Kamele.

"Today," she agreed.

Her mother nodded. "You are now eligible to celebrate your *Gigneri* and to be entrusted with the tale of your grandmothers," she said slowly. "If you will allow me to advise you, I would suggest that you choose to have a small, private ritual in the old style at the earliest possible moment." She tapped the packet on her lap. "This morning, in fact."

Theo thought about that. If she had her *Gigneri*, she would be a beginning adult, with increased advantages— and responsibilities. She could, for instance, decide whether or not she needed a mentor. Unless she was condemned as a public hazard, the safeties couldn't force her to do anything . . .

"I see the advantages," she said, her hand flat on Coyster's upturned belly. "But—'old style'?"

It was Father who answered. "Your First Pair would be put off until a time and place of your choosing," he murmured. "Fifty local years ago, the mode was to celebrate the coming-of-age first, with one's inaugural sexual encounter to be arranged by the beginning adult herself, taking such advice from her elders as she deemed necessary."

Theo blinked. "Well, *that* makes sense," she said, and wondered why Father laughed.

"If it's acceptable to you, Theo," Kamele said seriously. "We can celebrate your *Gigneri* right now. Just the three of us."

"With," Father added, "the appropriate announcement in the Scandal Sheet."

Theo nodded, and gave Kamele a smile. "It's acceptable."

"Good." Kamele stood, and Father did. Theo struggled briefly before she managed to push Coyster off her lap, and stood, too.

Kamele held the packet out on the palms of her hands.

"Here is the tale of those who went before," she said solemnly. "You are the sum and the total of us. We rejoice in you, daughter, and are amazed."

Theo swallowed in a throat gone suddenly tight; stepped forward and took the packet in both hands.

"I am humbled," she said, and the phrase she had memorized as mere rote was suddenly, achingly *true*. "I am humbled before my ancestors, Mother, and will strive to do my best, in honor of those who went before me."

She stepped back, the packet still cradled in her hands. There was silence. Kamele's face was wet with tears, through which Theo plainly saw pride, and love—and, yes, amazement.

"Congratulations, Theo," Father said quietly. "I am proud that you are my daughter."

# AFTERWORD

· · · · · · · · · · · · · · · · · · · ·

*Daughter of the Thing that Swallowed Georgia*
*or...*
*Why This Book is Special*

ALL BOOKS ARE SPECIAL. WRITERS INVEST SO EXTRAVA-
gantly in their work—time, love, money, worry—how
can the result be anything other than special? To say
that one story is more special than another... That's
a matter of taste, really.

So, when we say that *Fledgling* is something a little
out of the common way—*special*, in a word—we're
referring not so much to the story you've just read,
but to the circumstances of its birth.

*Fledgling* is a child born of necessity, fostered onto
the internet, and left to soar.

That it did... but we're getting ahead of ourselves.

In December 2006, it became apparent that our
long-time publisher's "cash-flow problems" had impacted
our household finances, and not in a good way. Our
situation was on the approach to dire, and we were seriously looking at having to live outdoors—not optimum

in a Maine winter. We needed to do something, fast, in order get that old cash flowing, and there's only one thing we really know how to do—

Tell stories.

The rights to the "main line" Liaden books rested with our publisher. But we had this character, this off-the-beaten-universe story, this *side book* that we felt—not only *confident* that we could write, but that it would *be fun* to write. Ghu knew, we needed a little fun in our lives about then.

So, we announced to our readers on the internet that we would be starting a new project: We would be writing the first draft of a novel, live on the web. We'd post the first chapter on January 22, 2007. Subsequent chapters would need to earn $300 in donations before the next was posted. Readers who donated $25 or more would receive one copy of the dead tree edition of the novel, if it was ever published.

We figured, you see, that we would start off strong, then donations would slope away, and we'd be posting a chapter every, oh, two or three weeks.

Before December was over, readers had funded ten chapters. By the time the first chapter was posted, we were committed to writing twenty weekly episodes in the life and times of Theo Waitley.

But our readers did more than donate; they took an interest—in Theo, in her problems, in her growing up, in the writing, and in the LiveJournal community created to discuss the progress of the plot. They nourished the story; encouraged the heroine like fond aunts and uncles, commiserated with her, and loved her, with all her faults and foibles.

They gave Theo her wings, and they cheered when she soared.

In between it all, we had put aside enough of that flowing cash to print a paper edition of *Fledgling* limited to those people who had donated $25 or more, through our own small publishing company, SRM Publisher, Ltd.

By then, though, our former publisher had returned the rights to the mainline novels, and Baen Books had expressed an interest in new Liaden material.

So, we asked our agent to contact Baen, to see if there was interest in publishing *Fledgling* for a wider audience.

The answer was a resounding *YES*.

And that—all of that—is what makes this book special. What makes it . . . magical, really. Without the eager participation of hundreds of readers, and a publisher's willingness to try something new, you would never have met Theo.

There's more, though.

Not only did the readers nourish Theo, they nourished us; and the writing—well, we'd *thought* it would be fun, and it was. Maybe even a little *too* much fun.

In January 2008, we commenced writing the second novel about Theo Waitley, *Saltation*. Watch for it soon, from Baen Books.

Thank you—all of you—so very much.

Sharon Lee and Steve Miller
Waterville, Maine
January 1, 2009

The following is an excerpt from:

# SALTATION

## A New Liaden Universe® Novel

# SHARON LEE & STEVE MILLER

Available from Baen Books
April 2010
hardcover

# ONE

· · · · · · ·

*Shuttle Approach*
*Anlingdin Piloting Academy*
*Eylot*

"CONSELEM!"

Theo didn't think that the gentle off-center nudge of reaction jets had deserved a sneeze, much less a cuss word. And the shouts and cackles of self-important glee when the second nudge was followed by a firmer push were just mean.

"We're all gonna die!"

Theo resisted the urge to look toward the front of the shuttle, having recognized *that* voice. Should've known. Sighing, she rested her head resolutely against well-worn padding. She'd drawn a seat without nearby viewports and was just as happy not to be sitting with the three student pilots, their flight wings shiny on their collars, who'd started chancing her back on the *Vestrin*. They were coming back to Anlingdin from the Short Break, so they said, and were determined to party as long as possible.

Snickiots.

At least she wasn't alone. Apparently they didn't much care for . . . Theo squinted at the legend scrolling across the main screen: "Student Pilot Kern Vallee at controls, please strap in." Right. They didn't much care for Kern Vallee, either.

"Conselem!" the ringleader yelled again, to the loud delight of his friends.

"You know," the second-rank snickiot said, sounding way too serious. "Kern flunked his first three landings. Good thing for us he's got Ablestum and the Short Wing sitting with him. We've got a good chance of getting down in one piece!"

There was another cycle of jets then, as if the pilot was testing controls, and then a tremble followed by a push Theo judged to be fairly firm, which brought more cuss words and shrieks from the front.

Eyes closed, Theo tried to ignore the noise and mentally recited her schedule. Landing, free time, then Admin Roundup. She sighed, longingly. In a half day or less she'd be in a quiet bunk. Alone. She hadn't been properly alone since she boarded *Vestrin* at Delgado Station, weeks ago. At least, she'd only had to put up with the three party-boys since Rooba, two ship-days.

And the descent to Eylot, of course.

She felt the jiggle of acceleration, the twisting on her gut as front and down changed place, guessed the maneuver upcoming, and grimaced.

"Oh, no! We're in for it now!"

The punch came in four distinct bursts of power, each one bringing shouts of fake terror from the three rowdies.

Theo felt her hands curl into fists. She took a

deep breath, and deliberately relaxed them, trying to distract herself by imagining Father—or, better, Captain Cho!—shutting them up. Instead, she saw Win Ton inside her closed eyelids, fingers flicking in his own *binjali* hand-talk rendition of *regard them as mere passengers*.

That thought led to others closer to her heart, and she regarded those things rather than the noise until the shuttle's very gentle touchdown on the Anlingdin Piloting Academy's own landing strip.

The newbies had been directed to the so-called passengers bay to collect their baggage, while the returning students—among them, the trio of snickiots from *Vestrin*—rushed off elsewhere. Theo breathed a sigh of relief. Good. That was probably the last she'd see of them—at least until year-end.

Someone jostled her, and she sighed again, this time in irritation. There was a lot of random motion going on, like everybody had a lot of energy to work off after the shuttle trip. She was feeling kind of jittery herself, like she wanted to dance and sleep at the same time. Still, milling around wasn't going to get their baggage out any sooner, so she tried to find a place to stand that was out of the way, but still gave her a good view of the gate.

The room was tall, and voices echoed noisily off of the ceiling, adding a headache-making depth to the nonstop chatter around her. She was apparently the only one among the newbies who didn't have a best friend with them. Well—her and a tall, awkward-looking girl in a bright green jacket, who was standing sort of in the middle of it all, adjusting her jacket with one hand, the other hand under her chin, like she was the only one in the bay, and wasn't too sure what to do next.

A baggage sled came through the gate, piled high with bags and crates. The crowd surged forward. Theo stood where she was, not wanting to get crushed. She could wait.

Another sled came through the gate; the crowds made way and re-formed with a minimum of fuss and a maximum of quick activity.

Theo looked about in sudden realization. This was so unlike either Delgado or Melchiza. On Delgado it felt like everyone older than her was in charge, and on Melchiza there was never any doubt who was in charge. Here, no one seemed in charge but everything was in motion. No one on guard, no one watching for miscreants, or antisocial conditions. It was . . . strange, she thought. And then she thought that she liked it, this tacit admission that they could sort themselves out. She relaxed, and watched, practicing advertency, like any good scholar, or traveler.

Around her were scores of young trainees standing by piles of baggage or looking hopelessly at the incoming field carts, watching for some last item among the confusion of the large hall. There were two large bags where the girl in the green jacket had been standing— and here she came back, dragging two more!

More carts arrived. Theo made herself stand patiently: her bag was well marked and would be easy enough to see once everything was brought in by the quick-moving workers. They all moved so easily, so much like pilots—

She lifted her eyes to the ceiling, feeling more than a little bit dumb. Of course they all moved like pilots:

she'd been told that most of the work at Anlingdin Piloting Academy was performed by pilots-in-training; eventually she'd be doing the same thing herself.

Looking around, Theo wondered how some of her fellow students could possibly have moved all their stuff between ship and shuttle. Could they really need piles and piles of whatever it was they'd brought?

True, she had shed some solemn tears in making the first hard decisions for herself, but as time went on she'd thought about the Melchiza trip and the extra carrying she'd done for that, and about how little of what was in her room would be going with her after she was a pilot, so it might as well stay home now. Like Coyster, and Father, and Kamele. They, like her things, would be there when she came home to visit; that would never change.

Kamele's reaction to Theo's first attempt at packing had been an astonished, "*Two* bags? But you have an allowance for three times that much!"

Father had laughed. "Be gentle—it is her first attempt! She'll soon learn better," he told Kamele, at the same time flashing a bright bit of hand-talk to Theo—*pilot to pilot*—and she'd laughed, then, though a heartbeat before she'd been ready to cry.

He'd managed to get much of the contents of her second bag into the first with astute repacking, and had eliminated other things with quick questions and comments like, "No library on Eylot?" and, "Outworld is not the same as frontier, youngster: I am almost certain that they will have tea;" and even "This mumu will be inappropriate on Eylot. Perhaps you should take your files with you and turn this back into the Wall for reuse."

She'd checked his face and seen only serious interest there: not a joke. And in the end, she'd copied her files and turned the mumu back to the Tech Department. In the end, she'd whittled things she brought to only the necessary.

Father said that pilots used the Three Pile Rule for deciding what to take with them. The first pile consisted of the things she really needed: ID, money, "your license, eventually, and a keep-safe, if you wish." Those things ought to fit into her jacket, vest or travel kit and always be to hand.

Things that she'd need later went into the second pile, and were packed in luggage.

Those things that she *might* need, except for extra air or water, went into the third pile—which was left behind.

Theo shifted from one foot to the other. She was getting tired of waiting in all the din and confusion, and was beginning to think longingly of her nice, quiet bunk, soon to be achieved— There!

Yet another sled came into the hall, her bag with its tag clearly visible perched on top of the pile. The gate snapped closed smartly behind it; a student work gang including—to her surprise and regret—the three troublemakers from *Vestrin,* ran for the cart to toss the last items off.

Ah, she thought, that explains it! The three knew exactly where their luggage was, and hauled it free with a fine disregard for physics. The surrounding bags shifted and tumbled. Her bag slid from its high perch, caught, and fell. Theo jumped forward—

Just before her bag hit the floor, one of the crew caught it, neatly and without flourish, looked down, blinked, and turned to display it to his friends. Maybe he was checking the tags, though she didn't know why they should care.

Theo continued toward them, and was almost knocked down by the tall girl in the bright green jacket, who had been looking lost earlier. She didn't look lost now. She looked mad.

"That box need not be thrown!" She sounded mad, too.

Indeed, the tallest of the three from the ship was hoisting a small box as if he meant to toss it to the floor.

He glared, put the box down hard on the cart, off-handedly caught another bag tossed to him by the stubbier guy, dropped it to the floor, and picked up Theo's bag. He made a show out of reading the tag, and laughed too loud.

"I'll take that, thank you."

Startlement.

Theo flushed; her words had come out louder than she'd expected, and into a lull in the racket of the hall, turning heads and dropping conversation levels all around.

"Yours? It's got a pilot tag on it!" This from the ringleader who'd offered, several times and pointedly, to permit Theo to accompany him—or all of them—to his cabin on the *Vestrin*. The oversize pilot's wings glittered on his shirt collar, just as it had when he'd leaned toward her conspiratorially on the ship, as if his offer had been some kind of favor.

"My bag." Theo nodded, trying for Kamele's crispest, most efficient voice. "Thank you."

A flick of fingers from the stubby one; quick and

with an accent she wasn't sure of, though she caught
the sense: *Throw me now run catch back toy's bag.*

"Don't!" Theo snapped, accompanying that with
a slashing *STOP ALL!* that brought a laugh from
an onlooker and a too-loudly muttered, "Miss Purity
strikes again!" from the ringleader.

"And *I* want my box," the girl in the green jacket
said imperiously. "You make me late for lunch."

The guy holding Theo's bag sat on the box and
looked down at her, ignoring the girl in the jacket.

"This tag—" He held the bag up and shook it at
her, like she needed help understanding which tag he
was talking about. "This tag is from Melchiza, in case
you don't know that. I can read the sight-code, and
that's a pilot-rated clearance. I bet you don't have a
pilot ID, do you? If you do, now's the time to show
it. If you don't, I'm filing this as stolen."

Theo glared, and touched the patch on her jacket,
that still carried her *Vestrin* photo pass-card and—

As if from all the walls at once came a lilting, if
loud, announcement.

"Attention. Registration jitney leaves in two minutes
from door four. Load now."

"This tag," Theo said, showing the strip she'd gotten
at Melchiza Station, "matches *that* tag. I got them on
Melchiza, and they're current for the Standard. My
name is on both. My bag. Sir."

She spoke calmly, and the *sir* was almost gentle,
but she couldn't stop herself from dropping into a
posture of alert waiting—nor, judging by the murmurs
behind her, was that lost on others. She sighed to
herself. Father had warned her—

"Oho, Wilsmyth, I think you ought to give the pretty

her bag," said someone Theo couldn't see. "Before she breaks you."

"I want my box!" snapped the girl in the green jacket. "Rise, oaf! I must have lunch! I must register!" She moved forward purposefully, jacket billowing.

Wilsmyth hesitated for another fraction of a second. He rose then, fast and sudden, and threw Theo's bag at her, hard. The other girl ducked beneath it to grab the box.

Theo fielded the bag one-handed, feeling a pull in her shoulder, and used the other hand to sign a curt *receipt acknowledged*, before she turned to seek door four.

# TWO

THE WOMAN IN THE PLAIN GREY UNIFORM HAD THE ROOM'S FULL attention as she strode about the low stage, left to right, right to left, talking at times as much to herself as to the group. The simple acts of walking on stage wearing a Jump pilot's jacket, slipping it off and casually throwing it over a nearby chair, had caught them as much as the quick hand-and-voice: *Welcome and listen up.* "I'm Commander Ronagy."

The basic intro was about what Theo had expected, a highly condensed repeat of the information in the school's orientation packet, but the follow-on was not.

Commander Ronagy came to the front of the stage and stood, legs braced, hands at ready, looking sternly out over the first four center rows, which was all the newbie class filled in this big auditorium.

"If you have any doubts about being here," she said soberly, "please, there's a shuttle scheduled to lift in the morning. If you're here under duress, come talk to me tonight, and we'll get you out of here as soon as we can, as neatly as we can. If you don't want to be here, we don't want you here."

Her right hand rose, fingers dancing briefly, several subdued metallic rings marking time in the spotlight, before she turned to pace again. Theo turned her head slightly and saw that tables and tray carts were being moved in the side door and rolling silently toward the back.

"I can tell you that not every pilot trainee has survived the course at Anlingdin Piloting Academy," the Commander continued. "The records speak for themselves and I suggest you avail yourselves of them if you haven't already. But you're here now, and this is what I can tell you without doubt: This will be one of the most physically and mentally challenging periods of your life. You may succumb to any of the hazards that claimed those of your less successful predecessors here at the academy: carelessness, bravado, inattention, suicide—these are the more common.

"You'll study some of the more dramatic errors in your training sims and if they don't leave you shaken, then perhaps you're in the wrong field. Our testing is designed to ensure that you're always at your peak, and always up to the next level of instruction. If you find you're falling behind, speak up."

Here she stopped in midstride, appeared to look at all the students at once and emphatically finger-yelled *GET HELP*. Her hands fluttered into a more subtle motion . . . she might, Theo thought, have been reminding herself of where she was in her presentation— *point six*.

"I can tell you that, statistically, your chance of survival and graduation is higher than the average. That's because you—this group—are something special. On the whole you're older than the school cohort groups we get for first and second semester. There's a compelling reason to start you now, rather than with the freshman class starting in a few months. Someone we trust told us you don't need to be babied or coddled, that you'll be able to do the job of becoming a pilot on your own terms. On the whole your recommendations have come directly from pilots who know you, and who are teachers in their own right.

"I can also tell you that if one of you errs to the point of death, it will greatly sadden us all, and we will mourn, but we will continue, as we have for three hundred years."

Theo caught the quick hand motion: *point seven*.

"Remember, yours is the interim group, and you're replacing those who washed themselves out, who flunked, who were asked not to return, who were claimed by their families for other duties, or who got drafted by their governments. Those ahead of you are technically your seniors. As we're at midyear, you will be moved into classes already in progress—and if necessary into remedial classes. Our charter with the planetary government requires the academy not only to enroll so many pilots per year, but to graduate so many a year. We are depending on you to be able to graduate, and while you'll get as much help as we can give to make you ready, your group is not supported by the general rebates and fees Anlingdin pays for local students and you'll generally not have the option to retake entire semesters."

Boy, was that ever true, Theo thought. She'd seen what the annual fee was, and it would have taken three years of Kamele's base salary to pay for her first year here . . . without Captain Cho's sponsorship she'd have never been able to enroll. And if she didn't keep her grades up, she wouldn't be able to afford to stay.

*Point eight.*

"If we were at the beginning of either half-term, I would be able to tell you how many of you will be sharing dormitory rooms, and give other housekeeping details. As it is, you will be scattered among existing housing arrangements, and might have anywhere from one to three other students with you. Generally, one student in each suite will clearly be the senior. Though we're not strictly military about these things—pilots are flexible, after all!—allow me to strongly suggest that the senior student be regarded as a mentor and guide, at least during your first semester. Your housing and meal information will be delivered at the tables which will be set up here while we all take advantage of the meal being laid at the back now. After the break, please have your Anlingdin cards at the ready and we'll get your piloting career under way. For the safety of all, please, no bowli balls in this room!"

There was an undercurrent of laughter as the Commander pointed out the tables piled with plates and food being being uncovered and set to serve.

The next signed but unspoken command was clearly *all eat.*

The buffet was surprisingly lavish, especially after the stifling sameness of *Vestrin's* menus. There was a mix of what Theo considered to be morning food and day food, to accommodate different personal times and preferences. Theo grabbed what looked like a cheese sandwich on dark bread, and a salad plate. Real, green vegetables! Carrots! And whole slices of tomato! She hadn't seen anything so good in weeks.

She located a vacant seat at a table for four, sent a nod and quick *seat taken?* to the sole occupant, a kid who was already deeply involved with a slice of pie. His unoccupied hand sent back a laconic *help yourself.*

"Thanks," Theo said, and parked her eatables before going off in search of a beverage.

The real tea was filed on a small table away from the coffee urns, fruit juice dispensers and carafes of water. Theo flipped open the keeper and flicked through the packets on offer. Again unlike *Vestrin*, which had offered Terran grades of so-called "tea," here were more familiar—and vastly more welcome!— packets interleaved with the Terran leaf.

Her hopes rose. Maybe they'd have— Yes! She grinned and plucked the packet of day tea from its cubby, turned—and all but fell into a man hardly any taller than she was. She danced sideways and made a recovery, the precious packet between her fingers.

The man smiled, and gave her a brief, pretty bow, murmuring something quick and lilting. The sound was so liquid that it took her a moment to realize that it was neither Terran—the official language of the academy—nor Trade, but Liaden.

She gave back a nod, found her hands had already asked *Say again?* while she blurted out in what she was sure was the wrong mode and probably the wrong tense, too, "Pardon, I have very small Liaden."

The man—the tag on his jacket read "Flight Instructor Orn Ald yos'Senchul," and the right sleeve of his crisp, tailored school jacket was empty—inclined his head.

"I'm sorry," she gasped, feeling her face heat. Using hand-talk to somebody with only one hand. *Way to be advertent, Theo!*

Flight Instructor yos'Senchul's fingers formed an elegant sign she read as *expectations betray*, while he smiled and murmured in accented Terran, "My pardon, as well. I was speaking a small Liaden jest, of two with exquisite taste who search for the same treasure." The fingers moved again, shaping the air effortlessly, *Apology unnecessary*.

"Oh, the tea!" Theo showed her packet. "This is the kind we drink at home."

"Is it, indeed? And you have so little Liaden?"

"Sleep learned, mostly," she confessed. "I know my accent's terrible. We speak Terran at home on Delgado, but the tea, I learned from my father."

His focus went distant a moment and the single hand signed a word she read as *wifechoice*. "Yes, of course. Delgado is quite cosmopolitan in its beverage choices, is it not, quite unlike . . . Melchiza."

She snorted, hands signing *squashed fruitwater* very nearly on their own, and he laughed.

"An excellent description, and their wines are not much better. Still, they do appreciate pilots . . . and I deduce, from rumor, that you must be Theo Waitley. I am pleased to make your acquaintance. You will be in my classes starting in two days. Enjoy your meal, and your tea!"

"Thank you, sir," she said, but he had already turned

to the tea chest to make his own choice. She caught up a brew-cup and moved off to her table, now full except for her place, and felt her face heat again as she went over the encounter.

Squashed fruitwater, she thought, and sighed. There must be a better sign that that!

"Erkes!" the van driver called out. "All excellent exopilots exit energetically…"

Theo went down the ramp on the heels of the tall girl in the green jacket from the baggage claim. The two of them pulled their bags from the rack, Theo wordlessly helping the other girl move her ridiculous pile out of the path of vehicular traffic.

"Thank you," the girl said as the van pulled away. She looked down at Theo and nodded. "I am Asu diamon Dayez," she said, pronouncing it like she expected Theo to recognize it, which she didn't. "And you are?"

"Theo Waitley." She hefted her bag, glad all over again to have only the one to deal with. "I'm in suite three-oh-two," she said, watching Asu diamon Dayez tether her bags together.

The taller girl looked up, shaking tumbled black curls out of her eyes. "So am I." She straightened, handle in one hand, and the all-important box tucked into the crook of her left arm. "Well! Let us be off, then, to discover this suite. If you will be so good as to open the door?"

Suite 302 was no bigger, Theo thought, than the apartment she and Kamele had in the Wall back on Delgado, but it was a lot better arranged. The door opened into a common room, with chairs, table, vid-screen, and a built-in counter already sporting a coffeepot and a minioven.

At the far end of the room, to the right, was another room, door open to reveal two bunks, two desks and lots of built-in storage space. To the left was a room slightly larger than the bunk room with a single bed and its own vid-screen.

She turned as the door to the hall opened to admit Asu, who was already sliding her key away into a pocket. "It works, and a good idea to test both at once," she said, giving an approving nod, which she probably meant to be friendly, but which for some reason irritated Theo.

*I must be really tired*, she thought, and swallowed her irritation, as she turned away to point at the bunk room.

"Which do you want, top or bottom?"

"Surely neither," Asu said crisply, steering her baggage train toward the single room. "I shall take this one."

Theo frowned. "That's probably the senior's room, do you think?"

The other girl turned her head, eyebrows up in surprise. "And I am senior, am I not? Eighteen Standards, plus a half."

She waited, her attitude one of challenge, and it wouldn't do to have an argument with her roommate on their first day, Theo reminded herself. She shrugged, hiding the sigh. "Plus a half? You're older than me," she conceded, and Asu nodded, apparently mollified.

"Please," she said, like she was giving Theo a present, "take whichever bunk pleases you." She glanced around again, frowning slightly. "Surely this can't be all the space. I will look more closely, but first, let us be secure."

She turned to the box she had placed on the table in the joint room. Theo carried her bag into the bunk room and set it down on one of the desks.

To her eye the top bunk was the best. The storage was good—more than she needed—the lighting abundant and directional, and twin fans—

"There!" Asu exclaimed.

Theo drifted out to the joint room, more curious about what was in the mysterious box than she was willing to admit even to herself.

"What is it?" she asked, blinking at the squat console with its array of varicolored lights.

Asu stared at her. "A Checksec, of course. Didn't you bring one? I mean, we've *got* to be careful. People are always snooping to see when you're traveling next, and if anyone's home, and intercepting the banking and everything. You never know if someone's listening with a vibcounter, or using a chipleak detector, or tapping net-calls. I mean, you can with a Checksec . . . but without one, all your business is public."

"But we're—" Theo swallowed the rest of her protest, suddenly remembering the "bug" Win Ton has found on board the *Vashtara*. Maybe Asu had a point, after all, she thought, warming to her roomie slightly.

That glow had faded by the time Asu had gone on to explain—at length—how in her house each room had a Checksec and they got calibrated every five days, and moved about randomly as well, so that anyone trying to spoof one would have a very hard time. And... it all sounded like too much trouble to Theo. She excused herself as soon as the Checksec had shown all its eyes green, which Asu said meant they were clean, "For now," she'd added darkly; and went to get settled in to quarters.

—end excerpt—

from *Saltation*
available in hardcover,
April 2010, from Baen Books